Praise for *New York Times* bestselling author Diana Palmer

"[Diana] Palmer demonstrates, yet again, why she's the queen of desperado quests for justice and true love."

—*Publishers Weekly* on *Dangerous*

"Diana Palmer is one of those authors whose books are always enjoyable. She throws in romance, suspense and a good story line."

—*The Romance Reader* on *Before Sunrise*

"The popular Palmer has penned another winning novel, a perfect blend of romance and suspense."

—*Booklist* on *Lawman*

Praise for *USA TODAY* bestselling author Delores Fossen

"[Delores] Fossen's stories are known for nonstop, explosive action with nail-biting close calls and impressive booby traps."

—*RT Book Reviews*

"Even if you think you've figured out whodunit, hang on till the end to get the full impact of the suspense, action and a family of sexy and lethal lawmen. From the shocking opening paragraph on, Fossen's tale just keeps getting better."

—*RT Book Reviews* on *Sawyer*

Author of over one hundred books, **Diana Palmer** is a multiple *New York Times* bestselling author and one of the top ten romance writers in America. She has a gift for telling even the most sensual tales with charm and humor. Diana lives with her family in Cornelia, Georgia. Visit her website at DianaPalmer.com.

A *USA TODAY* bestselling author, **Delores Fossen** has sold over fifty novels with millions of copies of her books in print worldwide. She's received a Booksellers' Best Award and an RT Reviewers' Choice Best Book Award. She was also a finalist for a prestigious RITA® Award. You can contact the author through her webpage at dfossen.net.

New York Times Bestselling Author

DIANA PALMER

THE MAVERICK

HARLEQUIN® BESTSELLING AUTHOR COLLECTION

ISBN-13: 978-0-373-01042-4

The Maverick
Copyright © 2016 by Harlequin Books S.A.

The publisher acknowledges the copyright holders of the individual works as follows:

The Maverick
Copyright © 2009 by Diana Palmer

Grayson
Copyright © 2011 by Delores Fossen

Recycling programs for this product may not exist in your area.

This edition published by arrangement with Harlequin Books S.A.

For questions and comments about the quality of this book, please contact us at CustomerService@Harlequin.com.

® and TM are trademarks of Harlequin Enterprises Limited or its corporate affiliates. Trademarks indicated with ® are registered in the United States Patent and Trademark Office, the Canadian Intellectual Property Office and in other countries.

Printed in U.S.A.

CONTENTS

Also available from Diana Palmer

For a complete listing of books by Diana Palmer, please visit DianaPalmer.com.

THE MAVERICK

Diana Palmer

To Julie Benefiel, who designed my cowboy quilt (hand pieced by Nancy Caudill),

To Nancy Mason, who quilted it,

And to Janet Borchert, who put together a 2007 hardcover book of all my covers, including foreign ones, along with Jade, Tracy, Nancy, Carey, Amy, Renata, Maria, LeeAnn, Efy, Kay, Peggy, Hang, Ronnie, Mona and Debbie of the Diana Palmer Bulletin Board.

Also to everyone who participated in the compendium summaries of all my books, and to Nancy for the quilted covers for the loose-leaf notebooks.

With many thanks and much love.

Chapter 1

Harley Fowler was staring so hard at his list of chores that he walked right into a young brunette as he headed into the hardware store in Jacobsville, Texas. He looked up, shocked, when she fell back against the open door, glaring at him.

"I've heard of men getting buried in their work, but this is too much," she told him with a speaking look. She smoothed over her short black hair, feeling for a bump where she'd collided with the door. Deep blue eyes glared up into his pale blue ones. She noticed that he had light brown hair and was wearing a baseball cap that seemed to suit him. He was sexy-looking.

"I'm not buried in my work," he said curtly. "I'm trying to get back to work, and shopping chores are keeping me from it."

"Which doesn't explain why you're assaulting women with doors. Does it?" she mused.

His eyes flared. "I didn't assault you with a door. You walked into me."

"I did not. You were staring at that piece of paper so hard that you wouldn't have seen a freight train coming." She peered over his arm at the list. "Pruning shears? Two new rakes?" She pursed her lips, but smiling blue eyes stared at him. "You're obviously somebody's gardener," she said, noting his muddy shoes and baseball cap.

His eyebrows met. "I am not a gardener," he said indignantly. "I'm a cowboy."

"You are not!"

"Excuse me?"

"You don't have a horse, you're not wearing a cowboy hat and you don't have on any chaps." She glanced at his feet. "You aren't even wearing cowboy boots!"

He gaped at her. "Did you just escape from intense therapy?"

"I have not been in any therapy," she said haughtily. "My idiosyncrasies are so unique that they couldn't classify me even with the latest edition of the DSM-IV, much less attempt to pyschoanalize me!"

She was referring to a classic volume of psychology that was used to diagnose those with mental challenges. He obviously had no idea what she was talking about.

"So, can you sing, then?"

He looked hunted. "Why would I want to sing?"

"Cowboys sing. I read it in a book."

"You can read?" he asked in mock surprise.

"Why would you think I couldn't?" she asked.

He nodded toward the sign on the hardware store's door that clearly said, in large letters, PULL. She was trying to push it.

She let go of the door and shifted her feet. "I saw that," she said defensively. "I just wanted to know if you were paying attention." She cocked her head at him. "Do you have a rope?"

"Why?" he asked. "You planning to hang yourself?"

She sighed with exaggerated patience. "Cowboys carry ropes."

"What for?"

"So they can rope cattle!"

"Don't find many head of cattle wandering around in hardware stores," he murmured, looking more confident now.

"What if you did?" she persisted. "How would you get a cow out of the store?"

"Bull. We run purebred Santa Gertrudis bulls on Mr. Parks's ranch," he corrected.

"And you don't have any cows?" She made a face. "You don't raise calves, then." She nodded.

His face flamed. "We do so raise calves. We do have cows. We just don't carry them into hardware stores and turn them loose!"

"Well, excuse me!" she said in mock apology. "I never said you did."

"Cowboy hats and ropes and cows," he muttered. He opened the door. "You going in or standing out here? I have work to do."

"Doing what? Knocking unsuspecting women in the head with doors?" she asked pleasantly.

His impatient eyes went over her neat slacks and wool jacket to the bag she was holding. "I said, are you going into the store?" he asked with forced patience, holding the door open.

"Yes, as a matter of fact, I am," she replied, moving closer. "I need some tape measures and Super Glue and matches and chalk and push pins and colored string and sticky tape."

"Don't tell me," he drawled. "You're a contractor."

"Oh, she's something a little less conventional than that, Harley," Police Chief Cash Grier said as he came up the steps to the store. "How's it going, Jones?" he asked.

"I'm overflowing in DBs, Grier," she replied with a grin. "Want some?"

He held up his hands. "We don't do a big business in homicides here. I'd like to keep it that way." He scowled. "You're out of your territory a bit, aren't you?"

"I am. I was asked down here by your sheriff, Hayes Carson. He actually does have a DB. I'm working the crime scene for him per his request through the Bexar County medical examiner's office, but I didn't bring enough supplies. I hope the hardware store can accommodate me. It's a long drive back to San Antonio when you're on a case."

"On a case?" Harley asked, confused.

"Yes, on a case," she said. "Unlike you, some of us are professionals who have real jobs."

"Do you know him?" Cash asked her.

She gave Harley a studied appraisal. "Not really. He came barreling up the steps and hit me with a door. He says he's a cowboy," she added in a confidential tone. "But just between us, I'm sure he's lying. He doesn't have a horse or a rope, he isn't wearing a cowboy hat or boots, he says he can't sing and he thinks bulls roam around loose in hardware stores."

Harley stared at her with more mixed emotions than he'd felt in years.

Cash choked back a laugh. "Well, he act... cowboy," Cash defended him. "He's Harley Fowl... Parks's foreman on his cattle ranch."

"Imagine that!" she exclaimed. "What a blow to the image of Texas if some tourist walks in and sees him dressed like that!" She indicated Harley's attire with one slender hand. "They can't call us the cowboy capital of the world if we have people working cattle in baseball caps! We'll be disgraced!"

Cash was trying not to laugh. Harley looked as if he might explode.

"Better a horseless cowboy than a contractor with an attitude like yours!" Harley shot back, with glittery eyes. "I'm amazed that anybody around here would hire you to build something for them."

She gave him a superior look. "I don't build things. But I could if I wanted to."

"She really doesn't build things," Cash said. "Harley, this is Alice Mayfield Jones," he introduced. "She's a forensic investigator for the Bexar County medical examiner's office."

"She works with dead people?" Harley exclaimed, and moved back a step.

"Dead bodies," Alice returned, glaring at his obvious distaste. "DBs. And I'm damned good at my job. Ask him," she added, nodding toward Cash.

"She does have a reputation," Cash admitted. His dark eyes twinkled. "And a nickname. Old Jab-'Em-in-the-Liver Alice."

"You've been talking to Marc Brannon," she accused.

"You did help him solve a case, back when he was still a Texas Ranger," he pointed out.

"Now they've got this new guy, transferred up from Houston," she said on a sigh. "He's real hard going. No sense of humor." She gave him a wry look. "Kind of like you used to be, in the old days when you worked out of the San Antonio district attorney's office, Grier," she recalled. "A professional loner with a bad attitude."

"Oh, I've changed." He grinned. "A wife and child can turn the worst of us inside out."

She smiled. "No kidding? If I have time, I'd love to see that little girl everybody's talking about. Is she as pretty as her mama?"

He nodded. "Oh, yes. Every bit."

Harley pulled at his collar. "Could you stop talking about children, please?" he muttered. "I'll break out in hives."

"Allergic to small things, are you?" Alice chided.

"Allergic to the whole subject of marriage," he emphasized with a meaningful stare.

Her eyebrows arched. "I'm sorry, were you hoping I was going to ask you to marry me?" she replied pleasantly. "You're not bad-looking, I guess, but I have a very high standard for prospective bridegrooms. Frankly," she added with a quick appraisal, "if you were on sale in a groom shop, I can assure you that I wouldn't purchase you."

He stared at her as if he doubted his hearing. Cash Grier had to turn away. His face was going purple.

The hardware-store door opened and a tall, black-haired, taciturn man came out it. He frowned. "Jones? What the hell are you doing down here? They asked for Longfellow!"

She glared back. "Longfellow hid in the women's restroom and refused to come out," she said haughtily.

"So they sent me. And why are you interested in Sheriff Carson's case? You're a fed."

Kilraven put his finger to his lips and looked around hastily to make sure nobody was listening. "I'm a policeman, working on the city force," he said curtly.

Alice held up both hands defensively. "Sorry! It's so hard to keep up with all these secrets!"

Kilraven glanced at his boss and back at Alice. "What secrets?"

"Well, there's the horseless cowboy there—" she pointed at Harley "—and the DB over on the Little Carmichael River…"

Kilraven's silver eyes widened. "On the river? I thought it was in town. Nobody told me!"

"I just did," Alice said. "But it's really a secret. I'm not supposed to tell anybody."

"I'm local law enforcement," Kilraven insisted. "You can tell me. Who is he?"

Alice gave him a bland look and propped a hand on her hip. "I only looked at him for two minutes before I realized I needed to get more investigative supplies. He's male and dead. He's got no ID, he's naked and even his mother wouldn't recognize his face."

"Dental records…" Kilraven began.

"For those, you need identifiable teeth," Alice replied sweetly.

Harley was turning white.

She glanced at him. "Are you squeamish?" she asked hopefully. "Listen, I once examined this dead guy whose girlfriend caught him with a hooker. After she offed him, she cut off his… Where are you going?"

Harley was making a beeline for the interior of the hardware store.

"Bathroom, I imagine." Grier grinned at Kilraven, who chuckled.

"He works around cattle and he's squeamish?" Alice asked, delighted. "I'll bet he's a lot of fun when they round up the calves!"

"Not nice," Kilraven chided. "Everybody's got a weak spot, Jones. Even you."

"I have no weak spots," she assured him.

"No social life, either," Grier murmured. "I heard you tried to conduct a postmortem on a turkey in North Carolina during a murder investigation there."

"It met with fowl play," she said, straight-faced.

Both men chuckled.

"I have to get to work," she said, becoming serious. "This is a strange case. Nobody knows who this guy is or where he came from, and there was a serious attempt to make him unidentifiable. Even with DNA, when I can get a profile back from state—and don't hold your breath on the timetable—I don't know if we can identify him. If he has no criminal record, he won't be on file anywhere."

"At least we don't get many of these," Kilraven said quietly.

Jones smiled at him. "When are you coming back up to San Antonio?" she asked. "You solved the Pendleton kidnapping and helped wrap up the perps."

"Just a few loose ends to tie up," he said. He nodded at her and his boss. "I'll get back on patrol."

"Brady's wife made potato soup and real corn bread for lunch. Don't miss it."

"Not me, boss."

Alice stared after the handsome officer. "He's a dish.

But isn't he overstaying his purpose down here?" she asked Cash.

He leaned down. "Winnie Sinclair works for the 911 center. Local gossip has it that he's sweet on her. That's why he's finding excuses not to leave."

Alice looked worried. "And he's dragging around a whole past that hardly anybody knows about. He's pretending it never happened."

"Maybe he has to."

She nodded. "It was bad. One of the worst cases I ever worked. Poor guy." She frowned. "They never solved it, you know. The perp is still out there, running around loose. It must have driven Kilraven and his brother, Jon Blackhawk, nuts, wondering if it was somebody they arrested, somebody with a grudge."

"Their father was an FBI agent in San Antonio, before he drank himself to death after the murders. Blackhawk still is," Cash replied thoughtfully. "Could have been a case any one of the three men worked, a perp getting even."

"It could," she agreed. "It must haunt the brothers. The guilt would be bad enough, but they wouldn't want to risk it happening again, to someone else they got involved with. They avoid women. Especially Kilraven."

"He wouldn't want to go through it again," Cash said.

"This Sinclair woman, how does she feel about Kilraven?"

Cash gave her a friendly smile. "I am not a gossip."

"Bull."

He laughed. "She's crazy about him. But she's very young."

"Age doesn't matter, in the long run," Alice said with

a faraway look in her eyes. "At least, sometimes." She opened the door. "See you around, Grier."

"You, too, Jones."

She walked into the hardware store. There at the counter was Harley, pale and out of sorts. He glared at her.

She held up both hands. "I wasn't even graphic," she said defensively. "And God only knows how you manage to help with branding, with that stomach."

"I ate something that didn't agree with me," he said icily.

"In that case, you must not have a lot of friends...."

The clerk doubled over laughing.

"I do not eat people!" Harley muttered.

"I should hope not," she replied. "I mean, being a cannibal is much worse than being a gardener."

"I am not a gardener!"

Alice gave the clerk a sweet smile. "Do you have chalk and colored string?" she asked. "I also need double-A batteries for my digital camera and some antibacterial hand cleaner."

The clerk looked blank.

Harley grinned. He knew this clerk very well. Sadly, Alice didn't. "Hey, John, this is a real, honest-to-goodness crime scene investigator," he told the young man. "She works out of the medical examiner's office in San Antonio!"

Alice felt her stomach drop as she noted the bright fascination in the clerk's eyes. The clerk's whole face became animated. "You do, really? Hey, I watch all those CSI shows," he exclaimed. "I know about DNA profiles. I even know how to tell how long a body's been dead just by identifying the insects on it...!"

"You have a great day, Ms. Jones," Harley told Alice, over the clerk's exuberant monologue.

She glared at him. "Oh, thanks very much."

He tipped his bibbed cap at her. "See you, John," he told the clerk. Harley picked up his purchases, smiling with pure delight, and headed right out the front door.

The clerk waved an absent hand in his general direction, never taking his eyes off Alice. "Anyway, about those insects," he began enthusiastically.

Alice followed him around the store for her supplies, groaning inwardly as he kept talking. She never ran out of people who could tell her how to do her job these days, thanks to the proliferation of television shows on forensics. She tried to explain that most labs were understaffed, under-budgeted, and that lab results didn't come back in an hour, even for a department like hers, on the University of Texas campus, which had a national reputation for excellence. But the bug expert here was on a roll and he wasn't listening. She resigned herself to the lecture and forced a smile. Wouldn't do to make enemies here, not when she might be doing more business with him later. She was going to get even with that smug cowboy the next time she saw him, though.

The riverbank was spitting out law enforcement people. Alice groaned as she bent to the poor body and began to take measurements. She'd already had an accommodating young officer from the Jacobsville Police Department run yellow police tape all around the crime scene. That didn't stop people from stepping over it, however.

"You stop that," Alice muttered at two men wearing deputy sheriff uniforms. They both stopped with one foot in the air at the tone of her voice. "No tramping around on my crime scene! That yellow tape is to keep people *out*."

"Sorry," one murmured sheepishly, and they both went back on their side of the line. Alice pushed away a strand of sweaty hair with the back of a latex-gloved hand and muttered to herself. It was almost Christmas, but the weather had gone nuts and it was hot. She'd already taken off her wool jacket and replaced it with a lab coat, but her slacks were wool and she was burning up. Not to mention that this guy had been lying on the riverbank for at least a day and he was ripe. She had Vicks Salve under her nose, but it wasn't helping a lot.

For the hundredth time, she wondered why she'd ever chosen such a messy profession. But it was very satisfying when she could help catch a murderer, which she had many times over the years. Not that it substituted for a family. But most men she met were repelled by her profession. Sometimes she tried to keep it to herself. But inevitably there would be a movie or a TV show that would mention some forensic detail and Alice would hold forth on the misinformation she noted. Sometimes it was rather graphic, like with the vengeful cowboy in the hardware store.

Then there would be the forced smiles. The excuses. And so it went. Usually that happened before the end of the first date. Or at least the second.

"I'll bet I'm the only twenty-six-year-old virgin in the whole damned state of Texas," she muttered to herself.

"Excuse me?" one of the deputies, a woman, exclaimed with wide, shocked eyes.

"That's right, you just look at me as if I sprouted

horns and a tail," she murmured as she worked. "I know I'm an anachronism."

"That's not what I meant," the deputy said, chuckling. "Listen, there are a lot of women our ages with that attitude. I don't want some unspeakable condition that I catch from a man who passes himself around like a dish of peanuts at a bar. And do you think they're going to tell you they've got something?"

Alice beamed. "I like you."

She chuckled. "Thanks. I think of it as being sensible." She lowered her voice. "See Kilraven over there?" she asked, drawing Alice's eyes to the arrival of another local cop—even if he really was a fed pretending to be one. "They say his brother, Jon Blackhawk, has never had a woman in his life. And we think we're prudes!"

Alice chuckled. "That's what I heard, too. Sensible man!"

"Very." The deputy was picking up every piece of paper, every cigarette butt she could find with latex gloves on, bagging them for Alice for evidence. "What about that old rag, Jones, think I should put it in a bag, too? Look at this little rusty spot."

Alice glanced at it, frowning. It was old, but there was a trace of something on it, something newer than the rag. "Yes," she said. "I think it's been here for a while, but that's new trace evidence on it. Careful not to touch the rusty-looking spot."

"Blood, isn't it?" She nodded.

"You're good," Alice said.

"I came down from Dallas PD," she said. "I got tired of big-city crime. Things are a little less hectic here. In fact, this is my first DB since I joined Sheriff Carson's department."

"That's a real change, I know," Alice said. "I work out of San Antonio. Not the quietest place in the world, especially on weekends."

Kilraven had walked right over the police tape and came up near the body.

"What do you think you're doing?" Alice exclaimed. "Kilraven...!"

"Look," he said, his keen silver eyes on the grass just under the dead man's right hand, which was clenched and depressed into the mud. "There's something white."

Alice followed his gaze. She didn't even see it at first. She'd moved so that it was in shadow. But when she shifted, the sunlight caught it. Paper. A tiny sliver of paper, just peeping out from under the dead man's thumb. She reached down with her gloved hand and brushed away the grass. There was a deep indentation in the soft, mushy soil, next to his hand; maybe a footprint. "I need my camera before I move it," she said, holding out her hand. The deputy retrieved the big digital camera from its bag and handed it to Alice, who documented the find and recorded it on a graph of the crime scene. Then, returning the camera, she slid a pencil gently under the hand, moving it until she was able to see the paper. She reached into her kit for a pair of tweezers and tugged it carefully from his grasp.

"It's a tiny, folded piece of paper," she said, frowning. "And thank God it hasn't rained."

"Amen," Kilraven agreed, peering at the paper in her hand.

"Good eyes," she added with a grin.

He grinned back. "Lakota blood." He chuckled. "Tracking is in my genes. My great-great-grandfather was at Little Big Horn."

"I won't ask on which side," she said in a loud whisper.

"No need to be coy. He rode with Crazy Horse's band."

"Hey, I read about that," the deputy said. "Custer's guys were routed, they say."

"One of the Cheyenne people said later that a white officer was killed down at the river in the first charge," he said. "He said the officer was carried up to the last stand by his men, and after that the soldiers seemed to lose heart and didn't fight so hard. They found Custer's brother, Tom, and a couple of ranking officers from other units, including Custer's brother-in-law, with Custer. It could indicate that the chain of command changed several times. Makes sense, if you think about it. If there was a charge, Custer would have led it. Several historians think that Custer's unit made it into the river before the Cheyenne came flying into it after them. If Custer was killed early, he'd have been carried up to the last stand ridge—an enlisted guy, they'd have left there in the river."

"I never read that Custer got killed early in the fight," the deputy exclaimed.

"I've only ever seen the theory in one book—a warrior was interviewed who was on the Indian side of the fight, and he said he thought Custer was killed in the first charge," he mused. "The Indians' side of the story didn't get much attention until recent years. They said there were no surviving eyewitnesses. Bull! There were several tribes of eyewitnesses. It was just that nobody thought their stories were worth hearing just after the battle. Not the massacre," he added before the deputy could speak. "Massacres are when you kill unarmed people. Custer's men all had guns."

The deputy grinned. "Ever think of teaching history?"

"Teaching's too dangerous a profession. That's why I joined the police force instead." Kilraven chuckled.

"Great news for law enforcement," Alice said. "You have good eyes."

"You'd have seen it for yourself, Jones, eventually," he replied. "You're the best."

"Wow! Did you hear that? Take notes," Alice told the deputy. "The next time I get yelled at for not doing my job right, I'm quoting Kilraven."

"Would it help?" he asked.

She laughed. "They're still scared of you up in San Antonio," she said. "One of the old patrolmen, Jacobs, turns white when they mention your name. I understand the two of you had a little dustup?"

"I threw him into a fruit display at the local supermarket. Messy business. Did you know that blackberries leave purple stains on skin?" he added conversationally.

"I'm a forensic specialist," Alice reminded him. "Can I ask why you threw him into a fruit display?"

"We were working a robbery and he started making these remarks about fruit with one of the gay officers standing right beside me. The officer in question couldn't do anything without getting in trouble." He grinned. "Amazing, how attitudes change with a little gentle adjustment."

"Hey, Kilraven, what are you doing walking around on the crime scene?" Cash Grier called from the sidelines.

"Don't fuss at him," Alice called back. "He just spotted a crucial piece of evidence. You should give him an award!"

There were catcalls from all the officers present.

"I should get an award!" he muttered as he went to join his boss. "I never take days off or vacations!"

"That's because you don't have a social life, Kilraven," one of the officers joked.

Alice stood up, staring at the local law enforcement uniforms surrounding the crime scene tape. She recognized at least two cars from other jurisdictions. There was even a federal car out there! It wasn't unusual in a sleepy county like Jacobs for all officers who weren't busy to congregate around an event like this. It wasn't every day that you found a murder victim in your area. But a federal car for a local murder?

As she watched, Garon Grier and Jon Blackhawk of the San Antonio district FBI office climbed out of the BuCar—the FBI's term for a bureau car—and walked over the tape to join Alice.

"What have you found?" Grier asked.

She pursed her lips, glancing from the assistant director of the regional FBI office, Grier, to Special Agent Jon Blackhawk. What a contrast! Grier was blond and Blackhawk had long, jet-black hair tied in a ponytail. They were both tall and well-built without being flashy about it. Garon Grier, like his brother Cash, was married. Jon Blackhawk was unattached and available. Alice wished she was his type. He was every bit as good-looking as his half brother Kilraven.

"I found some bits and pieces of evidence, with the deputy's help. Your brother," she told Jon, "found this." She held up the piece of paper in an evidence bag. "Don't touch," she cautioned as both men peered in. "I'm not unfolding it until I can get it into my lab. I won't risk losing any trace evidence out here."

Blackhawk pulled out a pad and started taking notes. "Where was it?" he asked.

"Gripped in the dead man's fingers, out of sight. Why are you here?" she asked. "This is a local matter."

Blackhawk was cautious. "Not entirely," he said.

Kilraven joined them. He and Blackhawk exchanged uneasy glances.

"Okay. Something's going on that I can't be told about. It's okay." She held up a hand. "I'm used to being a mushroom. Kept in the dark and fed with…"

"Never mind," Garon told her. He softened it with a smile. "We've had a tip. Nothing substantial. Just something that interests us about this case."

"And you can't tell me what the tip was?"

"We found a car in the river, farther down," Cash said quietly. "San Antonio plates."

"Maybe his?" Alice indicated the body.

"Maybe. We're running the plates now," Cash said.

"So, do you think he came down here on his own, or did somebody bring him in a trunk?" Alice mused.

The men chuckled. "You're good, Alice," Garon murmured.

"Of course I am!" she agreed. "Could you," she called to the female deputy, "get me some plaster of Paris out of my van, in the back? This may be a footprint where we found the piece of paper! Thanks."

She went back to work with a vengeance while two sets of brothers looked on with intent interest.

Chapter 2

Alice fell into her bed at the local Jacobsville motel after a satisfying soak in the luxurious whirlpool bathtub. Amazing, she thought, to find such a high-ticket item in a motel in a small Texas town. She was told that film crews from Hollywood frequently chose Jacobs County as a location and that the owner of the motel wanted to keep them happy. It was certainly great news for Alice.

She'd never been so tired. The crime scene, they found, extended for a quarter of a mile down the river. The victim had fought for his life. There were scuff marks and blood trails all over the place. So much for her theory that he'd traveled to Jacobsville in the trunk of the car they'd found.

The question was, why had somebody brought a man down to Jacobsville to kill him? It made no sense.

She closed her eyes, trying to put herself in the shoes of the murderer. People usually killed for a handful of reasons. They killed deliberately out of jealousy, anger or greed. Sometimes they killed accidentally. Often, it was an impulse that led to a death, or a series of acts that pushed a person over the edge. All too often, it was drugs or alcohol that robbed someone of impulse control, and that led inexorably to murder.

Few people went into an argument or a fight intending to kill someone. But it wasn't as if you could take it back even seconds after a human life expired. There were thousands of young people in prison who would have given anything to relive a single incident where they'd made a bad choice. Families suffered for those choices, along with their children. So often, it was easy to overlook the fact that even murderers had families, often decent, law-abiding families that agonized over what their loved one had done and paid the price along with them.

Alice rolled over, restlessly. Her job haunted her from time to time. Along with the coroner, and the investigating officers, she was the last voice of the deceased. She spoke for them, by gathering enough evidence to bring the killer to trial. It was a holy grail. She took her duties seriously. But she also had to live with the results of the murderer's lack of control. It was never pleasant to see a dead body. Some were in far worse conditions than others. She carried those memories as certainly as the family of the deceased carried them.

Early on, she'd learned that she couldn't let herself become emotionally involved with the victims. If she started crying, she'd never stop, and she wouldn't be effective in her line of work.

She found a happy medium in being the life of the party at crime scenes. It diverted her from the misery of her surroundings and, on occasion, helped the crime scene detectives cope, as well. One reporter, a rookie, had given her a hard time because of her attitude. She'd invited him to her office for a close-up look at the world of a real forensic investigator.

The reporter had arrived expecting the corpse, always tastefully displayed, to be situated in the tidy, high-tech surroundings that television crime shows had accustomed him to seeing.

Instead, Alice pulled the sheet from a drowning victim who'd been in the water three days.

She never saw the reporter again. Local cops who recounted the story, always with choked-back laughter, told her that he'd turned in his camera the same day and voiced an ambition to go into real estate.

Just as well, she thought. The real thing was pretty unpleasant. Television didn't give you the true picture, because there was no such thing as smell-o-vision. She could recall times when she'd gone through a whole jar of Vicks Salve trying to work on a drowning victim like the one she'd shown the critical member of the Fourth Estate.

She rolled over again. She couldn't get her mind to shut down long enough to allow for sleep. She was reviewing the meager facts she'd uncovered at the crime scene, trying to make some sort of sense out of it. Why would somebody drive a murder victim out of the city to kill him? Maybe because he didn't know he was going to become a murder victim. Maybe he got in the car voluntarily.

Good point, she thought. But it didn't explain the

crime. Heat of passion wouldn't cover this one. It was too deliberate. The perp meant to hide evidence. And he had.

She sighed. She wished she'd become a detective instead of a forensic specialist. It must be more fun solving crimes than being knee-deep in bodies. And prospective dates wouldn't look at you from a safe distance with that expression of utter distaste, like that gardener in the hardware store this afternoon.

What had Grier called him, Fowler? Harley Fowler, that was it. Not a bad-looking man. He had a familiar face. Alice wondered why. She was sure she'd never seen him before today. She was sure she'd remember somebody that disagreeable.

Maybe he resembled somebody she knew. That was possible. Fowler. Fowler. No. It didn't ring any bells. She'd have to let her mind brood on it for a couple of days. Sometimes that's all it took to solve such puzzles—background working of the subconscious. She chuckled to herself. *Background workings,* she thought, *will save me yet.*

After hours of almost-sleep, she got up, dressed and went back to the crime scene. It was quiet now, without the presence of almost every uniformed officer in the county. The body was lying in the local funeral home, waiting for transport to the medical examiner's office in San Antonio. Alice had driven her evidence up to San Antonio, to the crime lab, and turned it over to the trace evidence people, specifically Longfellow.

She'd entrusted Longfellow with the precious piece of paper that might yield dramatic evidence once unfolded. There had clearly been writing on it. The dead man had grasped it tight in his hand while he was being killed, and had managed to conceal it from his killer. It must have something on it that he was desperate to preserve. Amazing. She wanted to know what it was. Tomorrow, she promised herself, their best trace evidence specialist, Longfellow, would have that paper turned every which way but loose in her lab, and she'd find answers for Alice. She was one of the best CSI people Alice had ever worked with. When Alice drove right back down to Jacobsville, she knew she'd have answers from the lab soon.

Restless, she looked around at the lonely landscape, bare in winter. The local police were canvassing the surrounding area for anyone who'd seen something unusual in the past few days, or who'd noticed an out-of-town car around the river.

Alice paced the riverbank, a lonely figure in a neat white sweatshirt with blue jeans, staring out across the ripples of the water while her sneakers tried to sink into the damp sand. It was cooler today, in the fifties, about normal for a December day in south Texas.

Sometimes she could think better when she was alone at the crime scene. Today wasn't one of those days. She was acutely aware of her aloneness. It was worse now, after the death of her father a month ago. He was her last living relative. He'd been a banker back in Tennessee, where she'd taken courses in forensics. The family was from Floresville, just down the road from San Antonio. But her parents had moved away to Tennessee when she was in her last year of high school, and that had been a wrench. Alice had a crush on a boy in her class, but the move killed any hope of a relationship. She really had been a late bloomer, preferring to hang out in the biology lab rather than think about dating. Amoeba under the microscope were so much more interesting.

Alice had left home soon after her mother's death, the year she started college. Her mother had been a live wire, a happy and well-adjusted woman who could do almost anything around the house, especially cook. She despaired of Alice, her only child, who watched endless reruns of the old TV show *Quincy,* about a medical examiner, along with archaic *Perry Mason* episodes. Long before it was popular, Alice had dreamed of being a crime scene technician.

She'd been an ace at biology in high school. Her science teachers had encouraged her, delighting in her bright enthusiasm. One of them had recommended her to a colleague at the University of Texas campus in San Antonio, who'd steered her into a science major and helped her find local scholarships to supplement the small amount her father could afford for her. It had been an uphill climb to get that degree, and to add to it with courses from far-flung universities when time and money permitted; one being courses in forensic anthropology at the University of Tennessee in Knoxville. In between, she'd slogged away with other techs at one crime scene after another, gaining experience.

Once, in her haste to finish gathering evidence, due to a rare prospective date, she'd slipped up and mislabeled blood evidence. That had cost the prosecution staff a conviction. It had been a sobering experience for Alice, especially when the suspect went out and killed a young boy before being rearrested. Alice felt responsible for that boy's death. She never forgot how haste had put the nails in his coffin, and she never slipped up again. She gained a reputation for being precise and meticulous in evidence-gathering. And she never went home early again. Alice was almost always the last person to leave the lab, or the crime scene, at the end of the day.

A revved-up engine caught her attention. She turned as a carload of young boys pulled up beside her white van at the river's edge.

"Lookie there, a lonely lady!" one of them called. "Ain't she purty?"

"Shore is! Hey, pretty thing, you like younger men? We can make you happy!"

"You bet!" Another one laughed.

"Hey, lady, you feel like a party?" another one catcalled.

Alice glared. "No, I don't feel like a party. Take a hike!" She turned back to her contemplation of the river, hoping they'd give up and leave.

"Aww, that ain't no way to treat prospective boyfriends!" one yelled back. "Come on up here and lie down, lady. We want to talk to you!"

More raucous laughter echoed out of the car.

So much for patience. She was in no mood for teenagers acting out. She pulled out the pad and pen she always carried in her back pocket and walked up the bank and around to the back of their car. She wrote down the license plate number without being obvious about it. She'd call in a harassment call and let local law enforcement help her out. But even as she thought about it, she hesitated. There had to be a better way to handle this bunch of loonies without involving the law. She was overreacting. They were just teenagers, after all. Inspiration struck as she reemerged at the driver's side of the car.

She ruffled her hair and moved closer to the tow-headed young driver. She leaned down. "I like your tires," she drawled with a wide grin. "They're real nice. And wide. And they have treads. I *like* treads." She wiggled her eyebrows at him. "You like treads?"

He stared at her. The silly expression went into eclipse. "Treads?" His voice sounded squeaky. He tried again. "Tire…treads?"

"Yeah. Tire treads." She stuck her tongue in and out and grinned again. "I *reeaaally* like tire treads."

He was trying to pretend that he wasn't talking to a lunatic. "Uh. You do. Really."

She was enjoying herself now. The other boys seemed even more confused than the driver did. They were all staring at her. Nobody was laughing.

She frowned. "No, you don't like treads. You're just humoring me. Okay. If you don't like treads, you might like what I got in the truck," she said, lowering her voice. She jerked her head toward the van.

He cleared his throat. "I might like what you got in the truck," he parroted.

She nodded, grinning, widening her eyes until the whites almost gleamed. She leaned forward. "I got bodies in there!" she said in a stage whisper and levered her eyes wide-open. "Real dead bodies! Want to see?"

The driver gaped at her. Then he exclaimed, "Dead… bod.… Oh, good Lord, no!"

He jerked back from her, slammed his foot down on the accelerator and spun sand like dust as he roared back out onto the asphalt and left a rubber trail behind him.

She shook her head. "Was it something I said?" she asked a nearby bush.

She burst out laughing. She really did need a vacation, she told herself.

Harley Fowler saw the van sitting on the side of the road as he moved a handful of steers from one pasture to another. With the help of Bob, Cy Parks's veteran cattle dog, he put the little steers into their new area and closed the gate behind him. A carload of boys roared up beside the van and got noisy. They were obviously hassling the crime scene woman. Harley recognized her van.

His pale blue eyes narrowed and began to glitter. He didn't like a gang of boys trying to intimidate a lone woman. He reached into his saddlebag and pulled out his gunbelt, stepping down out of the saddle to strap it on. He tied the horse to a bar of the gate and motioned Bob to stay. Harley strolled off toward the van.

He didn't think he'd have to use the pistol, of course. The threat of it would be more than enough. But if any of the boys decided to have a go at him, he could put them down with his fists. He'd learned a lot from Eb Scott and the local mercs. He didn't need a gun to enforce his authority. But if the sight of it made the gang of boys a little more likely to leave without trouble, that was all right, too.

He moved into sight just at the back of Alice's van. She was leaning over the driver's side of the car. He couldn't hear what she said, but he could certainly hear what the boy exclaimed as he roared out onto the highway and took off.

Alice was talking to a bush.

Harley stared at her with confusion.

Alice sensed that she was no longer alone, and she turned. She blinked. "Have you been there long?" she asked hesitantly.

"Just long enough to see the Happy Teenager Gang take a powder," he replied. "Oh, and to hear you asking a bush about why they left." His eyes twinkled. "Talk to bushes a lot in your line of work, do you?"

She was studying him curiously, especially the low-slung pistol in its holster. "You on your way to a gun-fight and just stopped by to say hello?"

"I was moving steers," he replied. "I heard the teenagers giving you a hard time and came to see if you needed any help. Obviously not."

"Were you going to offer to shoot them for me?" she asked.

He chuckled. "Never had to shoot any kids," he said with emphasis.

"You've shot other sorts of people?"

"One or two," he said pleasantly, but this time he didn't smile.

She felt chills go down her spine. If her livelihood made him queasy, the way he looked wearing that sidearm made her feel the same way. He wasn't the easygoing cowboy she'd met in town the day before. He reminded her oddly of Cash Grier, for reasons she couldn't put into words. There was cold steel in this man. He had the self-confidence of a man who'd been tested under fire. It was unusual, in a modern man. Unless, she considered, he'd been in the military, or some paramilitary unit.

"I don't shoot women," he said when she hesitated.

"Good thing," she replied absently. "I don't have any bandages."

He moved closer. She seemed shaken. He scowled. "You okay?"

She shifted uneasily. "I guess so."

"Mind telling me how you got them to leave so quickly?"

"Oh. That. I just asked if they'd like to see the dead bodies in my van."

He blinked. He was sure he hadn't heard her right. "You asked if…?" he prompted.

She sighed. "I guess it was a little over the top. I was going to call Hayes Carson and have him come out and save me, but it seemed a bit much for a little catcalling."

He didn't smile. "Let me tell you something. A little catcalling, if they get away with it, can lead to a little harassment, and if they get away with that, it can lead to a little assault, even if drugs or alcohol aren't involved. Boys need limits, especially at that age. You should have called it in and let Hayes Carson come out here and scare the hell out of them."

"Well, aren't you the voice of experience!"

"I should be," he replied. "When I was sixteen, an older boy hassled a girl in our class repeatedly on campus after school and made fun of me when I objected to it. A few weeks later, after she'd tried and failed to get somebody to do something about him, he assaulted her."

She let out a whistle. "Heavy stuff."

"Yes, and the teacher who thought I was overreacting when I told him was later disciplined for his lack of response," he added coldly.

"We live in difficult times," she said.

"Count on it."

She glanced in the direction the car had gone. "I still have the license plate number," she murmured.

"Give it to Hayes and tell him what happened," he encouraged her. "Even if you don't press charges, he'll keep an eye on them. Just in case."

She studied his face. "You liked that girl."

"Yes. She was sweet and kind-natured. She…"

She moved a little closer. "She…?"

"She killed herself," he said tightly. "She was very religious. She couldn't live with what happened, especially after she had to testify to it in court and everyone knew."

"They seal those files…" she began.

"Get real," he shot back. "It happened in a small town just outside San Antonio, not much bigger than Jacobsville. I was living there temporarily with a nice older couple and going to school with her when it happened. The people who sat on the jury and in the courtroom were all local. They knew her."

"Oh," she said softly. "I'm sorry."

He nodded.

"How long did the boy get?"

"He was a juvenile," he said heavily. "He was under eighteen when it happened. He stayed in detention until he was twenty-one and they turned him loose."

"Pity."

"Yes." He shook himself as if the memory had taken him over and he wanted to be free of it. "I never heard anything about him after that. I hope he didn't prosper."

"Was he sorry, do you think?"

He laughed coldly. "Sorry he got caught, yes."

"I've seen that sort in court," she replied, her eyes darkening with the memory. "Cocky and self-centered, contemptuous of everybody around them. Especially people in power."

"Power corrupts," he began.

"And absolute power corrupts absolutely," she finished for him. "Lord Acton," she cited belatedly.

"Smart gent." He nodded toward the river. "Any new thoughts on the crime scene?"

She shook her head. "I like to go there alone and think. Sometimes I get ideas. I still can't figure how he died here, when he was from San Antonio, unless he came voluntarily with someone and didn't know they were going to kill him when they arrived."

"Or he came down here to see somebody," he returned, "and was ambushed."

"Wow," she said softly, turning to face him. "You're good."

There was a faint, ruddy color on his high cheekbones. "Thanks."

"No, I mean it," she said when she saw his expression. "That wasn't sarcasm."

He relaxed a little.

"We got off to a bad start, and it's my fault," Alice admitted. "Dead bodies make me nervous. I'm okay once I get started documenting things. It's the first sight of it that upsets me. You caught me at a bad time, at the hardware store. I didn't mean to embarrass you."

"Nothing embarrasses me," he said easily.

"I'm sorry, just the same."

He relaxed a little more.

She frowned as she studied his handsome face. He really was good-looking. "You look so familiar to me," she said. "I can't understand why. I've never met you before."

"They say we all have a doppelgänger," he mused. "Someone who looks just like us."

"Maybe that's it," she agreed. "San Antonio is a big city, for all its small-town atmosphere. We've got a lot of people. You must resemble someone I've seen."

"Probably."

She looked again at the crime scene. "I hope I can get enough evidence to help convict somebody of this. It was a really brutal murder. I don't like to think of people who can do things like that being loose in society."

He was watching her, adding up her nice figure and her odd personality. She was unique. He liked her. He wasn't admitting it, of course.

"How did you get into forensic work?" he asked. "Was it all those crime shows on TV?"

"It was the *Quincy* series," she confessed. "I watched reruns of it on TV when I was a kid. It fascinated me. I liked him, too, but it was the work that caught my attention. He was such an advocate for the victims." Her eyes became soft with reminiscence. "I remember when evidence I collected solved a crime. It was my first real case. The parents of the victim came over and hugged me after the prosecutor pointed me out to them. I always went to the sentencing if I could get away, in cases I worked. That was the first time I realized how important my work was." She grinned wickedly. "The convicted gave me the finger on his way out of the courtroom with a sheriff's deputy. I grinned at him. Felt good. Really good."

He laughed. It was a new sound, and she liked it.

"Does that make me less spooky?" she asked, moving a step closer.

"Yes, it does."

"You think I'm, you know, normal?"

"Nobody's really normal. But I know what you mean," he said, and he smiled at her, a genuine smile. "Yes, I think you're okay."

She cocked her head up at him and her blue eyes twinkled. "Would you believe that extraordinarily handsome Hollywood movie stars actually call me up for dates?"

"Do they, really?" he drawled.

"No, but doesn't it sound exciting?"

He laughed again.

She moved another step closer. "What I said, about not purchasing you if you were on sale in a groom shop... I didn't really mean it. There's a nice ring in that jewelry shop in Jacobsville," she said dreamily. "A man's wedding ring." She peered up through her lashes. "I could buy it for you."

He pursed his lips. "You could?"

"Yes. And I noticed that there's a minister at that Methodist Church. Are you Methodist?"

"Not really."

"Neither am I. Well, there's a justice of the peace in the courthouse. She marries people."

He was just listening now. His eyes were wide.

"If you liked the ring, and if it fit, we could talk to the justice of the peace. They also have licenses."

He pursed his lips again. "Whoa," he said after a minute. "I only met you yesterday."

"I know." She blinked. "What does that have to do with getting married?"

"I don't know you."

"Oh. Okay. I'm twenty-six. I still have most of my own teeth." She displayed them. "I'm healthy and athletic, I like to knit but I can hunt, too, and I have guns. I don't like spinach, but I love liver and onions. Oh, and I'm a virgin." She smiled broadly.

He was breathless by this time. He stared at her intently.

"It's true," she added when he didn't comment. She scowled. "Well, I don't like diseases and you can't look at a man and tell if he has one." She hesitated. Frowned worriedly. "You don't have any...?"

"No, I don't have any diseases," he said shortly. "I'm fastidious about women."

"What a relief!" she said with a huge sigh. "Well, that covers all the basics." Her blue eyes smiled up at him and she batted her long black eyelashes. "So when do we see the justice of the peace?"

"Not today," he replied. "I'm washing Bob."

"Bob?"

He pointed toward the cattle dog, who was still sitting at the pasture gate. He whistled. Bob came running up to him, wagging her long, silky tail and hassling. She looked as if she was always smiling.

"Hi, Bob," Alice said softly, and bent to offer a hand, which Bob smelled. Then Alice stroked the silky head. "Nice boy."

"Girl," he corrected. "Bob's a girl."

She blinked at him.

"Mr. Parks said if Johnny Cash could have a boy named Sue, he could have a girl dog named Bob."

"He's got a point," she agreed. She ruffled Bob's fur affectionately. "You're a beaut, Bob," she told the dog.

"She really is. Best cattle dog in the business, and she can get into places in the brush that we can't, on horseback, to flush out strays."

"Do you come from a ranching family?" she asked absently as she stroked the dog.

"Actually I didn't know much about cattle when I went to work for Mr. Parks. He had one of his men train me."

"Wow. Nice guy."

"He is. Dangerous, but nice."

She lifted her head at the use of the word and frowned slightly. "Dangerous?"

"Do you know anything about Eb Scott and his outfit?"

"The mercenary." She nodded. "We all know about his training camp down here. A couple of our officers use his firing range. He made it available to everyone in law enforcement. He's got friends in our department."

"Well, he and Mr. Parks and Dr. Micah Steele were part of a group who used to make their living as mercenaries."

"I remember now," she exclaimed. "There was a shoot-out with some of that drug lord Lopez's men a few years ago!"

"Yes. I was in it."

She let out a breath. "Brave man, to go up against those bozos. They carry automatic weapons."

"I noticed." That was said with a droll expression worth a hundred words.

She searched his eyes with quiet respect. "Now I really want to see the justice of the peace. I'd be safe anywhere."

He laughed. "I'm not that easy. You haven't even brought me flowers, or asked me out to a nice restaurant."

"Oh, dear."

"What?"

"I don't get paid until Friday, and I'm broke," she said sorrowfully. She made a face. "Well, maybe next week? Or we could go dutch…"

He chuckled with pure delight. "I'm broke, too."

"So, next week?"

"We'll talk about it."

She grinned. "Okay."

"Better get your van going," he said, holding out a palm-up hand and looking up. "We're going to get a rain shower. You could be stuck in that soft sand when it gets wet."

"I could. See you."

"See you."

She took off running for the van. Life was looking up, she thought happily.

Chapter 3

Harley went back to the ranch house with Bob racing beside his horse. He felt exhilarated for the first time in years. Usually he got emotionally involved with girls who were already crazy about some other man. He was the comforting shoulder, the listening ear. But Alice Jones seemed to really like him.

Of course, there was her profession. He felt cold when he thought about her hands working on dead tissue. That was a barrier he'd have to find some way to get past. Maybe by concentrating on what a cute woman she was.

Cy Parks was outside, looking over a bunch of young bulls in the corral. He looked up when Harley dismounted.

"What do you think, Harley?" he asked, nodding toward several very trim young Santa Gertrudis bulls.

"Nice," he said. "These the ones you bought at the auction we went to back in October? Gosh, they've grown!"

He nodded. "They are. I brought them in to show to J. D. Langley. He's looking for some young bulls for his own herd. I thought I'd sell him a couple of these. Good thing I didn't have to send them back."

Harley chuckled. "Good thing, for the seller. I remember the lot we sent back last year. I had to help you deliver them."

"Yes, I remember," Cy replied. "He slugged you and I slugged him."

Harley resisted a flush. It made him feel good, that Mr. Parks liked him enough to defend him. He could hardly recall his father. It had been years since they'd had any contact at all. He felt a little funny recalling how he'd lied to his boss about his family, claiming that his mother could help brand cattle and his father was a mechanic. He'd gone to live with an older couple he knew after a fight with his real folks. It was a small ranch they owned, but only the wife lived on it. Harley had stayed in town with the husband at his mechanic's shop most of the time. He hadn't been interested in cattle at the time. Now they were his life and Mr. Parks had taken the place of his father, although Harley had never put it into words. Someday, he guessed, he was going to have to tell his boss the truth about himself. But not today.

"Have any trouble settling the steers in their new pasture?" Cy asked.

"None at all. The forensic lady was out at the river."

"Alice Jones?"

"Yes. She said sometimes she likes to look around crime scenes alone. She gets impressions." He smiled.

"I helped her with an idea about how the murder was committed."

Parks looked at him and smiled. "You've got a good brain, Harley."

He grinned. "Thanks."

"So what was your idea?"

"Maybe the victim was here to see somebody and got ambushed."

Parks's expression became solemn. "That's an interesting theory. If she doesn't share it with Hayes Carson, you should. There may be somebody local involved in all this."

"That's not a comforting thought."

"I know." He frowned as he noted the gun and holster Harley was wearing. "Did we have a gunfight and I wasn't invited?"

"This?" Harley fingered the butt of the gun. "Oh. No! There were some local boys trying to harass Alice. I strapped it on for effect and went to help her, but she'd already sent them running."

"Threatened to call the cops, huh?" he asked pleasantly.

"She invited them to her van to look at bodies," he said, chuckling. "They left tread marks on the highway."

He grinned back. "Well! Sounds like she has a handle on taking care of herself."

"Yes. But we all need a little backup, from time to time," Harley said.

Cy put a hand on Harley's shoulder. "You were mine, that night we had the shoot-out with the drug dealers. You're a good man under fire."

"Thanks," Harley said, flushing a little with the

praise. "You'll never know how I felt, when you said that, after we got home."

"Maybe I do. See about that cattle truck, will you? I think it's misfiring again, and you're the best mechanic we've got."

"I'll do it. Just don't tell Buddy you meant it," he pleaded. "He's supposed to be the mechanic."

"Supposed to be is right," Cy huffed. "But I guess you've got a point. Try to tell him, in a nice way, that he needs to check the spark plugs."

"You could tell him," Harley began.

"Not the way you can. If I tell him, he'll quit." He grimaced. "Already lost one mechanic that way this year. Can't afford to lose another. You do it."

Harley laughed. "Okay. I'll find a way."

"You always do. Don't know what I'd do without you, Harley. You're an asset as a foreman." He studied the younger man quietly. "I never asked where you came from. You said you knew cattle, but you really didn't. You learned by watching, until I hooked you up with old Cal and let him tutor you. I always respected the effort you put in, to learn the cattle business. But you're still as mysterious as you were the day you turned up."

"Sometimes it's better to look ahead, and not backward," Harley replied.

Parks smiled. "Enough said. See you later."

"Sure."

He walked off toward the house where his young wife, Lisa, was waiting with one preschool-aged boy and one infant boy in her arms. Of all the people Harley would never have expected to marry, Mr. Parks was first on his list. The rancher had been reclusive, hard to get along with and, frankly, bad company. Lisa had changed him. Now it was impossible to think of him as anything except a family man. Marriage had mellowed him.

Harley thought about what Parks had said, about how mysterious he was. Maybe Mr. Parks thought he was running from the law. That was a real joke. Harley was running from his family. He'd had it up to his neck with monied circles and important people and parents who thought position was everything. They'd argued heatedly one summer several years ago, when Harley was sixteen, about Harley's place in the family and his lack of interest in their social life. He'd walked out.

He had a friend whose aunt and uncle owned a small ranch and had a mechanic's shop in Floresville. He'd taken Harley down there and they'd invited him to move in. He'd had his school files transferred to the nearest high school and he'd started his life over. His parents had objected, but they hadn't tried to force him to come back home. He graduated and went into the Army. But, just after he returned to Texas following his release from the Army, he went to see his parents and saw that nothing had changed at all. He was expected to do his part for the family by helping win friends and influencing the right people. Harley had left that very night, paid cash for a very old beat-up pickup truck and turned himself into a vagabond cowhand looking for work.

He'd gone by to see the elderly couple he'd lived with during his last year of high school, but the woman had died, the ranch had been sold and the mechanic had moved to Dallas. Discouraged, Harley had been driving through Jacobsville looking for a likely place to hire on when he'd seen cowboys working cattle beside the road. He'd talked to them and heard that Cy Parks was hiring. The rest was history.

He knew that people wondered about him. He kept his silence. It was new and pleasant to be accepted at face value, to have people look at him for who he was and what he knew how to do rather than at his background. He was happy in Jacobsville.

He did wonder sometimes if his people missed him. He read about them in the society columns. There had been a big political dustup just recently and a landslide victory for a friend of his father's. That had caught his attention. But it hadn't prompted him to try to mend fences. Years had passed since his sudden exodus from San Antonio, but it was still too soon for that. No, he liked being just plain Harley Fowler, cowboy. He wasn't risking his hard-won place in Jacobsville for anything.

Alice waited for Hayes Carson in his office, frowning as she looked around. Wanted posters. Reams of paperwork. A computer that was obsolete, paired with a printer that was even more obsolete. An old IBM Selectric typewriter. A battered metal wastebasket that looked as if it got kicked fairly often. A CB unit. She shook her head. There wasn't one photograph anywhere in the room, except for a framed one of Hayes's father, Dallas, who'd been sheriff before him. Nothing personal.

Hayes walked in, reading a sheet of paper.

"You really travel light, don't you?" Alice mused.

He looked up, surprised. "Why do you say that?"

"This is the most impersonal office I've ever walked into. Wait." She held up a hand. "I take that back. Jon

Blackhawk's office is worse. He doesn't even have a photograph in his."

"My dad would haunt me if I removed his." He chuckled, sitting down behind the desk.

"Heard anything from the feds?"

"Yes. They got a report back on the car. It was reported missing by a woman who works for a San Antonio politician yesterday. She has no idea who took it."

"Damn." She sighed and leaned back. "Well, Longfellow's working on that piece of paper I found at the crime scene and we may get something from the cast I made of the footprint. We did find faint sole markings, from a sneaker. FBI lab has the cast. They'll track down which company made the shoe and try to trace where it was sold."

"That's a damned long shot."

"Hey, they've solved crimes from chips of paint."

"I guess so."

She was deep in thought. "Odd, how that paper was pushed into the dirt under his hand."

"Somebody stepped on it," Hayes reminded her.

"No." Her eyes narrowed. "It was clenched in the victim's hand and hidden under it."

Hayes frowned. "Maybe the victim was keeping it hidden deliberately?"

She nodded. "Like, maybe he knew he was going to die and wanted to leave a clue that might bring his killer to justice."

Hayes chuckled. "Jones, you watch too many crime dramas on TV."

"Actually, to hear the clerk at the hardware tell it I don't watch enough," she sighed. "I got a ten-minute lecture on forensic entomology while he hunted up some supplies I needed."

"Bug forensics?" he asked.

She nodded. "You can tell time of death by insect activity. I've actually taken courses on it. And I've solved at least one murder with the help of a bug expert." She pushed back a stray wisp of dark hair. "But what's really interesting, Carson, is teeth."

He frowned. "Teeth?"

She nodded. "Dentition. You can tell so much about a DB from its teeth, especially if there are dental records available. For example, there's Carabelli's cusp, which is most frequently found in people of European ancestry. Then there's the Uto-Aztecan upper premolar with a bulging buccal cusp, which is found only in Native Americans. You can identify Asian ancestry in shovel-shaped incisors... Well, anyway, your ancestry, even the story of your life, is in your teeth. Your diet, your age..."

"Whether you got in bar fights," he interrupted.

She laughed. "Missing some teeth, are we?"

"Only a couple," he said easily. "I've calmed right down in my old age."

"You and Kilraven," she agreed dubiously.

He laughed. "Not that yahoo," he corrected. "Kilraven will never calm down, and you can quote me."

"He might, if he can ever slay his demons." She frowned thoughtfully and narrowed her eyes. "We have a lot of law enforcement down here that works in San Antonio." She was thinking out loud. "There's Garon Grier, the assistant SAC in the San Antonio field office. There's Rick Marquez, who works as a detective for San Antonio P.D. And then there's Kilraven."

"You trying to say something?" he asked.

She shook her head. "I'm linking unconnected facts. Sometimes it helps. Okay, here goes. A guy comes down here from San Antonio and gets whacked. He's driving somebody else's stolen car. He's messed up so badly that his own mother couldn't identify him. Whoever killed him didn't want him ID'd."

"Lots of reasons for that, maybe."

"Maybe. Hear me out. I'm doing pattern associations." She got up, locked her hands behind her waist and started pacing, tossing out thoughts as they presented themselves. "Of all those law enforcement people, Kilraven's been the most conspicuous in San Antonio lately. He was with his brother, Jon, when they tried to solve the kidnapping of Gracie Marsh, Jason Pendleton's stepsister…"

"Pendleton's wife, now," he interrupted with a grin.

She returned it. "He was also connected with the rescue of Rodrigo Ramirez, the DEA agent kidnapping victim whose wife, Glory, was an assistant D.A. in San Antonio."

Hayes leaned back in his chair. "That wasn't made public, any of it."

She nodded absently.

"Rick Marquez has been pretty visible, too," he pointed out. He frowned. "Wasn't Rick trying to convince Kilraven to let him reopen that murder case that involved his family?"

"Come to think of it, yes," she replied, stopping in front of the desk. "Kilraven refused. He said it would only resurrect all the pain, and the media would dine out on it. He and Jon both refused. They figured it was a random crime and the perp was long gone."

"But that wasn't the end of it."

"No," she said. "Marquez refused to quit. He promised to do his work on the QT and not reveal a word of it to anybody except the detective he brought in to help him sort through the old files." She grimaced. "But the investigation went nowhere. Less than a week into their project, Marquez and his fellow detective were told to drop the investigation."

Hayes pursed his lips. "Now isn't that interesting?"

"There's more," she said. "Marquez and the detective went to the D.A. and promised to get enough evidence to reopen the case if they were allowed to continue. The D.A. said to let him talk to a few people. The very next week, the detective who was working with Marquez on the case was suddenly pulled off Homicide and sent back to the uniformed division as a patrol sergeant. And Marquez was told politely to keep his nose out of the matter and not to pursue it any further."

Hayes was frowning now. "You know, it sounds very much as if somebody high up doesn't want that case reopened. And I have to ask why?"

She nodded. "Somebody is afraid the case may be solved. If I'm guessing right, somebody with an enormous amount of power in government."

"And we both know what happens when power is abused," Hayes said with a scowl. "Years ago, when I was still a deputy sheriff, one of my fellow deputies—a new recruit—decided on his own to investigate rumors of a house of prostitution being run out of a local motel. Like a lamb, he went to the county council and brought it up in an open meeting."

Alice grimaced, because she knew from long experience what most likely happened after that. "Poor guy!"

"Well, after he was fired and run out of town," Hayes said, "I was called in and told that I was not to involve myself in that case, if I wanted to continue as a deputy sheriff in this county. I'd made the comment that no law officer should be fired for doing his job, you see."

"What did you do?" she asked, because she knew Hayes. He wasn't the sort of person to take a threat like that lying down.

"Ran for sheriff and won," he said simply. He grinned. "Turns out the head of the county council was getting kickbacks from the pimp. I found out, got the evidence and called a reporter I knew in San Antonio."

"That reporter?" she exclaimed. "He got a Pulitzer Prize for the story! My gosh, Hayes, the head of the county council went to prison! But it was for more than corruption…"

"He and the pimp also ran a modest drug distribution ring," he interrupted. "He'll be going up before the parole board in a few months. I plan to attend the hearing." He smiled. "I do so enjoy these little informal board meetings."

"Ouch."

"People who go through life making their money primarily through dishonest dealings don't usually reform," he said quietly. "It's a basic character trait that no amount of well-meaning rehabilitation can reverse."

"We live among some very unsavory people."

"Yes. That's why we have law enforcement. I might add, that the law enforcement on the county level here is exceptional."

She snarled at him. He just grinned.

"What's your next move?" she asked.

"I'm not making one until I know what's in that note.

Shouldn't your assistant have something by now, even if it's only the text of the message?"

"She should." Alice pulled out her cell phone and called her office. "But I'm probably way off base about Kilraven's involvement in this. Maybe the victim just ticked off the wrong people and paid for it. Maybe he had unpaid drug bills or something."

"That's always a possibility," Hayes had to agree.

The phone rang and rang. Finally it was answered. "Crime lab, Longfellow speaking."

"Did you know that you have the surname of a famous poet?" Alice teased.

The other woman was all business, all the time, and she didn't get jokes. "Yes. I'm a far-removed distant cousin of the poet, in fact. You want to know about your scrap of paper, I suppose? It's much too early for any analysis of the paper or ink…"

"The writing, Longfellow, the writing," Alice interrupted.

"As I said, it's too early in the analysis. We'd need a sample to compare, first, and then we'd need a handwriting expert…"

"But what does the message *say?*" Alice blurted out impatiently. Honest to God, the other woman was so ponderously slow sometimes!

"Oh, that. Just a minute." There was a pause, some paper ruffling, a cough. Longfellow came back on the line. "It doesn't say anything."

"You can't make out the letters? Is it waterlogged or something?"

"It doesn't have letters."

"Then what does it have?" Alice said with the last of her patience straining at the leash. She was picturing Longfellow on the floor with herself standing over the lab tech with a large studded bat…

"It has numbers, Jones," came the droll reply. "Just a few numbers. Nothing else."

"An address?"

"Not likely."

"Give me the numbers."

"Only the last six are visible. The others apparently were obliterated by the man's sweaty palms when he clenched it so tightly. Here goes."

She read the series of numbers.

"Which ones were obliterated?" Alice asked.

"Looks like the ones at the beginning. If it's a telephone number, the area code and the first of the exchange numbers is missing. We'll probably be able to reconstruct those at the FBI lab, but not immediately. Sorry."

"No, listen, you've been a world of help. If I controlled salaries, you'd get a raise."

"Why, thank you, Jones," came the astonished reply. "That's very kind of you to say."

"You're very welcome. Let me know if you come up with anything else."

"Of course I will."

Alice hung up. She looked at the numbers and frowned.

"What have you got?" Hayes asked.

"I'm not sure. A telephone number, perhaps."

He moved closer and peered at the paper where she'd written those numbers down. "Could that be the exchange?" he asked, noting some of the numbers.

"I don't know. If it is, it could be a San Antonio number, but we'd need to have the area code to determine that, and it's missing."

"Get that lab busy."

She glowered at him. "Like we sleep late, take two-hour coffee breaks and wander into the crime lab about noon daily!"

"Sorry," he said, and grinned.

She pursed her full lips and gave him a roguish look. "Hey, you law enforcement guys live at doughnut shops and lounge around in the office reading sports magazines and playing games on the computer, right?"

He glowered back.

She held out one hand, palm up. "Welcome to the stereotype club."

"When will she have some more of those numbers?"

"Your guess is as good as mine. Has anybody spoken to the woman whose car was stolen to ask if someone she knew might have taken it? Or to pump her for information and find out if she really loaned it to him?" she added shrewdly.

"No, nobody's talked to her. The feds in charge of the investigation wanted to wait until they had enough information to coax her into giving them something they needed," he said.

"As we speak, they're roping Jon Blackhawk to his desk chair and gagging him," she pronounced with a grin. "His first reaction would be to drag her downtown and grill her."

"He's young and hotheaded. At least to hear his brother tell it."

"Kilraven loves his brother," Alice replied. "But he does know his failings."

"I wouldn't call rushing in headfirst a failing," Hayes pointed out.

"That's why you've been shot, Hayes," she said.

"Anybody can get shot," he said.

"Yes, but you've been shot twice," she rem... "The word locally is that you'd have a better ch... being named king of some small country than y... d have getting a wife. Nobody around here is rushing to line up and become a widow."

"I've calmed down," he muttered defensively. "And who's been saying that, anyway?"

"I heard that Minette Raynor was," she replied without quite meeting his eyes.

His jaw tautened. "I have no desire to marry Miss Raynor, now or ever," he returned coldly. "She helped kill my brother."

"She didn't, and you have proof, but suit yourself," she said when he looked angry enough to say something unforgivable. "Now, do you have any idea how we can talk to that woman before somebody shuts her up? It looks like whoever killed that poor man on the river wouldn't hesitate to give him company. I'd bet my reputation that he knew something that could bring down someone powerful, and he was stopped dead first. If the woman has any info at all, she's on the endangered list."

"Good point," Hayes had to admit. "Do you have a plan?"

She shook her head. "I wish."

"About that number, you might run it by the 911 operators," he said. "They deal with a lot of telephone traffic. They might recognize it."

"Now that's constructive thinking," she said with a grin. "But this isn't my jurisdiction, you know."

"The crime was committed in the county. That's my jurisdiction. I'm giving you the authority to investigate."

"Won't your own investigator feel slighted?"

"He would if he was here," he sighed. "He took his remaining days off and went to Wyoming for Christmas. He said he'd lose them if he didn't use them by the end of the year. I couldn't disagree and we didn't have much going on when I let him go." He shook his head. "He'll punch me when he gets back and discovers that we had a real DB right here and he didn't get to investigate it."

"The way things look," she said slowly, "he may still get to help. I don't think we're going to solve this one in a couple of days."

"Hey, I saw a murder like this one on one of those CSI shows," he said with pretended excitement. "They sent trace evidence out, got results in two hours and had the guy arrested and convicted and sent to jail just before the last commercial!"

She gave him a smile and a gesture that was universal before she picked up her purse, and the slip of paper, and left his office.

She was eating lunch at Barbara's Café in town when the object of her most recent daydreams walked in, tall and handsome in real cowboy duds, complete with a shepherd's coat, polished black boots and a real black Stetson cowboy hat with a brim that looked just like the one worn by Richard Boone in the television series *Have Gun Will Travel* that she used to watch videos of. It was cocked over his eyes and he looked as much like a desperado as he did a working cowboy.

He spotted Alice as he was paying for his meal at the counter and grinned at her. She turned over a cup of coffee and it spilled all over the table, which made his grin much bigger.

Barbara came running with a towel. "Don't worry, it happens all the time," she reassured Alice. She glanced at Harley, put some figures together and chuckled. "Ah, romance is in the air."

"It is not," Alice said firmly. "I offered to take him to a movie, but I'm broke, and he won't go dutch treat," she added in a soft wail.

"Aww," Barbara sympathized.

"I don't get paid until next Friday," Alice said, dabbing at wet spots on her once-immaculate oyster-white wool slacks. "I'll be miles away by then."

"I get paid this Friday," Harley said, straddling a chair opposite Alice with a huge steak and fries on a platter. "Are you having a salad for lunch?" he asked, aghast at the small bowl at her elbow. "You'll never be able to do any real investigating on a diet like that. You need protein." He indicated the juicy, rare steak on his own plate.

Alice groaned. He didn't understand. She'd spent so many hours working in her lab that she couldn't really eat a steak anymore. It was heresy here in Texas, so she tended to keep her opinions to herself. If she said anything like that, there would be a riot in Barbara's Café.

So she just smiled. "Fancy seeing you here," she teased.

He grinned. "I'll bet it wasn't a surprise," he said as he began to carve his steak.

"Whatever do you mean?" she asked with pretended innocence.

"I was just talking to Hayes Carson out on the street and he happened to mention that you asked him where I ate lunch," he replied.

She huffed. "Well, that's the last personal question I'll ever ask him, and you can take that to the bank!"

"Should I mention that I asked him where *you* ate lunch?" he added with a twinkle in his pale eyes.

Alice's irritated expression vanished. She sighed. "Did you, really?" she asked.

"I did, really. But don't take that as a marriage proposal," he said. "I almost never propose to crime scene investigators over lunch."

"Crime scene investigators?" a cowboy from one of the nearby ranches exclaimed, leaning toward them. "Listen, I watch those shows all the time. Did you know that they can tell time of death by…!"

"Oh, dear, I'm so sorry!" Alice exclaimed as the cowboy gaped at her. She'd "accidentally" poured a glass of iced tea all over him. "It's a reflex," she tried to explain as Barbara came running, again. "You see, every time somebody talks about the work I do, I just get all excited and start throwing things!" She picked up her salad bowl. "It's a helpless reflex, I just can't stop…"

"No problem!" the cowboy said at once, scrambling to his feet. "I had to get back to work anyway! Don't think a thing about it!"

He rushed out the door, trailing tea and ice chips, leaving behind half a cup of coffee and a couple of bites of pie and an empty plate.

Harley was trying not to laugh, but he lost it completely. Barbara was chuckling as she motioned to one of her girls to get a broom and pail.

"I'm sorry," Alice told her. "Really."

Barbara gave her an amused glance. "You don't like to talk shop at the table, do you?"

"No. I don't," she confessed.

"Don't worry," Barbara said as the broom and pail and a couple of paper towels were handed to her. "I'll make sure word gets around. Before lunch tomorrow," she added, still laughing.

Chapter 4

After that, nobody tried to engage Alice in conversation about her job. The meal was pleasant and friendly. Alice liked Harley. He had a good personality, and he actually improved on closer acquaintance, as so many people didn't. He was modest and unassuming, and he didn't try to monopolize the conversation.

"How's your investigation coming?" he asked when they were on second cups of black coffee.

She shrugged. "Slowly," she replied. "We've got a partial number, possibly a telephone number, a stolen car whose owner didn't know it was stolen and a partial sneaker track that we're hoping someone can identify."

"I saw a program on the FBI lab that showed how they do that," Harley replied. He stopped immediately as soon as he realized what he'd said. He sat with his fork poised in midair, eyeing Alice's refilled coffee mug.

She laughed. "Not to worry. I'll control my reflexes. Actually the lab does a very good job running down sneaker treads," she added. "The problem is that most treads are pretty common. You get the name of a company that produces them and then start wearing out shoe leather going to stores and asking for information about people who bought them."

"What about people who paid cash and there's no record of their buying them?"

"I never said investigation techniques were perfect," she returned, smiling. "We use what we can get."

He frowned. "Those numbers, it shouldn't be that hard to isolate a telephone number, should it? You could narrow it down with a computer program."

"Yes, but there are so many possible combinations, considering that we don't even have the area code." She groaned. "And we'll have to try every single one."

He pursed his lips. "The car, then. Are you sure the person who owned it didn't have a connection to the murder victim?"

She raised her eyebrows. "Ever considered a career in law enforcement?"

He laughed. "I did, once. A long time ago." He grimaced, as if the memory wasn't a particularly pleasant one.

"We're curious about the car," she said, "but they don't want to spook the car's owner. It turns out that she works for a particularly unpleasant member of the political community."

His eyebrows lifted. "Who?"

She hesitated.

"Come on. I'm a clam. Ask my boss."

"Okay. It's the senior U.S. senator from Texas who lives in San Antonio," she confessed.

Harley made an ungraceful movement and sat back in his chair. He stared toward the window without really seeing anything. "You think the politician may be connected in some way?"

"There's no way of knowing right now," she sighed. "Everybody big in political circles has people who work for them. Anybody can get involved with a bad person and not know it."

"Are they going to question the car owner?"

"I'm sure they will, eventually. They just want to pick the right time to do it."

He toyed with his coffee cup. "So, are you staying here for a while?"

She grimaced. "A few more days, just to see if I can develop any more leads. Hayes Carson wants me to look at the car while the lab's processing it, so I guess I'll go up to San Antonio for that and come back here when I'm done."

He just nodded, seemingly distracted.

She studied him with a whimsical expression. "So, when are we getting married?" she asked.

He gave her an amused look. "Not today. I have to move cattle."

"My schedule is very flexible," she assured him.

He smiled. "Mine isn't."

"Rats."

"Now that's interesting, I was just thinking about rats. I have to get cat food while I'm in town."

She blinked. "Cat food. For rats?"

"We keep barn cats to deal with the rat problem," he

explained. "But there aren't quite enough mice and rats to keep the cats healthy, so we supplement."

"I like cats," she said with a sigh and a smile. "Maybe we could adopt some stray ones when we get married." She frowned. "Now that's going to be a problem."

"Cats are?"

"No. Where are we going to live?" she persisted. "My job is in San Antonio and yours is here. I know," she said, brightening. "I'll commute!"

He laughed. She made him feel light inside. He finished his coffee. "Better work on getting the bridegroom first," he pointed out.

"Okay. What sort of flowers do you like, and when are we going on our first date?"

He pursed his lips. She was outrageously forward, but behind that bluff personality, he saw something deeper and far more fragile. She was shy. She was like a storefront with piñatas and confetti that sold elegant silverware. She was disguising her real persona with an exaggerated one.

He leaned back in his chair, feeling oddly arrogant at her interest in him. His eyes narrowed and he smiled. "I was thinking we might take in a movie at one of those big movie complexes in San Antonio. Friday night."

"Ooooooh," she exclaimed, bright-eyed. "I like science fiction."

"So do I, and there's a remake of a 1950s film playing. I wouldn't mind seeing it."

"Neither would I."

"I'll pick you up at your motel about five. We'll have dinner and take in the movie afterward. That suit you?"

She was nodding furiously. "Should I go ahead and buy the rings?" she asked with an innocent expression.

He chuckled. "I told you, I'm too tied up right now for weddings."

She snapped her fingers. "Darn!"

"But we can see a movie."

"I like movies."

"Me, too."

They paid for their respective meals and walked out together, drawing interest from several of the café patrons. Harley hadn't been taking any girls around with him lately, and here was this cute CSI lady from San Antonio having lunch with him. Speculation ran riot.

"They'll have us married by late afternoon," he remarked, nodding toward the windows, where curious eyes were following their every move.

"I'll go back in and invite them all to the wedding, shall I?" she asked at once.

"Kill the engine, dude," he drawled in a perfect imitation of the sea turtle in his favorite cartoon movie.

"You so totally rock, Squirt!" she drawled back.

He laughed. "Sweet. You like cartoon movies, too?"

"Crazy about them," she replied. "My favorite right now is *Wall-E,* but it changes from season to season. They just get better all the time."

"I liked *Wall-E,* too," he agreed. "Poignant story. Beautiful soundtrack."

"My sentiments, exactly. That's nice. When we have kids, we'll enjoy taking them to the theater to see the new cartoon movies."

He took off his hat and started fanning himself. "Don't mention kids or I'll faint!" he exclaimed. "I'm already having hot flashes, just considering the thought of marriage!"

She glared at him. "Women have hot flashes when they enter menopause," she said, emphasizing the first word.

He lifted his eyebrows and grinned. "Maybe I'm a woman in disguise," he whispered wickedly.

She wrinkled her nose up and gave him a slow, interested scrutiny from his cowboy boots to his brown hair. "It's a really good disguise," she had to agree. She growled, low in her throat, and smiled. "Tell you what, after the movie, we can undress you and see how good a disguise it really is."

"Well, I never!" he exclaimed, gasping. "I'm not that kind of man, I'll have you know! And if you keep talking like that, I'll never marry you. A man has his principles. You're just after my body!"

Alice was bursting at the seams with laughter. Harley followed her eyes, turned around, and there was Kilraven, in uniform, staring at him.

"I read this book," Kilraven said after a minute, "about a Scot who disguised himself as a woman for three days after he stole an English payroll destined for the turncoat Scottish Lords of the Congregation who were going to try to depose Mary, Queen of Scots. The family that sheltered him was rewarded with compensation that was paid for centuries, even after his death, they say. He knew how to repay a debt." He frowned. "But that was in the sixteenth century, and you don't look a thing like Lord Bothwell."

"I should hope not," Harley said. "He's been dead for over four hundred years!"

Alice moved close to him and bumped him with her hip. "Don't talk like that. Some of my best friends are dead people."

Harley and Kilraven both groaned.

"It was a joke," Alice burst out, exasperated. "My goodness, don't you people have a sense of humor?"

"He doesn't," Harley said, indicating Kilraven.

"I do so," Kilraven shot back, glaring. "I have a good sense of humor." He stepped closer. "And you'd better say that I do, because I'm armed."

"You have a great sense of humor," Harley replied at once, and grinned.

"What are you doing here?" Alice asked suddenly. "I thought you were supposed to be off today."

Kilraven shrugged. "One of our boys came down with flu and they needed somebody to fill in. Not much to do around here on a day off, so I volunteered," he added.

"There's TV," Alice said.

He scoffed. "I don't own a TV," he said huffily. "I read books."

"European history?" Harley asked, recalling the mention of Bothwell.

"Military history, mostly, but history is history. For instance," he began, "did you know that Hannibal sealed poisonous snakes in clay urns and had his men throw them onto the decks of enemy ships as an offensive measure?"

Harley was trying to keep a straight face.

Alice didn't even try. "You're kidding!"

"I am not. Look it up."

"I'd have gone right over the side into the ocean!" Alice exclaimed, shivering.

"So did a lot of the enemy combatants." Kilraven chuckled. "See what you learn when you read, instead of staying glued to a television set?"

"How can you not have a television set?" Harley exclaimed. "You can't watch the news…"

"Don't get me started," Kilraven muttered. "Corporate news, exploiting private individuals with personal problems for the entertainment of the masses! Look at that murder victim who was killed back in the summer, and the family of the accused is still getting crucified nightly in case they had anything to do with it. You call that news? I call it bread and circuses, just like the arena in ancient Rome!"

"Then how do you know what's going on in the world?" Alice had to know.

"I have a laptop computer with Internet access," he said. "That's where the real news is."

"A revolutionary," Harley said.

"An anarchist," Alice corrected.

"I am an upstanding member of law enforcement," Kilraven retorted. He glanced at the big watch on his wrist. "And I'm going to be late getting back on duty if I don't get lunch pretty soon."

Harley was looking at the watch and frowning. He knew the model. It was one frequently worn by mercs. "Blade or garrote?" he asked Kilraven, nodding at the watch.

Kilraven was surprised, but he recovered quickly. "Blade," he said. "How did you know?"

"Micah Steele used to wear one just like it."

Kilraven leaned down. "Guess who I bought it from?" he asked. He grinned. With a wave, he sauntered into the café.

"What were you talking about?" Alice asked curiously.

"Trade secret," Harley returned. "I have to get going. I'll see you Friday."

He turned away and then, just as suddenly turned back. "Wait a minute." He pulled a small pad and pencil out of his shirt pocket and jotted down a number. He tore off the paper and handed it to her. "That's my cell phone number. If anything comes up, and you can't make it Friday, you can call me."

"Can I call you anyway?" she asked.

He blinked. "What for?"

"To talk. You know, if I have any deeply personal problems that just can't wait until Friday?"

He laughed. "Alice, it's only two days away," he said.

"I could be traumatized by a snake or something."

He sighed. "Okay. But only then. It's hard to pull a cell phone out of its holder when you're knee-deep in mud trying to extract mired cattle."

She beamed. "I'll keep that in mind." She tucked the number in the pocket of her slacks. "I enjoyed lunch."

"Yeah," he said, smiling. "Me, too."

She watched him walk away with covetous eyes. He really did have a sensuous body, very masculine. She stood sighing over him until she realized that several pair of eyes were still watching her from inside the café. With a self-conscious grin in their direction, she went quickly to her van.

The pattern in the tennis shoes was so common that Alice had serious doubts that they'd ever locate the seller, much less the owner. The car was going to be a much better lead. She went up to the crime lab while they were processing it. There was some trace evidence that was promising. She also had Sergeant Rick Marquez, who worked out of San Antonio P.D., get as much information as he could about the woman the murdered man had stolen the car from.

The next morning in Jacobsville, on his way to work in San Antonio, Rick stopped by Alice's motel room to give her the information he'd managed to obtain. "She's been an employee of Senator Fowler for about two years," Rick said, perching on the edge of the dresser in front of the bed while she paced. "She's deeply religious. She goes to church on Sundays and Wednesdays. She's involved in an outreach program for the homeless, and she gives away a good deal of her salary to people she considers more needy." He shook his head. "You read about these people, but you rarely encounter them in real life. She hasn't got a black mark on her record anywhere, unless you consider a detention in high school for being late three days in a row when her mother was in the hospital."

"Wow," Alice exclaimed softly.

"There's more. She almost lost the job by lecturing the senator for hiring illegal workers and threatening them with deportation if they asked for higher wages."

"What a sweetheart," Alice muttered.

"From what we hear, the senator is the very devil to work for. They say his wife is almost as hard-nosed. She was a state supreme court judge before she went into the import/export business. She made millions at it. Finances a good part of the senator's reelection campaigns."

"Is he honest?"

"Is any politician?" Marquez asked cynically. "He sits on several powerful committees in Congress, and was once accused of taking kickbacks from a Mexican official."

"For what?"

"He was asked to oppose any shoring up of border security. Word is that the senator and his contact have their fingers in some illegal pies, most notably drug trafficking. But there's no proof. The last detective who tried to investigate the senator is now working traffic detail."

"A vengeful man."

"Very."

"I don't suppose that detective would talk to me?" she wondered aloud.

"She might," he replied surprisingly. "She and I were trying to get the Kilraven family murder case reopened, if you recall, when pressure was put on us to stop. She turned her attention to the senator and got kicked out of the detective squad." He grimaced. "She's a good woman. Got an invalid kid to look after and an ex-husband who's a pain in the butt, to put it nicely."

"We heard about the cold case being closed. You think the senator might have been responsible for it?" she wondered aloud.

"We don't know. He has a protégé who's just been elected junior senator from Texas, and the protégé has some odd ties to people who aren't exactly the crème of society. But we don't dare mention that in public." He smiled. "I don't fancy being put on a motorcycle at my age and launched into traffic duty."

"Your friend isn't having to do that, surely?" she asked.

"No, she's working two-car patrols on the night shift, but she's a sergeant, so she gets a good bit of desk work."

He studied her. "What's this I hear about you trying to marry Harley?"

She grinned. "It's early days. He's shy, but I'm going to drown him in flowers and chocolate until he says yes."

"Good luck," he said with a chuckle.

"I won't even need it. We're going to a movie together Friday."

"Are you? What are you going to see?"

"The remake of that fifties movie. We're going to dinner first."

"You are a fast worker, Alice," he said with respect. He checked his watch. "I've got to get back to the precinct."

She glanced at his watch curiously. "You don't have a blade or a wire in that thing, do you?"

"Not likely," he assured her. "Those watches cost more than I make, and they're used almost exclusively by mercs."

"Mercs?" She frowned.

"Soldiers of fortune. They work for the highest bidder, although our local crowd had more honor than that."

Mercs. Now she understood Harley's odd phrasing about "trade secrets."

"Where did you see a watch like that?" he asked.

She looked innocent. "I heard about one from Harley. I just wondered what they were used for."

"Oh. Well, I guess if you were in a tight spot, it might save your life to have one of those," he agreed, distracted.

"Before you go, can you give me the name and address of that detective in San Antonio?" she asked.

He hesitated. "Better let me funnel the questions

to her, Alice," he said with a smile. "She doesn't want anything to slip out about her follow-ups on that case. She's still working it, without permission."

She raised an eyebrow. "So are you, unless I miss my guess. Does Kilraven know?"

He shook his head. Then he hesitated. "Well, I don't think he does. He and Jon Blackhawk still don't want us nosing around. They're afraid the media will pick up the story and it will become the nightly news for a year or so." He shook his head. "Pitiful, how the networks don't go out and get any real news anymore. They just create it by harping on private families mixed up in tragedies, like living soap operas."

"That's how corporate media works," she told him. "If you want real news, buy a local weekly newspaper."

He laughed. "You're absolutely right. Take care, Alice."

"You, too. Thanks for the help."

"Anytime." He paused at the door and grinned at her. "If Harley doesn't work out, you could always pursue me," he invited. "I'm young and dashing and I even have long hair." He indicated his ponytail. "I played semi-professional soccer when I was in college, and I have a lovely singing voice."

She chuckled. "I've heard about your singing voice, Marquez. Weren't you asked, very politely, to stay out of the church choir?"

"I wanted to meet women," he said. "The choir was full of unattached ones. But I can sing," he added belligerently. "Some people don't appreciate real talent."

She wasn't touching that line with a pole. "I'll keep you in mind."

"You do that." He laughed as he closed the door.

Alice turned back to her notes, spread out on the desk in the motel room. There was something nagging at her about the piece of paper they'd recovered from the murder victim. She wondered why it bothered her.

Harley picked her up punctually at five on Friday night for their date. He wasn't overdressed, but he had on slacks and a spotless sports shirt with a dark blue jacket. He wasn't wearing his cowboy hat, either.

"You look nice," she said, smiling.

His eyes went to her neat blue sweater with embroidery around the rounded neckline and the black slacks she was wearing with slingbacks. She draped a black coat with fur collar over one arm and picked up her purse.

"Thanks," he said. "You look pretty good yourself, Alice."

She joined him at the door. "Ooops. Just a minute. I forgot my cell phone. I was charging it."

She unplugged it and tucked it into her pocket. It rang immediately. She grimaced. "Just a minute, okay?" she asked Harley.

She answered the phone. She listened. She grimaced. "Not tonight," she groaned. "Listen, I have plans. I never do, but I really have plans tonight. Can't Clancy cover for me, just this once? Please? Pretty please? I'll do the same for her. I'll even work Christmas Eve… okay? Thanks!" She beamed. "Thanks a million!"

She hung up.

"A case?" he asked curiously.

"Yes, but I traded out with another investigator." She shook her head as she joined him again at the door.

"It's been so slow lately that I forgot how hectic my life usually is."

"You have to work Christmas Eve?" he asked, surprised.

"Well, I usually volunteer," she confessed. "I don't have much of a social life. Besides, I think parents should be with children on holidays. I don't have any, but all my coworkers do."

He paused at the door of his pickup truck and looked down at her. "I like kids," he said.

"So do I," she replied seriously, and without joking. "I've just never had the opportunity to become a parent."

"You don't have to be married to have kids," he pointed out.

She gave him a harsh glare. "I am the product of generations of Baptist ministers," she told him. "My father was the only one of five brothers who went into business instead. You try having a modern attitude with a mother who taught Sunday School and uncles who spent their lives counseling young women whose lives were destroyed by unexpected pregnancies."

"I guess it would be rough," he said.

She smiled. "You grew up with parents who were free thinkers, didn't you?" she asked, curious.

He grimaced. He put her into the truck and got in beside her before he answered. "My father is an agnostic. He doesn't believe in anything except the power of the almighty dollar. My mother is just like him. They wanted me to associate with the right people and help them do it. I stayed with a friend's parents for a while and all but got adopted by them—he was a mechanic and they had a small ranch. I helped in the mechanic's shop. Then I went into the service, came back and tried to work things out with my real parents, but it wasn't possible. I ran away from home, fresh out of the Army Rangers."

"You were overseas during the Bosnia conflict, weren't you?" she asked.

He snapped his seat belt a little violently. "I was a desk clerk," he said with disgust. "I washed out of combat training. I couldn't make the grade. I ended up back in the regular Army doing clerical jobs. I never even saw combat. Not in the Army," he added.

"Oh."

"I left home, came down here to become a cowboy barely knowing a cow from a bull. The friends that I lived with had a small ranch, but I mostly stayed in town, working at the shop. We went out to the ranch on weekends, and I wasn't keen on livestock back then. Mr. Parks took me on anyway. He knew all along that I had no experience, but he put me to work with an old veteran cowhand named Cal Lucas, who taught me everything I know about cattle."

She grinned. "It took guts to do that."

He laughed. "I guess so. I bluffed a lot, although I am a good mechanic. Then I got in with this Sunday merc crew and went down to Africa with them one week on a so-called training mission. All we did was talk to some guys in a village about their problems with foreign relief shipments. But before we could do anything, we ran afoul of government troops and got sent home." He sighed. "I bragged about how much I'd learned, what a great merc I was." He glanced at her as they drove toward San Antonio, but she wasn't reacting critically. Much the reverse. He relaxed a little. "Then one of the drug lords came storming up to Mr. Parks's house with his men and I got a dose of reality—an automatic in my face. Mr. Parks jerked two combat knives out of his sleeves and threw them at the two men who were holding me. Put them both down in a heartbeat." He shook his head, still breathless at the memory. "I never saw anything like it, before or since. I thought he was just a rancher. Turns out he went with Micah Steele and Eb Scott on real merc missions overseas. He listened to me brag and watched me strut, and never said a word. I'd never have known, if the drug dealers hadn't attacked. We got in a firefight with them later."

"We heard about that, even up in San Antonio," she said.

He nodded. "It got around. Mr. Parks and Eb Scott and Micah Steele got together to take out a drug distribution center near Mr. Parks's property. I swallowed my pride and asked to go along. They let me." He sighed. "I grew up in the space of an hour. I saw men shot and killed, I had my life saved by Mr. Parks again in the process. Afterward, I never bragged or strutted again. Mr. Parks said he was proud of me." He flushed a little. "If my father had been like him, I guess I'd still be at home. He's a real man, Mr. Parks. I've never known a better one."

"He likes you, too."

He laughed self-consciously. "He does. He's offered me a few acres of land and some cattle, if I'd like to start my own herd. I'm thinking about it. I love ranching. I think I'm getting good at it."

"So we'd live on a cattle ranch." She pursed her lips mischievously. "I guess I could learn to help with brand-

ing. I mean, we wouldn't want our kids to th
mother was a sissy, would we?" she asked, laughi

Harley gave her a sideways glance and grinned. She really was fun to be with. He thought he might take her by the ranch one day while she was still in Jacobsville and introduce her to Mr. Parks. He was sure Mr. Parks would like her.

Chapter 5

The restaurant Harley took Alice to was a very nice one, with uniformed waiters and chandeliers.

"Oh, Harley, this wasn't necessary," she said quickly, flushing. "A hamburger would have been fine!"

He smiled. "We all got a Christmas bonus from Mr. Parks," he explained. "I don't drink or smoke or gamble, so I can afford a few luxuries from time to time."

"You don't have any vices? Wow. Now I really think we should set the date." She glanced at him under her lashes. "I don't drink, smoke or gamble, either," she added hopefully.

He nodded. "We'll be known as the most prudish couple in Jacobsville."

"Kilraven's prudish, too," she pointed out.

"Yes, but he won't be living in Jacobsville much longer. He's been reassigned, we're hearing. After all, he's really a fed."

She studied the menu. "I'll bet he could be a heartbreaker with a little practice."

"He's breaking Winnie Sinclair's heart, anyway, by leaving," Harley said, repeating the latest gossip. "She's really got a case on him. But he thinks she's too young."

"He's only in his thirties," she pointed out.

"Yes, but Winnie's the same age as her brother's new wife," he replied. "Boone Sinclair thought Keely Welsh was too young for him, too."

"But he gave in, in the end. You know, the Ballenger brothers in Jacobsville both married younger women. They've been happy together, all these years."

"Yes, they have."

The waiter came and took their orders. Alice had a shrimp cocktail and a large salad with coffee. Harley gave her a curious look.

"Aren't you hungry?" he asked.

She laughed. "I told you in Jacobsville, I love salads," she confessed. "I mostly eat them at every meal." She indicated her slender body. "I guess that's how I keep the weight off."

"I can eat as much as I like. I run it all off," he replied. "Working cattle is not for the faint of heart or the out-of-condition rancher."

She grinned. "I believe it." She smiled at the waiter as he deposited coffee in their china cups and left. "Why did you want to be a cowboy?" she asked him.

"I loved old Western movies on satellite," he said simply. "Gary Cooper and John Wayne and Randolph Scott. I dreamed of living on a cattle ranch and having animals around. I don't even mind washing Bob when she gets dirty, or Puppy Dog."

"What's Puppy Dog's name?" she asked.

"Puppy Dog."

She gave him an odd look. "Who's on first, what's on second, I don't know's on third?"

"I don't give a damn's our shortstop?" he finished the old Abbott and Costello comedy routine. He laughed. "No, it's not like that. His name really is Puppy Dog. We have a guy in town, Tom Walker. He had an outlandish dog named Moose that saved his daughter from a rattlesnake. Moose sired a litter of puppies. Moose is dead now, but Puppy Dog, who was one of his offspring, went to live with Lisa Monroe, before she married my boss. She called him Puppy Dog and figured it was as good a name as any. With a girl dog named Bob, my boss could hardly disagree," he added on a chuckle.

"I see."

"Do you like animals?"

"I love them," she said. "But I can't have animals in the apartment building where I live. I had cats and dogs and even a parrot when I lived at home."

"Do you have family?"

She shook her head. "My dad was the only one left. He died a few months ago. I have uncles, but we're not close."

"Did you love your parents?"

She smiled warmly. "Very much. My dad was a banker. We went fishing together on weekends. My mother was a housewife who never wanted to run a corporation or be a professional. She just wanted a houseful of kids, but I was the only child she was able to have. She spoiled me rotten. Dad tried to counterbalance her." She sipped coffee. "I miss them both. I wish I'd had brothers or sisters." She looked at him. "Do you have siblings?"

"I had a sister," he said quietly.

"Had?"

He nodded. He fingered his coffee cup. "She died when she was seven years old."

She hesitated. He looked as if this was a really bad memory. "How?"

He smiled sadly. "My father backed over her on his way down the driveway, in a hurry to get to a meeting."

She grimaced. "Poor man."

He cocked his head and studied her. "Why do you say that?"

"We had a little girl in for autopsy, about two years ago," she began. "Her dad was hysterical. Said the television fell over on her." She lifted her eyes. "You know, we don't just take someone's word for how an accident happens, even if we believe it. We run tests to check out the explanation and make sure it's feasible. Well, we pushed over a television of the same size as the one in the dad's apartment. Sure enough, it did catastrophic damage to a dummy." She shook her head. "Poor man went crazy. I mean, he really lost the will to live. His wife had died. The child was all he had left. He locked himself in the bathroom with a shotgun one night and pulled the trigger with his toe." She made a harsh sound. "Not the sort of autopsy you want to try to sleep after."

He was frowning.

"Sorry," she said, wincing. "I tend to talk shop. I know it's sickening, and here we are in a nice restaurant and all, and I did pour a glass of tea on a guy this week for doing the same thing to me..."

"I was thinking about the father," he said, smiling to relieve her tension. "I was sixteen when it happened. I grieved for her, of course, but my life was baseball and girls and video games and hamburgers. I never considered how my father might have felt. He seemed to just get on with his life afterward. So did my mother."

"Lots of people may seem to get over their grief. They don't."

He was more thoughtful than ever. "My mother had been a…lawyer," he said after a slight hesitation that Alice didn't notice. "She was very correct and proper. After my sister died, she changed. Cocktail parties, the right friends, the best house, the fanciest furniture… she went right off the deep end."

"You didn't connect it?"

He grimaced. "That was when I ran away from home and went to live with the mechanic and his wife," he confessed. "It was my senior year of high school. I graduated soon after, went into the Army and served for two years. When I got out, I went home. But I only stayed for a couple of weeks. My parents were total strangers. I didn't even know them anymore."

"That's sad. Do you have any contact with them?"

He shook his head. "I just left. They never even looked for me."

She slid her hand impulsively over his. His fingers turned and enveloped hers. His light blue eyes searched her darker ones curiously. "I never thought of crime scene investigators as having feelings," he said. "I thought you had to be pretty cold-blooded to do that sort of thing."

She smiled. "I'm the last hope of the doomed," she said. "The conscience of the murdered. The flickering candle of the soul of the deceased. I do my job so that murderers don't flourish, so that killers don't escape justice. I think of my job as a holy grail," she said solemnly.

"I hide my feelings. But I still have them. It hurts to see a life extinguished. Any life. But especially a child's."

His eyes began to twinkle with affection. "Alice, you're one of a kind."

"Oh, I do hope so," she said after a minute. "Because if there was another one of me, I might lose my job. Not many people would give twenty-four hours a day to the work." She hesitated and grinned. "Well, not all the time, obviously. Just occasionally, I get taken out by handsome, dashing men."

He laughed. "Thanks."

"Actually I mean it. I'm not shrewd enough to lie well."

The waiter came and poured more coffee and took their orders for dessert. When they were eating it, Alice frowned thoughtfully.

"It bothers me."

"What does?" he asked.

"The car. Why would a man steal a car from an upstanding, religious woman and then get killed?"

"He didn't know he was going to get killed."

She forked a piece of cheesecake and looked at it. "What if he had a criminal record? What if he got involved with her and wanted to change, to start over? What if he had something on his conscience and he wanted to spill the beans?" She looked up. "And somebody involved knew it and had to stop him?"

"That's a lot of ifs," he pointed out.

She nodded. "Yes, it is. We still don't know who the car was driven by, and the woman's story that it was stolen is just a little thin." She put the fork down. "I want to talk to her. But I don't know how to go about it. She works for a dangerous politician, I'm told. The feds have backed off. I won't do myself any favors if I charge in and start interrogating the senator's employee."

He studied her. "Let me see if I can find a way. I used to know my way around political circles. Maybe I can help."

She laughed. "You know a U.S. senator?" she teased.

He pursed his lips. "Maybe I know somebody who's related to one," he corrected.

"It would really help me a lot, if I could get to her before the feds do. I think she might tell me more than she'd tell a no-nonsense man."

"Give me until tomorrow. I'll think of something."

She smiled. "You're a doll."

He chuckled. "So are you."

She flushed. "Thanks."

They exchanged a long, soulful glance, only interrupted by the arrival of the waiter to ask if they wanted anything else and present the check. Alice's heart was doing double-time on the way out of the restaurant.

Harley walked her to the door of the motel. "I had a good time," he told her. "The best I've had in years."

She looked up, smiling. "Me, too. I turn off most men. The job, you know. I do work with people who aren't breathing."

"It doesn't matter," he said.

She felt the same tension that was visible in his tall, muscular body. He moved a step closer. She met him halfway.

He bent and drew his mouth softly over hers. When she didn't object, his arms went around her and pulled her close. He smiled as he increased the gentle pressure of his lips and felt hers tremble just a little before they relaxed and answered the pressure.

His body was already taut with desire, but it was too soon for a heated interlude. He didn't want to rush her. She was the most fascinating woman he'd ever known. He had to go slow.

He drew back after a minute and his hands tightened on her arms. "Suppose we take in another movie next week?" he asked.

She brightened. "A whole movie?"

He laughed softly. "At least."

"I'd like that."

"We'll try another restaurant. Just to sample the ones that are available until we find one we approve of," he teased.

"What a lovely idea! We can write reviews and put them online, too."

He pursed his lips. "What an entertaining thought."

"Nice reviews," she said, divining his mischievous thoughts.

"Spoilsport."

He winked at her, and she blushed.

"Don't forget," she said. "About finding me a way to interview that woman, okay?"

"Okay," he said. "Good night."

"Good night."

She stood, sighing, as he walked back to his truck. But when he got inside and started it, he didn't drive away. She realized belatedly that he was waiting until she went inside and locked the door. She laughed and waved. She liked that streak of protectiveness in him. It might not be modern, but it certainly made her feel cherished. She slept like a charm.

* * *

The next morning, he called her on his cell phone before she left the motel. "I've got us invited to a cocktail party tonight," he told her. "A fund-raiser for the senator."

"Us? But we can't contribute to that sort of thing! Can we?" she added.

"We don't have to. We're representing a contributor who's out of the country," he added with a chuckle. "Do you have a nice cocktail dress?"

"I do, but it's in San Antonio, in my apartment."

"No worries. You can go up and get it and I'll pick you up there at six."

"Fantastic! I'll wear something nice and I won't burp the theme songs to any television shows," she promised.

"Oh, that's good to know," he teased. "Got to get back to work. I told Mr. Parks I had to go to San Antonio this afternoon, so he's giving me a half day off. I didn't tell him why I needed the vacation time, but I think he suspects something."

"Don't mention this to anybody else, okay?" she asked. "If Jon Blackhawk or Kilraven find out, my goose will be cooked."

"I won't tell a soul."

"See you later. I owe you one, Harley."

"Yes," he drawled softly. "You do, don't you? I'll phone you later and get directions to your apartment."

"Okay."

She laughed and hung up.

The senator lived in a mansion. It was two stories high, with columns, and it had a front porch bigger than Alice's whole apartment. Lights burned in every

room, and in the gloomy, rainy night, it [...]
ing and beautiful.

Luxury sedans were parked up and down [...]
way. Harley's pickup truck wasn't in the same [...],
but he didn't seem to feel intimidated. He parked on the
street and helped Alice out of the truck. He was wearing evening clothes, with a black bow tie and highly
polished black wingtip shoes. He looked elegant. Alice
was wearing a simple black cocktail dress with her best
winter coat, the one she wore to work, a black one with
a fur collar. She carried her best black evening bag and
she wore black pumps that she'd polished, hoping to
cover the scuff marks. On her salary, although it was a
good one, she could hardly afford haute couture.

They were met at the door by a butler in uniform.
Harley handed him an invitation and the man hesitated
and did a double take, but he didn't say anything.

Once they were inside, Alice looked worriedly at
Harley.

"It's okay," he assured her, smiling as he cradled her
hand in his protectively. "No problem."

"Gosh," she said, awestruck as she looked around
her at the company she was in. "There's a movie star
over there," she said under her breath. "I recognize at
least two models and a Country-Western singing star,
and there's the guy who won the golf tournament…!"

"They're just people, Alice," he said gently.

She gaped at him. "Just people? You're joking,
right?" She turned too fast and bumped into somebody.
She looked up to apologize and her eyes almost popped.
"S-sorry," she stammered.

A movie star with a martial arts background grinned

at her. "No problem. It's easy to get knocked down in here. What a crowd, huh?"

"Y-yes," she agreed, nodding.

He laughed, smiled at Harley and drew his date, a gorgeous blonde, along with him toward the buffet table.

Harley curled his fingers into Alice's. "Rube," he teased softly. "You're starstruck."

"I am, I am," she agreed at once. "I've never been in such a place in my life. I don't hang out with the upper echelons of society in my job. You seem very much at home," she added, "for a man who spends his time with horses and cattle."

"Not a bad analogy, actually," he said under his breath. "Wouldn't a cattle prod come in handy around here, though?"

"Harley!" She laughed.

"Just kidding." He was looking around the room. After a minute, he spotted someone. "Let's go ask that woman if they know your employee."

"Okay."

"What's her name?" he whispered.

She dug for it. "Dolores."

He slid his arm around her shoulders and led her forward. She felt the warmth of his jacketed arm around her with real pleasure. She felt chilled at this party, with all this elegance. Her father had been a banker, and he hadn't been poor, but this was beyond the dreams of most people. Crystal chandeliers, Persian carpets, original oil paintings—was that a Renoir?!

"Hi," Harley said to one of the women pouring more punch into the Waterford crystal bowl. "Does Dolores still work here?"

The woman stared at him for a minute, but without

recognition. "Dolores? Yes. She's in the kitchen, making canapés. You look familiar. Do I know you?"

"I've got that kind of face," he said easily, smiling. "My wife and I know Dolores, we belong to her church. I promised the minister we'd give her a message from him if we came tonight," he added.

"One of that church crowd," the woman groaned, rolling her eyes. "Honestly, it's all she talks about, like there's nothing else in the world but church."

"Religion dies, so does civilization," Alice said quietly. She remembered that from her Western Civilization course in college.

"Whatever," the woman replied, bored.

"In the kitchen, huh? Thanks," Harley told the woman.

"Don't get her fired," came the quick reply. "She's a pain, sometimes, but she works hard enough doing dishes. If the senator or his wife see you keeping her from her job, he'll fire her."

"We won't do that," Harley promised. His lips made a thin line as he led Alice away.

"Surely the senator wouldn't fire her just for talking to us?" Alice wondered aloud.

"It wouldn't surprise me," Harley said. "We'll have to be circumspect."

Alice followed his lead. She wondered why he was so irritated. Perhaps the woman's remark offended his sense of justice.

The kitchen was crowded. It didn't occur to Alice to ask how Harley knew his way there. Women were bent over tables, preparing platters, sorting food, making canapés. Two women were at the huge double sink, washing dishes.

"Don't they have a dishwasher?" Alice wondered as they entered the room.

"You don't put Waterford crystal and Lenox china in a dishwasher," he commented easily.

She looked up at him with pure fascination. He didn't seem aware that he'd given away knowledge no working cowboy should even possess.

"How do we know which one's her?" he asked Alice.

Alice stared at the two women. One was barely out of her teens, wearing a nose ring and spiky hair. The other was conservatively dressed with her hair in a neat bun. She smiled, nodding toward the older one. She had a white apron wrapped around her. "The other woman said she was washing dishes," she whispered. "And she's a churchgoer."

He grinned, following her lead.

They eased around the curious workers, smiling.

"Hello, Dolores," Alice called to the woman.

The older woman turned, her red hands dripping water and soap, and started at the two visitors with wide brown eyes. "I'm sorry, do I know you?" she asked.

"I guess you've never seen us dressed up, huh? We're from your church," he told her, lying through his teeth. "Your minister gave us a message for you."

She blinked. "My minister...?"

"Could we talk, just for a minute?" Alice asked urgently.

The woman was suspicious. Her eyes narrowed. She hesitated, and Alice thought, *we've blown it.* But just then, Dolores nodded. "Sure. We can talk for a minute. Liz, I'm taking my break, now, okay? I'll only be ten minutes."

"Okay," Liz returned, with only a glance at the elegantly dressed people walking out with Dolores. "Don't be long. You know how he is," she added quickly.

Once they were outside, Dolores gave them a long look. "I know everyone in my church. You two don't go there," Dolores said with a gleam in her eyes. "Who are you and what do you want?"

Alice studied her. "I work for...out-of-town law enforcement," she improvised. "We found your car. And the man who was driving it."

The older woman hesitated. "I told the police yesterday, the car was stolen," she began weakly.

Alice stepped close, so that they couldn't be overheard. "He was beaten to death, so badly that his mother wouldn't know him," she said in a steely tone. "Your car was pushed into the river. Somebody didn't want him to be found. Nobody," she added softly, "should ever have to die like that. And his murderer shouldn't get away with it."

Dolores looked even sicker. She leaned back against the wall. Her eyes closed. "It's my fault. He said he wanted to start over. He wanted to marry me. He said he just had to do something first, to get something off his conscience. He asked to borrow the car, but he said if something happened, if he didn't call me back by the next morning, to say it was stolen so I wouldn't get in trouble. He said he knew about a crime and if he talked they might kill him."

"Do you know what crime?" Alice asked her.

She shook her head. "He wouldn't tell me anything. Nothing. He said it was the only way he could protect me."

"His name," Alice persisted. "Can you at least tell me his name?"

Dolores glanced toward the door, grimacing. "I don't know it," she whispered. "He said it was an alias."

"Then tell me the alias. Help me find his killer."

She drew in a breath. "Jack. Jack Bailey," she said. "He said he'd been in jail once. He said he was sorry. I got him going to church, trying to live a decent life. He was going to start over…" Her voice broke. "It's my fault."

"You were helping him," Alice corrected. "You gave him hope."

"He's dead."

"Yes. But there are worse things than dying. How long did you know him?" Alice asked.

"A few months. We went out together. He didn't own a car. I had to drive…"

"Where did he live?"

Dolores glanced at the door again. "I don't know. He always met me at a little strip mall near the tracks, the Weston Street Mall."

"Is there anything you can tell me that might help identify him?" Alice asked.

She blinked, deep in thought. "He said something happened, that it was an accident, but people died because of it. He was sorry. He said it was time to tell the truth, no matter how dangerous it was to him…"

"Dolores!"

She jumped. A tall, imposing figure stood in the light from the open door. "Get back in here! You aren't paid to socialize."

Harley stiffened, because he knew that voice.

"Yes, sir!" Dolores cried, rushing back inside. "Sorry. I was on my break…!"

She ran past the elegant older man. He closed the

door and came storming toward Alice and Harley, looking as if he meant to start trouble.

"What do you mean, interrupting my workers when I have important guests? Who the hell are you people and how did you get in here?" he demanded.

Harley moved into the light, his pale eyes glittering at the older man. "I had an invitation," he said softly.

The older man stopped abruptly. He cocked his head, as if the voice meant more to him than the face did. "Who...are you?" he asked huskily.

"Just a ghost, visiting old haunts," he said, and there was ice in his tone.

The older man moved a step closer. As he came into the light, Alice noticed that he, too, had pale eyes, and gray-streaked brown hair.

"H-Harley?" he asked in a hesitant tone.

Harley caught Alice's hand in his. She noticed that his fingers were like ice.

"Sorry to have bothered you, Senator," Harley said formally. "Alice and I know a pastor who's a mutual friend of Dolores. He asked us to tell her about a family that needed a ride to church Sunday. Please excuse us."

He drew Alice around the older man, who stood frozen watching them as they went back into the kitchen.

Harley paused by Dolores and whispered something in her ear quickly before he rejoined Alice and they sauntered toward the living room. The senator moved toward them before they reached the living room, stared after them with a pained expression and tried to speak.

It was too late. Harley walked Alice right out the front door. On the way, a dark-eyed, dark-haired man in an expensive suit scowled as they passed him. Har-

ley noticed that the senator stopped next to the other
man and started talking to him.

They made it back to the truck without being challenged, and without a word being spoken.

Harley put Alice inside the truck, got in and started
it.

"He knew you," she stammered.

"Apparently." He nodded at her. "Fasten your seat
belt."

"Sure." She snapped it in place, hoping that he might
add something, explain what had happened. He didn't.

"You've got something to go on now, at least," he
said.

"Yes," she agreed. "I have. Thanks, Harley. Thanks
very much."

"My pleasure." He glanced at her. "I told Dolores
what we said to the senator, so that our stories would
match. It might save her job."

"I hope so," she said. "She seemed like a really nice
person."

"Yeah."

He hardly said two words the whole rest of the way
to her apartment. He parked in front of the building.

"You coming back down to Jacobsville?" he asked.

"In the morning," she said. "I still have some investigating to do there."

"Lunch, Monday, at Barbara's?" he invited.

She smiled. "I'd like that."

He smiled back. "Yeah. Me, too. Sorry we didn't get
to stay. The buffet looked pretty good."

"I wasn't really hungry," she lied.

"You're a sweetheart. I'd take you out for a late supper, but my heart's not in it." He pulled her close and bent to kiss her. His mouth was hard and a little rough. "Thanks for not asking questions."

"No problem," she managed, because the kiss had been something, even if he hadn't quite realized what he was doing.

"See you Monday."

He went back to the truck and drove away. This time, he didn't wait for her to go in and close the door, an indication of how upset he really was.

Chapter 6

Harley drove back to the ranch and cut off the engine outside the bunkhouse. It had been almost eight years since he'd seen the senator. He hadn't realized what a shock it was going to be, to come face-to-face with him. It brought back all the old wounds.

"Hey!"

He glanced at the porch of the modern bunkhouse. Charlie Dawes was staring at him from a crack in the door. "You coming in or sleeping out there?" the other cowboy called with a laugh.

"Coming in, I guess," he replied.

"Well!" Charlie exclaimed when he saw how the other man was dressed. "I thought you said you were just going out for a drive."

"I took Alice to a party, but we left early. Neither of us was in the mood," he said.

"Alice. That your girl?"

Harley smiled. "You know," he told the other man, "I think she is."

Alice drove back down to Jacobsville late Sunday afternoon. She'd contacted Rick Marquez and asked if he'd do some investigating for her in San Antonio, to look for any rap sheet on a man who used a Jack Bailey alias and to see if they could find a man who'd been staying at a motel near the Weston Street Mall. He might have been seen in the company of a dark-haired woman driving a 1992 blue Ford sedan. It wasn't much to go on, but he might turn up something.

Meanwhile, Alice was going to go back to the crime scene and wander over it one more time, in hopes that the army of CSI detectives might have missed something, some tiny scrap of information that would help break the case.

She was dressed in jeans and sneakers and a green sweatshirt with CSI on it, sweeping the bank of the river, when her cell phone rang. She muttered as she pulled it out and checked the number. She frowned. Odd, she didn't recognize that number in any conscious way, but it struck something in the back of her mind.

"Jones," she said.

"Hi, Jones. It's Kilraven. I wondered if you dug up anything on the murder victim over the weekend?"

She sighed, her mind still on the ground she was searching. "Only that he had an alias, that he was trying to get something off his conscience, that he didn't own a car and he'd been in trouble with the law. Oh, and that he lived somewhere near the Weston Street Mall in San Antonio."

"Good God!" he exclaimed. "You got all that in one weekend?"

She laughed self-consciously. "Well, Harley helped. We crashed a senator's fund-raiser and cornered an employee of his who'd been dating the... Oh, damn!" she exclaimed. "Listen, your brother will fry me up toasty and feed me to sharks if you tell him I said that. The feds didn't want anybody going near that woman!"

"Relax. Jon was keen to go out and talk to her himself, but his office nixed it. They were just afraid that some heavy-handed lawman would go over there and spook her. You share what you just told me with him, and I guarantee nobody will say a word about it. Great work, Alice."

"Thanks," she said. "The woman's name is Dolores. She's a nice lady. She feels guilty that he got killed. She never even fussed about her car and now it's totaled. She said she loaned him the car, but he told her to say it was stolen if he didn't call her in a day, in case somebody went after him. He knew he could get killed."

"He said he wanted to get something off his conscience," he reminded her.

"Yes. He said something happened that was an accident but that people died because of it. Does that help?"

"Only if I had ESP," he sighed. "Any more luck on that piece of paper you found in the victim's hand?"

"None. I hope to hear something in a few days from the lab. They're working their fingers to the bone. Why are holidays such a great time for murders and suicides?" she wondered aloud. "It's the holidays. You'd think it would make people happy."

"Sadly, as we both know, it doesn't. It just emphasizes what they've lost, since holidays are prime time for families to get together."

"I suppose so."

"We heard that you were going out with Harley Fowler," he said after a minute, with laughter in his deep voice. "Is it serious?"

"Not really," she replied pertly. "I mean, I ask him to marry me twice a day, but that's not what you'd call serious, is it?"

"Only if he says yes," he returned.

"He hasn't yet, but it's still early. I'm very persistent."

"Well, good luck."

"I don't need luck. I'm unspeakably beautiful, have great language skills, I can boil eggs and wash cars and… Hello? Hello!"

He'd hung up on her, laughing. She closed the flip phone. "I didn't want to talk to you, anyway," she told the phone. "I'm trying to work here."

She walked along the riverbank again, her sharp eyes on the rocks and weeds that grew along the water's edge. She was letting her mind wander, not trying to think in any conscious way. Sometimes, she got ideas that way.

The dead man had a past. He was mixed up in some sort of accident in which a death occurred that caused more deaths. He wanted to get something off his conscience. So he'd borrowed a car from his girlfriend and driven to Jacobsville. To see whom? The town wasn't that big, but it was pretty large if you were trying to figure out who someone a man with a criminal past was trying to find. Who could it be? Someone in law enforcement? Or was he just driving through Jacobsville on his way to talk to someone?

No, she discarded that possibility immediately. He'd been killed here, so someone had either intercepted him or met him here, to talk about the past.

The problem was, she didn't have a clue who the man was or what he'd been involved in. She hoped that Rick Marquez came up with some answers.

But she knew more than she'd known a few days earlier, at least, and so did law enforcement. She still wondered at the interest of Jon Blackhawk of the San Antonio FBI office. Why were the feds involved? Were they working on some case secretly and didn't want to spill the beans to any outsiders?

Maybe they were working a similar case, she reasoned, and were trying to find a connection. They'd never tell her, of course, but she was a trained professional and this wasn't her first murder investigation.

What if the dead man had confessed, first, to the minister of Dolores's church?

She gasped out loud. It was like lightning striking. Of course! The minister might know something that he could tell her, unless he'd taken a vow of silence, like Catholic priests. They couldn't divulge anything learned in the confessional. But it was certainly worth a try!

She dug Harley's cell phone number out of her pocket and called him. The phone rang three times while she kicked at a dirt clod impatiently. Maybe he was knee-deep in mired cattle or something...

"Hello?"

"Harley!" she exclaimed.

"Now, just who else would it be, talking on Harley's phone?" came the amused, drawling reply.

"You, I hope," she said at once. "Listen, I need to talk to you…"

"You are," he reminded her.

"No, in person, right now," she emphasized. "It's about a minister…"

"Darlin', we can't get married today," he drawled. "I have to brush Bob the dog's teeth," he added lightly.

"Not that minister," she burst out. "Dolores's minister!"

He paused. "Why?"

"What if the murdered man confessed to him before he drove down to Jacobsville and got killed?" she exclaimed.

Harley whistled. "What if, indeed?"

"We need to go talk to her again and ask his name."

"Oh, now that may prove difficult. There's no party."

She realized that he was right. They had no excuse to show up at the senator's home, which was probably surrounded by security devices and armed guards. "Damn!"

"You can just call the house and ask for Dolores," he said reasonably. "You don't have to give your name or a reason."

She laughed softly. "Yes, I could do that. I don't know why I bothered you."

"Because you want to marry me," he said reasonably. "But I'm brushing the dog's teeth today. Sorry."

She glared at the phone. "Excuses, excuses," she muttered. "I'm growing older by the minute!"

"Why don't I bring you over here to go riding?" he wondered aloud. "You could meet my boss and his wife and the boys, and meet Puppy Dog."

She brightened. "What a nice idea!"

"I thought so myself. I'll ask the boss. Next week-end, maybe? I'll beg for another half day on Saturday and take you riding around the ranch. We've got plenty of spare horses." When she hesitated, he sighed. "Don't tell me. You can't ride."

"I can so ride horses," she said indignantly. "I ride horses at amusement parks all the time. They go up and down and round and round, and music plays."

"That isn't the same sort of riding. Well, I'll teach you," he said. "After all, if we get married, you'll have to live on a ranch. I'm not stuffing myself into some tiny apartment in San Antonio."

"Now that's the sort of talk I love to hear," she sighed.

He laughed. "Wear jeans and boots," he instructed. "And thick socks."

"No blouse or bra?" she exclaimed in mock outrage.

He whistled. "Well, you don't have to wear them on my account," he said softly. "But we wouldn't want to shock my boss, you know."

She laughed at that. "Okay. I'll come decently dressed. Saturday it is." She hesitated. "Where's the ranch?"

"I'll come and get you." He hesitated. "You'll still be here next Saturday, won't you?"

She was wondering how to stretch her investigation here by another week. Then she remembered that Christmas was Thursday and she relaxed. "I get Christmas off," she said. Then she remembered that she'd promised to work Christmas Eve already. "Well, I get Christmas Day. I'll ask for the rest of the week. I'll tell them that the case is heating up and I have two or three more people to interview."

"Great! Can I help?"

"Yes, you can find me two or three more people to

interview," she said. "Meanwhile, I'll call Dolores and ask her to give me her minister's name." She grimaced. "I'll have to be sure I don't say that to whoever answers the phone. We told everybody we were giving her a message from her minister!"

"Good idea. Let me know what you find out, okay?"

"You bet. See you." She hung up.

She had to dial information to get the senator's number and, thank God, it wasn't unlisted. She punched the numbers into her cell phone and waited. A young woman answered.

"May I please speak to Dolores?" Alice asked politely.

"Dolores?"

"Yes."

There was a long pause. Alice gritted her teeth. They were going to tell her that employees weren't allowed personal phone calls during the day, she just knew it.

But the voice came back on the line with a long sigh. "I'm so sorry," the woman said. "Dolores isn't here anymore."

That wasn't altogether surprising, but it wasn't a serious setback. "Can you tell me how to get in touch with her? I'm an old friend," she added, improvising.

The sigh was longer. "Well, you can't. I mean, she's dead."

Alice was staggered. "Dead?" she exclaimed.

"Yes. Suicide. She shot herself through the heart," the woman said sadly. "It was such a shock. The senator's wife found her... Oh, dear, I can't talk anymore, I'm sorry."

"Just a minute, just one minute, can you tell me where the funeral is being held?" she asked quickly.

"At the Weston Street Baptist Church," came the

reply, almost in a whisper, "at two tomorrow afternoon. I have to go. I'm very sorry about Dolores. We all liked her."

The phone went dead.

Alice felt sick. Suicide! Had she driven the poor woman to it, with her questions? Or had she been depressed because of her boyfriend's murder?

Strange, that she'd shot herself through the heart. Most women chose some less violent way to die. Most used drugs. Suicides by gun were usually men.

She called Harley back.

"Hello?" he said.

"Harley, she killed herself," she blurted out.

"Who? Dolores? She's dead?" he exclaimed.

"Yes. Shot through the heart, I was told. Suicide."

He paused. "Isn't that unusual for a woman? To use a gun to kill herself, I mean?"

"It is. But I found out where her pastor is," she added. "I'm going to the funeral tomorrow. Right now, I'm going up to San Antonio to my office."

"Why?" he asked.

"Because in all violent deaths, even those ascribed to suicide, an autopsy is required. I wouldn't miss this one for the world."

"Keep in touch."

"You bet."

Alice hung up and went back to her van. She had a hunch that a woman as religious as Dolores wouldn't kill herself. Most religions had edicts against it. That didn't stop people from doing it, of course, but Dolores didn't strike Alice as the suicidal sort. She was going to see if the autopsy revealed anything.

* * *

The office was, as usual on holidays, overworked. She found one of the assistant medical examiners poring over reports in his office.

He looked up as she entered. "Jones! Could I get you to come back and work for us in autopsy again if I bribed you? It's getting harder and harder to find people who don't mind hanging around with the dead."

She smiled. "Sorry, Murphy," she said. "I'm happier with investigative work these days. Listen, do you have a suicide back there? First name Dolores, worked for a senator...?"

"Yep. I did her myself, earlier this evening." He shook his head. "She had small hands and the gun was a .45 Colt ACP," he replied. "How she ever cocked the damned thing, much less killed herself with it, is going to be one of the great unsolved mysteries of life. Added to that, she had carpal tunnel in her right hand. She'd had surgery at least once. Weakens the muscle, you know. We'd already ascertained that she was right-handed because there was more muscle attachment there—usual on the dominant side."

"You're sure it was suicide?" she pressed.

He leaned back in his chair, eyeing her through thick corrective lenses. "There was a rim burn around the entrance wound," he said, referring to the heat and flare of the shot in close-contact wounds. "But the angle of entry was odd."

She jumped on that. "Odd, how?"

"Diagonal," he replied. He pulled out his digital camera, ran through the files and punched up one. He handed her the camera. "That's the wound, anterior view. Pull up the next shot and you'll see where it exited, posterior."

She inhaled. "Wow!"

"Interesting, isn't it? Most people who shoot themselves with an automatic handgun do it holding the barrel to the head or under the chin. This was angled downward. And as I said before, her hand was too weak to manage this sort of weapon. There's something else."

"What?" she asked, entranced.

"The gun was found still clenched in her left hand."

"So?"

"Remember what I said about the carpel tunnel? She was right-handed."

She cocked her head. "Going to write it up as suspected homicide?"

"You're joking, right? Know who she worked for?"

She sighed. "Yes. Senator Fowler."

"Would you write it up as a suspected homicide or would you try to keep your job?"

That was a sticky question. "But if she was murdered…"

"The 'if' is subjective. I'm not one of those TV forensic people," he reminded her. "I'm two years from retirement, and I'm not risking my pension on a possibility. She goes out as a suicide until I get absolute proof that it wasn't."

Alice knew when that would be. "Could you at least put 'probable suicide,' Murphy?" she persisted. "Just for me?"

He frowned. "Why? Alice, do you know something that I need to know?"

She didn't dare voice her suspicions. She had no proof. She managed a smile. "Humor me. It won't rattle any cages, and if something comes up down the line, you'll have covered your butt. Right?"

He searched her eyes for a moment and then smiled warmly. "Okay. I'll put probable. But if you dig up something, you tell me first, right?"

She grinned. "Right."

Her next move was to go to the Weston Street Baptist Church and speak to the minister, but she had to wait until the funeral to do it. If she saw the man alone, someone might see her and his life could be in danger. It might be already. She wasn't sure what to do.

She went to police headquarters and found Detective Rick Marquez sitting at his desk. The office was almost empty, but there he was, knee-deep in file folders.

She tapped on the door and walked in at the same time.

"Alice!" He got to his feet. "Nice to see you."

"Is it? Why?" she asked suspiciously.

He glanced at the file folders and winced. "Any reason to take a break is a good one. Not that I'm sorry to see you," he added.

"What are you doing?" she asked as she took a seat in front of the desk.

"Poring over cold cases," he said heavily. "My lieutenant said I could do it on my own time, as long as I didn't advertise why I was doing it."

"Why are you doing it?" she asked curiously.

"Your murder down in Jacobsville nudged a memory or two," he said. "There was a case similar to it, also unsolved. It involved a fourteen-year-old girl who was driving a car reported stolen. She was also unrecognizable, but several of her teeth were still in place.

They identified her by dental records. No witnesses, no clues."

"How long ago was this?" she asked.

He shrugged. "About seven years," he said. "In fact, it happened some time before Kilraven's family was killed."

"Could there be a connection?" she wondered aloud.

"I don't know. I don't see how the death of a teenage girl ties in to the murder of a cop's family." He smiled. "Maybe it's just a coincidence." He put the files aside. "Why are you up here?"

"I came to check the results of an autopsy," she said. "The woman who worked for Senator Fowler supposedly killed herself, but the bullet was angled downward, her hand was too weak to have pulled the trigger and the weapon was found clutched in the wrong hand."

He blew out his breath in a rush. "Some suicide."

"My thoughts exactly."

"Talk to me, Jones."

"She was involved with the murder victim in Jacobsville, remember?" she asked him. "She wouldn't tell me his name, she swore she didn't know it. But she gave me the alias he used—the one I called and gave you—and she said he'd spoken to the minister of her church. He told her there was an accident that caused a lot of other people to die. He had a guilty conscience and he wanted to tell what he knew."

Marquez's dark eyes pinned hers. "Isn't that interesting."

"Isn't it?"

"You going to talk to the minister?"

"I want to, but I'm afraid to be seen doing it," she told him. "His life may be in danger if he knows something. Whatever is going on, it's big, and it has ties to powerful people."

"The senator, maybe?" he wondered aloud.

"Maybe."

"When did you talk to her?"

"There was a fund-raiser at the senator's house. Harley Fowler took me…" She hadn't connected the names before. Now she did. The senator's name was Fowler. Harley's name was Fowler. The senator had recognized Harley, had approached him, had talked to him in a soft tone…

"Harley *Fowler?*" Marquez emphasized, making the same connection she did. "Harley's family?"

"I don't know," she said. "He didn't say anything to me. But the senator acted really strangely. He seemed to recognize Harley. And when Harley took me to my apartment, he didn't wait until I got inside the door. That's not like him. He was distracted."

"He comes from wealth and power, and he's working cattle for Cy Parks," Marquez mused. "Now isn't that a curious thing?"

"It is, and if it's true, you mustn't tell anybody," Alice replied. "It's his business."

"I agree. I'll keep it to myself. Who saw you talk to the woman at the senator's house?"

"Everybody, but we told them we knew her minister and came to tell her something for him."

"If she went to church every week, wouldn't that seem suspicious that you were seeing her to give her a message from her minister?"

Alice smiled. "Harley told them he'd asked us to give her a message about offering a ride to a fellow worshipper on Sunday."

"Uh, Alice, her car was pulled out of the Little Carmichael River in Jacobsville...?"

"Oh, good grief," she groaned. "Well, nobody knew that when we were at the party."

"Yes. But maybe somebody recognized you and figured you were investigating the murder," he returned.

She grimaced. "And I got her killed," she said miserably.

"No."

"If I hadn't gone there and talked to her...!" she protested.

"When your time's up, it's up, Jones," he replied philosophically. "It wouldn't have made any difference. A car crash, a heart attack, a fall from a high place...it could have been anything. Intentions are what matter. You didn't go there to cause her any trouble."

She managed a wan smile. "Thanks, Marquez."

"But if she was killed," he continued, "that fits into your case somehow. It means that the murderer isn't taking any chance that somebody might talk."

"The murderer...?"

"Your dead woman said the victim knew something damaging about several deaths. Who else but the murderer would be so hell-bent on eliminating evidence?"

"We still don't know who the victim is."

Marquez's sensuous lips flattened as he considered the possibilities. "If the minister knows anything, he's already in trouble. He may be in trouble if he doesn't know anything. The perp isn't taking any chances."

"What can we do to protect him?"

Marquez picked up the phone. "I'm going to risk my professional career and see if I can help him."

Alice sat and listened while he talked. Five minutes later, he hung up the phone.

"Are you sure that's the only way to protect him?" she asked worriedly.

"It's the best one I can think of, short of putting him in protective custody," he said solemnly. "I can't do that without probable cause, not to mention that our budget is in the red and we can't afford protective custody."

"Your boss isn't going to like it. And I expect Jon Blackhawk will be over here with a shotgun tomorrow morning, first thing."

"More than likely."

She smiled. "You're a prince!"

His eyebrows arched. "You could marry me," he suggested.

She shook her head. "No chance. If you really are a prince, if I kissed you, by the way the laws of probability work in my life, you'd turn right into a frog."

He hesitated and then burst out laughing.

She grinned. "Thanks, Marquez. If I can help you, anytime, I will."

"You can. Call my boss tomorrow and tell him that you think I'm suffering from a high fever and hallucinations and I'm not responsible for my own actions."

"I'll do that very thing. Honest."

The next morning, the local media reported that the pastor of a young woman who'd committed suicide was being questioned by police about some information that might tie her to a cold case. Alice thought it was a stroke of pure genius. Only a total fool would risk killing the pastor now that he was in the media spotlight. It was the best protection he could have.

Marquez's boss was, predictably, enraged. But Alice went to see him and, behind closed doors, told him what she knew about the murder in Jacobsville. He calmed down and agreed that it was a good call on his detective's part.

Then Alice went to see Reverend Mike Colman, early in the morning, before the funeral.

He wasn't what she expected. He was sitting in his office wearing sneakers, a pair of old jeans and a black sweatshirt. He had prematurely thinning dark hair, wore glasses and had a smile as warm as a summer day.

He got up and shook hands with Alice after she introduced herself.

"I understand that I might be a candidate for admittance to your facility," he deadpanned. "Detective Marquez decided that making a media pastry out of me could save my life."

"I hope he's right," she said solemnly. "Two people have died in the past two weeks who had ties to this case. We've got a victim in Jacobsville that we can't even identify."

He grimaced. "I was sorry to hear about Dolores. I never thought she'd kill herself, and I still don't."

"It's sad that she did so much to help a man tortured by his past, and paid for it with her life. Isn't there a saying, that no good deed goes unpunished?" she added with wan humor.

"It seems that way sometimes, doesn't it?" he asked with a smile. "But God's ways are mysterious. We aren't meant to know why things happen the way they do at all times. So what can I do to help you?"

"Do you think you could describe the man Dolores sent to talk to you? If I get a police artist over here with his software and his laptop, can you tell him what the man looked like?"

"Oh, I think I can do better than that."

He pulled a pencil out of his desk drawer, drew a thick pad of paper toward him, peeled back the top and proceeded with deft strokes to draw an unbelievably lifelike pencil portrait of a man.

"That's incredible!" Alice exclaimed, fascinated by the expert rendering.

He chuckled as he handed it over to her. "Thanks. I wasn't always a minister," he explained. "I was on my way to Paris to further my studies in art when God tapped me on the shoulder and told me He needed me." He shrugged. "You don't say no to Him," he added with a kind smile.

"If there isn't some sort of pastor/confessor bond you'd be breaking, could you tell me what you talked about with him?"

"There's no confidentiality," he replied. "But he didn't really tell me anything. He asked me if God could forgive any sin, and I told him yes. He said he'd been a bad man, but he was in love, and he wanted to change. He said he was going to talk to somebody who was involved in an old case, and he'd tell me everything when he got back." He grimaced. "Except he didn't get back, did he?"

"No," Alice agreed sadly. "He didn't."

Chapter 7

Alice took the drawing with her. She phoned Marquez's office, planning to stop by to show the drawing to him, but he'd already gone home. She tucked it into her purse and went to her own office. It was now Christmas Eve, and she'd promised to work tonight as a favor to the woman who'd saved her date with Harley.

She walked into the medical examiner's office, waving to the security guard on her way inside. The building, located on the University of Texas campus, was almost deserted. Only a skeleton crew worked on holidays. Most of the staff had families. Only Alice and one other employee were still single. But the medical examiner's office was accessible 24/7, so someone was always on call.

She went by her colleague's desk and grimaced as she saw the caseload sitting in the basket, waiting for her. It was going to be a long night.

She sat down at her own desk and started poring over the first case file. There were always deaths to investigate, even when foul play wasn't involved. In each one, if there was an question as to how the deceased had departed, it was up to her to work with the detectives to determine a cause of death. Her only consolation was that the police detectives were every bit as overloaded as she, a medical examiner investigator, was. Nobody did investigative work to get rich. But the job did have other rewards, she reminded herself. Solving a crime and bringing a murderer to justice was one of the perks. And no amount of money would make up for the pleasure it gave her to see that a death was avenged. Legally, of course.

She opened the first file and started working up the notes on the computer into a document easily read by the lead police detective on the case, as well as the assistant district attorney prosecuting it. She waded through crime scene photographs, measurements, witness statements and other interviews, but as she did, she was still wondering about the coincidence of Harley's last name and the senator's. The older man had recognized him, had called him Harley. They obviously knew each other, and there was some animosity there. But if the senator was a relation, why hadn't Harley mentioned it when he and Alice stopped by the house for the fund-raiser?

Maybe he hadn't wanted Alice to know. Maybe he didn't want anyone to know, especially anyone in Jacobsville. Perhaps he wanted to make it on his own, without the wealth and power of his family behind him. He'd said that he no longer felt comfortable with the things his parents wanted him to do. If they were in politics and expected him to help host fund-raisers and hang out with the cream of high society, he might have felt uncomfortable. She recalled her own parents and how much she'd loved them, and how close they'd been. They'd never asked her to do anything she didn't feel comfortable with. Harley obviously hadn't had that sort of home life. She was sad for him. But if things worked out, she promised herself that she'd do what she could to make up for what he missed. First step in that direction, she decided, was a special Christmas present.

She slept late on Christmas morning. But when she woke up, she got out her cell phone and made a virtual shopping trip around town, to discover which businesses were open on a holiday. She found one, and it carried just the item she wanted. She drove by there on her way down to Jacobsville.

Good thing she'd called ahead about keeping her motel room, she thought when she drove into the parking lot. The place was full. Obviously some locals had out-of-town family who didn't want to impose when they came visiting on the holidays. She stashed her suitcase and called Harley's number.

"Hello," came a disgruntled voice over the line.

"Harley?" she asked hesitantly.

There was a shocked pause. "Alice? Is that you?"

She laughed. "Well, you sound out of sorts."

"I am." There was a splash. "Get out of there, you walking steak platter!" he yelled. "Hold the line a minute, Alice, I have to put down the damn…phone!"

There was a string of very unpleasant language, most of which was mercifully muffled. Finally Harley came back on the line.

"I hate the cattle business," he said.

She grimaced. Perhaps she shouldn't have made that shopping trip after all. "Do you?" she asked. "Why?"

"Truck broke down in the middle of the pasture while I was tossing out hay," he muttered. "I got out of the truck and under the hood to see what was wrong. I left the door open. Boss's wife had sent me by the store on the way to pick up some turnip greens for her. Damned cow stuck her head into the truck and ate every damned one of them! So now, I'm mired up to my knees in mud and the truck's sinking, and once I get the truck out, I've got to go all the way back to town for a bunch of turnips on account of the stupid cow... Why are you laughing?"

"I thought you ran purebred bulls," she said.

"You can't get a purebred bull without a purebred cow to drop it," he said with exaggerated patience.

"Sorry. I wasn't thinking. Say, I'm just across the street from a market. Want me to go over and get you some more turnips and bring them to you?"

There was an intake of breath. "You'd do that? On Christmas Day?"

"I sort of got you something," she said. "Just a little something. I wanted an excuse to bring it to you, anyway."

"Doggone it, Alice, I didn't get you anything," he said shamefully.

"I didn't expect you to," she said at once. "But you took me to a nice party and I thought... Well, it's just a little something."

"I took you to a social shooting gallery and didn't even buy you supper," he said, feeling ashamed.

"It was a nice party," she said. "Do you want turnips or not?"

He laughed. "I do. Think you can find Cy Parks's ranch?"

"Give me directions."

He did, routing her the quickest way.

"I'll be there in thirty minutes," she said. "Or I'll call for more directions."

"Okay. Thanks a million, Alice."

"No problem."

She dressed in her working clothes, jeans and boots and a coat, but she added a pretty white sweater with a pink poinsettia embroidered on it, for Christmas. She didn't bother with makeup. It wouldn't help much anyway, she decided with a rueful smile. She bought the turnips and drove the few miles to the turnoff that led to Cy Parks's purebred Santa Gertrudis stud ranch.

Harley was waiting for her less than half a mile down the road, at the fork that turned into the ranch house. He was covered in mud, even his once-brown cowboy hat. He had a smear of mud on one cheek, but he looked very sexy, Alice thought. She couldn't think of one man out of thirty she knew who could be covered in mud and still look so good. Harley did.

He pushed back his hat as he walked up to the van, opening the door for her.

She grabbed the turnips in their brown bag and handed it to him. She jumped down with a small box in her hand. "Here," she said, shoving it at him.

"Wait a sec." He put the turnips in his truck and handed her a five-dollar bill. "Don't argue," he said at once, when she tried to. "I had money to get them with, even allowing for cow sabotage." He grinned.

She grinned back. "Okay." She put the bill in her slacks pocket and handed him the box.

He gave her an odd look. "What's it for?"

"Christmas," she said.

He laughed. "Boss gives me a bonus every Christmas. I can't remember the last time I got an actual present."

She flushed.

"Don't get self-conscious about it," he said, when he noticed her sudden color. "I just felt bad that I didn't get you something."

"I told you, the party…"

"Some party," he muttered. He turned the small box in his hands, curious. He pulled the tape that held the sides together and opened it. His pale eyes lit up as he pulled the little silver longhorn tie tack out of the box. "Hey, this is sweet! I've been looking for one of these, but I could never find one small enough to be in good taste!"

She flushed again. "You really like it?"

"I do! I'll wear it to the next Cattlemen's Association meeting," he promised. "Thanks, Alice."

"Merry Christmas."

"It is now," he agreed. He slid an arm around her waist and pulled her against him. "Merry Christmas, Alice." He bent and kissed her with rough affection.

She sighed and melted into him. The kiss was warm, and hard and intoxicating. She was a normal adult woman with all the usual longings, but it had been a long time since a kiss had made her want to rip a man's clothes off and push him down on the ground.

She laughed.

He drew back at once, angry. "What the hell…!"

"No, it's not… I'm not laughing at you! I was wondering what you'd think if I started ripping your clothes off…!"

He'd gone from surprise to anger to indignation, and now he doubled over laughing.

"Was it something I said?" she wondered aloud.

He grabbed her up in his arms and spun her around, catching her close to kiss her hungrily again and again. He was covered in mud, and now she was covered in it, too. She didn't care.

Her arms caught around his neck. She held on, loving the warm crush of his mouth in the cold rain that was just starting to fall. Her eyes closed. She breathed, and breathed him, cologne and soap and coffee…

After a few seconds, the kiss stopped being fun and became serious. His hard mouth opened. His arm dragged her breasts against his broad chest. He nudged her lips apart and invaded her mouth with deliberate sensuality.

He nibbled her lower lip as he carried her to the pickup truck. He nudged the turnips into the passenger seat while he edged under the wheel, still carrying Alice. He settled her in his lap and kissed her harder while his hands slid under the warm sweater and onto her bare back, working their way under the wispy little bra she was wearing.

His hands were cold and she jumped when they found her pert little breasts, and she laughed nervously.

"They'll warm up," he whispered against her mouth.

She was going under in waves of pleasure. It had been such a long time since she'd been held and kissed, and even the best she'd had was nothing compared to this. She moaned softly as his palms settled over her breasts and began to caress them, ever so gently.

She held on for dear life. She hoped he wasn't going to suggest that they try to manage an intimate session on the seat, because there really wasn't that much room. On the other hand, she wasn't protesting...

When he drew back, she barely realized it. She was hanging in space, so flushed with delight that she was feeling oblivious to everything else.

He was looking at her with open curiosity, his hands still under her top, but resting on her rib cage now, not intimately on her breasts.

She blinked, staring up at him helplessly. "Is something wrong?" she asked in a voice that sounded drowsy with passion.

"Alice, you haven't done much of this, have you?" he asked very seriously.

She bit her lip self-consciously. "Am I doing it wrong?"

"There's no right or wrong way," he corrected gently. "You don't know how to give it back."

She just stared at him.

"It's not a complaint," he said when he realized he was hurting her feelings. He bent and brushed his warm mouth over her eyelids. "For a brash woman, you're amazingly innocent. I thought you were kidding about being a virgin."

She went scarlet. "Well, no, I wasn't."

He laughed softly. "I noticed. Here. Sit up."

She did, but she popped back up and grabbed the turnips before she sat on them. "Whew," she whistled. "They're okay."

He took them from her and put them up on the dash.

She gave him a mock hurt look. "Don't you want to ravish me on the truck seat?" she asked hopefully.

He lifted both eyebrows. "Alice, you hussy!" He laughed.

She grimaced. "Sorry."

"I was teasing!"

"Oh."

He drew her close and hugged her with rough affection. "Yes, I'd love to ravish you on the seat, but not on Christmas Day in plain view of the boss and any cowhand who wandered by."

"Are they likely to wander by?" she wondered out loud.

He let her go and nodded in the direction of the house. There were two cowboys coming their way on horseback. They weren't looking at them. They seemed to be talking.

"It's Christmas," she said.

"Yes, and cattle have to be worked on holidays as well as workdays," he reminded her.

"Sorry. I forgot."

"I really like my tie tack," he said. "And thanks a million for bringing me the turnips." He hesitated. "But I have to get back to work. I gave up my day off so that John could go and see his kids," he added with a smile.

She beamed. "I gave up my Christmas Eve for the same reason. But that's how I got to go to the party with you. I promised to work for him last night."

"We're both nice people," he said, smiling.

She sighed. "I could call a minister right now."

"He's busy," he said with a grin. "It's Christmas."

"Oh. Right."

He got out of the truck and helped her down. "Thanks for my present. Sorry I didn't get you one."

"Yes, you did," she said at once, and then laughed and flushed.

He bent and kissed her softly. "I got an extra one myself," he whispered. "Are we still going riding Saturday?"

"Oh, yes," she said. "At least, I think so. I've got to run up to San Antonio in the morning to talk to Rick Marquez. The minister of the murdered woman was able to draw the man she sent to him."

"Really?" he asked, impressed.

"Yes, and so now we have a real lead." She frowned thoughtfully. "You know, I wonder if Kilraven might recognize the guy. He works out of San Antonio. He might make a copy and show it to his brother, too."

"Good idea." He drew in a long breath. "Alice, you be careful," he added. "If the woman was killed because she talked to us, the minister might be next, and then you." He didn't add, but they both knew, that he could be on the firing line, too.

"The minister's okay. Marquez called a reporter he knew and got him on the evening news." She chuckled. "They'd be nuts to hurt him now, with all the media attention."

"Probably true, and good call by Marquez. But you're not on the news."

"Point taken. I'll watch my back. You watch yours, too," she added with a little concern.

"I work for a former mercenary," he reminded her drolly. "It would take somebody really off balance to come gunning for me."

"Okay. That makes me feel better." She smiled. "But if this case heats up in San Antonio, I may have to go back sooner than Saturday…"

"So? If you can't come riding, I can drive up there and we can catch a movie or go out to eat."

"You would?" she exclaimed, surprised.

He glowered at her. "We're going steady. Didn't you notice?"

"No! Why didn't you tell me?" she demanded.

"You didn't ask. Go back to the motel and maybe we can have lunch tomorrow at Barbara's. I'll phone you."

She grinned. "That would be lovely."

"Meanwhile, I've got more cattle to feed," he said on a weary sigh. "It was a nice break, though."

"Yes, it was."

He looked at the smears of mud on her once-pristine shirt and winced. "Sorry," he said.

She looked down at the smears and just laughed. "It'll wash," she said with a shy smile.

He beamed. He loved a woman who didn't mind a little dirt. He opened her van door and she climbed up into it. "Drive carefully," he told her.

She smiled. "I always do."

"See you."

"See you."

She was halfway back to the motel before she realized that she hadn't mentioned his connection to Senator Fowler. Of course, that might be just as well, considering that the newest murder victim had ties to the senator, and the original murder victim did, too, in a roundabout way.

On her way to see Hayes Carson at the sheriff's office, Alice phoned Marquez at home—well, it was a holiday, so she thought he might be at home with his foster mother, Barbara. She found out that Marquez had been called back to San Antonio on a case. She grimaced. She was never going to get in touch with him, she supposed.

She walked into Carson's office. He was sitting at his desk. He lifted both eyebrows. "It's December twenty-fifth," he pointed out.

She lifted both eyebrows. "Ho, ho, ho?" she said.

He chuckled. "So I'm not the only person who works holidays. I had started to wonder." He indicated the empty desks around his office in the county detention center.

"My office looked that way last night, too," she confessed. She sat down by his desk. "I questioned a woman who worked for Senator Fowler about the man who drove her car down here and got killed next to the river."

"Find out much?" he asked, suddenly serious.

"That I shouldn't have been so obvious about questioning her. She died of an apparent suicide, but I pestered the attending pathologist to put 'probable' before 'suicide' on the death certificate. She shot herself through the heart with the wrong hand and the bullet was angled down." She waited for a reaction.

He leaned back in his chair. "Wonders will never cease."

"I went to see her minister, who spoke to the man we found dead by the river. The minister was an art student. He drew me this." She pulled out a folded sheet of paper from her purse and handed it to him.

"Hallelujah!" he burst out. "Alice, you're a wonder! You should be promoted!"

"No, thanks, I like fieldwork too much," she told him, grinning. "It's good, isn't it? That's what your murder victim looks like." Her smile faded. "I'm just sorry I got the woman killed who was trying to help him restart his life."

He looked up with piercing eyes. "You didn't. Life happens. We don't control how it happens."

"You're good for my self-esteem. I was going to show that to Rick Marquez, but he's become rather elusive."

"Something happened in San Antonio. I don't know what. They called in a lot of off-duty people."

"Was Kilraven one of them, or do you know?" she asked.

"I don't, but I can find out." He called the dispatch center and gave Kilraven's badge number and asked if Kilraven was on duty.

"Yes, he is. Do you want me to ask him to place you a twenty-one?" she asked, referring to a phone call.

"Yes, thanks, Winnie," he said, a smile in his voice as he recognized dispatcher Winnie Sinclair.

"No problem. Dispatch out at thirteen hundred hours."

He hung up. "She'll have him call me," he told Alice. "What did the minister tell you about the murdered man?" he asked while they waited.

"Not much. He said the guy told him he'd been a bad man, but he wanted to change, that he was going to speak to somebody about an old case and that he'd talk to the minister again after he did it. It's a real shame. Apparently he'd just discovered that there was more to life than dodging the law. He had a good woman friend, he was starting to go to church—now he's lying in the morgue, unidentifiable."

"Not anymore," Hayes told her, waving the drawing.

"Yes, but he could be anybody," she replied.

"If he has a criminal background, he's got fingerprints on file and a mug shot. I have access to face recognition software."

"You do? How?" she asked, fascinated.

"Tell you what," he said, leaning forward. "I'll give you my source if you'll tell me how you got hold of that computer chip emplacement tech for tagging bodies."

She caught her breath. "Well! You do get around, don't you? That's cutting-edge and we don't advertise it."

"My source doesn't advertise, either."

"We'll trade," she promised. "Now, tell me…"

The phone rang. Hayes picked it up. He gave Alice a sardonic look. "Yes, the sheriff's office is open on Christmas. I just put away my reindeer and took off my red suit… Yes, Alice Jones is here with an artist's sketch of the murdered man… Hello? Hello?" He hung up with a sigh. "Kilraven," he said, answering the unasked question.

Alice sighed. "I get that a lot, too. People hanging up on me, I mean. I'll bet he's burning rubber, trying to get here at light speed."

"I wouldn't doubt it." He chuckled.

Sure enough, just a minute or two later, they heard squealing tires turning into the parking lot outside the window. A squad car with flashing blue lights slammed to a stop just at the front door and the engine went dead. Seconds later, Kilraven stormed into the office.

"Let's see it," he said without preamble.

Hayes handed him the drawing.

Kilraven looked at it for a long time, frowning.

"Recognize him?" Alice asked.

He grimaced. "No," he said gruffly. "Damn! I thought it might be somebody I knew."

"Why?" Hayes asked.

"I work out of San Antonio as a rule," he said. "And I was a patrol officer, and then a detective, on the police force there for some years. If the guy had a record in San Antonio, I might have had dealings with him. But I don't recognize this guy."

Hayes took the sketch back. "If I make a copy, could you show it to Jon and see if he looks familiar to him?"

"Sure." He glanced at Alice. "How'd you get a sketch of the dead man? Reconstructive artist?"

"No. That woman I talked to about him killed herself..."

"Like hell she did," Kilraven exclaimed. "That's too pat!"

"Just what I thought. I talked to the forensic pathologist who did the autopsy," she added. "He said she was right-handed, but shot herself through the heart with her left hand. Good trick, too, because she had carpal tunnel syndrome, plus surgery, and the gun was a big, heavy .45 Colt ACP. He said she'd have had hell just cocking it."

"He labeled it a suicide?"

She shook her head. "He's trying not to get caught up in political fallout. She worked for the senator, you know, and he's not going to want to be a media snack over a possible homicide that happened on his own property."

"The pathologist didn't label it a suicide?" he persisted.

"I got him to add 'probable' to the report."

"Well, that's something, I guess. Damned shame about the woman. She might have been able to tell us more, in time." He smiled at Alice. "I'm glad you went to see her, anyway. What we have is thanks to you." He frowned. "But how did you get the sketch?"

"The woman's minister," she said simply. "He'd

talked to the man who was killed and before he became a minister, he was an artist. He didn't add much to what the woman had already told me. He did say that the guy had a guilty conscience and he was going to talk to somebody about an old case."

Kilraven was frowning again. "An old case. Who was he going to talk to? People in law enforcement, maybe?"

"Very possibly," Alice agreed. "I'm not through digging. But I need to identify this man. I thought I might go to the motel where he was staying and start interviewing residents. It's a start."

"Not for you," Kilraven said sternly. "You've put yourself in enough danger already. You leave this to me and Jon. We get paid for people to shoot at us. You don't."

"My hero," Alice sighed, batting her eyelashes at him and smiling. "If I wasn't so keen to marry Harley Fowler, I swear I'd be sending you candy and flowers."

"I hate sweets and I'm allergic to flowers," he pointed out.

She wrinkled her nose. "Just as well, then, isn't it?"

"I'll copy this for you," Hayes said, moving to the copy machine in the corner. "We're low on toner, though, so don't expect anything as good as the original drawing."

"Why don't you get more toner?" Alice asked.

Hayes glowered. "I have to have a purchase order from the county commission, and they're still yelling at me about the last several I asked for."

"Which was for…?" Kilraven prompted.

Hayes made the copy, examined it and handed it to

Kilraven. "A cat, and an electrician, and an exterminator."

Alice and Kilraven stared at him.

He moved self-consciously back to his desk and sat
down. "I bought this cheap cat," he emphasized. "It
only cost fifteen bucks at the pet store. It wasn't purebred or anything."

"Why did you buy a cat?" Alice asked.

He sighed. "Do you remember the mouse that lived
in Tira Hart's house before she became Simon Hart's
wife?"

"Well, I heard about it," Kilraven admitted.

"One of my deputies caught two field mice and was
going to take them home to his kids for a science project. He put them in a wood box and when he went to
get them out, they weren't there." Hayes sighed. "They
chewed their way out of the box, they chewed up the
baseboards and two electrical wires, and did about three
hundred dollars' worth of damage to county property.
I called an electrician for that. Then I tried traps and
they wouldn't work, so I bought a cat."

"Did the cat get the mice?" Alice asked.

Hayes shook his head. "Actually," he replied, "the
mice lay in wait for the cat, chomped down on both his
paws at the same time and darted back into the hole in
the wall they came out of. Last time I saw the cat, he
was headed out of town by way of the city park. The
mice are still here, though," he added philosophically.
"Which is why I had to have authorization to pay for
an exterminator. The chairman of our county commission found one of the mice sitting in his coffee cup." He
sighed. "Would you believe, I got blamed for that, too?"

"Well, that explains why the commission got mad

at you," Alice said. "I mean, for the cat and the electrician."

"No, that's not why they got mad."

"It wasn't?"

He looked sheepish. "It was the engine for a 1996 Ford pickup truck."

Alice stared at him. "Okay, now I'm confused."

"I had to call an exterminator. While he was looking for the mice, they got under the hood of his truck and did something—God knows what, but it was catastrophic. When he started the truck, the engine caught fire. It was a total loss."

"How do you know the mice did it?" Kilraven wanted to know.

"One of my deputies—the same one who brought the damned rodents in here in the first place—saw them coming down the wheel well of the truck just before the exterminator got in and started it."

Alice laughed. She got to her feet. "Hayes, if I were you, I'd find whoever bought Cag Hart's big albino python and borrow him."

"If these mice are anything like Tira's mouse, fat chance a snake will do what a cat can't."

As he spoke, the lights started dimming. He shook his head. "They're back," he said with sad resignation.

"Better hide your firearms," Kilraven advised as he and Alice started for the door.

"With my luck, they're better shots than I am." Hayes laughed. "I'm going to show this drawing around town and see if anybody recognizes the subject. If either of you find out anything else about the murdered man, let me know."

"Will do," Alice promised.

Chapter 8

Alice followed Kilraven out the door. He stood on the steps of the detention center, deep in thought.

"Why did you think you might know the murder victim?" Alice asked him.

"I told you…"

"You lied."

He looked down at her with arched eyebrows.

"Oh, I'm psychic," she said easily. "You know all those shows about people with ESP who solve murders, well, I get mistaken for that dishy one all the time…"

"You're not psychic, Alice," he said impatiently.

"No sense of humor," she scoffed. "I wonder how you stay sane on the job! Okay, okay—" she held up both hands when he glowered "—I'll talk. It was the way you rushed over here to look at the drawing. Come on, give me a break. Nobody gets in that sort of hurry without a pretty sturdy reason."

He rested his hand on the holstered butt of his pistol. His eyes held that "thousand-yard stare" that was so remarked on in combat stories. "I've encouraged a former San Antonio detective to do some digging into the files on my cold case," he said quietly. "And you aren't to mention that to Marquez. He's in enough trouble. We're not going to tell him."

She wouldn't have dared mention that she already knew about the detective working on the case, and so did Marquez. "Have you got a lead?" she asked.

"I thought this case might be one," he said quietly. "A guy comes down here from San Antonio, and gets killed. It's eerie, but I had a feeling that he might have been looking for me. Stupid, I know..."

"There are dozens of reasons he might have driven down here," she replied. "And he might have been passing through. The perp might have followed him and ambushed him."

"You're right, of course." He managed a smile. "I keep hoping I'll get lucky one day." The smile faded into cold steel. "I want to know who it was. I want to make him pay for the past seven miserable years of my life."

She cocked her head, frowning. "Nothing will make up for that," she said quietly. "You can't take two lives out of someone. There's no punishment on earth that will take away the pain, or the loss. You know that."

"Consciously, I do," he said. He drew in a sharp breath. "I worked somebody else's shift as a favor that night. If I hadn't, I'd have been with them..."

"Stop that!" she said in a tone short enough to shock him. "Lives have been destroyed with that one, stupid word. *If!* Listen to me, Kilraven, you can't appropriate the power of life and death. You can't control the world. Sometimes people die in horrible ways. It's not right, but it's just the way things are. You have to go forward. Living in regret is only another way the perp scores off you."

He didn't seem to take offense. He was actually listening.

"I hear it from victims' families all the time," she continued. "They grieve, they hate, they live for vengeance. They can't wait for the case to go to trial so they can watch the guilty person burn. But, guess what, juries don't convict, or perps make deals, or sometimes the case even gets thrown out of court because of a break in the chain of evidence. And all that anger has no place to go, except in sound bites for the six-o'clock news. Then the families go home and the hatred grows, and they end up with empty lives full of nothing. Nothing at all. Hate takes the place that healing should occupy."

He stared down at her for a long moment. "I guess I've been there."

"For about seven years," she guessed. "Are you going to devote your life to all that hatred? You'll grow old with nothing to show for those wasted years except bitter memories."

"If my daughter had lived," he said in a harsh tone, "she'd be ten years old next week."

She didn't know how to answer him. The anguish he felt was in every word.

"He got away with it, Jones," he said harshly.

"No, he didn't," she replied. "Someone knows what happened, and who did it. One day, a telephone will ring in a detective's office, and a jilted girlfriend or boyfriend will give up the perp out of hurt or revenge or greed."

He relaxed a little. "You really think so?"

"I've seen it happen. So have you."

"I guess I have."

"Try to stop living in the past," she counseled gently. "It's a waste of a good man."

He lifted an eyebrow, and the black mood seemed to drop away. His silver eyes twinkled. "Flirting with me?"

"Don't go there," she warned. "I've seen too many wives sitting up watching the late show, hoping their husbands would come home. That's not going to be me. I'm going to marry a cattle rancher and sleep nights."

He grinned. "That's no guarantee of sleep. Baby bulls and cows almost always get born in the wee hours of the morning."

"You'd know," she agreed, smiling. "You and Jon have that huge black Angus ranch in Oklahoma, don't you?"

He nodded. "Pity neither of us wants to sit around and babysit cattle. We're too career conscious."

"When you get older, it might appeal."

"It might," he said, but not with any enthusiasm. "We hold on to it because Jon's mother likes to have company there." He grimaced. "She's got a new prospect for Jon."

"I heard." Alice chuckled. "He had her arrested in his own office for sexual harassment. I understand Joceline Perry is still making him suffer for it."

"It really was sexual harassment," Kilraven corrected. "The woman is a call girl. We both tried to tell my stepmom, but her best friend is the woman's mother. She won't believe us. Mom keeps trying to get her to the ranch, with the idea that Jon will like her better if he sees her in blue jeans."

"Fat chance," Alice said. "Jon should tell Joceline the truth."

"He won't lower his dignity that far. He said if she wants to think he's that much of a scoundrel, let her. They don't get along, anyway."

"No offense, but most women don't get along with your brother," she replied. "He doesn't really like women very much."

He sighed. "If you had my stepmother as a mom, you wouldn't, either." He held up a hand. "She has her good qualities. But she has blind spots and prejudices that would choke a mule. God help the woman who really falls in love with Jon. She'll have to get past Jon's mother, and it will take a tank."

She pursed her lips. "I hear Joceline has the personality of a tank."

He chuckled. "She does. But she hates Jon." He hesitated. "If you get any new leads, you'll tell me, right?"

"Right."

"Thanks for the lecture," he added with twinkling eyes. "You're not bad."

"I'm terrific," she corrected. "Just you wait. Harley Fowler will be rushing me to the nearest minister any day now."

"Poor guy."

"Hey, you stop that. I'm a catch, I am. I've got movie stars standing in line trying to marry me… Where are you going?"

"Back to work while there's still time," he called over his shoulder.

Before she could add to her bragging, he hopped into his squad car and peeled out of the parking lot.

Alice stared after him. "You'd be lucky if I set my sights on you," she said to nobody in particular. "It's your loss!" she called after the retreating squad car.

A deputy she hadn't heard came up behind her. "Talking to yourself again, Jones?" he mused.

She gave him a pained glance. "It's just as well that I do. I'm not having much luck getting people to listen to me."

"I know just how that feels," he said with a chuckle.

He probably did, she thought as she went back to her van. People in law enforcement were as much social workers as law enforcers. They had to be diplomatic, keep their tempers under extraordinary provocation, hand out helpful advice and firm warnings, sort out domestic problems, handle unruly suspects and even dodge bullets.

Alice knew she was not cut out for that sort of life, but she enjoyed her job. At least, she chuckled, she didn't have to dodge bullets.

Saturday, she was still in Jacobsville, waiting for one last piece of evidence that came from the site of the car that was submerged in the river. A fisherman had found a strange object near the site and called police. Hayes Carson had driven out himself to have a look. It was a metal thermos jug that the fisherman had found in some weeds. It looked new and still had liquid in it. Could have been that some other pedestrian lost it, Hayes confided, but it paid to keep your options open. Hayes had promised that Alice could have it, but she'd promised to go riding with Harley. So she'd told Hayes she'd pick it up at his office late that afternoon.

"And you think the sheriff himself sits at his desk waiting for people on a Saturday?" Hayes queried on the phone in mock horror.

"Listen, Hayes, I have it on good authority that you practically sleep at the office most nights and even keep a razor and toothbrush there," she said with droll humor. "So I'll see you about seven."

He sighed. "I'll be here, working up another budget proposal."

"See?" She hung up.

Cy Parks wasn't what she'd expected. He was tall and lean, with black hair showing just threads of gray, and green eyes. His wife, Lisa, was shorter and blonde with light eyes and glasses. They had two sons, one who was a toddler and the other newborn. Lisa was holding one, Cy had the oldest.

"We've heard a lot about you," Cy mused as Alice stood next to Harley. They were all wearing jeans and long-sleeved shirts and coats. It was a cold day.

"Most of it is probably true," Alice sighed. "But I have great teeth—" she displayed them "—and a good attitude."

They laughed.

"We haven't heard bad things," Lisa assured her, adjusting her glasses on her pert nose.

"Yes, we have." Cy chuckled. "Not really bad ones. Harley says you keep proposing to him, is all."

"Oh, that's true," Alice said, grinning. "I'm wearing him down, day by day. I just can't get him to let me buy him a ring."

Cy pursed his lips and glanced at Harley. "Hey, if you can get him in a suit, I'll give him away," he promised.

Harley grinned at him. "I'll remind you that you said that," he told his boss.

Cy's eyes were more kind than humorous. "I mean it."

Harley flushed a little with pleasure. "Thanks."

"Does that mean yes?" Alice asked Harley, wide-eyed.

He gave her a mock glare. "It means I'm thinking about it."

"Darn," she muttered.

"How's your murder investigation coming?" Cy asked suddenly.

"You mean the DB on the river?" she asked. "Slowly. We've got evidence. We just can't puzzle out what it means."

"There are some messed-up people involved, is my guess," Cy said, somber. "I've seen people handled the way your victim was. It usually meant a very personal grudge."

Alice nodded. "We've found that most close-up attacks, when they aren't random, are done by people with a grudge. I never cease to be amazed at what human beings are capable of."

"Amen." Cy slid an arm around Lisa. "We'd better get these boys back into a warm house. We've been through the mill with colds already." He chuckled. "Nice to meet you, Alice. If you can get him—" he pointed at Harley "—to marry you, I've already promised him some land and a seed herd of my best cattle."

"That's really nice of you," Alice said, and meant it.

Cy glanced at Harley warmly. "I'd kind of like to keep him close by," he said with a smile. "I'd miss him."

Harley seemed to grow two feet. "I'm not going anywhere," he drawled, but he couldn't hide that he was flattered.

"Come back again," Lisa told Alice. "It's hard to find two minutes to talk with little guys like these around—" she indicated her babies "—but we'll manage."

"I'd love to," Alice told her.

The Parks family waved and went into the house.

"They're nice," Alice said to Harley.

He nodded. "Mr. Parks has been more of a father to me than my own ever was."

Alice wanted to comment, to ask about the senator. But the look on Harley's face stopped her. It was traumatic. "I haven't been on a horse in about two years," she told him. "I had to go out with the Texas Rangers to look at some remains in the brush country, and it was the only way to get to the crime scene." She groaned. "Six hours on horseback, through prickly pear cactus and thorny bushes! My legs were scratched even through thick jeans and they felt like they were permanently bowed when I finally got back home."

"I've been there, too." He laughed. "But we won't go six hours, I promise."

He led her into the barn, where he already had two horses saddled. Hers was a pinto, a female, just the right size.

"That's Bean," he said. "Colby Lane's daughter rides her when she comes over here."

"Bean?" she asked as she mounted.

"She's a pinto," he said dryly.

She laughed. "Oh!"

He climbed into the saddle of a black Arabian gelding and led off down the trail that ran to the back of the property.

It was a nice day to go riding, she thought. It had rained the night before, but it was sunny today, if cold. There were small mud patches on the trail, and despite the dead grass and bare trees, it felt good to be out-of-doors on a horse.

She closed her eyes and smelled the clean scent of country air. "If you could bottle this air," she commented, "you could outsell perfume companies."

He chuckled. "You sure could. It's great, isn't it? People in cities don't even know what they're missing."

"You lived in a city once, didn't you?" she asked in a conversational tone.

He turned his head sideways. Pale blue eyes narrowed under the wide brim of his hat as he pondered the question. "You've been making connections, Alice."

She flushed a little. "No, I really haven't. I've just noticed similarities."

"In names," he replied.

"Yes," she confessed.

He drew in a breath and drew in the reins. So did she. He sat beside her quietly, his eyes resting on the horizon.

"The senator is your father," she guessed.

He grimaced. "Yes."

She averted her gaze to the ground. It was just faintly muddy and the vegetation was brown. The trees in the distance were bare. It was a cold landscape. Cold, like Harley's expression.

"My parents were always in the middle of a cocktail party or a meeting. All my life. I grew up hearing the sound of ice clinking in glasses. We had politicians and other rich and famous people wandering in and out. I was marched out before bedtime to show everybody what a family man the politician was." He laughed coldly. "My mother was a superior court judge," he added surprisingly. "Very solemn on the bench, very strict at home. My sister died, and suddenly she was drinking more heavily than my father at those cocktail parties. She gave up her job on the bench to become an importer." He shook his head. "He changed, too. When he was younger, he'd play ball with me, or take me to the movies. After my sister died, everything was devoted to his career, to campaigning, even when he wasn't up for reelection. I can't tell you how sick I got of it."

"I can almost imagine," she said gently. "I'm sorry."

He turned back to her, frowning. "I never connected those two facts. You know, my sister's death with the changes in my parents. I was just a kid myself, not really old enough to think deeply." He glanced back at the horizon. "Maybe I was wrong."

"Maybe you were both wrong," she corrected. "Your father seemed very sad when he saw you."

"It's been almost eight years," he replied. "In all that time, not one card or phone call. It's hard to square that with any real regret."

"Sometimes people don't know how to reach out," she said. "I've seen families alienated for years, all because they didn't know how to make the first contact, take the first step back to a relationship that had gone wrong."

He sighed, fingering the bridle. "I guess that describes me pretty well."

"It's pride, isn't it?" she asked.

He laughed faintly. "Isn't it always?" he wondered aloud. "I felt that I was the wronged party. I didn't think it was up to me to make the first move. So I waited."

"Maybe your father felt the same way," she suggested.

"My father isn't the easiest man to approach, even on his good days," he said. "He has a temper."

"You weren't singing happy songs the day I called you, when the cow ate your turnips," she replied, tongue-in-cheek.

He laughed. "I guess I've got a temper, too."

"So do I. It isn't exactly a bad trait. Only if you carry it to extremes."

He looked down at his gloved hands. "I guess."

"They're not young people anymore, Harley," she said quietly. "If you wait too much longer, you may not get the chance to patch things up."

He nodded. "I've been thinking about that."

She hesitated. She didn't want to push too hard. She nudged her horse forward a little, so that she was even with him. "Have you thought about what sort of ring you'd like?"

He pursed his lips and glanced over at her. "One to go on my finger, or one to go through my nose?"

She laughed. "Stop that."

"Just kidding." He looked up. "It's getting cloudy. We'd better get a move on, or we may get caught in a rain shower."

She knew the warning was his way of ending the

conversation. But she'd got him thinking. That was enough, for now. "Suits me."

He walked her back to the van, his hands in his pockets, his thoughts far away.

"I enjoyed today," she told him. "Thanks for the riding lesson."

He stopped at the driver's door of the van and looked down at her, a little oddly. "You don't push, do you?" he asked solemnly. "It's one of the things I like best about you."

"I don't like being pushed, myself," she confided. She searched his eyes. "You're a good man."

He drew his hand out of his pocket and smoothed back her windblown dark hair, where it blew onto her cheek. The soft leather of the glove tickled. "You're a good woman," he replied. "And I really mean that."

She started to speak.

He bent and covered her mouth with his before she could say anything. His lips parted, cold and hungry on her soft, pliable lips. She opened them with a sigh and reached around him with both arms, and held on tight. She loved kissing him. But it was more than affection. It was a white-hot fire of passion that made her ache from head to toe. She felt swollen, hot, burning, as his arms contracted.

"Oh, God," he groaned, shivering as he buried his mouth in her neck. "Alice, we're getting in too deep, too quick."

"Complaints, complaints," she grumbled into his coat.

He laughed despite the ache that was almost doubling him over. "It's not a complaint. Well, not exactly." He drew in a calming breath and slowly let her go. His eyes burned down into hers. "We can't rush this," he said. "It's too good. We have to go slow."

Her wide, dark blue eyes searched his languidly. She was still humming all over with pleasure. "Go slow." She nodded. Her eyes fell to his mouth.

"Are you hearing me?"

She nodded. Her gaze was riveted to the sensuous lines of his lips. "Hearing."

"Woman…!"

He caught her close again, ramming his mouth down onto hers. He backed her into the door of the van and ground his body against hers in a fever of need that echoed in her harsh moan.

For a long time, they strained together in the misting rain, neither capable of pulling back. Just when it seemed that the only way to go was into the back of the van, he managed to jerk his mouth back from hers and step away. His jaw was so taut, it felt as if his mouth might break. His pale blue eyes were blazing with frustrated need.

Her mouth was swollen and red. She leaned back against the door, struggling to breathe normally as she stared up at him with helpless adoration. He wasn't obviously muscular, but that close, she felt every taut line of his body. He was delicious, she thought. Like candy. Hard candy.

"You have to leave. Now." He said it in a very strained tone.

"Leave." She nodded again.

"Leave. Now."

She nodded. "Now."

"Alice," he groaned. "Honey, there are four pairs of

eyes watching us out the window right now, and two pairs of them are getting a hell of a sex education!"

"Eyes." She blinked. "Eyes?"

She turned. There, in the living-room window, were four faces. The adult ones were obviously amused. The little ones were wide-eyed with curiosity.

Alice blushed. "Oh, dear."

"You have to go. Right now." He moved her gently aside and opened the door. He helped her up onto the seat. He groaned. "I'm not having supper in the big house tonight, I can promise you that," he added.

She began to recover her senses and her sense of humor. Her eyes twinkled. "Oh, I see," she mused. "I've compromised you. Well, don't you worry, sweetheart," she drawled. "I'll save your reputation. You can marry me tomorrow."

He laughed. "No. I'm trimming horses' hooves."

She glowered at him. "They have farriers to do that."

"Our farrier is on Christmas vacation," he assured her.

"One day," she told him, "you'll run out of excuses."

He searched her eyes and smiled softly. "Of course I will." He stepped back. "But not today. I'll phone you." He closed the door.

She started the engine and powered down the window. "Thanks for the ride."

He was still smiling. "Thanks for the advice. I'll take it."

"Merry Christmas."

He cocked his head. "Christmas is over."

"New Year's is coming."

"That reminds me, we have a New Year's celebration here," he said. "I can bring you to it."

"I'll be back in San Antonio then," she said miserably.

"I'll drive you down here and then drive you home."

"No. I'll stay in the motel," she said. "I don't want you on the roads after midnight. There are drunk drivers."

His heart lifted. His eyes warmed. "You really are a honey."

She smiled. "Hold that thought. See you."

He winked at her and chuckled when she blushed again. "See you, pretty girl."

She fumbled the van into gear and drove off jerkily. It had been a landmark day.

Chapter 9

Alice was back in her office the following week. She'd turned the thermos from the river in Jacobsville over to Longfellow first thing in the morning. She was waiting for results, going over a case file, when the door opened and a tall, distinguished-looking gentleman in an expensive dark blue suit walked in, unannounced. He had black hair with silver at the temples, and light blue eyes. She recognized him at once.

"Senator Fowler," she said quietly.

"Ms. Jones," he replied. He stood over the desk with his hands in his pockets. "I wonder if you could spare me a few minutes?"

"Of course." She indicated the chair in front of her desk.

He took his hands out of his pockets and sat down, crossing one long leg over the other. "I believe you know my son."

She smiled. "Yes. I know Harley."

"I... My wife and I haven't seen him for many years," he began. "We made terrible mistakes. Now it seems that we'll never be able to find our way back to him. He's grown into a fine-looking young man. He...has a job?"

She nodded. "A very good one. And friends."

"I'm glad. I'm very glad." He hesitated. "We didn't know how to cope with him. He was such a cocky youngster, so sure that he had all the answers." He looked down at his shoes. "We should have been kinder."

"You lost your daughter," Alice said very gently.

He lifted his eyes and they shimmered with pain and grief. "I killed...my daughter," he gritted. "Backed over her with my car rushing to get to a campaign rally." He closed his eyes. "Afterward, I went mad."

"So did your wife, I think," Alice said quietly.

He nodded. He brushed at his eyes and averted them. "She was a superior court judge. She started drinking and quit the bench. She said she couldn't sit in judgment on other people when her own mistakes were so terrible. She was on the phone when it happened. She'd just told our daughter, Cecily, to stop interrupting her and go away. You know, the sort of offhand remark parents make. It doesn't mean they don't love the child. Anyway, Cecily sneaked out the door and went behind the car, unbeknownst to me, apparently to get a toy she'd tossed under it. I jumped in without looking to see if there was anybody behind me. I was late getting to a meeting... Anyway, my wife never knew Cecily was outside until I started screaming, when I knew what I'd done." He leaned forward. "We blamed each other.

We had fights. Harley grieved. He blamed me, most of all. But he seemed to just get right on with his life afterward."

"I don't think any of you did that," Alice replied. "I don't think you dealt with it."

He looked up. His blue eyes were damp. "How do you know so much?"

"I deal with death every day," she said simply. "I've seen families torn apart by tragedies. Very few people admit that they need help, or get counseling. It is horrible to lose a child. It's traumatic to lose one the way you did. You should have been in therapy, all of you."

"I wasn't the sort of person who could have admitted that," he said simply. "I was more concerned with my image. It was an election year, you see. I threw myself into the campaign and thought that would accomplish the same thing. So did my wife." He shook his head. "She decided to start a business, to keep busy." He managed a smile. "Now we never see each other. After Harley left, we blamed each other for that, too."

She studied the older man curiously. "You're a politician. You must have access to investigators. You could have found Harley any time you wanted to."

He hesitated. Then he nodded. "But that works both ways, Ms. Jones. He could have found us, too. We didn't move around."

"Harley said you wanted him to be part of a social set that he didn't like."

"Do you think I like it?" he asked suddenly and gave a bitter laugh. "I love my job. I have power. I can do a lot of good, and I do. But socializing is part of that job. I do more business at cocktail parties than I've ever done in my office in Washington. I make contacts, I get

networks going, I research. I never stop." He sighed. "I
tried to explain that to Harley, but he thought I meant
that I wanted to use him to reel in campaign workers."
He laughed. "It's funny now. He was so green, so naive.
He thought he knew all there was to know about politics and life." He looked up. "I hope he's learned that
nothing is black or white."

"He's learned a lot," she replied. "But he's been running away from his past for years."

"Too many years. I can't approach him directly. He'd
take off." He clasped his hands together. "I was hoping
you might find it in your heart to pave the way for me.
Just a little. I only want to talk to him."

She narrowed her eyes. "This wouldn't have anything to do with the woman we talked to at your fund-
raising party...?"

He stared at her with piercing blue eyes just a shade
lighter than Harley's. "You're very quick."

"I didn't start this job yesterday," she replied, and
smiled faintly.

He drew in a long breath. "I gave Dolores a hard time.
She was deeply religious, but she got on my nerves. A
man who's forsaken religion doesn't like sermons," he
added, laughing bitterly. "But she was a good person.
My wife had a heart attack earlier this year. I hired a
nurse to sit with her, when she got home from the hospital. Unknown to me, the nurse drugged my wife and
left the house to party with her boyfriend. Dolores made
sure I found out. Then she sat with my wife. They found
a lot to talk about. After my wife got back on her feet,
she began to change for the better. I think it was Dolores's influence." He hung his head. "I was harsh to
Dolores the night of the fund-raiser. That's haunted me,

too. I have a young protégé, our newest senator. He's got a brother who makes me very nervous…" He lifted his eyes. "Sorry. I keep getting off the track. I do want you to help me reconnect with my son, if you can. But that's not why I'm here."

"Then why are you here, Senator?" she asked.

He looked her in the eye. "Dolores didn't commit suicide."

Her heart jumped, but she kept a straight face. She linked her hands in front of her on the desk and leaned forward. "Why do you think that?"

"Because once, when I was despondent, I made a joke about running my car into a tree. She was eloquent on the subject of suicide. She thought it was the greatest sin of all. She said that it was an insult to God and it caused so much grief for people who loved you." He looked up. "I'm not an investigator, but I know she was right-handed. She was shot in the right side of her body." He shook his head. "She wasn't the sort of person to do that. She hated guns. I'm sure she never owned one. It doesn't feel right."

"I couldn't force the assistant medical examiner to write it up as a homicide. He's near retirement, and it was your employee who died. He's afraid of you, of your influence. He knows that you stopped the investigation on the Kilraven case stone-cold."

"I didn't," he said unexpectedly, and his mouth tightened. "Will Sanders is the new junior senator from Texas," he continued. "He's a nice guy, but his brother is a small-time hoodlum with some nasty contacts, who mixes with dangerous people. He's involved in illegal enterprises. Will can't stop him, but he does try to protect him. Obviously he thinks Hank knows something about the Kilraven case, and he doesn't want it discovered."

Alice's blue eyes began to glitter. "Murder is a nasty business," she pointed out. "Would you like to know what was done to Kilraven's wife and three-year-old daughter?" she added. "He saw it up close, by accident. But I have autopsy photos that I've never shown anyone, if you'd like to see what happened to them."

The senator paled. "I would not," he replied. He stared into space. "I'm willing for Kilraven to look into the case. Rick Marquez's colleague was sent to work in traffic control. I'm sorry for that. Will persuaded me to get her off the case. She's a bulldog when it comes to homicide investigation, and she stops at nothing to solve a crime." He looked up. "Will's rather forceful in his way. I let him lead me sometimes. But I don't want either of us being shown as obstructing a murder investigation, even one that's seven years old. He's probably afraid that his brother, Hank, may have knowledge of the perpetrator and Will's trying to shield him. He's done that all his life. But he has no idea what the media would do to him if it ever came out that he'd hindered the discovery of a murderer, especially in a case as horrific as this."

"I've seen what happens when people conceal evidence. It's not pretty," Alice said. "How can you help Kilraven?"

"For one thing, I can smooth the way for Marquez's colleague. I'll go have a talk with the police commissioner when I leave here. He'll get her reassigned to Homicide. Here." He scribbled a number on a piece of paper and handed it to her. "That's my private cell number. I keep two phones on me, but only a few people have access to this number. Tell Kilraven to call me. Or do you have his number?"

"Sure." She pulled out her own cell phone, pushed a few buttons and wrote down Kilraven's cell phone number on a scrap of paper. Odd, how familiar that number looked on paper. She handed it to the senator. "There."

"Thanks. Uh, if you like," he added with a smile as he stood up, "you could share my private number with Harley. He can call me anytime. Even if I'm standing at a podium making a speech somewhere. I won't mind being interrupted."

She stood up, too, smiling. "I'm going down there Wednesday for the New Year's Eve celebration in town, as it happens, with Harley. I'll pass it along. Thanks, Senator Fowler."

He shook hands with her. "If I can pave the way for you in the investigation into Dolores's death, I'll be glad to," he added.

"I'll keep you in mind. Kilraven will be grateful for your help, I'm sure."

He smiled, waved and left.

Alice sat down. Something wasn't right. She pulled up her notes on the Jacobsville murder investigation and scrolled down to the series of numbers that Long-fellow had transcribed from the piece of paper in the victim's hand. Gasping, she pulled up Kilraven's cell phone number on her own cell phone and compared them. The digits that were decipherable were a match for everything except the area code, which was missing. It wasn't conclusive, but it was pretty certain that the murder victim had come to contact Kilraven. Which begged the question, did the victim know something about the old murder case?

Her first instinct was to pick up the phone and call Kilraven. But her second was caution. Without the missing numbers, it could be a coincidence. Better to let the senator call Kilraven and get him some help—Marquez's detective friend—and go from there. Meanwhile, Alice would press Longfellow about the faded, wet portion of the paper where the first few numbers were, so far, unreadable. The FBI lab had the technology enabling them to pull up the faintest traces of ink. They might work a miracle for the investigation.

The thermos contained a tiny residue of coffee laced with a narcotic drug, Longfellow told Alice. "If it's connected to your case," the assistant investigator told Alice, "it could explain a lot. It would make the victim less able to defend himself from an attacker."

"Fingerprints?"

Longfellow shook her head. "It was clean. Wiped, apparently, and just tossed away. It's as if," she added, frowning, "the killer was so confident that he left the thermos deliberately, to show his superiority."

Alice smiled faintly. "I love it when perps do that," she said. "When we catch them, and get them into court, that cockiness usually takes a nosedive. It's a kick to see it."

"Indeed," Longfellow added. "I'll keep digging, though," she assured Alice.

"You do that. We'll need every scrap of evidence we have to pin this murder on somebody. The killer's good. Very good." She frowned. "He's probably done this before and never got caught."

"That might explain his efficiency," the other woman

agreed. "But he missed that scrap of paper in the victim's hand."

"Every criminal slips up eventually. Let's hope this is his swan song."

"Oh, yes."

Alice drove down to Jacobsville in her personal car, a little Honda with terrific gas mileage, and checked in at the motel. She'd reserved a room, to make sure she got one, because out-of-town people came for the New Year's Eve celebration. Once she was checked in, she phoned Harley.

"I was going to come up and get you," he protested.

"I don't want you on the roads at night, either, Harley," she replied softly.

He sighed. "What am I going to do with you, Alice?"

"I have several suggestions," she began brightly.

He laughed. "You can tell me tonight. Barbara's Café is staying open for the festivities. Suppose I come and get you about six, and we'll have supper. Then we'll go to the Cattlemen's Association building where the party's being held."

"That sounds great."

"It's formal," he added hesitantly.

"No worries. I brought my skimpy little black cocktail dress and my sassy boa."

He chuckled. "Not a live one, I hope."

"Nope."

"I'll see you later, then," he said in a low, sexy tone.

"I'll look forward to it."

He hung up. So did she. Then she checked her watch. It was going to be a long afternoon.

* * *

Harley caught his breath when she opened the door. She was dressed in a little black silk dress with spaghetti straps and a brief, low-cut bodice that made the most of her pert breasts. The dress clung to her hips and fell to her knees in silky profusion. She wore dark hose and black slingback pumps. She'd used enough makeup to give her an odd, foreign appearance. Her lips, plumped with glossy red stay-on lipstick, were tempting. She wore a knitted black boa with blue feathery wisps and carried a small black evening bag with a long strap.

"Will I do?" Alice asked innocently.

Harley couldn't even speak. He nudged her back into the room, closed and locked the door, took off his hat and his jacket and pushed her gently onto the bed.

"Sorry," he murmured as his mouth took hers like a whirlwind.

She moaned as he slid onto her, teasing her legs apart so that he could ease up her skirt and touch the soft flesh there with a lean, exploring hand.

His mouth became demanding. His hands moved up and down her yielding body, discovering soft curves and softer flesh beneath. With his mouth still insistent on her parting lips, he brushed away the spaghetti straps and bared her to the waist. He lifted his head to look at her taut, mauve-tipped breasts. "Beautiful," he whispered, and his mouth diverted to the hardness, covered it delicately, and with a subtle suction that arched her off the bed in a stab of pleasure so deep that it seemed to make her swell all over.

She forced his head closer, writhing under him as the

hunger built and built in the secret silence of the room. All she wanted was for him never to stop. She whispered it, moaning, coaxing, as the flames grew higher and higher, and his hands reached under her, searching for a waistband…

Her cell phone blared out the theme from the original *Indiana Jones* movie. They both jumped at the sound. Harley, his mind returning to normal, quickly drew his hands out from under Alice's skirt with a grimace, and rolled away. He lay struggling to get his breath while she eased off the bed and retrieved her purse from the floor where she'd dropped it.

"Jones," she managed in a hoarse tone.

"Alice?" Hayes Carson asked, because she didn't sound like herself.

"Yes," she said, forcing herself to breathe normally. "Hayes?"

"Yes. I wanted to know if you found out anything about that thermos." He hesitated. "Did I call at a bad time?"

She managed a laugh. "We could debate that," she said. "Actually the thermos was clean. No fingerprints, but the liquid in it had traces of a narcotic laced in it," she replied. "But Longfellow's still looking. We've got the note at the FBI lab. Hopefully they'll be able to get the missing numbers for us. But they've got a backlog and it's the holidays. Not much hope for anything this week."

"I was afraid of that."

"Well, we live in hope," she said, and glanced at Harley, who was now sitting up and looking pained.

"We do. Coming to the celebration tonight?"

"Sure am. You coming?"

"I never miss it. Uh, is Harley bringing you?"

She laughed. "He is. We'll see you there."

"Sure thing." He hung up.

She glanced at Harley with a wicked smile. "Well, we can think of Hayes as portable birth control tonight, can't we?"

He burst out laughing despite his discomfort. He managed to get to his feet, still struggling to breathe normally. "I can think of a few other pertinent adjectives that would fit him."

"Unprintable ones, I'll bet." She went up to him and put her hands on his broad chest. She reached up to kiss him softly. "It was good timing. I couldn't have stopped."

"Yeah. Me, neither," he confessed, flushing a little. "It's been a long dry spell." He bent and brushed his mouth over hers. "But we've proven that we're physically compatible," he mused.

"Definitely." She pursed her lips. "So how about we get married tomorrow morning?"

He chuckled. "Can't. I'm brushing bulls for a regional show."

"Brushing bulls?" she wondered aloud.

"Purebred herd sires. They have to be brushed and combed and dolled up. The more ribbons we win, the higher we can charge for their, uh, well, for straws."

Of semen, he meant, but he was too nice to say it bluntly. "I know what straws are, Harley." She grinned. "I get the idea."

"So not tomorrow."

"I live in hope," she returned. She went to the mirror in the bathroom to repair her makeup, which was royally smeared. "Better check your face, too," she called.

"This never-smear lipstick has dishonest publicity. It does smear."

He walked up behind her. His shirt was undone. She remembered doing that, her hands buried in the thick hair that covered his chest, tugging it while he kissed her. She flushed at the memory.

He checked his face, decided it would pass, and lowered his eyes to Alice's flushed cheeks in the mirror. He put his hands on her shoulders and tightened them. "We can't get married tomorrow. But I thought, maybe next week. Friday, maybe," he said softly. "I can take a few days off. We could drive down to Galveston. To the beach. Even in winter, it's beautiful there."

She'd turned and was staring up at him wide-eyed. "You mean that? It isn't you're just saying it so I'll stop harassing you?"

He bent and kissed her forehead with breathless tenderness. "I don't know how it happened, exactly," he said in a husky, soft tone. "But I'm in love with you."

She slid her arms around his neck. "I'm in love with you, too, Harley," she said in a wondering tone, searching his eyes.

He lifted her up to him and kissed her in a new way, a different way. With reverence, and respect, and aching tenderness.

"I'll marry you whenever you like," she said against his mouth.

He kissed her harder. The passion returned, riveting them together, locking them in a heat of desire that was ever more formidable to resist.

He drew back, grinding his teeth in frustration, and moved her away from him. "We have to stop this," he said. "At least until after the wedding. I'm really old-fashioned about these things."

"Tell me about it," she said huskily. "I come from a whole family of Baptist ministers. Need I say more?"

He managed a smile. "No. I know what you mean." He drew a steadying breath and looked in the mirror. He grimaced. "Okay, now I believe that publicity was a load of bull," he told her. "I'm smeared, too, and it's not my color."

"It definitely isn't," she agreed. She wet a washcloth and proceeded to clean up both of them. Then, while he got his suit coat back on, and his hair combed, she finished her own makeup. By the time she was done, he was waiting for her at the door. He smiled as she approached him.

"You look sharp," he said gently.

She whirled the boa around her neck and smiled from ear to ear. "You look devastating," she replied.

He stuck out an arm. She linked her hand into it. He opened the door and followed her out.

There was a band. They played regional favorites, and Harley danced with Alice. Practically the whole town had gathered in the building that housed the local Cattlemen's Association, to celebrate the coming of the new year. A pair of steer horns, the idea of Calhoun Ballenger, their new state senator, waited to fall when midnight came.

Hayes Carson was wearing his uniform, and Alice teased him about it.

"Hey, I'm on duty," he replied with a grin. "And I'm only here between calls."

"I'm not arguing. It's a big turnout. Is it always like this?"

"Always," Hayes replied. He started to add to that when a call came over his radio. He pressed the button on his portable and told the dispatcher he was en route to the call. "See what I mean?" he added with a sigh. "Have fun."

"We will," Harley replied, sliding an arm around her.

Hayes waved as he went out the door.

"Is he sweet on you?" Harley asked with just a hint of jealousy in his tone.

She pressed close to him. "Everybody but Hayes knows that he's sweet on Minette Raynor, but he's never going to admit it. He's spent years blaming her for his younger brother's drug-related death. She wasn't responsible, and he even knows who was because there was a confession."

"That's sad," Harley replied.

"It is." She looked up at him and smiled. "But it's not our problem. You said we'd get married next Friday. I'll have to ask for time off."

He pursed his lips. "So will I. Do you want to get married in church?"

She hesitated. "Could we?"

"Yes. I'll make the arrangements. What sort of flowers do you want, for your bouquet?"

"Yellow and white roses," she said at once. "But, Harley, I don't have a wedding gown. You don't want a big reception?"

"Not very big, no, but you should have a wedding gown," he replied solemnly. "If we have a daughter, she could have it for her own wedding one day. Or it could be an heirloom, at least, to hand down."

"A daughter. Children…" She caught her breath. "I hadn't thought about… Oh, yes, I want children! I want them so much!"

His body corded. "So do I."

"I'll buy a wedding gown, first thing when I get home," she said. "I'll need a maid of honor. You'll need a best man," she added quickly.

"I'll ask Mr. Parks," he said.

She smiled. "I don't really have many women friends. Do you suppose Mrs. Parks would be my matron of honor?"

"I think she'd be honored," Harley replied. "I'll ask them."

"Wow," she said softly. "It's all happening so fast." She frowned. "Not too fast, is it?" she worried aloud.

"Not too fast," he assured her. "We're the same sort of people, Alice. We'll fit together like a puzzle. I promise you we will. I'll take care of you all my life."

"I'll take care of you," she replied solemnly. "I want to keep my job."

He smiled. "Of course you do. You can commute, can't you?"

She smiled. "Of course. I have a Honda."

"I've seen it. Nice little car. I've got a truck, so we can haul stuff. Mr. Parks is giving me some land and some cattle from his purebred herd. There's an old house on the land. It's not the best place to set up housekeeping, but Mr. Parks said the minute I proposed, to let him know and he'd get a construction crew out there to remodel it." He hesitated. "I told him Saturday that I was going to propose to you."

Her lips parted. "Saturday?"

He nodded. "That's when I knew I couldn't live without you, Alice."

She pressed close into his arms, not caring what anybody thought. "I felt that way, too. Like I've always known you."

He kissed her forehead and held her tight. "Yes. So we have a place to live. The boss will have it in great shape when we get back from our honeymoon." He lifted his head. "Will you mind living on a ranch?"

"Are you kidding? I want to keep chickens and learn to can and make my own butter."

He laughed. "Really?"

"Really! I hate living in the city. I can't even keep a cat in my apartment, much less grow things there." She beamed. "I'll love it!"

He grinned back. "I'll bring you one of my chicken catalogs. I like the fancy ones, but you can get regular hens, as well."

"Chicken catalogs? You like chickens?"

"Boss keeps them," he said. "I used to gather eggs for Mrs. Parks, years ago. I like hens. I had my mind on a small ranch and I thought chickens would go nicely with cattle."

She sighed. "We're going to be very happy, I think."

"I think so, too."

The Parkses showed up, along with the Steeles and the Scotts. Harley and Alice announced their plans, and the Parkses agreed with delightful speed to take part in the wedding. Other local citizens gathered around to congratulate them.

Midnight came all too soon. The steer horns lowered to the loud count by the crowd, out under the bright

Texas stars to celebrate the new year. The horns made it to the ground, the band struck up "Auld Lang Syne" and everybody kissed and cried and threw confetti.

"Happy New Year, Alice," Harley whispered as he bent to kiss her.

"Happy New Year." She threw her arms around him and kissed him back.

He left her at her motel with real reluctance. "I won't come in," he said at once, grinning wickedly. "We've already discovered that I have no willpower."

"Neither do I," she sighed. "I guess we're very strange. Most people who get married have been living together for years. We're the odd couple, waiting until after the ceremony."

He became serious. "It all goes back to those old ideals, to the nobility of the human spirit," he said softly. "Tradition is important. And I love the idea of chastity. I'm only sorry that I didn't wait for you, Alice. But, then, I didn't know you were going to come along. I'd decided that I'd never find someone I wanted to spend my life with." He smiled. "What a surprise you were."

She went close and hugged him. "You're the nicest man I've ever known. No qualms about what I do for a living?" she added.

He shrugged. "It's a job. I work with cattle and get sunk up to my knees in cow manure. It's not so different from what you do. We both get covered up in disgusting substances to do our jobs."

"I never thought of it like that."

He hugged her close. "We'll get along fine. And we'll wait, even if half the world thinks we're nuts."

"Speaking for myself, I've always been goofy."

"So have I."

"Besides," she said, pulling back, "I was never one to go with the crowd. You'll call me?"

"Every day," he said huskily. "A week from Friday."

She smiled warmly. "A week from Friday. Happy New Year."

He kissed her. "Happy New Year."

He got back into his car. He didn't drive away until she was safely inside her room.

Chapter 10

Alice had forgotten, in the excitement, to tell Harley about the senator's message. But the following day, when he called, he didn't have time to talk. So she waited until Friday, when he phoned and was in a chatty mood.

"I have a message for you," she said hesitantly. "From your father."

"My father?" he said after a minute, and he was solemn.

"He said that he'd made some dreadful mistakes. He wants the opportunity to apologize for them. Your sister's death caused problems for both your parents that they never faced."

"Yes, and I never realized it. When did you talk to him?"

"He came to see me Monday, at my office. I like him," she added quietly. "I think he was sincere, about wanting to reconnect with you. He gave me his private cell phone number." She hesitated. "Do you want it?"

He hesitated, too, but only for a moment. "Yes."

She called out the numbers to him.

"I'm not saying I'll call him," he said after a minute. "But I'll think about it."

"That's my guy," she replied, and felt warm all over at the thought. She'd had some worries, though. "Harley?"

"Hmm?"

"You know that we've only known each other for a few weeks…" she began.

"And you're afraid we're rushing into marriage?"

She shrugged. "Aren't we?"

He laughed softly. "Alice, we can wait for several months or several years, but in the end, we'll get married. We have so much in common that no sane gambler would bet against us. But if you want to wait, honey, we'll wait." He cleared his throat. "It's just that my willpower may not be up to it. Just don't expect to get married in a white gown, okay?"

She remembered their close calls and laughed. "Okay, I'm convinced. We'll get married a week from Friday."

"Wear a veil, will you," he added seriously. "It's old-fashioned, but it's so beautiful."

"Say no more. I'll shop veils-are-us this very day."

"There's such a place?" he asked.

"I'll let you know."

"Deal. I'll call you tonight."

She felt a flush of warmth. "Okay."

"Bye, darlin'," he drawled, and hung up.

Alice held the phone close, sighing, until Longfellow walked by and gave her a strange look.

Alice removed the phone from her chest and put it

carefully on the desk. "Magnetism, Longfellow," she said facetiously. "You see, a burst of magnetism caught my cell phone and riveted it to my chest. I have only just managed to extricate it." She waited hopefully for the reply.

Longfellow pursed her lips. "You just stick to that story, but I have reason to know that you have recently become engaged. So I'll bet your boyfriend just hung up."

"Who told you I was engaged?" Alice demanded.

Longfellow started counting them off on her fingers. "Rick Marquez, Jon Blackhawk, Kilraven, Hayes Carson…"

"How do you know Kilraven?" Alice wanted to know.

"He keeps bugging me about that telephone number," she sighed. "As if the FBI lab doesn't have any other evidence to process. Give me a break!" She rolled her eyes.

"If they call you, get in touch with me before you tell Kilraven anything, okay?" she asked. "I want to make sure he's not running off into dead ends on my account."

"I'll do that," Longfellow promised. She stared at Alice. "If you want to shop for a wedding gown, I know just the place. And I'll be your fashion consultant."

Alice looked dubious.

"Wait a sec," Longfellow said. "I have photos of my own wedding, three years ago." She pulled them up on her phone and showed them to Alice. "That's my gown."

Alice caught her breath. "Where in the world did you find such a gown?"

"At a little boutique downtown, would you believe it? They do hand embroidery—although in your case, it will probably have to be machined—and they have a pretty good selection for a small shop."

"Can we go after work?" Alice asked enthusiastically.

Longfellow laughed. "You bet."

"Thanks."

"Not a problem."

Alice picked out a dream of a gown, white satin with delicate pastel silk embroidery on the hem in yellow and pink and blue. There was a long illusion veil that matched it, with just the ends embroidered delicately in silk in the same pastel colors. It wasn't even that expensive.

"Why aren't you on the news?" Alice asked the owner, a petite little brunette. "I've never seen such beautiful wedding gowns!"

"We don't appeal to everybody," came the reply. "But for the few, we're here."

"I'll spread the word around," Alice promised.

"I already have." Longfellow chuckled.

Outside the shop, with her purchase safely placed in the backseat of her car, Alice impulsively hugged Longfellow. "Thanks so much."

"It was my pleasure," Longfellow replied. "Where will you live?"

"He's got a small ranch," she said proudly. "We're going to raise purebred Santa Gertrudis cattle. But until we make our first million at it, he's going to go on working as a ranch foreman, and I'll keep my job here. I'll commute."

"You always wanted to live in the country," Longfellow recalled.

Alice smiled. "Yes. And with the right man. I have definitely found him." She sighed. "I know it sounds like a rushed thing. We've known each other just a short time..."

"My sister met her husband and got married in five days," Longfellow said smugly. "They just celebrated their thirty-seventh wedding anniversary."

"Thirty-seven years?" Alice exclaimed.

"Well, he liked *Star Trek,* she said," Longfellow explained. "She said that told her everything she needed to know about him—that he was intelligent, tolerant, inquisitive, optimistic about the future, unprejudiced and a little quirky." She shrugged and laughed. "Not bad for a quick character reading, was it?"

"Not at all. Good for her!"

"You do the same," Longfellow lectured. "I don't want to see you in divorce court a month after you say your vows."

"I believe we can safely say that won't happen," Alice replied, and she felt and sounded confident. She frowned. "I wonder if he likes *Star Trek,*" she wondered aloud.

In fact, she asked him when he called that night. "I do," he replied. "All the series, all the movies, and especially the new one, about Kirk, Spock and McCoy as cadets." He paused. "How about you?"

"I love it, too." She laughed, and then explained why she'd asked the question.

He was serious then. "That's a long time," he said of Longfellow's sister's marriage. "We'll give her a run for her money, won't we, Alice?"

She smiled. "Yes, we will."

There was a long pause. "You're wondering if I called that number you gave me," Harley said.

She laughed in surprise. "You read minds! That's great! If we ever have an argument, you'll know why I was mad and just what to do about it!"

"I only read minds occasionally," he told her, "so let's not have arguments. But I did call my father. We had a long talk. I think we may get together one day, with my mother, and try to iron things out."

"That's wonderful," she said softly.

"It won't be easy to get over the past, but at least we're all willing to try. I did mention the wedding to him."

"And?"

"He said that if he showed up, we'd be a media lunch. I have to agree," he added. "I don't want that. Neither do you. But we're invited to their house for a potluck dinner the day we get back from our honeymoon."

"I'd enjoy that."

"Me, too."

"I bought a wedding gown. With a veil. It's beautiful."

"On you, any gown would be. You're delicious, Alice."

She laughed softly. "That's just the right thing to say."

"I mean it, too."

"I know."

"Game for a movie tomorrow night?" he asked. "There's a Christmas-themed one we could go see."

"That would be fun. Yes."

"I'll pick you up at six and we'll have supper first."

"That's a date."

"Uh, and no stopping by your apartment after. I go home."

"Yes, Harley. You go home."

There was a brief pause and they both burst out laughing.

He did go home, but only after a heated session on her sofa that ended with him actually pulling away and running for the door. He waved as he slammed it behind him, leaving a disheveled Alice laughing her head off.

It was raining on their wedding day. Alice carried an umbrella over her gown and Lisa Parks held up the train as they rushed into the church just ahead of a thunderbolt. Cy Parks was waiting at the altar with Harley, who looked devastating in a tuxedo, a conventional black one with a white shirt and black bow tie. Harley couldn't take his eyes off Alice.

Lisa went to her seat. The full church quieted. Alice smiled as the Wedding March struck up on the organ and she adjusted her train before she picked up the pretty bouquet he'd ordered for her. The fingertip veil just hid the wetness in her eyes as she wished with all her heart that her parents had been here to see her marry.

She walked slowly down the aisle, aware of friendly, curious eyes admiring her dress. Leo Hart and his wife, Janie, were sitting on the aisle. Alice didn't know, but Janie had dated Harley while she was trying to get over Leo. It hadn't been serious. In fact, Harley had dated several local women, including one who'd cast him off like a wet shoe and hurt his pride. It had seemed to many people as if Harley would always be the stand-in for some other man. But here he was with a really pretty, professional woman, and she had a reputation as a keen investigator. Many people in Jacobsville watched the crime scene investigation shows. They grinned as they considered how nice it was going to be, having somebody local who could answer all those questions they wanted to ask about homicide investigation.

Alice paused at the altar, looked up at Harley and felt a moment of panic. They hardly knew each other. They were almost strangers. This was insane…!

Just then, as if he knew what she was feeling, Harley's big hand reached over and linked itself unobtrusively into her cold fingers and pressed them, very gently. She looked into his eyes. He was smiling, with love and pride and confidence. All at once, she relaxed and smiled back.

The minister cleared his throat.

"Sorry," Alice mouthed, and turned her attention to him instead of Harley.

The minister, who had a daughter just Alice's age, grinned at her and began the service.

It was brief, but poignant. At the end of it, Harley lifted the exquisite veil and kissed his bride. Alice fought back tears as she returned the tender kiss.

They ran out of the church amid a shower of confetti and well wishes.

"Good thing you aren't having a reception," Cash Grier remarked as they waited for the limousine Cy Parks had ordered to take them to the airport, one of several wedding presents.

"A reception?" Alice asked, curious. "Why?"

"Our local district attorney, Blake Kemp, had one," Cash explained. "He and his wife went home instead to dress for their honeymoon. While they were gone, there was an altercation. One of my officers was wearing the punch, another salvaged just the top layer of the wedding cake and most of the guests went to jail." He grinned. "Jacobsville weddings are interesting."

They both laughed, and agreed that it was probably a good thing after all.

Cy Parks paused with Lisa when the limo drove up and the driver came around to open the rear door.

Cy shook hands with Harley. "Your house will be ready when you get back," he told Harley. "You did good."

Harley beamed. "You'll never know how much it meant to me, that you and Lisa stood up with us. Thanks."

Cy was somber. "You're a good man, Harley. I hope my sons will be like you."

Harley had to bite down hard. "Thanks," he managed.

"Go have a nice honeymoon," Cy told the couple. He grinned. "I won't let the Hart boys near your house, either."

"The Hart boys?" Alice parroted.

Leo Hart leaned over her shoulder. "We have a reputation for making weddings interesting," he told her, and grinned.

"Not so much these days." Janie grinned from beside him.

A tall, silver-eyed man in a police uniform walked up beside them. Kilraven. Grinning. "I'm giving the limo a police escort to the airport," he told them.

"That's very nice of you," Alice told him.

He sighed. "Might as well, since there's no reception. Weddings are getting really somber around here."

"Why don't you get married and have a reception?" Cash Grier suggested.

Kilraven gave him a look. "And have women throwing themselves over cliffs because I went out of circulation? In your dreams, Grier!"

Everybody laughed.

Corpus Christi was a beautiful little city on the Gulf of Mexico. It had a sugar-sand beach and seagulls and a myriad of local shops with all sorts of souvenirs and pretty things to buy. Harley and Alice never noticed.

They'd managed to get checked in and they looked out the window at the beach. Then they looked at each other.

Clothes fell. Buttons popped. Intimate garments went everywhere. Alice threw back the covers and dived in just a few seconds ahead of her brand-new husband. In a tangle of arms and legs, they devoured each other in a surging crescendo of passion that lasted for what seemed hours.

"What are you waiting for?" Alice groaned. "Come back here!"

"I was only…trying to make it easier…" he began.

"Easier, the devil!" She arched up, grimacing, because it really did hurt. But only for a few seconds. She stiffened, but then the fever burned right back up again, and she dragged him down with a kiss that knocked every single worry right out of his mind.

"Oh, wow," she managed when the room stopped spinning around them. She was lying half under Harley, covered in sweat even in the cool room, shivering with delight. "Now that was a first time to write about!" she enthused.

He laughed. "I was trying not to hurt you," he pointed out.

She pushed him over and rolled onto him. "And I appreciate every single effort, but it wasn't necessary," she murmured as she kissed him. "I was starving for you!"

"I noticed."

She lifted up and gave him a wicked look.

"I was starving for you, too," he replied diplomatically, and chuckled. "You were incredible."

"So were you." She sighed and laid her cheek on his broad, hairy chest. "No wonder people don't wait for wedding nights anymore."

"Some of them do."

"It isn't night, yet," she reminded him.

He laughed softly. "I guess not."

She kissed his chest. "Should we go down to the restaurant to eat?"

"Mr. Parks gave us a one-week honeymoon with room service. I do not think we should insult the man by not using it," he replied.

"Oh, I do agree. I would hate to insult Mr. Parks. Besides," she murmured, shifting, "I just thought of something we can do to pass the time until supper!"

"You did?" He rolled her over, radiant. "Show me!"

She did.

They arrived home bleary-eyed from lack of sleep and with only a few photos and souvenirs of where they'd been. In actuality, they'd hardly seen anything except the ceiling of their hotel room.

The ranch house was one level. It was old, but well-kept, and it had new steps and porch rails, and a porch swing. It also had a new coat of white paint.

"It's just beautiful," Alice enthused. "Harley, it looks like the house I lived in when I was a little girl, growing up in Floresville!"

"You grew up in Floresville?" he asked as he unlocked the door and opened it.

She looked up at him. "We don't know a lot about each other, do we? It will give us something to talk about when we calm down just a little."

He grinned and swept her up in his arms, to carry her into the house. "Don't hold your breath waiting for that to happen," he advised.

She smiled and kissed him.

He put her down in the living room. She sighed. "Oh, my," she said softly.

There were roses everywhere, vases full of them, in every color. There were colorful afghans and two sweaters (his and hers), a big-screen color television set, a DVD player, an Xbox 360 gaming system and several games, and a basket of fruit. On the dining-room table, there were containers of breads and a propped-up note pointing to the refrigerator. It was full of cooked food. There was even a cake for dessert.

"Good grief." Harley whistled. He picked up the note and read it. "Congratulations and best wishes from the Scotts, the Parkses, the Steeles, all the Harts and the Pendletons." He gaped at her. "The Pendletons! Jason Pendleton is a multimillionaire! I thought he was going to deck me in San Antonio…" He hesitated to tell his new wife that he'd tried to date Jason's stepsister Gracie, who was now Mrs. Pendleton. He chuckled. "Well,

I guess he forgave me. His mother has a craft shop and she knits. I'll bet she made the afghans for us."

Alice fingered the delicate stitches. "I'll be still writing thank-you notes when our kids are in grammar school," she remarked. "Harley, you have so many friends. I never realized." She turned and smiled at him. "We're going to be so happy here."

He beamed. He opened his arms and Alice ran into them, to be held close and hugged.

"Are you hungry?" he asked.

She peered up at him and laughed. "We didn't get breakfast."

"And whose fault was that, Mrs. Fowler?" he teased.

"I said I was hungry, it just wasn't for food. Well, not then. I could eat," she added, peering past him at the cake on the table.

"So could I, and I noticed fried chicken in the fridge. It's my favorite."

"Mine, too," she agreed. "I don't cook much on the weekdays because I'm on call so often." She looked up at him worriedly.

"I can cook, Alice," he assured her, smiling. "And I will, when I need to."

"You're just the best husband," she sighed.

"Glad you think so." He chuckled. "Let's find some plates."

They watched television while they nibbled on all sorts of delicious things. It was a treat that they both liked the same sort of shows. But they didn't watch it for long. The trip back had been tiring, and in many ways, it had been a long week. They slept soundly.

The next day, Alice had to drive up to her office to

check on what progress had been made into the murder investigation while Harley got back to work on the ranch. He had things to do, as well, not to mention getting his own present of purebred cattle fed and watered and settled before he went over to Mr. Parks's house to do his job.

Longfellow welcomed her at the door with a hug. "Did you have a nice trip?"

"Lovely," Alice assured her. "But it's good to get home. We had food and presents waiting for us like you wouldn't believe. Mr. Parks had Harley's house renovated and he actually gave him a small herd of purebred cattle for a wedding gift—not to mention the honeymoon trip. What a boss!"

Longfellow smiled. "Surprising, isn't it, how generous he is. Considering the line of work he used to be in, it's a miracle he survived to get married and have a family."

"Yes, I know what you mean," Alice replied. "Any word yet on that scrap of paper we sent to the FBI lab?"

She shook her head. "The holidays, you know, and we're not at the top of the line for quick results." She pursed her lips. "Didn't you once bribe people to get faster service?" she teased.

Alice laughed. "I did, but I don't think my new husband would appreciate it if I did that sort of thing now."

"Probably not."

"Anything on the woman who died at Senator Fowler's house?" Alice added.

Longfellow frowned. "Actually, the senator stopped by and left you a note. I think I put it in your middle desk drawer. He said you were going to be a terrific daughter-in-law… Oops, I'm not supposed to know that, am I?"

Alice's eyes widened. She hadn't considered that she was now the daughter-in-law of the senior senator from Texas. She sat down, hard. "Well, my goodness," she said breathlessly. "I hadn't thought about that."

"You'll have clout in high places, if you ever need it," the other woman said wickedly. "You can threaten people with him!"

Alice laughed. "You idiot."

"I'd threaten people with him," came the reply. She frowned. "Especially Jon Blackhawk," she added.

"What's Jon done to you?"

"He called me at home at midnight to ask if we had lab results back on that thermos that Sheriff Hayes gave you."

"Now why would he want to know about that?"

Longfellow's eyes sparkled. "The investigator who was working with Marquez on the Kilraven case recalled seeing one like it."

"Where? When?"

"At the home of her ex-husband, actually," she said. "Remember that spiral design on the cup? It was rather odd, I thought at the time, like somebody had painted it with acrylics."

"Can we find out who her ex-husband is?" Alice asked excitedly.

"I did. He died a few weeks ago. The woman he was living with couldn't tell her anything about his friends or visitors, or about the thermos. The investigator told me that the woman was so strung out on coke that she hardly knew where she was."

"Pity," Alice replied sadly.

"Yes, and apparently the ex-husband had a drug problem of his own. Poor woman," she added softly. "She worked her way up to sergeant in the homicide division, and lost her promotion when she helped Marquez reopen the Kilraven cold case files."

Alice was only half listening now. She recalled the note the senator had left, pulled it out, opened it and read it. He'd talked to the police commissioner, he wrote, who had promised the reinstatement of the investigator on the Kilraven case. He'd also spoken to his colleague, the junior senator, and informed him that they were not going to try to hinder any murder investigations, regardless of how old they were. He'd talked to the coroner as well, and the autopsy on the senator's kitchen worker had been reclassified as a homicide. He hoped this would help. He reminded her that she and Harley should call and let them know when they were coming to supper. They had a wedding gift to present.

Alice whistled softly. "He's been busy." She told Longfellow the results of the senator's intercession. "What a nice man."

"Lucky you, to be related to him." The other woman chuckled. "See, I told you that... Wait a sec."

Her phone was ringing. She picked it up, raised her eyebrows at Alice and pulled a pen and paper toward her. "That's very nice of you! We didn't expect to hear back so soon. Yes, I'm ready. Yes." She was writing. She nodded. "I've got it. Yes. Yes, that will be fine. Thank you!" She hung up. "The FBI lab!" she exclaimed. "They've deciphered the rest of the numbers on that slip of paper you found in the victim's hand in Jacobsville!"

"Really? Let me see!"

Alice picked up the slip of paper and read the numbers with a sinking feeling in her stomach. Now there was no doubt, none at all, who the victim had come to Jacobsville to see. The number was for Kilraven's cell phone.

Chapter 11

Kilraven waited for Alice in the squad room at the Jacobsville Police Department. Alice had driven down in
the middle of the day. She didn't want him to have to
wait for the news, but she didn't want to tell him over
the phone, either.

He stood up when she walked in and closed the door
behind her. "Well?" he asked.

"The number on that slip of paper in the dead man's
hand," she said. "It was your cell phone number."

He let out a breath. His eyes were sad and bitter. "He
knew something about the murder. He came to tell me.
Somebody knew or suspected, and they killed him."

"Then they figured that Dolores, who worked for
Senator Fowler, might have heard something from the
man, and they killed her, too. This is a nasty business."

"Very," Kilraven replied. "But this case is going to

break the older one," he added. "I'm sure of it. Thanks, Alice," he added quietly. "I owe you one."

"I'll remember that," she said, smiling. "Keep me in the loop, will you? Oh, there's another thing, I almost forgot. That thermos that Sheriff Hayes found, the one wiped clean of prints? Your investigator in San Antonio actually recognized it! It belonged to her ex-husband!"

"Oh, boy," he said heavily. "That's going to cause some pain locally."

"It is? Why?"

"Her ex-husband is the uncle of Winnie Sinclair."

"Does Winnie know?" Alice asked, stunned.

"No. And you can't tell her." His eyes had an odd, pained look. "I'll have to do it, somehow."

"Was he the sort of person who'd get mixed up in murder?"

"I don't know. But he's dead now. Whatever he knew died with him. Thanks again, Alice. I will keep you in the loop," he promised.

She nodded and he left her standing there. She felt his pain. Her own life was so blessed, she thought. Kilraven's was a study in anguish. Maybe he could solve the case at last, though. And maybe little Winnie Sinclair would have a happier future than she expected. Certainly, Kilraven seemed concerned about her feelings.

Alice and Harley went to supper with the senator and his wife. They were hesitant at first, with Harley, but as the evening wore on, they talked. Old wounds were reopened, but also lanced. By the time the younger Fowlers left, there was a détente.

"It went better than I expected it to," Harley said. "I suppose all three of us had unrealistic expectations."

She smiled. "They were proud of you when they heard what you'd done with your life. You could tell."

He smiled. "I grew up. I was such a cocky brat when I went to work for Cy Parks." He chuckled. "But I grew up fast. I learned a lot. I'm still learning." He glanced at her as he drove. "Nice presents they gave us, too. A little unexpected."

"Yes. A telescope." She glanced through the back window of the pickup at it, in its thick cardboard box, lying in the bed of the truck. "An eight-inch Schmidt-Cassegrain, at that," she mused.

He stood up on the brakes. "You know what it is?" he burst out.

"Oh, yes, I took a course in astronomy. I have volumes in my office on…" She stopped. The senator had been in her office. She laughed. "My goodness, he's observant!"

"My present isn't bad, either."

They'd given Harley a new saddle, a very ornate one that he could use while riding in parades. "Somebody must have told them what you were doing for a living while we were on our honeymoon," she guessed.

"My father is a digger." He laughed. "I'm sure he asked around."

"We have to spend time with them," she told him. "Family is important. Especially, when you don't have any left."

"You have uncles," he reminded her.

"Yes, but they all live far away and we were never close. I'd like very much to have children. And they'll need a granny and granddaddy, won't they?"

He reached across the seat and linked her hand into his. "Yes." He squeezed her fingers. "We're going to be happy, Alice."

She leaned her head back and stared at him with utter delight. "We're going to be very happy, Harley," she replied. She closed her eyes with a sigh, and smiled. "Very happy."

* * * * *

GRAYSON

Delores Fossen

Chapter 1

Silver Creek, Texas

Sheriff Grayson Ryland couldn't shake the feeling that someone was watching him.

He slid his hand over the Smith & Wesson in his leather shoulder holster and stepped from his patrol truck. He lifted his head, listening, and glanced around the thick woods that were practically smothering the yellow cottage. The front door and curtains were closed.

No sign of the cottage's owner, Eve Warren.

No sign of anyone for that matter, but just twenty minutes earlier Eve had called his office to report that she had seen someone *suspicious* in the area.

Grayson knew this part of the county like the back of his hand. Along with his brothers, he had fished in the creek at the bottom of the hill. He'd camped these woods. There were a lot of places to duck out of sight....

Plenty of memories, too.

That required a deep breath, and he cursed himself for having to take it.

The front door opened, and he spotted Eve. She was a five-foot-six-inch memory of a different kind. She'd obviously known he was there. Maybe that was the reason his brain was firing warnings on all cylinders.

"Grayson," she said, her tongue flickering over her bottom lip. "You came."

That nervous little tongue flicker and the too-hopeful look in her misty blue eyes riled him. "You called the sheriff's office and asked for me," he reminded her. "You said you thought you saw someone."

"Of course." She nodded, swallowed hard. "But I wasn't sure you'd come."

Neither was he, especially since he was neck-deep in a murder investigation, but when he'd gotten her message, he'd decided not to send a deputy, that he would be the one to personally respond.

Well, respond to the call anyway.

Not to the woman.

Not ever again.

It'd been over sixteen years since he'd last seen Eve. She'd been standing in a doorway then, too. Her blond hair had been well past her shoulders back in those days, but it was short now and fashionably rumpled. The last decade and a half had settled nicely on her curvy body.

Something he decided not to notice.

Since his eyes and body seemed to have a different idea about that not-noticing part, Grayson got down to business.

"You reported someone suspicious?" he prompted.

"I did." She scrubbed her hands down the sides of her

pearl-gray dress. The cold December wind caught the hem, making it flutter around the tops of her knees. "I was about to call you anyway...about something else... and then I saw him. A man. He was down by the creek."

Grayson lifted his shoulder and wondered why the heck she'd intended to call him, but he didn't ask. "Could have been a neighbor." Even though there weren't any close ones to the Warren cottage.

"I don't think it was a neighbor," Eve insisted. "I got a bad feeling when I spotted him."

Yeah. Grayson knew all about bad feelings. The one he had about this situation was getting worse with each passing moment.

"I didn't want to take any chances," she continued. "What with the murder you had here a few days ago. How are you handling that, by the way?"

She probably hadn't meant to irritate him with that question, but she did. Hell, no matter what she said, she would irritate him. But Grayson didn't want anyone, including Eve, questioning his ability to handle a murder investigation, even if it was only the third one in his twelve years as sheriff of Silver Creek.

"I heard you haven't identified the body, or the killer," she added.

"Not yet." And Grayson got back on target. "You have any idea who this person was you saw?"

Eve shook her head. "No. But for the past couple of days I've been getting hang-up calls at my condo in San Antonio. And there's been a time or two when I thought someone was following me. Nothing specific. Just a feeling. It was one of the reasons I decided to come out to the cottage. So I could get away."

Well, that explained that. Eve had inherited the cottage from her grandmother eighteen months ago, but to the best of Grayson's knowledge, this was her first visit to the place. And she hadn't just come to relax. She'd planned on calling him.

Why?

Again, he didn't ask. He kept this conversation focused on the job he'd been called out to do.

"Any reason you know of why someone would follow you or make those hang-up calls?" he asked.

Another head shake. "I've been under a lot of stress lately," she admitted. "The job. And some personal stuff. Until I saw the man, I kept telling myself that it was all in my head. But he was real, Grayson."

He mentally groaned at the way she said his name. It was intimate, the way she used to murmur it after one of their scalding hot kissing sessions.

He glanced at the woods, then the creek. "I'll have a look around," Grayson let her know. "But if you're worried, you probably shouldn't be staying out here alone."

He turned to have that look around.

"Wait," Eve called out. "Don't go. I wanted to ask about your family. How are your brothers?"

He had four living brothers. Four sets of news, updates and troubles. Since it would take the better part of an hour to catch her up on everything, Grayson settled for saying, "They're all fine."

Grayson turned again, but again Eve stopped him.

"Even Nate?" she questioned. "I heard his wife was killed a few months ago."

Yeah. That was all part of the troubles. The worst of them. "Nate's coping." But Grayson knew that wasn't true. If Nate didn't have his baby daughter to care for, his brother wouldn't make it out of bed each morning.

Grayson was still trying to figure out how to take care of that.

"And the ranch?" Eve continued. "I read somewhere that the ranch won a big award for your quarter horses."

Fed up with the small talk, Grayson decided to put an end to this. Chitchat was an insult at this stage of the game. However, when he looked back at her, he saw that she had her hands clenched around the door frame. Her knuckles were turning white.

Grayson cursed under his breath. "Okay. What's wrong?" But he didn't just ask. He went closer so he could see inside the cottage to make sure someone wasn't standing behind her, holding her at gunpoint. Because Eve wasn't the white-knuckle type. He had never known anything to scare her.

The place was small so he was able to take in most of it with one sweeping glance. There was no one in the living and eating area, and the loft/bedroom was empty, too.

Grayson looked her straight in the eyes. "Eve, are you all right?"

She hesitated and nibbled some more on her lip. "I really did see someone about a half hour ago, I swear, and he ran away when he spotted me."

Since that sounded like the beginning of an explanation that might clarify the real reason for her call, Grayson just stood there and waited for the rest of it.

"Could you come in?" Eve finally said. "I need to talk to you."

Oh, hell. This couldn't be good. "Talk?" he challenged.

He was about to remind her that it was long over between them, that they had no past issues to discuss, but she kept motioning for him to come in.

"Eve," he warned.

"Please." Her voice was all breath and no sound.

Grayson cursed that *please* and the look in her eyes. He knew that look. He'd seen it when she was thirteen and had learned her mother was dying from bone cancer. He'd seen it again sixteen years ago when on her twenty-first birthday she'd stood in the doorway of the ranch and demanded a commitment from him or else.

Because he'd had no choice, Grayson had answered *or else.*

And Eve had walked out.

Now, Grayson walked in. She stepped back so he could enter the cottage, and she shut the door behind him. He didn't take off his Stetson or his jacket because he hoped he wouldn't be here that long.

It was warm inside, thanks to the electric heater she had going near the fireplace. No fire, though. And it would have been a perfect day for it since the outside temp was barely forty degrees.

With a closer look, Grayson could see the place was in perfect order. Definitely no signs of any kind of struggle or hostage situation. There was no suitcase that he could spot, but Eve's purse was on the coffee table, and her camera and equipment bag were on the small kitchen counter. Several photographs were spread out around the bag. Since Eve was a newspaper photographer, that wasn't out of the ordinary, either.

"The pictures," she mumbled following his gaze. "I was trying to work while I waited for you."

Trying. And likely failing from the way they were scattered around. "Are you in some kind of trouble?"

"Yes," she readily admitted.

Surprised, and more worried than he wanted to be, he turned around to face her. "Trouble with the law?"

"I wish," Eve mumbled. She groaned softly and threaded her fingers through both sides of her hair. That stretched her dress over her breasts and gave Grayson a reminder he didn't want or need.

He'd been attracted to Eve for as long as he could remember. But he refused to let that attraction play into whatever the hell this was.

"Trouble at work?" he tried next.

She lifted her shoulder but answered, "No."

He glanced at the photos on the table again.

"I took those at a charity fund-raising rodeo in San Antonio," she explained.

So, they were work, but judging from the casual way she'd mentioned them, they weren't the source of the worry in her eyes. "Look, I could play twenty questions and ask about a stalker, an ex or whatever. But let's save ourselves some time and you just tell me what you have to say."

She nodded, paused, nodded again. "It's personal. And it has to do with you. I need to ask you something."

Grayson braced himself for some kind of rehashing of the past. After all, he was thirty-eight now, and Eve was thirty-seven. Hardly kids. And since neither of them had ever married, maybe this was her trip back down memory lane.

Well, he didn't want to take this trip with her.

"I've been having some medical problems," she continued. But then paused again.

That latest pause caused Grayson to come up with some pretty bad conclusions. Conclusions he didn't want to say aloud, but his first thought was cancer or some other terminal disease. Hell.

Had Eve come home to die?

"What's wrong?" he settled for repeating.

She shook her head, maybe after seeing the alarm in his eyes. "No. Not that kind of medical problem."

Grayson silently released the breath he'd been holding.

"I'm, uh, going through, well, menopause," she volunteered.

Of all the things Grayson had expected her to say, that wasn't one of them. "Aren't you too young for that?"

"Yes. Premature menopause." She swallowed hard again. "There's no way to stop it."

Well, it wasn't a cancer death sentence like her mother's, but Grayson could understand her concern. "So, is that why you're here, to try to come to terms with it?"

He'd asked the question in earnest, but he checked his watch. Talking with him wouldn't help Eve come to terms with anything, and he had work to do. That included a look around the place and then he had to convince her to head back to San Antonio. It was obvious she was too spooked and worried to be out in the woods all alone.

"I don't have much time," she said before he could speak. "That's why I came to Silver Creek today. And that's why I'll need your answer right away. I know this isn't fair, but if you say no, I'll have to try to find someone else…though I'm not sure I can." She didn't stop long enough to draw breath, and her words bled together. "Still, I'll understand if you want to say no, but Grayson, I'm praying you won't—"

"What are you talking about?" he finally said, speaking right over her.

Now Eve stopped and caught on to the back of the chair. "Perhaps you should sit down for this."

The rushed frantic pace was gone, but her eyes told him this particular storm was far from being over.

"I'd rather stand," he let her know.

"No. Trust me on this. You need to be sitting."

That took him several steps beyond just being curious, and Grayson sank into the chair across from her. Eve sat as well, facing him. Staring at him. And nibbling on her lip.

"I'm not sure how to say this," she continued, "so I'm just going to put it out there."

But she still didn't do that. Eve opened her mouth, closed it and stared at him.

"Grayson," she finally said and looked him straight in the eyes. "I need you to get me pregnant. *Today.*"

Chapter 2

Eve had tried to brace herself for Grayson's reaction.

She'd anticipated that he might just walk out. Or curse. Or even ask her if she'd lost her mind. He might still do those things, but at the moment he just sat there while his jaw practically hit his knees.

Other than his slack-jaw reaction, there was no sign of the storm that she must have stirred up inside him. Not that Eve had expected him to show any major signs of what he was feeling.

Grayson was Grayson.

Calm, reliable, levelheaded, responsible.

Hot.

In those well-worn Wranglers, black Stetson, black shirt and buckskin jacket, he looked like a model for some Western ad in a glossy magazine.

A comparison he would have hated if he had known what she was thinking.

Even though he had that scarred silver badge clipped to his rawhide rodeo belt, Grayson was first and foremost a cowboy and, along with his brothers, owner of one of the most successful ranches in central Texas. That success was due in large part to Grayson.

There was nothing glossy about him.

Eve forced herself away from that mental summary of Grayson's attributes. His hot cowboy looks and ranching success weren't relevant here. It had been the calm, reliable, levelheaded and responsible aspects of his personality that had caused her to want him to father her child.

Maybe it was her desperation, but Eve had hoped that Grayson would also be cooperative. That slack jaw gave her some doubts about that though.

"When I was at my doctor's office this morning, I found out I'm ovulating," she continued. That seemed way too personal to be sharing with anyone except maybe a spouse or best friend, but she didn't have time for modesty here.

Time was literally ticking away.

"The fact that I'm ovulating is nothing short of a miracle," she continued. "The doctor didn't think it would happen, and it almost certainly won't happen again."

Grayson just kept staring.

She wished he would curse or yell, but no, not Grayson. Those silver-gray eyes drilled right into her, challenging her to give him an explanation that he could wrap his logical mind around.

There wouldn't be anything logical about this. Well, not on his part anyway. To Eve, it was pure logic.

"I desperately want a child, and I'm begging you to help me," she clarified in case the gist had gotten lost in all her babbling. "I don't have time to find anyone else. I've got twenty-four hours, maybe less."

Grayson dropped the stare, blew out a long breath and leaned back in the chair. He was probably glad that she had insisted on the being seated part.

He flexed his eyebrows. "How can you possibly ask me to do this?"

"You're the first person I thought of," she admitted.

Actually, he was the *only* person. Those Ryland genes were prime stuff, and all the Ryland males were able-bodied, smart as whips and drop-dead gorgeous with their midnight-black hair and crystal-gray eyes. Again, the looks were just icing.

Grayson wasn't just her first choice for this. He was her *only* choice.

"Don't say no," Eve blurted out when she was certain Grayson was about to do exactly that.

Now he cursed. This time it wasn't under his breath. "No," he stated simply, but it had not been simply said. There was a flash of emotion in all those swirls of gray in his eyes. "You already know I don't want to be a father."

It was an argument that Eve had anticipated, and she had a counterargument for it. "Yes, because you had to raise your younger brothers after your father walked out and your mother died."

Now *she* cursed. She should have rehearsed this. Bringing up Grayson's reckless father was not the way to earn points here even though it'd happened over twenty years ago when Grayson was barely eighteen. A lifetime wouldn't be long enough to forget or forgive that kind of hurt, and it had shaped Grayson to the very core of who he was now.

Yes, he'd been a father figure to his five younger siblings. Head of the ranch and the family. And he'd sacrificed so much for both that by the time Eve had been looking to settle down and have a family with him, Grayson no longer had anything to give anyone.

Including her.

Still, she wanted him for this massive favor.

"I'm not asking you to be a father." Eve tried and failed to keep the emotion out of her argument, but her voice broke. "I only need you to get me pregnant, Grayson. Nothing else. In fact, I would insist on nothing else."

She hated to put him into a corner as she'd done all those years ago. That had been a massive mistake. But she did need an immediate answer.

Grayson shook his head again and eased to the edge of the chair so they were closer. And eye to eye.

"I can't." He held up his hand when she started to interrupt him. "I know the difference between fathering a child and being a father. I can't say yes to either."

Oh, mercy. He wasn't even giving it any thought or consideration. He had doled out an automatic refusal. Eve had thought she had prepared herself for this, but she obviously hadn't. That sent her desperation to a whole new level. Everything inside her started to race and spin as if she were on the verge of a panic attack.

She immediately tried to come up with other ways she could persuade him. First and foremost, she could try to use their past. Their connection. They'd been close once. Once, they'd been in love.

Well, she had been in love with him anyway.

Grayson never quite let himself take that leap of the heart, and he'd certainly never said the words.

She had hoped the close-to-love feelings that he had once had for her would be a trump card she could use here to convince him. Heck, she wasn't too proud to beg.

But she shook her head.

Begging might work. *Might.* However, this was Grayson, and because in the past she had loved him, Eve owed him more than that. She reined in her feelings and tried to say something that made sense. Something that would make him see that she wasn't crazy, just desperate.

"I'm sorry," she somehow managed to say. Her breath suddenly felt too thick to push out of her lungs, and she understood that whole cliché about having a heavy heart. Hers weighed a ton right now. "When the doctor told me I was ovulating and that I probably had a day or two at most, I thought of you. I jumped right in my car and drove straight to Silver Creek."

"I'm flattered. I think." The corner of his mouth lifted a fraction.

Ah, there it was. The biggest weapon in the Grayson Ryland arsenal. That half smile. Even now, after his refusal, it made her feel all warm and golden inside.

Since he'd attempted some levity, Eve did, too, but she doubted the smile made it to her eyes. God, this hurt. She wanted this baby more than her own life, and it was slipping away as the seconds ticked off.

"You can find someone else?" Grayson asked.

"I hope." But that was being overly optimistic. She'd lost a lot of time by driving out to Silver Creek, but then she'd had no choice. She very well couldn't have explained this with a phone call. Plus, she had prayed that she would be able to convince him once they were face-to-face.

She'd obviously been wrong.

Eve felt the raw blush on her cheeks and got to her feet. "I need to hurry back into San Antonio."

Grayson stood, as well. "Maybe you can use a sperm bank or fertility clinic?"

"No." She tried to blink back the tears, but failed at that, too. "Not enough time. The doctor said it takes days, even weeks to go through the screening and get an appointment. Plus, many of the clinics are closed because Christmas is only three days away."

He acknowledged that with a shrug. "A friend then?"

The drive had given her time to consider that, as well. It was sad but true that she was seriously lacking male companionship. Heck, she hadn't had a real date in nearly a year, and her last boyfriend was married now. As for male friends and coworkers, none had fit the bill as well as Grayson Ryland.

She shook her head and hurried to the kitchen where she crammed the photos back into her bag. The pictures were yet another kettle of fish, but they would have to wait. Eve wasn't ready to give up her baby mission just yet, even if she'd failed with Grayson.

She put on her red wool coat and hoisted both her purse and equipment bag onto her shoulder. Moving as fast as she could, she shut off the heater, unplugged it and turned back around to face Grayson. Even after his refusal, she couldn't help feeling that jolt of attraction when she looked at him.

Drop-dead gorgeous was right.

And for several brief moments Eve considered tossing the little bit of pride she had left. She could just throw herself at him and try to seduce him.

But she rethought that.

Grayson would resist. He had already shown her that he had a mountain of willpower and discipline to go along with those looks.

"What will you do?" he asked.

Because she felt the tears start to burn in her eyes, Eve dodged his gaze and grabbed her keys. "Maybe I can hire a friend of a friend."

She could make some calls the second she was back in her car, but she had no idea where to start.

"Hire someone?" Grayson questioned. He stepped outside the cottage with her.

Eve nodded. She closed and locked the door before she headed for her car. It wasn't below freezing, but the icy wind sliced right through her.

"You'd hire someone?" Grayson repeated when she didn't answer. He caught on to her arm and whirled her around to face him. "Eve, listen to yourself. Yes, I know you're desperate, and this baby must be important to you or you wouldn't have come here, but you can't just hire someone to sleep with you."

"To provide semen so I can be inseminated," she corrected, maneuvering herself out of his grip. She couldn't look at him and didn't want him to look at her. Eve hurried across the yard. "I have no intentions of sleeping with anyone to get pregnant. I was serious about not having a biological father in the picture. I'll make some calls, find a donor, pay him for his sperm and, if necessary, I'll do the insemination at home."

Grayson made a sound of relief, or something. Probably because he'd thought she was indeed crazy enough to jump into bed with the first guy she ran across on the drive home. Eve's biological clock was screaming for her to do that, but she wanted a healthy baby and body.

"I want to raise a baby on my own," she continued. "And if I find someone, he'll have to agree to giving up his paternal rights."

No need to rehash the emotional baggage that had brought her to that conclusion. Besides, Grayson knew about her absentee father and the abusive stepfather that she'd had as a kid. He didn't know about the three failed relationships she'd had since leaving Silver Creek, and that included one episode of her being an honest-to-goodness runaway bride.

It was just as well he didn't know that.

Best not to spell it out that she considered Grayson and only Grayson for a life partner. He was literally the only man she trusted, even if he had crushed her heart all those years ago. And now he'd managed to do it again.

Frustrated with herself and her situation, Eve threw open the back door of her car so she could dump her bag and equipment onto the seat. She hesitated for just a moment because she knew Grayson was right behind her. If she turned around, she'd have to face him once more.

"I'm sorry I bothered you," Eve mumbled.

She turned and, still dodging his gaze, she tried to sidestep around Grayson.

He sidestepped, too, and blocked her path. She hadn't thought it possible, but he looked more uncomfortable than she felt.

"I can call the Silver Creek Hospital," Grayson suggested. "Doc Hancock might be able to pull some strings and speed up things with a sperm bank. Or I could talk to my brothers. They might know—"

"Don't involve your brothers," Eve interrupted.

Anything but that. Just talking about this would be hard enough for Grayson, especially telling them that he had turned her down. Eve didn't want to be the subject of conversation at the Ryland dinner table.

"Best not to involve anyone from Silver Creek," she added. "I'll go to a hospital in San Antonio and, well, beg." And she would. This pregnancy was going to happen, even if she didn't have a clue how she would manage it.

She stepped around him and hurried to the driver's side of the car. Since she wasn't looking at Grayson, that was probably the reason she saw the movement.

In the cluster of trees about fifty yards from her car.

"What?" Grayson asked when she froze.

Eve looked around the trees, trying to figure out what had caught her attention.

There.

She saw the man.

Dressed in a dark shirt and pants, he had a black baseball cap sitting low on his head so that it obstructed his face. He quickly ducked out of sight, but from just that quick glimpse, Eve recognized him.

"That's the same man I saw earlier, by the creek," she told Grayson.

Grayson drew his gun from the shoulder holster beneath his jacket. The metal whispered against the leather, and he moved in front of her. "Any idea who he is?"

"No." But she knew that he was hiding, and that couldn't be good.

Did this have anything to do with the hang-up calls she'd been getting? Or could it be her imagination working overtime? Everything suddenly seemed to be going against her.

"I'm Sheriff Grayson Ryland," Grayson called out. "Identify yourself."

Eve stood there and held her breath, waiting. But the man said nothing.

"You think it's a local kid playing a prank?" she whispered, praying that was all there was to this.

Grayson fastened his attention to those trees. "No. A local kid would have answered me."

True. Grayson commanded, and got, respect in Silver Creek. And that caused her heart to pound against her chest. After all, there was a killer on the loose. Eve almost hoped this was connected to the hang-up calls. Better that than having a killer just yards away.

Grayson lifted his gun, and he took aim. "Well?" he prompted, his voice loud enough that the person hiding wouldn't have any trouble hearing him. "Come out so I can see who you are."

Still nothing.

"Get in your car," Grayson instructed from over his shoulder. "I'll get a closer look."

Eve wanted to latch on to him, to stop him from walking toward those trees, but this was his job. Plus, Grayson wouldn't stop. Not for her. Not for anyone.

"Just be careful," she whispered, her voice cracking a little. Eve eased open her car door and ducked down to get inside.

The sound stopped her.

It was a loud blast, and it shook the ground beneath them. Her stomach went to her knees, and her breath stalled in her throat. For a split second she thought someone had shot at them.

But this was much louder than a gunshot.

"Get down!" Grayson shouted.

He didn't give her a chance to do that on her own. He hooked his arm around her waist and pulled her behind her car door and to the ground.

Eve glanced behind her, at the cottage, and she saw what had caused that nightmarish sound.

An explosion.

Her grandmother's cottage was on fire.

Chapter 3

What the hell was going on?

That was Grayson's first thought, quickly followed by the realization that if Eve and he had stayed inside the house just a few more minutes, they would have both been blown to bits.

Behind them, the cottage had orangey flames shooting from it, and there was debris plunging to the ground. Maybe a propane tank had exploded or something, but Grayson wasn't sure it was an accident.

After all, there was a guy hiding in the trees.

Grayson figured it was too much to hope that the two things weren't related.

Had this person somehow rigged the explosion? If so, that meant the man would have had to have gotten close enough to the cottage to tamper with the tank that was just outside the kitchen window, but Grayson hadn't heard him. Of course, he'd been so involved with Eve's baby bombshell that he might not have noticed a tornado bearing down on them. He would berate himself for that later.

Now, he had to do something to protect Eve.

Grayson took cover in front of her and behind the car door, and he re-aimed his gun in the direction of the person he'd seen just moments before the explosion.

"Get out here!" he shouted to the person.

After hearing no response to his last demand, Grayson didn't expect the guy to comply this time. And he didn't.

No answer.

No sign of him.

Grayson kept watch behind them to make sure no one was coming at them from that direction. Other than the falling debris, the fire and black smoke smearing against the sky, there was nothing.

Except Eve, of course.

Her eyes were wide with fear, and he could feel her breath whipping against his back and neck. "We could have died," she mumbled.

Yeah. They'd been damn lucky. A few minutes wasn't much of a window between life and death, and her storming out had literally saved them.

Because she looked to be on the verge of panicking, Grayson wanted to reassure her that all would be fine, but he had no idea if that was true. The one thing he did know was that it wasn't a good idea for them to be in the open like this. There could be a secondary explosion, and he needed to get Eve someplace safe so he could try to figure out what had just happened.

He glanced at his truck, but it was a good thirty

feet away. Too far. He didn't want Eve to be out in the open that long. There wasn't just the worry of a second explosion but of their tree-hiding *friend* and what he might try to do.

"Get inside your car," he told Eve, "and slide into the passenger's seat so I can drive."

"Oh, God," he heard her say.

And Grayson silently repeated it. He didn't know just how bad this situation could get, and he didn't want to find out with Eve in tow.

"Put the keys in the ignition," Grayson added when he felt her scramble to get into the car. "And stay down. Get on the floor."

No *Oh, God* this time, but he heard her breath shiver as it rushed past her lips. He wasn't exactly an old pro at facing potentially lethal situations, but he had the training and some experience during his time as sheriff. This had to be a first for Eve.

Not too many people had ever come this close to dying.

Grayson glanced behind him to make sure she had followed his orders. She had. Eve had squeezed herself in between the passenger's seat and the dashboard. It was safer than sitting upright, but Grayson knew a car wouldn't be much protection if anything was about to happen. A secondary explosion could send fiery debris slamming right into them.

He tried to keep watch all around them while he eased into the driver's seat and adjusted it so he'd fit. He needed to put some distance between the cottage, woods and them, and then he would call for assistance. Someone could take Eve to the sheriff's office, and

Grayson could figure out why all of this didn't feel like an accident.

While keeping a firm grip on his gun, he shut the car door and started the engine. He took out his phone and handed it to Eve. "Call the fire department."

She did but without taking her stunned gaze off the flames that were eating their way through what was left of the cottage. It had to break her heart to see the damage, and later the full loss would hit her.

As if she hadn't had enough to deal with for one day.

Even now, with the chaos of the moment, he still had her request going through his head.

I need you to get me pregnant.

He'd made it clear that wasn't going to happen, so the situation was over for him. But not for Eve. He had seen that determination in her eyes, and one way or another, she was going to get this dream baby. Hell, this near-death experience might even make her more determined.

"Hang on," Grayson warned her as he drove away— fast. He didn't exactly gun the engine, but he didn't dawdle, either.

The narrow road was dirt, gravel and mud since it had rained hard just that morning. With the sinkholes poxing the surface, it was impossible to have a smooth ride. But a smooth ride was an insignificant concern. Right now, he just wanted Eve out of there so he could deal with this situation on his own terms.

In other words, *alone.*

"The gas was turned off," Eve murmured. "It's been turned off for months. So what caused the explosion?"

"Maybe a leak in the gas line." And if so, that would be easy to prove.

"Call the first number on my contact list," Grayson instructed. It was for the emergency dispatcher in the sheriff's building. "I want at least one deputy out here with the fire department. Have them meet me at the end of the road."

Once help arrived, he could hand off Eve to whichever deputy responded, and Grayson could escort the fire department and others to the scene. He didn't want anyone walking into a potential ambush.

Eve made the call, and he heard her relay his instructions to the emergency dispatcher. Just ahead, Grayson spotted the first curve of the snaky road. He touched the brakes.

And nothing happened.

Nothing!

The car continued to barrel toward the curve. So Grayson cursed and tried again, but this time he added a lot more pressure.

Still nothing.

Hell.

"What's wrong?" Eve asked.

Grayson dropped his gun onto the console between them so he could use both hands to steer. "I think someone cut the brake line."

Eve put her hand against her chest. "W-hat?"

She sounded terrified and probably was, but Grayson couldn't take the time to reassure her that he was going to try to get them out of this without them being hurt. The curve was just seconds away, and the road surface was as slick as spit. But his biggest concern was the trees. The road was lined with them, and if he crashed into one of them, Eve and he could both be killed on impact.

"Get in the seat and put on your seat belt," he told her, fastening his attention on the curve.

She scrambled to do just that, but he figured there wasn't enough time. To buy them a little more of that precious time, Grayson lifted the emergency brake lever, even though it wouldn't help much. The emergency brake would only work on the rear brake, and it wouldn't slow them down enough. Still, he had to try anything to reduce the speed.

"Hold on," he warned her.

Eve was still fumbling with the seat belt when the car went into the curve. Grayson had no choice but to try to keep the vehicle on the road since the trees were just yards away.

The right tires caught the gravel-filled shoulder, kicking up rocks against the metal undercarriage. The sound was nearly deafening, and it blended with his own heartbeat, which was pounding in his ears.

Eve's car went into a slide, the back end fishtailing. Grayson steered into the slide. Or rather that's what he tried to do, but he soon learned he had zero control. He saw the trees getting closer and closer, and there wasn't a damn thing he could do about it.

For just a split second, he made eye contact with Eve. Her gaze was frozen on him while her hands worked frantically to fasten the seat belt. Her eyes said it all.

She thought they were going to die, and she was silently saying goodbye.

Grayson didn't say goodbye back because he had no intention of dying today.

He heard the click of her seat belt, finally. And Grayson jerked the steering wheel to the left. The car careened in that direction, but not before the back end smashed into a live oak tree. The jolt rattled the entire vehicle and tossed them around like rag dolls.

Thank God they were wearing their seat belts.

He also thanked God that he was able to hang on to the steering wheel. They'd dodged a head-on collision, and the impact with the tree had slowed them down some, but they literally weren't out of the woods yet.

The car went into a skid in the opposite direction.

More trees.

Grayson didn't even bother to curse. He just focused all his energy on trying to control an out-of-control car.

And it was a battle he was losing.

There was a trio of hackberry trees directly in front of them. If he managed to miss one, he would no doubt just plow into the others, or one of their low-hanging limbs.

He fought with the wheel, trying to make it turn away, but they were in another skid, the mud and rocks helping to propel them in a direction he didn't want to go.

"There's the man we saw earlier," Eve said, her voice filled with fear.

She pointed to Grayson's right, but he didn't look in that direction. Not because he doubted her. No. The hiding man probably was there, but Grayson had to give it one last-ditch effort to get the car into the best position for what would almost certainly be a collision.

"Cover your face," Grayson managed to warn her. Because the limbs would probably break the glass.

His life didn't exactly flash before his eyes, but Grayson did think of his family. His brothers. His little niece, Kimmie.

And Eve.

She was there, right smack-dab in the middle of all of his memories.

He watched the front end of the car slide toward the middle tree, but at the last second, the vehicle shifted. No longer head-on. But the driver's side—his side— careened right into the hackberry.

Grayson felt the air bags slam into his face and side. The double impact combined with the collision rammed him into Eve and her air bag. There were the sounds of broken glass and the metal crunching against the tree trunk. The radiator spewed steam.

"We're alive," he heard Eve say.

Grayson did a quick assessment. Yeah, they were alive all right, and the car was wrapped around the hackberry.

"Are you hurt?" he asked Eve, trying to assess if he had any injuries of his own. His shoulder hurt like hell, but he was hoping it was just from the air-bag punch and that it hadn't been dislocated. He would need that shoulder to try to get them out of this crumpled heap of a car.

When Eve didn't answer, Grayson's stomach knotted, and he whipped his head in her direction. Her hands were on the air bag that she was trying to bat down, but her attention was fixed on the side window.

Grayson soon saw why.

The man, the one who'd hidden in the trees, was running straight toward them.

Chapter 4

The man was armed, a pistol in his right hand.

Eve heard Grayson yell for her to get down, but she didn't have time to react. Grayson pushed her down, her face and body colliding with the partially inflated air bag.

"My gun," he snarled.

Grayson cursed and punched at the air bags. He was obviously trying to find his weapon. When Eve had last seen it, Grayson had put it on the console, but the crash had probably sent it flying.

Oh, mercy.

That meant they were sitting ducks, unarmed, with a gunman bearing down on them. She couldn't get out of the car, not with the man so close and on her side of the vehicle. They couldn't get out on the driver's side because it was literally crunched around a tree. Thank

God for the air bags, or Grayson would have been seriously injured or killed.

Eve glanced up at the approaching man. The person
who was likely responsible for the explosion that had
destroyed her grandmother's cottage. The fear raced
through her.

Still, she felt anger, too.

This idiot had endangered them and was continuing
to do so. She wouldn't just stand by and let him shoot
Grayson and her. Neither would Grayson.

They both grappled around the interior of her car,
and Eve remembered her own gun in the glove com-
partment. It took some doing to get the air bag out of
the way, but she finally managed it. She threw open
the glove box door, latched on to the gun and handed
it to Grayson.

He immediately took aim.

The man must have seen him do that because he
ducked behind a tree. She wasn't sure if that was a good
or bad thing. If the man had stayed out in the open,
Grayson would have had a clean shot. This way, they
were still trapped.

"One of the deputies will be here soon," Grayson
reminded her.

Probably one of his brothers. Both Dade and Mason
were Silver Creek deputy sheriffs, and since Grayson
had requested backup, they would no doubt get there
as soon as humanly possible.

But that might not be soon enough.

Using his left hand Grayson continued to bat away
the air bag, but he kept his attention pinned to the tree
where the man had ducked out of sight. Eve kept watch
as well, but there were other trees near that one, and it

wouldn't take much for the man to move behind one of those closer trees and sneak right up on them.

"Who is he?" Eve meant to ask herself that question, but she said it aloud.

"I don't know," Grayson answered. "But he could be the killer we're after."

Yes. Eve was aware that there was an unidentified killer on the loose.

Thanks to the newspaper coverage, she was also aware that just a few days ago a young woman's body had been found in the creek. The woman had been fully clothed, no signs of sexual assault, but her fingerprints and face had been obliterated. That's the term the press had used, *obliterated,* and Eve had assumed the killer had done that to prevent her from being identified.

It had worked.

So why would this killer come after Grayson and her now?

Until the body was identified, and that might never happen, it wasn't likely that Grayson would be able to come up with a list of suspects.

But Eve had a sickening thought.

Perhaps the man had killed the woman in or near the cottage. Maybe he was destroying any potential physical evidence that would link him to the crime. And here she'd walked in with so much on her mind that she hadn't even considered a trip home could be dangerous. This in spite of her knowing about the murder that possibly happened just a stone's throw away from the cottage.

That oversight could be deadly.

She choked back a sob. Only minutes earlier her main worry had been getting pregnant, but for that to happen Grayson and she had to survive this. If something went wrong and he got hurt, it would be her fault because he wouldn't have been out here in these woods if she hadn't called him.

"I'll get you out of here," she heard Grayson say.

It sounded like a promise. But Eve knew backup was still a few minutes away. A lot could happen in those few short minutes.

Because she had her attention pinned to that tree, she saw the man lean out. Or rather she saw his gun.

"Get down!" she warned Grayson.

Just as the shot slammed through the window directly above Eve's head. The sound was deafening, and the bullet tore through the safety glass.

Grayson moved forward, his body and forearm pushing her deeper onto the floor so that she could no longer see what was going on.

And Grayson fired.

Eve automatically put her hands over her ears, but the blast was so loud that it seemed to shake the entire car. What was left of the safety glass in the window came tumbling down on top of her.

Grayson elbowed the chunk of glass aside and fired another shot. All Eve could do was pray, and her prayers were quickly answered. Even with the roaring in her ears from the shots, she heard a welcome sound.

A siren.

Maybe the fire department. Maybe a deputy. She didn't care which. She just wanted Grayson to have backup. Her gun was fully loaded, but Eve didn't have any other ammunition with her, and she didn't want to risk a gun battle with the man who had a better position behind the tree.

"The SOB's getting away," Grayson growled.

Eve hadn't thought this situation could get more frightening, but that did it. If he managed to escape, he might try to come after her again.

She didn't need this, and neither did Grayson.

Grayson obviously agreed because he climbed over her and caught on to the door handle. He turned it, but it didn't budge. Eve didn't relish the idea of Grayson running after a possible killer, but the alternative was worse. Besides, the gunman had quit shooting.

For now, anyway.

Eve rammed her weight against the door to help Grayson open it. It took several hard pushes, but with their combined effort the door finally flew open.

"Be careful," she warned him.

"You, too," Grayson warned back. "Stay put and try to find my gun. I figure he's trying to get as far away from that siren as he can, but if this guy is stupid and doubles back, shoot him."

That didn't help with her ragged nerves, but as Grayson sprang from the car, Eve made a frantic search for the gun. She also kept watch, blindly running her hands over the floor and seats.

The sirens got closer, and she saw the flashes of blue lights at the end of the road. Backup was just seconds away, but Grayson was already running past the tree that the gunman had hidden behind.

Her fingers brushed over the cold gunmetal, finally, and Eve snatched up Grayson's Smith & Wesson. Her hands were shaking like crazy, but she positioned the gun so it would be easier for her to take aim. But she was hoping that might not be necessary.

A Silver Creek cruiser came to a screeching stop

next to her wrecked car, and she recognized the man who jumped out. It was Dade, Grayson's brother. Like Grayson, he wore jeans and a badge clipped to his belt, and he had his gun ready. He was lankier than Grayson, but Eve didn't doubt Dade's capabilities. From everything she'd heard, he was a good lawman.

"Eve?" he asked. Dade was clearly surprised to see her in Silver Creek. Then his gaze flashed to the cottage. Or rather what remained of it. It was still on fire, but there wasn't much left to burn.

Soon, very soon, it would be just a pile of ashes.

"Someone blew up the cottage. And then he fired a shot at us," she explained. "He might be the killer you're looking for." Mercy, her voice was shaking as badly as her hands, and she tried to rein in her fear so she could point toward the tree. "Grayson went after him."

Concern flashed through Dade's eyes, and he snapped his attention in the direction where she'd pointed. "Stay here," Dade said, repeating Grayson's earlier order. "The fire crew is right behind me. And keep that gun ready, just in case."

She watched him run toward the spot where she'd last seen Grayson, and Eve added another prayer for Dade's safety, too. Like all the Rylands, she'd known Dade her entire life, and even though he was only two years younger than she was, she had always thought of him as her kid brother. That probably had something to do with all the meals she'd helped cook for Dade and the others after their mother committed suicide.

"The dark ages," she mumbled.

That's how she'd always thought of that time twenty years ago when Grayson and his brothers had basically become orphans. During the years that followed, Eve had gotten close with all of Grayson's brothers, closer than she had been with her own family.

She blinked back the tears. And here she'd endangered yet another *family* member. Heck, Mason was probably on the way, too. Before the hour was up, she might have put all three of them at risk.

Eve heard a second set of sirens and knew that the fire department was close by. She stayed in the car, as both Grayson and Dade had warned her to do, but she moved to the edge of the seat, closer to the open door, so she could try to pick through the woods and see Grayson. She still had sight of Dade, but Grayson was nowhere to be seen.

She glanced behind her at the fire engine as it made the final turn from the farm road onto the gravel drive that led to the cottage. The driver turned off the sirens, and everything suddenly went silent.

Eve could hear the wind assaulting the trees. She could hear her own heartbeat in her ears.

She also heard Dade shout, "Get down!"

And the sound of a gun going off ripped through the silence.

Chapter 5

Grayson cursed and dove to the ground.

He'd already had enough surprises today, and he didn't need this SOB firing any more shots at him. Besides, Eve wasn't that far away, and he darn sure didn't want a stray bullet traveling in her direction.

"You okay?" Dade called out. His brother had dropped to the ground, too, but was crawling toward Grayson.

"Yeah. I'm just fine and dandy," Grayson barked. "You see him?"

Dade didn't answer right away, giving Grayson some hope, but that hope went south when his brother finally said, "No."

Grayson lifted his head and examined the woods. Since it was the dead of winter, a lot of the foliage was gone, but that didn't mean there weren't plenty of places to hide.

And then Grayson heard something he didn't want to hear.

The sound of water.

Hell. This guy was in the creek, and that meant he was getting away.

Dade apparently heard it, too, because he cursed and got to his feet. So did Grayson, and they started to run toward the sound of that splashing. Of course, the splashing was long gone before they arrived on the creek bank.

And there was no sign of the gunman.

Dade and Grayson stood there, looking hard, but there was no way to tell which direction he went. If the guy was smart, he could have just floated downstream and out of sight. Of course, he could have scrambled over the outcropping of rocks on the other side of the creek bed and then disappeared into the dense woods.

"We need a tracking dog," Dade mumbled.

Yeah. And they needed their brother Mason out here on horseback. Mason was a better tracker than any dog or any of the local Texas Rangers, but Grayson intended to ask for their help, too. He wanted this gunman caught *now,* and he would use any resource available.

"I got a good look at his face," Grayson let Dade know. "If he's in the system, I think I can pick out his photo."

Though that would take time. Maybe lots of time. Something Grayson wasn't sure he had.

This guy would be back.

The question was why? Grayson was sure if he could figure that out, then he would have a better chance of identifying him and stopping another attack.

"Why don't you get Eve away from here? She's pretty

shaken up," Dade suggested. He took out his cell phone. "I'll start making calls."

Grayson started to say no, that he wanted to stay. If they got lucky with the search, he wanted to be the one to put the cuffs on this piece of slime, but Dade was right. Eve didn't need to be here. Neither did he. His brothers could handle it and handle it well. So he turned and headed back toward Eve and her car.

He spotted her the moment he came out of the thick cluster of trees. She was out of the wrecked car, talking to Dusty Bullock, the fire chief. She looked calm enough, but Grayson knew that underneath her nerves had to be raw since to the best of his knowledge this was the first time she'd experienced anyone trying to kill her.

And there was no doubt that the killing attempt had been aimed at Eve.

When she saw Grayson, Eve ran toward him, but he quickly closed the distance between them because he didn't want her out in the open.

"Did you catch him?" she asked.

Grayson shook his head and watched her expression go from shock to fear. Yeah. She understood how important it was for them to find this gunman *today*.

Since she looked ready to launch herself into his arms, or cry, he took his gun from her, reholstered it and handed Eve her handgun. She slipped it into her coat pocket. And Grayson caught on to her shoulder so he could lead her in the direction of his truck.

"I need to get you back to my office," he grumbled. Grayson hated the gruffness in his voice. Hated even more that he couldn't comfort her at a time when she needed comforting, but after the conversation they'd had in the cottage, it was best if he kept his distance.

"But what about the gunman?" she challenged. "He's still out there."

"Dade's looking for him, and we'll bring in help." Grayson stopped next to the fire chief. "Call me the minute you know what caused the explosion in the cottage."

"You're thinking it was foul play?" Dusty asked, his craggy face bunched up with concern.

"Yeah," Grayson answered honestly, though he knew that would cause Eve more panic. "I want the brake line on Eve's car checked, too, because I'm sure someone cut it."

"Oh, God," Eve mumbled.

He got her moving again, but she stopped first to retrieve her purse and equipment bag from her car. Since she looked ready to fall apart, Grayson decided to use the drive to his office to get her to concentrate on how they could bring this nightmarish day to a good conclusion.

A conclusion that would end with an arrest.

"Did you see the gunman's face?" Grayson asked. He drove away from her cottage, which would soon be taped off and processed as a crime scene.

"Not really." When she couldn't get her seat belt on after two tries, Grayson reached over and helped her. His hand brushed against hers, and he quickly pulled back. With the energy between them already on edge, it was best to avoid touching her.

And *thinking* about touching her.

Something he didn't quite accomplish.

Grayson huffed and continued. "The gunman had

brownish-red hair. About six-two. Around a hundred and seventy pounds. Ring any bells?"

She shook her head. "Should it?"

"Maybe. I figure you've crossed paths with him. Why else would he want to come after you that way?"

Eve mumbled another "Oh, God," and plowed her fingers through the sides of her hair. "I don't recognize him." She pressed hard against her temples and head. "What could I have done to make him want to kill me?"

That was the million-dollar question, and Grayson had to explore all possibilities. "An old boyfriend, maybe? Maybe he altered his appearance so that you didn't easily recognize him?"

Her hands slipped from her hair and dropped into her lap. She stared at him. "You're the only boyfriend I have who's riled at me."

"I'm not riled," Grayson protested.

She huffed. "You're riled all right."

He huffed, too. "Just because I turned down your offer to make a baby doesn't mean I'm pissed off." But when he heard his tone, he realized he was. Grayson cursed. "I just wasn't expecting you to ask anything like that, okay? You surprised the hell out of me."

"Yes, I figured that out. But you can't blame me for trying. I just thought… Well, I just thought *wrong*."

She was right about that. So, why did Grayson feel so blasted guilty for turning her down? Since that was something he didn't want to think or talk about, he went back to the investigation. They were still fifteen minutes out from his office, and he wanted to put that time to good use instead of adding to that guilt trip.

"I heard you were engaged but broke things off,"

Grayson tossed out there. "Could your ex be holding a grudge?"

She mumbled something he didn't catch. "No. It's true, I called things off the day of the wedding, but he's moved on and already married to someone else."

Maybe her ex-fiancé had indeed moved on, but Grayson wanted to verify that was true. Love and love-scorned were motives for a lot of crimes.

And a lot of questions.

He wanted to ask Eve why she'd waited until her wedding day to end things, but it was none of his business.

"How about a member of your ex's family?" he pressed. "Sometimes family members or friends think they need to avenge a broken heart."

She sat quietly a moment. And she didn't deny that broken heart part. "Why wait over a year to get revenge?" She shook her head again. "I was thinking maybe what happened today has to do with the killer. Maybe he was trying to destroy evidence by destroying the cottage?"

Yes. That was the next theory on Grayson's list. Perhaps the killer had left some kind of forensic evidence in or near the cottage. That was a solid reason to destroy it.

"But then why would he want to kill you?" Grayson pressed. He turned off the ranch road and onto the highway that would take him back into town. "Is it possible you know something about the murder?"

"How could I? I wasn't in Silver Creek when it happened. I was in San Antonio."

"The murder might not have happened in Silver Creek," he reminded her. "In fact, I suspect it didn't. I think the body was just dumped there."

She gave him a flat look. "Trust me, I would have remembered if I'd witnessed someone being murdered."

True. But there had to be a reason this guy was after her. Grayson really needed to get an ID on that body because he couldn't shake the feeling that the dead woman and this attack were connected.

"We don't have an identity on the dead woman, but she was five-six and was in her early twenties." Grayson hoped that would spur Eve to remember something.

Eve nodded. "I read that in the paper. Her face and fingerprints had been obliterated." She paused. "What does that mean exactly?"

"You don't want to know." But Grayson would never forget the sight of what was left of the woman. Someone had literally bashed in her face so that none of her features had been recognizable, and then cut off the pads of her fingertips. He'd also broken off her teeth, probably so that dental records couldn't be used to identify her. "But the killer didn't obliterate her hair, and it's unique. Three colors—red, black and blond. Remember seeing anyone with hair like that?"

She shrugged. "It's possible. That type of hair isn't so rare in a city the size of San Antonio."

True. But it was the only thing he had to go on. Now it was time to grasp at a few straws. "When did you start getting hang-up calls?" Grayson pressed.

"Four days ago," she answered without hesitation.

Four days. According to the ME, that was an estimate of when the woman had been killed.

He was about to continue his questions when Grayson spotted the familiar rust-scabbed red truck barreling down the highway. It was his brother Mason, responding to the scene. Grayson didn't slow down.

Neither did Mason. They exchanged a glance, and in that split-second glance, Grayson saw exactly what he wanted to see: Mason's determination to find the man who'd taken shots at Eve and him.

Sometimes keeping Mason's intense moods under control was like trying to keep a leash on a rogue bull. But it was that intensity that made Mason a good cop. Mason wasn't the sort of man Grayson would go to with his personal problems—he wouldn't get much empathy there—but for everything else Mason was the brother he knew he could rely on the most.

Grayson stopped in the parking lot of his office and turned to Eve. "I need to get your statement about what just happened and ask you a few more questions about those hang-up calls. Then I can take you to the ranch. You can stay there until we catch this guy."

She was already shaking her head before he finished. "I can't go to your ranch."

No. He didn't have time for this argument. "Look, I know it might be a little uncomfortable for you there, what with Dade and Mason around—"

"It's not that. I'm comfortable with your family. Always have been."

Grayson couldn't argue with that. Heck, his brothers had, and probably always would, consider Eve a sister. His youngest brother, Kade, often said that Eve was more like a mother to him than his own mother had been.

So what was Eve's issue?

She stared at him. "I need to get back to San Antonio, and I intend to do that as soon as I can arrange for transportation. Your reports will have to wait. I have to find a place where I can be inseminated *today*."

Grayson was sure he looked at her as if she'd lost her mind. "Eve, someone tried to kill you," he reminded her, though he was positive she hadn't forgotten that.

Her hand was still shaking when she touched her fingers to her lips. She paused a moment, still trembling, and her gaze came back to his. "If I don't do the insemination today, I'll never have a baby. And yes, I know there's a killer out there. And yes, that killer might have been the one to take shots at us today. But I don't have time to wait for him to be caught."

Grayson broke his no-touching rule and caught on to her shoulders. He wanted to make this very clear. But for a moment he lost his train of thought when he saw the nicks and scrapes on her face. From the air bag, no doubt. But even with the superficial damage, Eve was still the most beautiful woman he'd ever seen.

He pushed that thought aside with all the rest of the carnal things that came to mind whenever he looked at Eve. She had, and always would have, his number.

Grayson met her eye to eye. "The killer could come after you in San Antonio."

She blinked, swallowed hard. "So, I'll hire a bodyguard as soon as I call the rental car company to come and get me. I want to be on the road within the next thirty minutes."

He didn't know whether to curse or try to shake some sense into her. "Eve, is this baby worth your life?"

Her breath rattled in her throat. Tears sprang to her eyes. "Yes," she whispered.

And with that, she grabbed her equipment bag and purse and got out of his truck. The bag went on one shoulder. Her purse on the other.

Well, he'd asked the question, and even though it

hadn't been the answer he wanted to hear, Grayson knew it was Eve's final answer. She wasn't going to budge on this.

Hell.

That meant he had to drive back into San Antonio with her. Or else send Dade or Mason. Now Grayson cursed because he sure didn't have time for this.

He got out, slammed the truck door with far more force than necessary and followed her into the back entrance of the law enforcement building. It wasn't a huge place—especially considering how much time he spent there. It had a reception area, four offices, two interrogation rooms and a holding cell on the bottom floor. There was an apartment-style break room on the top floor where there'd once been jail cells before a new facility had been built on the edge of town.

Grayson stepped inside and heard the day shift dispatcher, Tina Fox, talking from her desk in the reception area. An area roped off with twinkling Christmas lights and a miniature tree that played annoying tinny carols when anyone walked past it. Mason had already kicked it once. Grayson was considering the same. As far as he was concerned, this was a bah-humbug kind of Christmas, and this attempt to kill Eve wasn't doing much to change his opinion about that.

Tina looked back at him and waved. From the sound of it, she was getting an update from Dade. Soon Grayson would want that update as well, but first he had to deal with the most hardheaded woman in Texas.

Ahead of him, Eve made her way to his office while she fished for something in her purse. She finally pulled out her cell phone when she came to a quick stop. Her hand and phone had been moving toward her ear, but that stopped, as well. She stood there frozen, her gaze fixed on something in his office.

Grayson cursed and hurried to pull her aside because he knew what had shocked her. The crime board in his office had photos of the dead woman. Or rather what was left of her. To put it mildly, they weren't pretty.

"Sorry about that," he mumbled. And he crossed the room to turn the board around so that the gruesome pictures would be facing the wall.

"Wait!" Eve insisted.

She walked closer, her attention nailed to the grisliest of the photos. It was a close-up view of the dead woman's bashed-in face and had been taken several hours after her body had been fished out of the creek.

"There's no need for you to see these," Grayson assured her. When he tried to turn the board again, she caught on to his arm to stop them.

She moved even closer, until her face was just inches from the photo. Eve mumbled something and then dropped her equipment bag onto his desk. Frantically, she began to rummage through it, pulling out the pictures that Grayson had seen earlier on the counter at the cottage.

"What is it?" he asked.

"I've seen her before." Her voice was all breath now. "Well, I've seen that hair anyway."

Grayson glanced back at the dead woman's hair, though the image was already embedded into his mind. He wasn't sure he'd ever be able to forget it. But the hair was certainly distinctive. Three colors. Red, blond, black, and the black was only on the ends of her choppily cut hair.

Eve continued to pull photos from her bag, glancing at each and then tossing them aside on the tops of folders and reports that Grayson had spread out on his desk. She plucked another from the bag and froze again.

Grayson looked at the shot from over her shoulder. He recognized the location—it had been taken at the indoor rodeo arena in San Antonio. There were at least a dozen people standing at the railings, their eyes fixed on the bull rider who had just been tossed into the air.

Then he saw the woman.

And her hair.

"When did you take this?" Grayson couldn't ask the question fast enough. He grabbed the picture from her so he could study it.

"Four days ago at the fund-raiser rodeo. I had these printed because I wanted to take a better look at them to see which to include in the story. But I didn't use this one." She paused. "It's her, isn't it?"

Grayson paused, too, but not because he wasn't sure. He was.

The image of the dead woman stared back at him.

Chapter 6

Eve hadn't realized she was holding her breath until her lungs began to ache. "Is that the murdered woman?" she asked Grayson.

"Yeah," he finally said, his attention still glued to that photo. "Any idea who she is?"

"No, I took dozens of random shots that day. She was just someone in the crowd."

"Yes. But if the medical examiner is right, this is also the day she was murdered." He tipped his head to her bag. "I need to look at all the pictures."

She gave a shaky nod, and while she was doing that, Grayson peeled off his jacket and tossed it over the back of his chair. Then he put the photo on his fax machine. "I'm sending it to the Ranger crime lab in Austin with a request for immediate processing."

Good. Soon he might have a name to go with that face.

Eve continued to dump pictures onto his desk, but with each one she mumbled a no. She huffed. "That's it. The only one I have of her."

"Then I'll have to get what I can from it."

He made several more copies of the picture, one that he pinned on to the corkboard with the other photos. The others, he put in his in-basket so he'd have them for other law enforcement agencies. Then he sat at his desk, placing the original picture right next to him, and he fired off that request message to the Ranger crime lab.

While he did that, Eve took herself back to that photo session. It had been routine, something she'd done dozens of times.

"Four days ago," she said softly. "That's when my hang-up calls started."

That got Grayson's attention. He stood and stared at her, and Eve knew what he was thinking. Was there something in the photo that had caused the hang-up calls, the fire at the cottage and the shooting?

Was the killer in the photo?

Eve rifled through her equipment bag and came up with a small magnifying glass. She handed it to Grayson, and he used it to zoom in. She hurried beside him so she could take a look, as well.

Unlike the rest of the spectators, the woman wasn't looking at the bull rider. She had her attention on the man wearing a baseball cap on her left. Her face was tight, as if she was angry. *Very* angry. And the man had his hand gripped on to her arm.

"I'm pretty sure that's the guy who shot at us today," Grayson mumbled, tapping his finger to the guy in the baseball cap.

Eve sucked in her breath. She hadn't gotten a good look at him, but the build was right. So was that baseball cap.

Grayson turned back to his keyboard. "I'll ask the lab to put the entire picture into the facial recognition program. It's the fastest way for us to get an ID."

Good. Eve wanted that. But she also wanted to get out of there and on the road. It was already past noon, and time was running out. She took out her cell to call for a car rental, but before she could make the call, Grayson's phone rang.

"Sheriff Ryland," he answered, and she knew from his expression that whoever was on the other end of the line was telling him something important. Was it possible the Rangers had already managed to ID the dead woman? Eve prayed they had. Because the sooner that happened, the sooner Grayson could proceed with the investigation.

"Yeah. I'll let Eve know," Grayson mumbled several seconds later. "What about the search? Any sign of the gunman?" He paused. "Keep looking."

"What happened?" she asked the moment he hung up.

"That was the fire chief." Grayson pulled in a long breath. "He said he's positive someone tampered with both your brakes and the gas line that led to the cottage. Plus, there was a tracking device on your car."

Eve had tried to brace herself for bad news. After all, it was a logical conclusion about the brakes and gas line, but it still sent an icy chill through her. So did the fact that someone had tracked her out to the cottage.

God, did someone really want her dead because she'd taken a photo?

"Do you park your car in a garage in San Antonio?" Grayson asked.

"No. I use the lot adjacent to my condo."

In other words, her vehicle had been out in the open. Not just there but at her downtown office, as well. Obviously, someone could have planted that tracking device at any time in the past four days. And during those four days, the person had no doubt watched her, plotting the best way to get the picture and eliminate her.

She held on to Grayson's desk to steady herself.

Grayson cursed, moved out of his chair, grabbed her arm and forced her to sit down. "I hope now you realize that going back to San Antonio is a bad idea."

Yes. She did. But that wouldn't stop her. "Then I'll go to Austin. I'm sure they have fertility clinics there."

Grayson didn't curse again, but the look he gave her showed the profanity he was choking back.

"I don't expect you to understand." She got to her feet and squared her shoulders. She looked him straight in the eye. "You're burned out with the whole idea of fatherhood so how could you understand that for me having a baby, *my* baby, is the most important thing in my life?"

Grayson looked her straight in the eyes, too. "Eve, what I understand is this killer knows you took his picture, and he'll do anything to get it back. I can keep you safe here in Silver Creek until we can get the picture printed in tomorrow's paper. That way, the killer won't have a reason to come after you because thousands of people will have seen his face, along with the woman he probably murdered."

She tried to shrug. Eve wasn't immune to the fear, but she wasn't giving in to it, either. "Then print the photo, and tomorrow I can celebrate both my insemination and my safety."

He didn't answer that and just kept glaring as if searching for the right argument to change her mind. There wasn't an argument that could do that.

Eve adjusted her cell again, ready to make her call. "I'll get a car rental, and on the drive to Austin, I'll phone clinics and start begging. One way or another, I'm getting pregnant today."

Now he cursed and shook his head. "Give me a few minutes, and I'll drive you to Austin myself."

Eve hadn't thought the day could have any more surprises, but that was a big one, and she knew just how massive a concession that was for Grayson.

"You can't," she argued. "You have too much to do to babysit me."

"Save your breath," he growled. He grabbed his coat and put it on as if he taking his anger out on the garment. He also snatched the rodeo photo of the dead woman. "You're not the only hardheaded person in this room. And if you can make calls on the drive over, then so can I. If I have to, I'll run this investigation from my truck."

He brushed past her and headed for his door, and she heard him tell the dispatcher that he had to leave. Eve didn't want to think of what kind of complications this might cause for Grayson, but she knew it would. She also knew this was another huge compromise for him. Maybe Dade and Mason could find this gunman today so this would all be over.

She gathered up the pictures and stuffed them into the equipment bag. Her hand knocked against another photo. The only framed one on Grayson's desk. It was of his maternal grandfather, Sheriff Chet McLaurin.

Despite her own horrible circumstances, she smiled when she saw the man's face. Eve had known him well, and he'd become like her own grandfather. When he'd been murdered twenty years ago, Eve had grieved right along with the Ryland clan.

She wondered if Grayson and his brothers realized that the man in the photo was the reason they'd all gotten into law enforcement. An unsolved murder could do that. It was a wound that would not heal.

Eve spotted another wound.

The silver concho hooked on to the top of the frame. She recognized it, as well. Grayson's father had given all six of his sons a concho with the double *R* symbol of their family's ranch. He'd done that, and then less than a week later, he'd left Silver Creek and abandoned the very family that he claimed to have loved.

No wonder Grayson didn't want kids of his own.

He'd witnessed firsthand that parenthood could cut to the core. Eve swore she would never do that to her child.

"Ready?" Grayson said from the doorway.

She'd been so caught up in the picture of his grandfather and the concho that she hadn't noticed Grayson was there. He had also noticed what had caught her attention.

"Yeah," he mumbled as if he'd known exactly what she'd been thinking.

Eve silently cursed the legacy that Grayson's father had left him, and she stuffed the rest of her things into the equipment bag.

"You kept the concho he gave you," she commented as they went to his truck.

He didn't answer until they were both inside the cab of his truck. "Sometimes it helps to remember how much I hate my father."

She stared at him. "How could that possibly help?"

"It's a reminder that sometimes the easy way out can hurt a lot of people."

He didn't look at her when he said that, and if Eve hadn't known him so well she might have thought that was a jab at her decision to go through with this insemination. But since she did know him, she figured he was talking about his family duties. For Grayson, family came first, and that hadn't always been easy for him.

"Mason put a bullet in his concho," Grayson said under his breath. He drove out of the parking lot and onto the road that would take them out of town and to the highway. "Then he nailed it to the wall directly in front of his bed so he could curse it every morning when he woke up."

Eve sighed. So much hurt caused by one man. Their father, Boone Ryland. "I remember Dade told me that he threw his away."

"Yeah." And for a moment, Grayson seemed lost in those bad memories. The dark ages. However, his cell rang, and he morphed from the wounded son to steely sheriff.

"Sheriff Ryland," he answered. He put the phone on speaker and slipped it into a stand that was mounted to the dashboard. He also kept watch around them as they passed the last of the town shops.

"It's me, Dade. I just got off the phone with the Ranger lab. They got a match on the photo."

"Already?" Grayson questioned.

"It wasn't that hard. Her name is Nina Manning, age

twenty-two, from Houston, and she had a record for drug possession and prostitution. There's also a year-old missing person's report complete with pictures."

"Nina Manning," Eve repeated. It didn't ring any bells.

"Is Eve still with you?" Dade asked.

Eve looked at Grayson and waited for him to answer. "Yeah. I have to drive her, uh, somewhere. But I want to know everything that's happening with the case. Any sign of the gunman?"

"No. But Mason's out here. If the guy's still in the area, Mason will find him."

Eve doubted the gunman was still around. Heck, he'd probably parked his car on one of the ranch trails and was now probably long gone. Or maybe he was looking for her. Despite the importance of Dade's call, that caused her to look in the rearview mirror. No one was following them. The rural road behind them was empty.

"Were the Rangers able to identify the other man in the picture who had hold of Nina's arm?" Grayson asked.

"There was no immediate match."

Grayson shook his head. "I think he's the guy who tried to kill us today so we need an ID."

"The Rangers are still trying," Dade assured him. "But they did get a match on the man to the woman's right. His name is Sebastian Collier."

Now that rang some bells. Eve had seen the surname many times in the newspaper, mainly in the business and society sections. "He's related to Claude Collier, the San Antonio real estate tycoon?" Eve asked.

"Sebastian is his son," Dade answered. "And sonny-boy has a record, too, for a DWI and resisting arrest.

Guess his millionaire daddy didn't teach him to call the family chauffeur when he's had too much to drink."

Eve picked up the photo that Grayson had brought along, and she zoomed in on the man to Nina Manning's right. Sebastian Collier looked like a preppy college student in his collared cream-colored shirt and dark pants. It certainly didn't seem as if he was with the woman with multicolored hair.

But then Eve looked closer.

Sebastian's attention was certainly on Nina. His eyes were angled in her direction, or rather in the direction of the grip the other man had on Nina's arm. Sebastian looked uncomfortable with the encounter.

"Keep pushing the Rangers," she heard Grayson tell his brother. "I want that other man identified. I also want someone out to question this Sebastian Collier." He looked at his watch, mumbled something in disgust. "I'll try to get to San Antonio myself as soon as I'm sure Eve will be safe."

Dade assured Grayson he would do everything to get a name to go with that face in the photo, and he ended the call.

Eve hadn't missed Grayson's mumble of disgust, and she was positive she was the cause. He wanted to be in the heat of this investigation, but here he was driving her to Austin instead. She turned to face him, to tell him that he could just drop her off in Austin and leave. Not that it would do any good—he would insist on staying. But she had to try. This investigation was important to both of them.

However, before she could launch into another argument, she heard the sound.

It was a thick, hard blast.

At first she thought maybe they'd had a blowout. But the second sound was identical.

"Get down!" Grayson shouted.

Just as a third blast ripped through the truck window.

Chapter 7

Grayson slammed his foot onto the accelerator to get Eve and him out of there, but it was already too late.

He heard the fourth shot, and he also heard Eve repeat his shouted command of *get down*. But he couldn't duck out of sight. He had to fight to keep them alive. He pushed Eve down onto the seat so that she wouldn't be hit with the bullet or the broken glass.

But the bullet didn't crash through the glass.

It hit the tire.

Grayson's stomach knotted, and he felt his truck jerk to the right. He fought with the steering wheel and tried to stay on the road, but it was impossible. The now-flat tire and metal rim scraped against the gravel shoulder.

"Hang on," he warned Eve.

They were going to crash.

He couldn't avoid that. However, the crash was the

least of Grayson's worries. Someone had shot out the tire, and that someone was no doubt waiting for them. That meant Eve was in danger all over again, and Grayson cursed the bastard responsible for that.

There were no trees near the road, thank God, but there were clusters about a hundred yards off the road. That's probably where the gunman was hiding. And then there was the creek directly in front of them. He didn't want to go there because there were some deep spots in the water that could swallow them up.

"We have to jump," Grayson told her, and he pumped the brakes to slow the truck as much as he could. However, he didn't have much control of the vehicle.

Jumping was a risk, but the greater risk would be to remain inside so the gunman would have an easier chance of killing them. Besides, there was that potential for drowning.

Eve didn't answer, but she nodded and caught on to the door handle.

"When you jump out, run toward the trees to the right," he added. "And grab my cell phone."

Grayson took out his gun. Eve grabbed the phone.

"Now!" He barreled out at the same time as Eve, and he hit the soggy ground ready to fire. The truck gave Eve some cover for just a few seconds, until it plunged nose-first into the creek.

The gunman fired, the shot kicking up mud and a clump of grass several yards in front of Grayson. Grayson returned fire, a single shot, praying it would buy Eve enough time. He could hear her running, but he had to do everything to keep the gunman's attention on him.

Grayson spotted the gunman, or rather the sleeve of his jacket. He spotted Eve, too. She had ducked behind an oak and had taken out her own gun from her coat pocket. She leaned out and took aim at the gunman.

What the hell was she doing?

That knot in his stomach twisted even harder. She had purposely left cover, the very thing he didn't want her to do. Grayson frantically motioned for her to get back. But she didn't. She fired. Her shot slammed into the tree where the gunman was hiding. The bullet didn't hit him, but it caused the man to jump back.

Even though Eve's diversion could have been deadly, it was exactly what Grayson needed because he scrambled toward Eve and dove behind the tree. He also caught on to her and pulled her deeper into the woods. He damn sure didn't want her to get hurt trying to protect him.

"Stay back," Grayson warned her in a rough whisper. But he soon realized that staying back might be just as dangerous as staying put. That's because the gunman was on the move. He dropped back into the thick patch of trees. The SOB was trying to circle behind them.

Grayson had faced danger alone and had even faced it with other lawmen, but being under fire with a civilian was a first. And to make matters worse, that civilian was Eve. He wished he could go back in time and save her from this.

He repositioned Eve behind him and went deeper into the woods as well, but not toward the gunman. They needed to get into a better position, so with Eve in tow, he started moving, going at a right angle. He tried to keep his steps light so that it wouldn't give them away, but that wasn't easy with the dead limbs and leaves littering the grounds.

Eve and he ran, until he lost sight of the road and truck, and he didn't stop until he reached a small clearing.

Another shot came at them.

It wasn't close, at least twenty feet away, but the gunman had sent it in their direction. However, Grayson now knew the gunman's direction, too.

He moved Eve to the right, and they followed the thick woods until they reached the other side of the clearing. Grayson glanced back at Eve to make sure she was okay.

Her breath was gusting now, she was pale, but she didn't appear to be on the verge of panicking. There was some fear there in her eyes, but there was also determination to get out of this alive.

Eve motioned across the clearing, and Grayson saw the gunman duck behind another tree. He caught just a glimpse of the man's face, but Grayson was more convinced than ever that this was the same person in the photo with the dead woman. Grayson hadn't had many doubts left that this was connected to the photograph Eve had taken, and he certainly didn't doubt it now.

The gunman continued to work his way to his right, and Grayson did the same. It was a risk taking Eve deeper and deeper into the woods, but he had to figure out a way to stop this guy. Preferably alive. But he was more than willing to take him out if it meant Eve and he could get out of there.

When they'd made it all the way to a new section of the creek, Grayson stopped and waited.

He didn't have to wait long.

Grayson spotted the gunman just as the man spotted them.

The gunman lifted his weapon, but Grayson was already braced for the attack. He shoved Eve back, took aim and fired before the gunman could. It was a sickening sound of the bullet slamming into human flesh.

A deadly thud.

Clutching his chest, the man flew backward and landed among the dense underbrush.

"Is he...dead?" Eve whispered.

"Maybe." The moments crawled by, and Grayson waited. Watching. He looked for any movement, but he didn't see it. "Stay here."

Eve caught on to his arm and looked ready to launch into an argument about why he should stay put, but her gaze dropped to his badge. Resignation went through her eyes as a worried sigh left her mouth. "Be careful."

"That's the plan," he mumbled, and he headed in the direction of the fallen gunman.

He kept watch on Eve and tried to push aside all the other things that crept into his mind, but Grayson knew once this threat was over, he had a dozen other things to deal with—especially Eve.

Grayson reached the spot he'd last seen the gunman, and he cursed. The gunman was still there, in the exact place where he'd taken his last breath. His gun had dropped from his hand.

"He's dead," Grayson relayed to Eve.

She started toward him, practically running. "You're sure?"

Grayson leaned down and checked for a pulse, but that was just to keep everything straight for the reports he'd have to write up later. "Yeah."

Eve was nearly out of breath by the time she made it to him. She took one look at the man's ash-white face, and she shivered and leaned against Grayson.

He'd seen death before, maybe Eve had, too, but it was different seeing it like this. She was trembling hard now, and there were tears in her eyes, so he took her arm and led her away. There was no need for her to see any more of this.

"Why did he try to kill us?" she whispered, her voice clogged with emotion.

Grayson didn't know for sure, but he figured it had something to do with the dead woman in the photos. Maybe this gunman had killed her. "I'll find out," he promised Eve.

Since she looked ready to collapse, Grayson pulled her into his arms. She didn't put up a fight, probably because there was no fight left in her. This had taken, and would continue to take, a lot out of her. Grayson regretted that, but he didn't regret that this guy was dead.

Or that he was able to give some small comfort to Eve.

She was still trembling, but her breathing started to level. What she didn't do was move away, and Grayson was thankful for it. He hated to admit it, but the shooting had shaken him, and being this close to Eve was giving him as much comfort as he was hopefully giving her.

Even now, under the worst of circumstances, he couldn't help but notice how nicely Eve still fit in his arms. Her body practically molded against his.

"We're not bad people," she mumbled. "This shouldn't happen to us."

Yeah. But Grayson knew that neither good nor bad had anything to do with this. The dead man was likely trying to cover up a murder, and in his experience people would do anything and everything to avoid jail.

She pulled back and stared up at him. Their gazes connected, and that *fit,* too. He could read her so well and knew the tears were about to spill again. She had a good reason to cry, and later he would lend her his shoulder, but for now, he had things to do.

"This guy might not be the one who killed Nina Manning. He could be just a triggerman," Grayson explained, trying to keep his voice void of emotion so that she would stay calm.

He failed.

Despite her leveled breathing, Eve still looked anything but calm. So, to soothe himself and her, he brushed a kiss on her temple and then eased back so that she was no longer in his embrace.

"The only way we make this better," Grayson whispered to her, "is to end it. I have to find out why this man came after us."

Eve's bottom lip trembled, and she nodded. Seconds later, she nodded again. "I'm not weak," she assured him. Something he already knew.

"You just saw me kill a man. There's nothing weak about your reaction. Truth is, I'm shaking inside." And that was the truth. Killing didn't come easy to him, and he hoped like hell that it never did.

Another nod. Eve blinked back tears and reached out to him, but neither of her hands was free. She had her gun in her right hand. The cell phone in the other.

He took the cell from her and motioned for her to move even farther away from the body. "I'll call Dade," he let her know. And he tried. But the signal was so low that the call wouldn't go through. Grayson sent him a text instead and gave Dade their location.

Eve slipped her gun into her pocket and pulled her

coat tightly against her. It wasn't freezing, but it wasn't warm, either. Besides, she was battling adrenaline and nerves, and that was no doubt contributing to the trembling.

"What now?" she asked.

Grayson took a deep breath before he answered. "We wait."

She blinked. "For how long?"

He heard the unasked questions, and he knew she wouldn't like the answers to any of them. "The text will eventually get through to Dade, and he'll come after us."

"Good." Her face relaxed a little. "Then we should walk back to the road to meet him."

Grayson glanced back at the body. "The coyotes won't leave a fresh kill alone for long. I need to preserve the crime scene as much as possible because I need an ID on this guy."

Eve started shaking her head. "But I need to get to Austin."

He nodded and settled for saying, "I know."

"No. You don't know." She huffed and blinked back more tears.

Hell.

Well, at least she wasn't shaking so hard, but this was about to get ugly.

"You don't know," she repeated, and she just kept on repeating it until the words and the tears got the best of her. She sagged against a tree.

"Eve," he said reaching out to her, but she just moved away.

Her breath broke on a sob. "I've made some terrible mistakes in my life. First, giving you that ultimatum. And then I promised my heart and life to a man I didn't love. I'm the Typhoid Mary of relationships, Grayson, but I know I'm meant to be a mother."

She was. Grayson didn't doubt that. Heck, she'd practically been a mother to his youngest brother. Grayson, however, didn't have a good track record. And he tried one last time to convince Eve of that.

"I'm not the man you want to father your baby," he insisted.

She opened her mouth to say something, but Grayson didn't want her to tell him something along the lines of his being the only man she wanted for that job. He couldn't hear that. Not now. Not with Eve falling apart like this.

"I sucked as a father," he continued, trying to snag her gaze. Eye contact might help her see the determination. "My brother Gage is dead."

"Gage died doing a job he loved," she clarified. "You couldn't and wouldn't have stopped him from joining the Justice Department any more than he could have stopped you from being sheriff of Silver Creek."

Maybe. But that didn't change things. Besides, Gage was just one of his failures.

"Dade has got so much rage inside him. Nate's just one bad day away from needing professional help. And Mason? Hell, I wouldn't be surprised if he hunted our father down just so he could kill him in cold blood." Grayson paused because he had to. "That's the kind of family I raised."

Now she made eye contact, and the jolt was like a head-on collision. Grayson had hoped she would see his emotion, and maybe she did, but he saw hers in complete vivid detail. The pain. The need.

The hopelessness of her situation.

"If I helped you," he managed to say, "I'd just screw things up again."

She swiped away the tears and stared at him. "If you don't help me, I'll never know what it's like to be a mother. I'll never have a part of my life that I want more than my next breath." She walked closer. "Grayson, you would have no responsibility in this, other than having sex with me. I swear, *no responsibility.*"

He had to say no. Had to. And Grayson just kept repeating that.

But he knew the reality here.

Even if Dade got the text and responded right away, it would be an hour or more before they could get this body out of the woods. Grayson would need another vehicle since his truck was in the creek. It would be nightfall or later before he could get Eve to a clinic in Austin. Since it was just three days before Christmas, it was likely the clinics had already closed for the day. Maybe for the rest of the holiday week.

Still, Grayson had to say no.

Didn't he?

"Don't think too much," she whispered, walking closer.

The cold air mixed with her breath and created a misty fog around her face. It seemed unreal. Like a dream. And Grayson had had so many dreams about her that he nearly got lost in the moment.

Oh, man.

She could still make him burn.

Eve stopped, directly in front of him. So close he could take in her scent. She leaned in and put her mouth to his ear. She didn't touch him. Didn't have to touch him. Her scent was enough. He fought to hang on to the denial he intended to give her, but it was a battle that Grayson knew he was losing.

Worse, he *wanted* to lose.

"Just consider this a big favor for an old friend," she whispered.

A friend? Eve was plenty of things, but she wasn't a friend. Whatever she was, she was pulling him closer. And closer.

"Please," she said. Just that one word. Her warm breath brushed against his mouth like a kiss.

He looked into her eyes and didn't look beyond that. Yeah. He could say no. He could turn and walk away.

But that wasn't what Grayson was going to do.

What he did was exactly as Eve had said. He didn't think too much. He didn't look beyond this moment and the bad mistake he was about to make.

Grayson cursed and pulled her to him.

Chapter 8

Eve was too afraid to ask Grayson if he was sure about this. She was too afraid to delay even a second because she couldn't risk that he would change his mind.

This had to happen, and it had to happen now.

Grayson was obviously with her on the *now* part. He slid down, his back against the tree, and he pulled her down with him.

Eve's breath was racing already. Her heart pounded against her ribs so hard that it felt her bones would break. She was trembling, scared and cold, but she pushed all those uncomfortable things aside and pressed her mouth to his.

Big mistake.

She felt him stiffen, and the air between them changed. He'd agreed to the sex, to the making a baby part, but that stiff mouth told her that he wasn't ready or willing to go back to where they'd been.

"All right," she mumbled, hoping the sound of her own voice would steady her nerves.

It didn't, but Eve didn't let raw nerves or Grayson's steely look get to her. She worked fast, sliding up her dress and moving onto his lap in the same motion. She didn't meet his gaze. Didn't want to. This was already difficult enough without seeing the proof of what he was thinking.

And he was no doubt thinking this was a big mistake.

Eve didn't let him voice that. She knew what she had to do. She'd had years of experience making out with Grayson. After all, they'd had their first kiss when she was fifteen, and they had spent years driving each other crazy.

She knew how to make him crazy.

Eve didn't kiss him again, but she put her mouth right next to his ear. He liked the breath and heat. He liked the pressure and the touch of her tongue there. Well, at least that's what used to fire him up. She had another moment of panic when she realized that her mouth might not have the same effect on him as it had back then. He might push her—

Grayson made a slight, familiar sound.

If she'd been any other woman, she might not have even heard the catch in his chest, the small burst of breath that he tried to choke back. But Eve heard those things, and she knew exactly what they meant. This was still a fire spot for him. So were her hands on his chest. Since his shirt was already partially unbuttoned, she ran her fingers through his chest hair. And lower.

Grayson liked lower.

Still did, apparently.

Because by the time she trailed her fingers from his

stomach and to the front of his jeans, she found him already huge and hard. She pressed her sex against his.

Eve suddenly didn't feel so cold.

A thought flashed through her head—this was like riding a bicycle. Well, better actually. Her body knew exactly what Grayson could do to her, how he could make her soar. And fall. That wouldn't happen now. It couldn't. She had to keep this as clinical as possible. He was merely a sperm donor here and not her lover.

Eve fumbled with his zipper and finally managed to lower it. No thanks to her hands. She was trembling. So was her mouth, but that didn't seem to affect the kisses she lowered to his neck.

She reached to take off her panties, but Grayson latched on to her hand. His grip was as hard as the part of him she was pressed against.

Her gaze snapped to his, and again Eve was terrified that he was stopping this. But Grayson didn't look her in the eyes. He made another of those sounds, a growl from deep within his throat, and he grabbed her with his other hand. He turned her, shoving her back against the tree. The impact and her surprise nearly knocked the breath out of her.

Grayson seemed to have no trouble breathing. He yanked off her panties and pushed his hips between her legs. He was on his knees now, and the weight of him pinned her to the tree.

For just a moment, she registered the rough bark against her back and bottom. His raw grip. The harsh profanity he was mumbling. Then, he thrust into her. One long stroke that was nearly as rough as the hold he had on her wrists.

Her body gave way to his sex. Welcoming him. Yes,

he was rough, and the thrusts inside her didn't become gentle, either. Of course, he knew her body as well as she knew his. And Grayson knew her. Gentle didn't work for *her*. She had always been in such a hurry to have him that she had begged for hard and fast.

Exactly what he was giving her now.

The man knew what he was doing, that was for sure. He'd learned to make love with her. He knew how to bring her to climax within seconds. Normally, Eve would have gladly surrendered to that climax. She would have surrendered to Grayson, but she instinctively knew that would make the aftermath even worse than it already would be.

And it would be *bad*.

This would cut her off from Grayson forever. Once he'd had time to apply his logical no-shades-of-gray mind to this, he would feel that she'd manipulated him. And she had. Later, Eve would deal with it, too. But for now, she pressed her mouth to the spot just below his ear. She whispered his name.

"Grayson."

The trigger, he had once called it. To finish him off, all she had to do was say his name. It had just the effect she knew it would.

He thrust into her one last time and said her name, too. *Almost.*

"Damn you, Eve," Grayson cursed.

And he finished what he'd started.

Chapter 9

Grayson got up as soon as he could move. He fixed his clothes and then put some distance between Eve and him. He couldn't go far, but even a few yards would help.

He hoped.

Behind him, he could hear Eve milling around. She was also mumbling. Grayson didn't want to figure out what she was saying. He didn't want to figure out anything except why he'd snapped and done the very thing he'd sworn he wouldn't do.

"If you're waiting for me to say I'm sorry, then you'll be waiting a long time," Eve let him know. "Because I'm not sorry, and I hope you're not, either."

Oh, he was. Sorry and stupid. But that wouldn't change what had happened. There was no way he could justify having sex with Eve. Yes, she might get pregnant. She might finally get that baby she wanted, but that put him right in a position he didn't want to be.

He didn't want to be a father.

Of course, the odds were against Eve having conceived. Grayson had no idea of the stats, but even with her at the prime time of the month, this had to be a long shot.

Hell.

That bothered him, too.

He wanted Eve to have this chance at motherhood, but Grayson wanted what he wanted, as well. Too bad he couldn't quite put a finger on what he did want. Nor did he have time to figure it out. His phone beeped, and he glanced down at the message as it came onto the screen.

"Is it Dade?" Eve asked, hurrying to his side. She was still fixing her clothes, and she smelled like sex. Looked like it, too, Grayson noticed when he risked glancing at her. He looked away as fast as he could.

"Yeah." Grayson worked his way through the abbreviations Dade had used in the message and gave her a summary. "He used my cell phone to pinpoint our location and will be here soon."

She made a sound of relief. So different from the sound she'd made just minutes ago when he'd taken her against the tree. The memory of it flashed through his head, and Grayson knew that memory would give him no peace.

His phone beeped again, and there was a new message from Dade. "He wants me to take a picture of the body," Grayson relayed to Eve. "As soon as we have a better signal, I can send it to the Rangers and they can feed it through the facial recognition program."

Something that Grayson should have already thought of, but then he'd had sex with Eve on his mind.

He cursed himself again.

"Wait here," he ordered, and Grayson walked across the woods to the body. Even the mini break from Eve might help because right now his stomach was knotted even harder than it had been in the middle of the attack.

The dead man was still there, of course, sprawled out among the clumps of dried leaves and fallen tree limbs. Grayson snapped a couple of pictures and checked the signal. Still too weak to send the photos, but he made a mental note to keep checking. He made another mental note not to do any more looking at Eve. No thinking about Eve. No more need for her that was generated below the belt.

Hard to do with her standing there in that body-hugging dress.

"Thank you," she whispered when he went back to her.

He didn't want to hear this. "Don't," Grayson warned. "Don't say anything." He wasn't a man who dwelled on regrets, but by God he could make an exception.

She stepped in front of him and forced eye contact. "Thank you," Eve repeated, and she leaned in pressed a chaste kiss on his cheek.

His cheek!

Here his body was still burning for her, and she had risked giving him a brotherly kiss like that. The woman really was playing with fire.

Grayson stepped back and fastened his attention on the area where the dead man was. "Did I hurt you?" he growled.

"No." Eve answered it so quickly that she'd probably

anticipated the question. Which meant he'd been too rough. Grayson shot her an over-the-shoulder glance to let her know that.

She shrugged. "I don't mind a little rough. But you're aware of that."

Yeah, he was. He knew every inch of her body and could have gotten her off with just a touch. But Grayson had tried to keep the pleasure factor out of this. For him that was impossible. His body was humming, and well satisfied, even though his brain was confused as hell.

"How long before you know if this worked?" he asked.

"I'm not sure. I'll have to ask my doctor." She hesitated. "I figured I wouldn't call you or anything with the results. I thought it would be easier that way. Is that okay?"

Was it? Grayson didn't have a clue what was okay. His brain was a mess right now. "Yeah," he settled for saying.

She pulled her coat around her and shivered. Eve was obviously cold, but Grayson intended to do nothing about that. He'd already done enough for the day.

"I don't want you to tell your family about this," she insisted. "As soon as we're out of here, I'll leave so you won't have to see me."

He gave her another look that was probably more scowl than anything else.

She huffed. "Grayson, I'm not stupid. I know what's going on in your head, and you'll want to put as much distance between us as possible."

True. But distance was going to be a problem until he figured out why the man had wanted her dead. Grayson was about to remind her of that when he heard Dade call out to them.

"Over here!" Grayson answered. With Eve right behind him, he went in the direction of his brother's voice.

Eve raked her hand through her hair, trying to fix it, and she brushed off the bits of leaves and twigs from her coat. Grayson tried to do the same.

He soon spotted Dade, and he wasn't alone. Deputy Melissa Garza was with him. Mel, as she liked to be called. And Grayson was thankful Dade had brought her along.

"You okay?" Dade asked when he was still a good twenty yards away.

Grayson nodded, but he was far from okay. He tipped his head to the body. "Single gunshot wound to the chest, and he bled out. It's the man we chased into the woods behind Eve's cottage."

Mel began to trudge her way through to the dead man, but Dade stayed on the path that led directly toward Grayson. As his brother walked closer, he glanced at both Eve and him. Not an ordinary glance but a suspicious one.

"I have the photos," Grayson said showing Dade his cell. Best to get Dade's suspicious mind back where it belonged—on the investigation. "Is the medical examiner on the way?"

"Yeah. He and his crew are right behind us." Dade volleyed more glances between the two of them.

"Good. Mel can stay with the body, and you can get Eve and me out of here," Grayson instructed. "I want to get the photos to the Rangers."

Dade called out Grayson's instructions to Mel, and the deputy nodded.

"Are you really okay?" Dade asked Eve as the three of them headed back toward the road.

"You mean other than the raw nerves, the tear-stained cheeks and adrenaline crash?" The corner of her mouth lifted. "Yes, I'm okay."

Dade hooked his arm around her shoulders. "I wish you could have had a better homecoming." He shifted his attention to Grayson but didn't say anything. Dade's left eyebrow lifted.

Grayson ignored him and kept on walking. Thankfully, they soon reached a spot where the cell signal was stronger, and he fired off the photos. If the dead man had a police record, then it wouldn't take the Rangers long to come up with an ID.

It took a good ten minutes for them to get back to the road where Dade had a cruiser waiting. Dade helped Eve into the front passenger's seat, closed the door and turned back around to stare at Grayson.

"Don't ask," Grayson growled in a whisper.

Dade lifted his shoulder. "Hey, you got my vote if you're getting back together with Eve."

"It's not a vote." Grayson cursed. "And what part of 'don't ask' didn't you understand?"

"The *don't* part." Dade smirked as only a younger brother could manage to do.

Grayson cursed some more. "Look, I'm in a bad mood. The kind of mood where I'd love to beat someone senseless. My advice? Stay out of my way, or that someone will be you." He threw open the door and climbed into the driver's seat.

As soon as Dade got in, Grayson sped back toward town. His mood improved a little when he saw the ME's van approaching from the opposite direction. That meant Mel wouldn't have to stay out there very long, and that was good. He needed all his deputies back at the station so he could figure out what the heck was going on.

"Any idea how the dead man tracked you down?" Dade asked from the backseat.

Grayson was about to say no, but then he groaned. "Probably a tracking device. He put one on Eve's car, we know that, and I'm guessing he put one on the truck, too."

Eve made a small gasping sound of surprise.

"I'll have someone check when they fish your truck from the creek," Dade assured him. But Grayson heard the hesitation in his brother's voice. Dade was no doubt wondering why Grayson hadn't thought of the possibility of a tracking device before he'd driven the truck away from his office.

Grayson didn't need another reason to put some distance between Eve and him, but there it was. He was thinking like a rookie, and the stakes were too high for him to make another mistake.

This mistake could have gotten Eve killed.

He wouldn't forget that.

Since Eve was shivering, Grayson decided to turn up the heat, though the adrenaline was probably more responsible than the chilly temperature. Eve apparently had the same idea because she reached at the same time he did. Their hands collided. And she pulled back as if he'd scalded her. Ironic, since just a half hour earlier he'd been deep inside her. Still, it was good they were in agreement about this no-touching thing.

"Uh, I'm guessing Eve's in protective custody?" Dade wanted to know. It sounded like a loaded question.

Eve turned in the seat to look at Dade, and Grayson nodded. "She can stay at the ranch."

"At the ranch?" She shook her head. "That's probably not a good idea."

Yeah. He was in agreement with that, too. The sex against the tree had only created more tension and friction between them, but there couldn't be any more mistakes.

"You might not have to be there long," Grayson explained. "We just need to tie up some loose ends on this case." He looked in the rearview mirror so he could see Dade. "Any more news on our DB, Nina Manning?"

"Still waiting on the preliminaries. Once we have the next of kin identified, we can talk to them, as well."

Grayson shook his head. "You said there was a missing person's report filed on her a year ago. Who filed that?"

"Her mother, Theresa Manning. She was a single parent, no record of the father, and Theresa died about a month ago. Yeah," Dade added when Grayson glanced at him in the mirror. "Theresa was diabetic and died from an insulin overdose. Could have been an accident, but I asked the Houston cops to look into it."

Yes, because the timing was suspicious.

Grayson's phone buzzed, and he saw the caller was from the Texas Ranger lab. "Sheriff Ryland," he answered and put the call on speaker so Dade could hear.

"Ranger Egan Caldwell," the man identified himself. "I have a match on the photos of the dead man."

Grayson released the breath he'd been holding. "Who is he?"

"Leon Ames. He has a record, obviously. Seven years

ago for assault with a deadly weapon. He spent two years in a Bexar county jail and is still on probation."

Well, prison hadn't rehabilitated him, that's for sure. "He tried to kill me twice today, and he's in the photograph with the dead woman, Nina Manning. Is there a connection?"

"Nothing obvious, but he's got a history with the other man in the photo, Sebastian Collier."

"How?" Dade and Grayson asked in unison. Eve leaned closer to the phone and listened.

"Leon Ames works…worked for Sebastian's father, Claude. He was a handyman at their San Antonio estate."

Handyman. That was an interesting word, considering the photograph with the dead woman and the attempts to kill Eve and him.

"I'm faxing you the rest of the report," the ranger continued. "For what it's worth, I don't think Leon Ames was working alone. From everything I can see, he was nothing more than a lackey."

"What makes you think that?" Grayson asked.

"A large sum of money deposited into his bank account the day after the murder. Twenty thousand dollars. We can't trace the money because he made the deposit in cash. My guess is that money was a payoff for services rendered."

Grayson suspected as much. "So, who hired Leon— Claude or Sebastian?"

"Either is possible," the ranger answered. "But I think all roads in this investigation lead to the Colliers, and that you'll find a killer at the estate."

Chapter 10

Eve needed a friendly face, and she saw one the moment Grayson pulled to a stop in front of the Collier estate. His brother, Lieutenant Nate Ryland, was there waiting for them on the sidewalk in front of the towering black-iron fence that fronted the equally towering Collier estate.

Nate smiled, his dimples flashing, and the moment she stepped from the car, he pulled her into his arms. "Even under these circumstances, it's good to see you," Nate whispered.

"It's good to see you, too." And Eve meant it. She'd never felt more at home than in the arms of a Ryland, and Nate was no exception.

She inched back to meet his gaze and return the smile. The Ryland DNA was there all right, etched over his perfectly chiseled face, black hair and storm-gray eyes. But Nate was smooth around the cowboy-edges in his dark blue suit, which was a job requirement for San Antonio P.D. Like the rest of the Ryland clan, he was more at home in Wranglers and on the back of a horse.

Would her baby be the same?

Her baby, she mentally repeated. And she felt her smile deepen. Yes, a pregnancy was a long shot, but it was possible that she was well on her way to getting the child she'd always wanted.

"Eve?" Nate said, drawing her out of her daydream. "You okay?"

"Of course. I was just distracted for a moment." Eve stared at him, and her smile faded when she remembered what Nate had gone through. "I'm sorry about your wife's death," she whispered.

Eve was even sorrier that she hadn't gone to the funeral or spoken to him about it before now. Nate had always felt like a brother to her, and she'd let him down at a time when he no doubt needed all of his friends. "How are you handling things?"

His smile faded, too. "It's, uh, complicated," he mumbled. Nate's gaze swung in Grayson's direction, an indication to her that this conversation was over. "Are you ready to do battle with the Colliers?"

"Considering their hired gun tried to kill us, yeah, I'm ready."

Nate gave a crisp nod. As a lieutenant, he'd no doubt done his share of interrogations. He was also a cop with some clout when it came to handling an investigation.

And Grayson.

If Nate hadn't had some influence, Eve wouldn't have been allowed to tag along. As it was, she'd practically had to beg Grayson to let her come. He'd wanted to tuck her safely away at the ranch. Eve wanted to be safe, but she didn't want that at the expense of learning the truth. She had taken the incriminating photo, and she wanted to confront the person responsible for what was going on.

"Anything I should know before we go inside?" Grayson asked his brother.

"Well, they haven't lawyered up. But I doubt that means you'll get a lot of cooperation, especially when you link the dead woman to their now dead employee."

Eve hoped Nate was wrong. She wanted answers today so she could start distancing herself from Grayson. She couldn't keep leaning on these Ryland shoulders.

"So, Claude and Sebastian know that Leon was killed?" she clarified.

"They do. And when I spoke to them over the phone, I also told them that Leon tried to murder both of you." Nate walked toward the gate and flashed his badge at the monitor. Seconds later, the gate creaked open.

"I'd like to handle the interview myself," Grayson insisted.

"Figured you would. But if we learn anything we can use to hold either one of them, I need to make the arrest since we're not sure where this murder occurred."

An arrest. Eve hoped that would happen, and then things could finally get back to normal. Well, maybe. If she was indeed pregnant, then nothing would be *normal* again.

Nate shot her a glance. "And I hoped you would say as little as possible. I want them to see you, so they'll know that the picture you took is no longer a reason to come after you. That's the only reason I'm allowing you in the middle of a murder investigation."

She nodded, mumbled a thanks.

"Eve knows the rules," Grayson said, and it sounded like a warning. He walked ahead of them toward the porch that stretched the entire width of the three-story house. There were dozens of white columns, each of them ringed with fresh holly, and a five-foot-tall vertical wreath hung on the door.

Nate fell in step alongside her. "Did something happen between you two?" he asked.

What—did she have a big sign stuck to her back proclaiming that she'd had sex with Grayson? Of course, *sex* was a very loose term for what had happened between them. It had seemed more like a biology experiment.

And that, she reminded herself, was exactly what she'd asked of Grayson.

No strings attached. No emotion. No discussion.

Well, she'd gotten all of that. He had hardly said two words to her when they'd gone back to the sheriff's office to change his clothes. Or on the drive from Silver Creek to her San Antonio condo so she could get a change of clothes, as well. Ditto for more of his silence on the drive to the Collier estate.

And that was just as well.

He was making it easier for her to walk away.

"Nothing happened," she lied.

Nate made a sound that could have meant anything and joined Grayson on the porch as he rang the doorbell. Eve stayed just behind them. A maid wearing a uniform opened the door, and without saying a word, she ushered them through the marble-floored foyer and into a sitting room where two men waited for them.

The room was decorated in varying shades of white and cream. A stark contrast to the floor-to-ceiling Christmas tree that was practically smothered in shiny blood-red ornaments. After the real blood she'd seen today, the sight of those ornaments twisted her stomach a little.

Eve recognized both men in the room—Claude from his photos in the newspapers and Sebastian from the picture she'd taken of him at the rodeo. Both men were dressed in suits. Claude's was black. His son's, a dark gray. Both men were sipping something from cut-crystal glasses that looked and smelled expensive.

"Sheriff Grayson Ryland," he said, stepping ahead of Nate and her. "This is my brother, Lt. Nate Ryland from SAPD, and Eve Warren."

"Ah, Ms. Warren, the woman who took the photo in question," Sebastian quickly supplied. He crossed the room and shook all of their hands. His expression and greeting were friendly enough, but Eve wondered just how long that would last.

The friendly demeanor didn't extend to the other Collier in the room. Claude was a carbon copy of his son, but he was at least twenty pounds thinner and his scowl bunched up his otherwise classic features. His navy blue eyes were narrowed, and he watched them as if they were thieves about to run off with the family silver. He also didn't ask them to sit, probably because he hoped this would be a short visit. Or maybe he was just naturally rude.

"Yes, I took the picture," Eve answered when Sebastian continued to stare at her. "How did you know about that?"

That question earned her scolding looks from Nate and Grayson, who obviously didn't want her involved in this questioning, but Sebastian only flashed that thousand-watt smile. A smile that probably worked wonders on his business associates, but to her it felt slimy.

Just like the man himself.

"A journalist friend told me," Sebastian volunteered. "I understand it was going to be printed in tomorrow's newspaper. But then you managed to ID the unfortunate victim."

"Yes," Grayson verified. He kept his gaze pinned to Sebastian. "Mind explaining what you and your *handyman* were doing in the photo with Nina Manning?"

Sebastian opened his mouth to answer, but his father's voice boomed through the room. "Leon Ames is not my handyman. I fired him three days ago."

Grayson and Nate exchanged glances. "Why?" Grayson demanded.

Claude shrugged as if the answer wasn't important. He responded only after Grayson continued to stare at him. "Erratic behavior," Claude finally supplied. The man couldn't have sounded snootier if he'd tried. "I expect impeccable behavior from my employees, and Leon didn't live up to that."

"How so?" Grayson pressed.

Claude blew out an irritated breath. "If you must know, he used one of the family cars to run a personal errand. I questioned him, he lied about it and I dismissed him. End of story."

Grayson matched the irritated breath response. "No.

It's not the end of it. Because the day before you fired him, Leon and your son were photographed with a woman who was murdered."

"I can explain that," Sebastian offered, still sounding very cooperative. "I went to the charity rodeo, and I ran into Leon and the woman. I believe they were lovers."

"Lovers?" Grayson again. "Leon was twice her age."

Claude flexed his eyebrows. "Then, maybe *lover* isn't the right term. I think the woman was a pro. She was hitting up Leon for cash."

Since Nina did indeed have a record for prostitution, that could be true, but Eve wasn't about to believe him. Sebastian almost certainly wouldn't admit if he'd been the one who hired Nina for her *services*.

"Tell me everything you remember about the meeting," Grayson demanded, looking directly at Sebastian.

Sebastian took a sip of his drink and gave another nonchalant lift of his shoulder. "As I said, I went to the charity rodeo so I could make a donation and ran into Leon. The woman was with him, and they seemed to be, well, cozy."

"In the picture they appeared to be angry," Grayson fired back.

"That came later." Sebastian didn't hesitate. "The woman's attitude became less friendly when Leon refused to give her money."

Grayson stepped closer to Sebastian. "Did she say what the money was for?"

Sebastian shook his head. "I didn't listen to their conversation, Sheriff. The woman was obviously low-rent. Probably high on drugs. Once I realized that, I moved away and let them finish their discussion. I didn't want to be seen in that kind of company."

"Did it seem as if Leon knew Nina before this meeting?" Nate asked.

"I'm not sure." Sebastian finished his drink in one gulp.

"You should be talking to Leon's friends about that," Claude interrupted. "I won't have my family's good name dragged through the mud for the likes of Leon Ames."

Grayson gave him a flat look. "I don't suppose you have the names of Leon's friends?"

Claude's mouth twisted as if he'd tasted something bitter. "I do not make it a habit of delving into the personal lives of my employees." He slapped his glass onto the table. "And that's the end of this interview. Anything else goes through our family attorneys."

Sebastian gave an embarrassed smile. "I've already told you everything I know."

"Not quite." Despite Claude's rude dismissal, Grayson stayed put. "When's the last time you saw Leon and the dead woman?"

"Probably just a few minutes after Miss Warren here snapped the photo. I left, and I have no idea where they went." Sebastian checked his watch. "Now, if you'll excuse me, I need to get ready for our guests. We're having a small Christmas gathering here tonight."

"If you remember anything else about the encounter with Nina and Leon," Grayson said to Sebastian, "I want you to call me." He extracted a business card from his jacket pocket and dropped it on the glass end table. "I'll also need you to go to SAPD and give a written statement."

Sebastian groaned softly. "Please tell me that can

wait until after the holidays. Christmas is only three days away."

"And SAPD will be open all day," Grayson fired back. "A woman is dead, and she deserves justice. I need that statement and anything else you can remember about Leon's friends."

"Of course," Sebastian finally agreed, but he was no longer so cordial. His mouth tightened.

Both father and son turned to walk out, but they stopped when the sound of a woman's high heels echoed through the room. They all turned in the direction of the sound, and Eve spotted a curvy blonde in a plunging liquid-silver dress, who was making her way toward them. She, too, had a drink in a crystal highball glass, and she was teetering on five-inch red heels that were the exact color of the Christmas ornaments.

"Claude, you didn't tell me that we had guests." She clucked her tongue and smiled first at Grayson. Then Nate. She didn't even spare Eve a glance.

"They're not guests," Claude snapped. "They're cops. And they were just leaving."

"Leaving?" The woman gave a quick fake pout. "Well, let me introduce myself. I'm Annabel Collier, Claude's wife." Her cherry-lacquered smile went south when she glanced at Sebastian. "And I'm his stepmother."

Eve hadn't studied the background info on Annabel, but she was betting that stepmother and son were close to the same age. Annabel was clearly a trophy wife.

A drunk one.

"The maid was about to show them out," Claude reiterated, and just like that, the maid appeared in the doorway of the sitting room.

"I can do that," Annabel volunteered. She hooked her arm through Grayson's, and Eve didn't think it was her imagination that the woman pressed the side of her double Ds against Grayson's chest.

"Isn't the estate beautiful this time of year?" Annabel babbled on. Some of her drink sloshed onto the floor and the toes of those red stilettos. "I love all the sparkles and the presents. Claude is very generous with presents, you know. I peeked, and all I can say is five carats, platinum setting." She punctuated that with a drunken giggle.

Behind them, Eve heard Claude mumble something, but both Sebastian and he stayed put as Annabel escorted Grayson to the door. Nate and Eve followed, and Eve wondered if she could trip the bimbo who was hanging all over Grayson. Since Grayson and she weren't together, it didn't make sense to be jealous, but Eve felt it anyway.

Annabel threw open the door, and the cold December wind poured into the foyer and rustled the shimmering gold wreath. Despite her strapless dress she stepped onto the porch with them. She glanced over her shoulder, and when her gaze returned to them, she was a changed woman. No bimbo smile, and her sapphire-blue eyes were suddenly intense.

Eve was too dumbfounded to do anything but watch, which was probably a good thing.

Annabel plucked something from her cleavage and pressed it into Grayson's hand, which she pretended to shake. "The Colliers have secrets," she whispered, her bottom lip trembling. "Deadly ones."

Annabel giggled again, sliding right back into the persona of the drunken trophy wife. "Happy holidays," she told them as she stepped back inside. She gave Grayson one last pleading look, and then shut the door.

"What was that all about?" Nate mumbled.

But Grayson didn't answer. He hurried off the porch and toward the car. So did Nate and Eve. He waited until they were outside the gates and away from the security cameras that dotted the fence.

Then Grayson opened his hand so that Nate and Eve could see what Annabel had given him.

Eve stared it and shook her head.

What the heck was going on, and why had Annabel given them *this?*

Chapter 11

Grayson was several steps beyond exhaustion, but he kept his eyes on the road. It was nearly dark, and the temperature had dropped, and the last thing he needed was to wreck another car today.

"Anything?" he asked Eve again.

It was a question he'd asked her several times since they'd left San Antonio nearly a half hour earlier. Most of that time, Eve had been using the laptop that she'd picked up from her condo so she could view the pictures.

Pictures on the tiny memory card that Annabel had given them.

Grayson had already emailed a copy of the card's contents to the crime lab in Austin, but he wanted to have a closer look for himself as to what Annabel had considered important enough to pass along to a sheriff who was investigating her husband and stepson.

Eve shifted the laptop to a position so that Grayson could see. He glanced at the screen and saw the thumbnails of the photographs. There were dozens of them.

"Annabel obviously likes to take pictures, but I think I finally have them sorted," Eve mumbled. She tapped the ones in the first row. "These are shots taken in what appears to be Claude's office. My guess is Annabel took them with a hidden camera mounted somewhere in the room because the angle never changes."

"Anything incriminating?" Grayson asked.

"Hard to tell. Claude's obviously having a discussion with this dark-haired woman, but there's nothing sexual going on. I think they're arguing."

Grayson agreed. Everything about their body language conveyed anger, not romance. "I need to find out who that woman is." And the crime lab could maybe help with that.

"Well, I think we can rule her out as a mistress. Claude seems to prefer women half his age, and this woman looks to be about fifty." Eve enlarged the photos on the next row, and she made a sound of surprise.

"What?" Grayson asked. He didn't want to fully take his eyes off the road, but Eve's reaction grabbed his attention.

"There are a dozen or more shots taken in a hotel lobby. An expensive hotel, judging from the decor. And there's Nina." She pointed to the next series of pictures. "Nina's not alone, either. Both Claude and Sebastian are there with her."

Eve met his gaze. "That means Sebastian lied about never having seen Nina."

Yeah. Annabel had been right about family secrets. Was this what she'd meant?

"Is a lie enough to arrest Sebastian?" Eve asked.

"No. With his money and connections, we need more. We need a motive." Grayson turned off the highway and onto the ranch road that would take him home.

She huffed and pushed her hair from her face. Eve was obviously exhausted, too. Even with the watery light from the laptop screen, he could see the dark circles beneath her eyes. He could also see how damn attractive she was, and he wondered if there was ever a time he wouldn't look at her and think just that.

"Maybe Sebastian and Nina were lovers?" Eve tossed out there. She was obviously unaware that he was sneaking glimpses of not just the photographs but of her. "Maybe Sebastian snapped when he found out his lover also had a romantic interest in his father?"

Grayson shook his head. "That doesn't look like a lover's encounter. Even though it's possible that one or both had sex with her, and Nina was trying to blackmail them. After all, Claude did say he wouldn't have his family's good name dragged through the mud. Maybe this was his way of making sure that didn't happen."

And Claude could have hired Leon to kill a blackmailing Nina.

But then why was Sebastian in the picture?

Better yet, why had Annabel given him this incriminating evidence?

Grayson wasn't sure, but he intended to find out. He'd already requested a more detailed background check on Nina and all the Colliers, including Annabel.

"There are some pictures taken at the charity rodeo," Eve let him know. "Not mine. These are ones that Annabel or someone else shot. High angle, zoom lens. She was probably in the top seats of the stadium."

Maybe so that the men wouldn't notice her, which meant that Annabel probably knew she was snapping pictures of something incriminating.

"Did she photograph the encounter with Leon, Nina and Sebastian?" Grayson asked.

He took the last turn to the ranch and could see the lights of the sprawling two-story house just ahead. Sometimes, he took home for granted. But not tonight. It was a welcome sight.

"Not that I can readily see," Eve answered, her attention still nailed to the computer screen. "I need to enlarge the photos and study them."

"Later." The pictures were important, perhaps even critical, but he wanted to get her settled into the guest-room first. He'd already called the housekeeper, Bessie Watkins, to let her know they were on the way so that she could prepare the guestroom.

Eve looked up as if surprised to see they were already at the ranch. "Wow," she mumbled.

That reaction was no doubt for the Christmas lights. There were hundreds of them lining the fence that led all the way to the main house. Even the shrubs had been decked with twinkling lights, and there were two fully decorated Christmas trees on each end of the porch.

"Bessie did this," Grayson explained. "For Nate's daughter, Kimmie. It's her first Christmas."

Grayson felt a tightness in his chest. Because it was a Christmas that his niece wouldn't be able to spend with her mother. It made him even more determined to keep Eve safe. And he'd taken measures to make sure that happened.

The ranch was huge, over three thousand acres, but it was equipped with a full security system that monitored all parts of the house and property. There were also at least a dozen ranch hands in quarters on the grounds.

Then, there were his brothers.

Mason and Dade were still at work in town, but soon they would return for the night. Nate, too, even though Kimmie and he lived in a separate wing of the ranch house. The youngest, Kade, was at his apartment in Austin where he worked for the FBI, but he could be at the ranch in an hour if necessary.

Grayson hoped it wouldn't be necessary.

He stopped the car in the circular drive and looked around. It was pitch-dark now, but there were enough security and Christmas lights for him to see that no one was lurking around, ready to strike. Still, he didn't want to dawdle. Grayson grabbed the suitcase that Eve had taken from her place in San Antonio. She latched on to the laptop, and they hurried up the flagstone porch steps.

Other than the Christmas lights, there was no glitz here like at the Collier estate. The porch was painted white, and the rocking chairs weren't just for show. They used them often.

"You're finally here," Bessie said the moment she threw open the door. And despite the laptop between them, Bessie hugged Eve. "Girl, you are a sight for sore eyes."

"It's great to see you, too, Bessie," Eve answered.

"I got a room all made up for you." Bessie caught on to Eve's arm and led her across the foyer. Not marble, but Texas hardwood.

The furnishings here and in the rest of the house leaned more toward a Western theme with pine tables and oil paintings of the various show horses and livestock they'd had over the years. One of Dade's girl-friends had joked that it was cowboy chic.

Eve glanced around and took a deep breath. She was probably thinking things hadn't changed much since she'd last been here. Grayson's thoughts went in a different direction. As always, she looked as if she belonged there.

Under different circumstances, she would have.

But it hadn't been different circumstances since his father had walked out on his family twenty years ago. Since then Grayson hadn't wanted a wife or a family. Of course, that hadn't stopped him from having sex with Eve in the woods.

Later, he'd have to figure out how to deal with that.

Bessie directed Eve toward the stairs to the right of the entry. "I can run you a bath. And then you can have something to eat. I made chili and pecan pie, your favorites."

Eve looked back at Grayson as if she expected him to rescue her. "I need to go over these pictures," she insisted.

Grayson took the laptop from her, balancing it in his left hand since he had her suitcase in his right. "The pictures can wait a few minutes. Besides, I'm starving. Take your bath so we can eat."

That wasn't exactly true. Eve and he had grabbed some fast food on the way out to the Collier estate, but Grayson knew he could get Eve's cooperation if she thought the dinner and bath breaks were for him and not her.

It worked. Eve didn't argue.

While Bessie chattered away about the Christmas dinner plans, she led Eve into the bathroom of the guest suite. Grayson deposited Eve's suitcase in the bedroom and went to his suite directly across the hall so he, too, could grab a quick shower.

Grayson tossed his clothes and Stetson onto the bed and hurried because he wanted to get back to the pictures. He also needed to find out the status of the background checks on Annabel, Claude, Sebastian and Nina. However, he wasn't nearly as quick as Eve because he had barely dried off and put on a pair of clean jeans when there was a knock at the door.

"It's me," Eve said, but she didn't wait. She threw open the door just as Grayson was zipping his jeans.

"Oh, sorry," she mumbled. Her hair was wet, no makeup, and she was wearing a dark green sweater top and pants. She wasn't wearing shoes but rather a pair of socks.

She fluttered her fingers behind her as if indicating that she was about to return to her room so he could finish dressing. But she stayed put with her gaze pinned to his bare chest and stomach.

She pulled in her breath and held it for a second. "You have a scar," she whispered.

For a moment Grayson had thought that breathless reaction was for his half-naked body. It's a good thing it wasn't.

And he was pretty sure he believed that.

She walked toward him, slowly, leaned down and touched the six-inch scar that started at his chest and ended on his right side. "How did it happen?"

"I broke up a fight at the cantina on the edge of town. Didn't see the switchblade until it was too late."

Another deep breath. "You could have been killed." Her voice was suddenly clogged with emotion.

Yeah. But Grayson kept that to himself. He also caught her hand to move it off his stomach, but somehow their fingers ended up laced together.

And neither of them pulled away.

Their eyes met. She was so familiar to him, but those eyes always held a surprise or two. Sometimes they were a misty blue. Other times, the color of a spring Texas sky.

Grayson cursed that last analogy.

He was a cowboy, and the last thing he should be doing was thinking poetic thoughts about the color of Eve's eyes.

His thoughts weren't so poetic when it came to the rest of her.

Grayson knew exactly how she looked beneath those winter clothes. He knew how much she liked it when he kissed her belly. And the inside of her thighs. He knew the way she smelled. The way she tasted. The sounds that she made when he was driving her hot and crazy. And it was because he knew all those things that he had to back away.

But he didn't.

They stood there, gazes locked, as if paralysis had set in and neither could move. Eve's breath became thin. Her face flushed. She glanced at his bed, and Grayson knew exactly what she was thinking.

He'd made love to her in that bed.

Things had been different then. Ten years ago they'd remodeled the house and turned all the bedrooms into suites. But the black lacquered wrought-iron bed was the same. It'd been his grandfather's, and Grayson had staked claim to it twenty years ago after his grandfather had been killed. He'd gone through several mattresses in those twenty years, but the bed itself had remained unchanged.

No telling how many times Grayson had sneaked Eve up to his room. To this very bed.

In the beginning, neither had had a clue what they were doing. They had followed their instincts. Did the things that felt good. And plenty of those times, he'd had to kiss her hard and deep to muffle the sounds she made when she climaxed.

Grayson could hear those sounds now echoing through his head.

He couldn't help but respond to those memories. To the touch of her fingers linked with his.

Part of him, the part straining against the zipper of his jeans, started to rationalize that he could put her on that bed again. He knew how to get those sounds from her. Knew the delicious heat of her body.

"Mercy," she mumbled, but it didn't have any sound. She shook her head. Moistened her lips.

He wanted to hear her voice. Those sounds. But most of all, he just wanted to kiss her.

"It would be a mistake," Grayson said more to himself than her.

"Oh, yeah. A big one." But she inched closer. So close that he tasted her breath on his mouth. That taste went straight through him.

Something inside him snapped, and he latched on to the back of her neck and hauled her to him. Their mouths met, and he heard the sound all right. A little bit of whimper mixed with a boatload of relief.

Grayson knew exactly how she felt.

Helpless. Stupid.

And hot.

"Should I close the door and give you time alone?" someone snarled from the doorway. It was his brother Mason.

Eve and Grayson flew apart as if they'd just been caught doing something wrong. Which was true. They couldn't lust after each other. Sex against the tree to make a baby was one thing. But real sex would turn their status from *it's complicated* to *it's damn impossible.*

"Well?" Mason prompted in that surly noninterested way that only Mason could manage. "You need time to do something about that kiss or what?"

"Did you want something?" Grayson fired back at his brother.

Mason lifted the papers he had in his hand and dropped them onto the table near the door. "Background reports on the Colliers and the dead girl. You should read them. There's some interesting stuff in there." He tipped his head to the laptop. "Anything with the photos?"

"Not yet," Eve and Grayson said in unison.

If that frustrated Mason, he didn't show it. He turned but then stopped. "Good to see you, Eve." From Mason, that was a warm, fuzzy welcome.

"It's good to see you, too." Eve's was considerably warmer. Strange, most people steered clear of Mason, but Eve went to him and planted a kiss on his cheek.

Now Mason looked uncomfortable. "Yell if you need me." And with that mumbled offer, he strolled away.

Both Eve and he hurried to the reports that Mason had dropped on the table, and Grayson snatched them up. There were at least thirty pages, and with Eve right at his shoulder, they started to skim through them. It didn't take long for Grayson to see what Mason had considered *interesting stuff.*

There was a photo of Claude's first wife, Cicely, and it was the same woman in the photos taken in his office. So that was one thing cleared up. Claude's ex had visited him. Nothing suspicious about that. Since she was the mother of his son, they would always have a connection.

That required Grayson to take a deep breath because he couldn't help but think that one day, soon, Eve and he might have that same connection.

"Cicely had twins," Eve read, touching her finger to that part of the background. "Sebastian and Sophia."

This was the first Grayson had heard of it, but then he'd only had a preliminary report of Sebastian before the interview at the Collier estate.

Grayson read on. "When Sophia was six months old, the nanny, Helen Bolton, disappeared with her, and even though Helen turned up dead three months later, Sophia was never found."

On the same page of the report, there was a photo of baby Sophia that had obviously been taken right before she went missing.

"You have a scanner in the house?" Eve asked, her attention nailed to the picture of the baby.

"Sure. In my office."

Eve grabbed the laptop and headed up the hall. She practically raced ahead of him, and the moment they were inside, she fed the picture into the scanner and loaded it onto the laptop with the other photos they'd gotten from Annabel.

"What are you doing?" Grayson wanted to know.

While she typed frantically on the keyboard, Eve

sank down in the leather chair behind his desk. "I have age progression software. It's not a hundred percent accurate, but it might work."

Grayson watched Eve manipulate the copied image of the baby, and soon it began to take shape. The adult version of Sophia Collier appeared on the screen.

Grayson cursed under his breath. The hair was different, but there were enough similarities.

"Oh, God," Eve mumbled. She leaned away from the laptop and touched her fingers to her mouth. "Do you see it?" she asked.

"Yeah." Grayson saw it all right.

And it meant this investigation had just taken a crazy twist.

Because the dead woman, Nina Manning, hadn't been Claude's mistress as they'd originally thought. She was Sophia Collier, Claude's missing daughter.

Chapter 12

"I wished you'd stayed at the ranch," Grayson mumbled again. He kept his attention pinned to the San Antonio downtown street that was clogged with holiday shoppers and traffic.

Eve ignored him. She'd already explained her reasons for tagging along for this visit to Cicely Collier. She wanted the truth about the dead woman, and when that happened, the danger would be over. She could go home and, well, wait until she could take a pregnancy test.

It had been less than twenty-four hours since Grayson had agreed to have sex with her, but she'd read enough of the pregnancy books to know that conception could have already happened.

She could be pregnant.

Despite everything else going on, Eve smiled and slid her hand over her stomach. Even though it was a long shot, she wanted to hang on to the possibility as long as she could.

Even if she couldn't hang on to Grayson.

That kiss in his bedroom had felt so much like old times, and as stupid as it sounded, it had felt more intimate than the sex. It had been real, not some gesture that she'd had to talk Grayson into doing.

And that's why it couldn't happen again.

She could coax him into kissing her again. Maybe even talk him into coming to her bed. But he would soon feel trapped, and he would blame himself—and her—for feeling that way. She cared for him too much to make him go through that. Grayson already had enough duty forced on him in his life without making him feel even a shred of obligation to her. More kissing would make him feel obligated.

"You okay?" Grayson asked.

She glanced at him and realized he'd seen her hand on her stomach. "I'm fine."

He seemed suspicious of her answer, but he didn't press it. Nor would he. A discussion about the baby was off-limits for both of them, and Eve was thankful for it. Conversation wasn't going to help with this matter. No. The only thing that would help was to put some distance between them.

The voice on the GPS directed them toward another turn, and Grayson drove into the upscale San Antonio neighborhood. Of course, she hadn't expected Cicely to live in a shack, but it was obvious the woman had done well in the divorce settlement.

Grayson parked in the driveway of the two-story Victorian-style home. It was painted a soft buttery yellow with white trim, and despite the fact that it was the dead of winter, the lawn was as pristine as the house.

"I have a warrant for Cicely's DNA," Grayson explained, grabbing the large padded envelope that earlier he'd put on the backseat. "I can compare it to Nina's. If it's a match, we'll have proof that Nina is really Sophia Collier."

"What about Claude's DNA?" Eve asked.

"There's a warrant for that, too. Nate's over there now collecting it."

Poor Nate. She doubted Claude would make the process easy. For that matter, maybe Cicely wouldn't either, especially when they told her that her long-lost daughter was likely dead. Murdered, at that.

Eve was bracing herself for the worst.

Grayson and she got out of the car and went to the door. Unlike at the Collier estate, Cicely already had the door open and was waiting for them.

Cicely looked exactly as she had in the photographs that Annabel had taken of her in Claude's office. Her short, dark brown hair was perfect, not a strand out of place, and she wore a simple olive-green wool suit. She was nothing like Annabel, her curvy young replacement, but it was easy to see that Cicely had once been stunningly beautiful.

"Sheriff Ryland," Cicely greeted. Her nerves were there in her voice and the worry etched on her face.

"Mrs. Collier. This is Eve Warren. She's helping with the investigation."

"Yes." She stared at Eve and repeated it. "Sebastian called and told me that Ms. Warren had taken a picture that you have some questions about."

Cicely stepped back, motioning for them to enter.

She didn't say anything else until she led them into a cozy room off the back of the foyer. The painting over the stone fireplace immediately caught Eve's eye. It was an oil painting of two babies. One was definitely Sophia, and she guessed the other one was Sebastian.

"My children," Cicely explained, following Eve's gaze. "Won't you please have a seat?" She motioned toward the pair of chairs.

There was a gleaming silver tray with a teapot and cookies on the coffee table. Cicely sat on a floral sofa and began to serve them. Eve sat across from her.

"Sebastian dropped by earlier, and we had a long chat." Cicely's hands were trembling when she passed Eve the tea that she'd poured in a delicate cup painted with yellow roses. "He's worried. And so am I. You think Sebastian had something to do with Nina Manning's death."

"Did he?" Grayson asked. He waved off the tea when Cicely offered it to him and sat in the chair next to Eve.

"No." Cicely's pale green eyes came to Eve's. "But of course, that means nothing. I would say that because he's my son."

Eve was more than a little surprised that a mother would admit that. Of course, despite her comment about *being worried,* maybe Cicely and Sebastian weren't that close.

Grayson took out the warrant and the DNA kit from the envelope and handed them to Cicely. "I need a sample of your DNA."

Cicely's forehead bunched up, and for a moment Eve thought she would refuse, but she only refused the warrant. She pushed it aside, took the swab and without questions, she used it on the inside of her mouth.

"It's not necessary, you know," she said, handing the kit back to Grayson.

Yes, it was, and Eve figured Grayson was about to tell her why. Eve held her breath.

"Mrs. Collier—" But that was as far as Grayson got.

"Yes," Cicely interrupted. "I know that Nina Manning is…was my daughter."

Eve didn't know who looked more surprised—Grayson or her.

Cicely took a sip of tea, but her hand was trembling so much that some of it sloshed into the saucer. "I've already done the DNA test, and I can provide a copy of the results if you need them."

Grayson stayed quiet a moment. "How long have you known that she was your daughter?"

Cicely dodged his gaze. "About a month."

"A month?" Grayson mumbled something under his breath. "And you didn't think you should tell the police that your kidnapped daughter had returned?"

"I considered many things but not that." Cicely let the vague comment hang in the air for several seconds. "About a month ago, Nina showed up here and claimed to be Sophia. She said that as a baby she'd been abandoned at a church and had been raised in foster care. I didn't believe her, of course. Not until I got back the results from the DNA test."

Cicely blinked back tears. "I thought my daughter was dead."

After twenty-two years, that was reasonable, but Eve knew if she'd been in Cicely's shoes, she would have never stopped looking. *Never.*

"What happened when you found out Nina was telling the truth?" Grayson asked.

Balancing her cup on her lap, she picked at a non-existent piece of lint on her jacket. "I begged her to come home. It was obvious that she needed help. Rehab. Counseling. Did you know that she'd been selling her body to support her drug habit?"

Grayson nodded. "She had a record."

Cicely pulled in her breath as if it were physically painful to hear her suspicions confirmed. "She refused my help. She only wanted money, and I didn't want to hand over cash because I knew she'd just use it for drugs. So I called Claude to see if he would help me convince her to go to rehab."

Grayson and Eve exchanged a glance.

"Claude knew that Nina was your daughter?" Grayson asked.

"Of course," Cicely said without hesitation. "What? Did he deny it?"

"He did," Grayson confirmed.

Her mouth tightened. "Well, apparently he wasn't just a weasel of a husband, he's also a weasel of a father." She practically dumped her teacup onto the table and got up. She folded her arms over her chest and paced. "Did you meet his new tart of a wife?"

"Yes, we met Annabel." Grayson didn't say a word about the photos Annabel had provided. Without them, it might have taken a lot longer to make the connection between Nina and Sophia. However, Eve wasn't sure that had been Annabel's intention.

"Annabel." Cicely repeated the name like it was a profanity. "You can put her at the top of the list of suspects as my daughter's killer. She probably hired her lapdog, Leon Ames, to murder my baby in cold blood."

Eve set her tea aside also. This conversation was

definitely loaded with bombshells. "Why would Annabel do that?" Eve wanted to know.

Cicely rubbed her fingers together. "Money, plain and simple. Claude's dying, you know?"

Grayson shook his head. "You're sure?"

"Positive. Sebastian told me all about it. Claude has a malignant nonoperable brain tumor. Probably has less than two months to live. And when they put Claude in the ground, the tart will inherit half of his estate. If Sophia had lived, the split would have been three ways. Apparently, that wasn't enough money for her."

Mercy. If that was true, then Cicely had not only just given Annabel a motive but Sebastian, as well. After all, Sebastian certainly hadn't volunteered anything about the dead woman being his sister. In fact, he'd lied to Grayson from the very start.

"I need to re-interview Claude and Sebastian," Grayson said, standing.

"Annabel, too," Cicely insisted. "She's the one who had my baby killed, and I'm going to prove it. I want her surgically perfected butt tossed in jail."

Cicely wasn't so shaky now. She looked like a woman on a mission of revenge.

"You need to stay out of the investigation," Grayson reminded her. "If Annabel is guilty, I'll figure out a way to prove it."

Cicely didn't respond, and Eve wondered just how much trouble the woman would be. She wasn't just going to drop this.

"You can see yourselves out," Cicely said with ice in her voice. She'd apparently worked herself into a frenzy and was no longer in the hostess mode.

Grayson and Eve did just that. They saw themselves

out, but Eve was reeling from what they'd just learned. Reeling and frustrated.

"I thought by now we'd have just one suspect," Eve whispered to Grayson on the way to the door. "Instead we have two—Annabel and Sebastian."

"We have four," Grayson whispered back, and he didn't say more until they were outside. "Claude might not have been so happy to see his drug-addicted, prostitute daughter return to the family fold."

True. He had a thing about keeping mud off his good name. "And the fourth suspect?"

Grayson opened the car door for her, and she got inside. "Cicely."

Eve shook her head. "You think she would kill her own daughter?"

"I don't know, but I'm going to find out." He shut her door, got in behind the wheel and drove away. He took a deep breath. "I could drop you off at SAPD headquarters while I re-interview the Colliers."

Eve gave him a flat look. "I'm going with you."

Grayson matched her look and added a raised eyebrow. "There could be a killer in the house."

She wasn't immune to the fear, mainly because Eve believed that one of the Colliers was indeed a killer. But she was stuck on this investigation treadmill until Grayson made an arrest. Eve wanted to confront the danger head-on, and the sooner that happened, the better.

Grayson mumbled something about her being stubborn and grabbed his phone. "Then I'll have Nate bring the Colliers into the police station."

Eve didn't have to guess how this would play out. "They aren't going to like that."

"Good. Because I don't like the lies they've told us.

Plus, I'd like to see how Claude reacts when I show him the memory card his wife gave us."

Eve almost felt sorry for Annabel. *Almost*. But then, Annabel did have a strong motive for murder— her soon-to-be-dead husband's money. And it was as if Annabel was trying to put the blame on either Claude or her stepson with those pictures she'd taken.

Grayson made the call to Nate, and while he was arranging the follow-up interview with the Colliers, Eve grabbed her laptop because she wanted to continue studying the photos. Before she could do that, however, she noticed the email from her doctor, Alan Stephenson.

The message was simple. "I've been trying to reach you. Call me."

Eve automatically reached for her cell, only to re-member she didn't have one. It was in Grayson's truck, which had gone into the creek. She hadn't checked her answering machine at the condo either, mainly because Grayson had been in such a hurry to get her out of there.

"I need to use your phone," she told Grayson the mo-ment he ended his call with Nate.

"Anything wrong?" he asked.

"I'm not sure." Eve took the cell and frantically pressed in the phone number at the bottom of the email. A dozen things went through her mind, most of them bad. Had the doctor been wrong about her ovulating? Had she put Grayson through all of this for nothing? Her heart broke at the thought of her being too late to have a child of her own.

She got the doctor's answering service first, but Dr. Stephenson had left word to put her call through to him. Moments later, the doctor picked up.

"Eve," he greeted, but she could hear something in his voice. This was not good news.

"I got your email. You've been trying to call me?"

"Most of yesterday afternoon. I found a private sperm donor, but as you probably already know, it's already too late. I'm sorry."

Her lungs were aching so she released the breath she'd been holding. "I found a donor." She didn't look at Grayson, but she sensed he was looking at her.

"That's wonderful." The doctor sounded both surprised and relieved. "Did you use artificial insemination?"

The image of Grayson in the woods flashed through her mind. "No. There wasn't time."

The doctor cleared his throat. "Well, the old-fashioned way works, too."

And was a lot more pleasurable. But Eve kept that to herself. "I know it's probably a long shot."

"Maybe not. Having sex when you're ovulating substantially increases the odds. Come in next week, and I'll run a test. We should be able to tell if you're pregnant."

Everything inside Eve began to spin. "Next week? That soon?"

"That soon," the doctor assured her. "Call the office and make an appointment. I'll see you then."

The doctor ended the call, and Eve just sat there and stared at the phone. It was exactly the news she wanted. The doctor was hopeful that she had conceived, and she wouldn't have to wait long. Seven days. That was it. And she would know if Grayson and she had made a baby.

But she immediately shook her head. She couldn't think of this as Grayson's baby.

Only hers.

"My doctor can do the pregnancy test next week," she relayed to Grayson, though he was looking at everything but her now.

He didn't respond. Which was just as well. Best not to mention pregnancy tests or the baby again because if this interview with the Colliers went well, maybe Grayson could make an arrest. Then, they would go their separate ways.

That stung.

But it was necessary. A baby had to be enough. She couldn't go weaving a fantasy life with Grayson when the last thing he wanted was to raise another child.

Eve cursed the tears that sprang to her eyes, and then she cursed Grayson for being able to detach so easily. She glanced at him to see if he'd had any reaction whatsoever to the test news, but he was volleying his attention between the street ahead and the rearview mirror.

That wasn't a detached look on his face.

"What's wrong?" she asked, turning in her seat to follow his gaze.

He reached inside his jacket and drew his gun. "Someone's following us."

Chapter 13

Next week

The timing of Eve's pregnancy results should have been the last thing on Grayson's mind, but he was having a hard time pushing it aside.

"That dark blue car is the one following us?" Eve asked. She apparently wasn't thinking baby tests, either. She had her attention on the vehicle behind them.

"Yeah." It wasn't right on their tail, but the blue car had stayed several vehicles back and had made the last three turns that Grayson had taken.

"Can you see the driver?" she asked.

"No." The noon sun was catching the tint of the windows at the wrong angle, and Grayson couldn't even tell how many people there were in the car. Heck, he wasn't positive they were even being followed.

So Grayson did a test of his own.

Without signaling, he took a right turn so quickly that the driver behind him honked. But Grayson got his answer. The blue car made the same turn.

"What now?" There was a tremble in Eve's voice, and it had been that way since she'd spoken to her doctor. But now it was heavy with concern.

"We drive to SAPD headquarters as planned." Grayson only hoped the car followed them into the parking lot so he could confront this moron. Of course, he didn't want to do that with Eve around, but maybe he could get her inside the headquarters building first.

Grayson made his way through the side streets and spotted the SAPD parking lot just ahead. He pulled in, heading straight toward the drop-off that would put Eve just a few yards from the front door.

"The driver didn't turn," Eve relayed.

A glance in the rearview mirror verified that. Maybe this idiot hadn't wanted to risk arrest, but that didn't mean he wouldn't follow them when they left. Grayson would have to take extra precautions. He damn sure didn't want someone trying to shoot out their tires again.

"I'll park and be inside in a minute," Grayson told Eve and was thankful she didn't argue with him about that. The instant he came to a stop, Eve hurried inside the building.

Nate was there, just inside the door waiting for her, and Grayson caught a glimpse of Nate pulling her into his arms for a hug. It was ironic. His brothers had always loved Eve, had always thought of her as part of the family. How would they react if it turned out that she was indeed pregnant with his child?

Grayson groaned.

Maybe the better question was, how would *he* react?

Well, next week he'd know. By then, he'd hopefully have Nina Manning's killer behind bars and would be able to have some time to think this all through.

He parked and went inside to join Eve and Nate who were waiting for him in the reception area.

"Eve said someone was following you?" Nate asked.

"Yeah. But he apparently got cold feet. I got a description but not the plates."

Nate's forehead bunched up. "When you get ready to take Eve back to the ranch, I'll have one of the cruisers accompany you. That should deter anyone from following or launching another attack."

You'd think, but this investigation was twisting and turning too much for Grayson's liking. He just wanted it to end so that Eve could be safe.

"Sebastian Collier is already here," Nate announced, leading them through the headquarters toward the interview rooms. "Claude and Annabel are on the way."

"Did they give you any hassle about coming?" Eve asked.

The flat look Nate gave her indicated they had. "Claude says he'll sue us for harassment."

Grayson figured the man would use that threat, but if the DNA proved that Nina was his biological child, then that might get SAPD authorization for a search warrant to start going through not just the Collier estate, but Claude and Sebastian's financials. After all, someone had paid off Leon Ames, and Grayson was betting it was a Collier. Unfortunately, if they used cash, then the financial records might be a dead end.

"Eve and I can watch through the two-way mirror

in the adjacent room," Nate suggested. Both Grayson and he looked at Eve, and she opened her mouth, probably to argue.

"Give yourself a break from the stress," Grayson told her, and he dropped his gaze to her stomach.

Her eyes widened and just like that, she nodded. Yeah, it was a dirty trick considering she might not even be pregnant, but there was no reason for her to go a second round with this pack of jackals. Just being in the same room with them spiked his blood pressure.

Nate maneuvered them through the maze of halls until they reached the interview room, and he took Eve next door. Sebastian was seated, but he didn't offer the smile and warm welcome that he had earlier.

"I'm assuming this is important?" Sebastian asked. Everything about his body language revealed his impatience and annoyance. His face was tight, and his breath was coming out in short bursts.

"It's important," Grayson assured him. He didn't sit. He wanted to stand so he could violate Sebastian's personal space and make him even more uncomfortable. "Did you have someone follow me a few minutes ago?"

"Please." Sebastian stretched out the syllables. "I have better things to do, like last-minute shopping. Tomorrow's Christmas Eve." He stared at them, and then he mumbled a profanity under his breath. "Look, I don't know why I'm suddenly a suspect, but I did nothing wrong."

"You lied to me."

The staring match continued, and Sebastian was the first to look away. More profanity came. "About two weeks ago Nina Manning called me and asked to meet her. She claimed she was my long-lost sister. The timing was suspicious because her call came less than twenty-four hours after my father found out he was dying."

Grayson reserved judgment on the suspicious part. "Did you meet with her?"

"Yes. At a hotel in downtown San Antonio. I didn't believe her. I thought she was running a scam, but because I didn't want her upsetting my father, I was prepared to pay her off. Then, my father showed up, and after they argued, Nina ran out."

Well, that explained Annabel's pictures. "How did your father know about the meeting?"

"Nina called him, too. I guess she figured if she couldn't get the money from me, then she'd get it from my father."

Something about this didn't sound right. "If Nina wanted money, why did she run off after the so-called argument?"

"Because she was a drug-addicted, lying little witch," someone said from the doorway. It was Claude, and Annabel was by his side. Both looked about as thrilled to be there as Sebastian was.

Sebastian got to his feet. "You should sit, Father."

"I don't intend to be here that long," Claude fired back. "My attorney is on the way, and I've already put a call in to the mayor. I will not be treated like a common criminal." He aimed that remark and an accompanying glare at Grayson.

"Besides, Claude isn't well enough for this," Annabel added. The words were right, but the emotion didn't quite make it to her eyes. No glare for her, but she did look uncomfortable.

"A woman is dead," Grayson stated, looking at Claude. "She was last seen alive with your son and former employee. That employee tried to kill me and the woman who photographed Nina Manning." He paused. "Or maybe I should call the dead woman Sophia Collier."

"Never!" Claude's voice boomed through the hall, and with his index finger pointed at Grayson, he stepped into the room. "That piece of trash has no blood of mine in her."

Grayson shrugged. "Your ex-wife thought differently. She believed Nina was Sophia."

Annabel huffed. Now, there was real emotion. "Of course Cicely would believe that. She's mentally unstable, you know."

"She is," Sebastian agreed.

Grayson glanced at Claude to see if he had a comment about his ex, but Claude's jaw was so tight that Grayson figured he wasn't capable of speaking. Grayson made a mental note to do some digging to see if Cicely was indeed suffering from any form of mental illness.

"Since Nina's paternity is in question, we needed the DNA sample from you," Grayson told Claude.

"Which I gave," Claude spat out. "But there's no test that will convince me that she was my Sophia."

"Your son must have thought it was at least possible," Grayson disputed, "because he met with her again at the charity rodeo."

"I didn't meet with her," Sebastian insisted. "I already told you she was there with Leon. I simply ran into them."

Grayson just looked at them, waiting for an explanation he could actually believe—because he didn't buy the running into them story. His stony look didn't stop with just Sebastian, either. When Grayson let his intense stare stay on Annabel, her breath began to tremble, and she actually dropped back a step, probably because she thought she was about to be outed about the memory disk she'd given him. And Grayson considered it, but if either Sebastian or Claude was the killer, then that might make Annabel the next victim.

There was a soft knock, and since the door was still open, Grayson didn't have any trouble seeing who'd made the sound.

Cicely.

She was holding her leather purse in front of her like a shield, and she looked at them as if trying to figure out what was going on. Grayson knew how she felt.

"By any chance were you the one who followed Ms. Warren and me?" Grayson asked.

"Yes." And Cicely didn't hesitate, either. "I wanted to see if you'd run to Claude and tell him everything I said to you." She gave a smug nod. "But instead you ordered him to come here. Did he deny it?" Cicely asked, sliding her venomous gaze at Claude.

Claude had some venom of his own. The veins on his forehead and neck started to bulge. "If you're talking about that woman claiming to be Sophia, of course I denied it. She wasn't our daughter."

"I told you that I did a DNA test," Cicely said between clenched teeth.

"A test that could have been faked," Sebastian interrupted. "You're so eager to find your long-lost daughter that you're willing to believe anything."

"I faked nothing, and neither did Sophia." Cicely was so angry now that she was shaking, and she opened her purse and snatched something from it. Something encased in a plastic zip bag. She slapped it onto the table.

Grayson walked closer to see what it was. He'd expected a photo or something else that might shed light on this.

But it was a diamond bracelet.

Grayson frowned. "Is this connected to the investigation?"

"It is." Cicely pointed to Annabel. "She gave the bracelet to Sophia as a bribe to get her to leave."

Annabel, Sebastian and Claude all disagreed, and they weren't quiet about it, either. "I've never seen that bracelet before," Annabel insisted. She reached for the bag, but Cicely snagged her wrist.

"Sophia said you gave it to her and demanded that she sell it and use the money to get out of town. I sealed it up because I'm betting the police can find your DNA on it."

Maybe. But that wouldn't prove anything other than perhaps Annabel had told him another lie. It didn't mean she was a killer.

"How did you get the bracelet?" Grayson asked Cicely.

And with that one simple question, the room fell silent, and all eyes were on Cicely.

Cicely lifted her chin as if insulted by the implication of the question. "When Sophia came to my house, she had the bracelet with her and said it was a bribe from Annabel. She also said she was scared, that she thought Annabel would kill her if she didn't leave town and not try to stake a claim to her rightful inheritance."

"It's only a rightful claim if she was my sister," Sebastian tossed at her. "And she wasn't."

That started up another round of accusations, and Cicely was loud and liberal with the name calling—especially the names she called Annabel.

"Shut up!" Grayson practically yelled. And he turned back to Cicely. "Why would Sophia leave the bracelet with you?"

Cicely didn't jump to answer that. In fact, she swallowed hard. "She didn't say, exactly, but I think she knew something bad was going to happen to her. I think she wanted me to have it so I could prove that Annabel was her killer."

Annabel gasped and caught on to Grayson's arm. "I didn't kill her. I…" But she didn't finish, and the grip she had on his arm melted away. "I didn't kill her," she repeated.

Sebastian moved closer as if checking to make sure Annabel was okay. When his attention came back to Cicely, his eyes were narrowed. "Mother, why don't you tell the sheriff about your association with Leon Ames?"

"Association?" Cicely pulled back her shoulders. "I don't know what you mean."

"Really?" Sebastian challenged. He walked toward his mother. Slow, calculated steps. "Leon visited you often. In fact, he visited you in the past week."

Cicely didn't deny it, and when she tried to look away, Grayson got right in her face. "Is it true?"

The woman finally nodded, prompting an I-told-you-so huff from Sebastian. Neither Annabel nor Claude seemed surprised with Cicely's admission, which meant they had likely known.

"Leon was my friend." Cicely's voice was practically a whisper.

Friend. That was an interesting relationship, especially considering Leon worked for Claude. Of course, that didn't mean he hadn't been secretly working for Cicely, as well. Since Grayson believed that Leon had likely killed Nina, now he had to figure out who had given the man orders to kill.

"Leon was your lover and would have done anything for you," Sebastian accused. He was smirking when he looked at Grayson. "My mother has an affinity for associating with lowlifes. That's probably why she was so eager to believe that woman when she claimed she was Sophia."

That put some fire back into Cicely, and she opened her mouth, probably to verbally blast her son into the next county.

But a sound stopped her.

A gasp.

Not just any ordinary gasp, either. It was as if all the air swooshed out of Claude's lungs.

"Sebastian," Claude managed to say. A split second before he clamped his hands to the sides of his head and dropped to the floor.

Chapter 14

Eve got out of Grayson's car and made her way up the steps of the ranch house. Despite the fact that someone had tried to kill them twice today, her nerves were no longer firing on all cylinders.

Thank God.

The bone-weary fatigue was no doubt responsible for that. The Christmas lights helped, too. Hard to think of murders and attacks when there were hundreds of multicolored lights twinkling around her. And then she stepped inside and knew this was the main source of her calmer nerves.

For reasons she didn't want to explore, the Ryland ranch always had and always would feel like home to her. So many memories, and they flooded through her, easing away the rest of the tension.

Grayson walked in right behind her. He had his

phone sandwiched between his ear and shoulder, a place it'd been during most of their drive from San Antonio back to the ranch. Along the way, he'd gotten several updates on the investigation.

And Claude.

Judging from the part of this particular conversation, Grayson was talking with Claude's doctor.

When the man had first collapsed at the SAPD precinct, Eve had thought he was faking it so he could put a quick end to the interview. But after he'd been rushed to the hospital in an ambulance, the doctors had informed Grayson that Claude's condition was critical. So, no more interviews until the man was stable. Whenever that would be.

"Claude is still touch and go," Grayson relayed to her when he ended the call. "He might not make it through the night." He slapped his phone shut and pulled in a long, weary breath.

Eve understood that weariness. She wasn't fond of Claude, but if he died, he might take his secrets to the grave. Especially one secret.

Had he been the one responsible for Nina's death?

Or did that guilt lie with Sebastian, Annabel or even Cicely?

"What about the DNA results?" Eve wanted to know because she'd heard Grayson's phone conversation with Nate about that, as well.

Grayson shook his head. "Nothing yet, but we should have preliminary results in an hour or two." He used the keypad on the wall to arm the security system. "Nate's also checking to see if anyone else, including Cicely, ran a DNA test on Nina."

She thought about that for a moment. "But Cicely

said she'd done the test. Why would she lie about something like that?"

"Who knows? I'm still working that out, but I'm not ready to believe anything a Collier says."

Eve agreed. All of them seemed to have something to hide, but the DNA results might be a start toward learning the truth. If Nina was indeed Sophia, then that only strengthened Sebastian and Annabel's motives for murder. They might not have wanted to split Claude's estate three ways.

Still, there were some things Eve hadn't been able to grasp. "I understand why Claude might have had Nina killed," she commented. "With his elitist attitude, he would never admit to having a drug addict daughter. But what about Cicely? She seems more than willing to admit that Nina was hers. So, why would she kill her?"

"Seems," Grayson emphasized. "That's why I want to see when and if Cicely ran the DNA test."

Ah, Eve got it then. Because the test could have been a cover-up. Nina could have confronted or even attempted to blackmail Cicely, and Cicely could have refused to believe this was her long-lost daughter. Cicely could have had Nina killed out of anger. However, the woman wouldn't look like a major murder suspect if she told everyone that she knew Nina was truly Sophia.

If Cicely had done that, it was a smart move.

"Anyone home?" Grayson called out. When no one answered, he headed for the kitchen, and Eve followed.

She immediately spotted the note from Bessie on the double-door stainless-steel fridge. "Mason called. He and Dade are staying in town to work on the case," Grayson read aloud. "Nate and the baby won't be home, either. Haven't heard a peep from Kade. Dinner's in the fridge and I'm headed out for girls' night at my sister's place in Saddle Springs. Give Eve a good-night kiss for me." Bessie had added a smiley face.

The woman's attempt at humor didn't cause either Grayson or Eve to smile. But it did give Eve an uneasy feeling because she realized that Grayson and she were alone in the house. She glanced at Grayson, and his quick look away convinced her that he was aware of it, as well.

"You'll need to eat," he reminded her.

"You, too," she reminded him right back.

But neither of them moved. They both stood there, staring at Bessie's note, while the air zinged around them. For a moment Eve wondered if Grayson might act on that good-night kiss after all, but he mumbled something about being hungry and pulled open the fridge door.

There was a large baking dish with lasagna on the center shelf. She was suddenly starving. She knew from experience that Bessie was an amazing cook, but Eve decided both Grayson and she could use a little space to clear their heads. After all, in the past twenty-four hours, they'd nearly been killed and had then gotten embroiled in a murder investigation.

They'd also had sex.

Even the fatigue couldn't erase the too-familiar tingling she still felt. And that was another huge reason for a little head-clearing space.

"I think I'll take a shower before I eat," Eve told him.

Grayson didn't have time to respond because his cell phone rang. Eve waited just a few seconds to make sure it wasn't critical, but when she realized it was the youngest Ryland, Kade, calling for an update about the investigation, she excused herself and went to the guest suite.

Eve intended to head straight for the shower, but she saw the photo album on the guest bed. The leather cover had probably once been white but had aged to a rich cream color, and it was thick, at least three inches.

"Here's your Christmas present. Thought you'd like copies of some old memories," was written on the sticky note attached. "Love, Bessie."

She was reasonably sure she didn't need any more memories or copies of memories, but Eve sat on the edge of the bed and opened it. The first picture was of Boone and Marcie Ryland, Grayson's parents, on their wedding day. They were both smiling, and there were no hints of the troubles to come nineteen years later when Boone would walk out on Marcie and his six sons. A few months after that, Marcie would take her own life.

What a waste. So many lives had been changed because of Boone's departure. Especially Grayson's. If he hadn't had to raise his brothers, he might have wanted a family of his own. But it hurt Eve too much to dwell on that particular *if*.

Eve turned the page to Grayson's baby picture— probably taken when he was no more than a day or two old. She smiled. If she was indeed pregnant, then this was a glimpse of how her baby could look.

She flipped through the pages, each of them snapshots of time. Grayson's first horseback ride—barely a toddler in the saddle. His first day of school.

And then Eve was in the picture—literally.

Nearly all the subsequent pages had photos of her with the Ryland family. Christmas. Easter. Birthdays.

She'd been a part of them. Always engulfed in those strong arms that had always given her so much love.

She ached to be part of that again but knew it was lost forever. The ultimatum she'd given Grayson all those years ago had sealed her fate and separated her from him, and his family, forever.

Or had it?

Her mind began to spin with the possibility of her baby being part of this. Not permanently part of the family but maybe visits so the baby would know his or her bloodline.

But she forced herself to stop.

She'd made the deal with Grayson—if he got her pregnant, that would be it. No strings attached. So, her fate was sealed. Her baby's fate, too. One way or another, she would leave as soon as it was safe.

Eve blinked back tears, but more followed. She was still swiping them away when the house phone rang. She glanced at the caller ID screen and saw that it was Annabel Collier. Since this could be important, she lay the album aside and hurried downstairs.

Grayson was in the kitchen where he was already talking to Annabel, and he had put the call on speaker. "I'm listening," he said to Annabel.

Annabel didn't say anything for several seconds. "I'm not sure how to say this."

Grayson huffed. "Try," he insisted. He looked at Eve then, and his right eyebrow slid up, questioning her about something. When she shook her head, Grayson went to her and touched her cheek. Or so she thought. But not a real touch. He wiped away a stray tear.

"You okay?" he mouthed.

Eve moved away from him, and thankfully didn't have to explain anything because Annabel continued.

"I lied to you," the woman confessed.

Grayson didn't huff this time, but he looked as if he wanted to do just that. "Which lie would that be?"

"About the diamond bracelet. It was mine. I figured you would discover that when you had it tested so I decided to come clean. I gave it to Nina, hoping it would convince her to leave."

Now Eve was the one to huff. The Colliers were certainly free with their lies, and she didn't think it was a coincidence that the lies seemed to be attempts to prevent them from being charged with murder.

"Then Cicely was right." Grayson took out a plate of heated lasagna from the microwave and handed it to Eve.

"Cicely was trying to make me sound guilty. That's the only reason she had the bracelet. She wants to incriminate me."

Eve got them both out some silverware and paper napkins and sat at the counter. Grayson got out two longneck beers and his plate. He looked at her. Studied her. Maybe trying to figure out what had caused those tears.

"The question you should be asking yourself is how Cicely got that bracelet in the first place," Annabel went on. "Because I seriously doubt Nina freely gave it to her. That bracelet was worth thousands, and a druggie like Nina wouldn't have handed it over without a fight."

"Are you saying Cicely killed Nina and took the bracelet?" Grayson didn't wait. He sat and started to eat.

"Yes, that's exactly what I'm saying." But then Annabel paused. "Or maybe Sebastian killed her and gave the bracelet to his mother. He could have done it to try to incriminate me, too."

"Sebastian," Grayson repeated. "I wondered when this conversation would turn to him."

"What do you mean?" Annabel accused.

He had a gulp of beer first. And another look at Eve. "I mean your husband is dying. By tomorrow morning, you could be a wealthy widow—thanks to your huge inheritance. If Sebastian were out of the picture, you'd have double the wealth and no pesky stepchildren around to cash in on their daddy's will."

Annabel made a sound of outrage. "I didn't kill anyone!" she practically shouted.

"Maybe. Can you say the same for your husband?" Grayson challenged.

Silence. The moments crawled by, and Grayson continued to sip his beer. The glances at her continued, too. What didn't happen was a denial from Annabel about her husband's innocence.

"If Claude recovers, you'll have to ask him that." Annabel's voice was no longer hot with anger. It was ice-cold and impatient.

"I will," Grayson assured her. "Now, tell me why you gave me the memory card with the photos."

She paused again. "Because I knew something wasn't right when Nina showed up. Claude and Sebastian were having secret conversations. And Cicely kept calling. I didn't know Nina was going to die, but I thought I might need proof."

"Proof of what?" Grayson pressed.

"That I didn't have anything to do with her, her life or her death."

"Well, the pictures don't prove that." Of course, they

did prove that all their suspects had had close contact with a woman who was murdered. Even if Annabel hadn't taken the pictures herself, she had certainly been aware of them.

"I didn't kill her," Annabel insisted. "Now that I've told you about the bracelet, we have nothing further to discuss." And she hung up.

Without taking his attention off Eve, he leaned over and pressed the end button on the phone. Since his stare was making her uncomfortable, Eve focused on the square of lasagna in front of her.

"Why are you looking at me like that?" she finally asked.

Grayson opened his mouth. Closed it. And the staring continued.

Eve decided she'd just spill it. "I was crying because I'd been looking at a photo album that Bessie gave me for Christmas. Old memories," she settled for saying.

"Oh." And judging from his tone, that was not the answer he'd expected. "I thought maybe...well, I thought you'd learned you weren't pregnant."

Now, it was her turn to say "Oh." He'd seen the tears and assumed the worst. Or maybe in his case, the best—that maybe she'd gotten her period. However, that wouldn't be just bad news. It would break her heart.

"No." Since the lasagna suddenly wasn't settling well in her stomach, Eve got up so she could put it back in the fridge. "I won't know until next week."

"Okay." He nodded, repeated it.

She could feel his regret. His doubts. And Eve was just too tired to go there. She whirled back around to remind him that from here on out he wasn't part of her life.

But Grayson stood and whirled around at the same time, and they practically smacked right into each other. Eve started to move back, way back, but Grayson caught on to her arm, anchoring her in place. She could have shaken off his grip, of course, but she didn't.

"I can't do this," she managed to say.

His eyebrow came up again, and he was obviously waiting for an explanation of what specifically she couldn't do, but Eve hesitated one second too long, and in that second she got caught up in Grayson's eyes. His scent.

His touch.

She'd never been able to resist him, never, and apparently tonight was no different.

"I can't, either," he answered. Though she had no idea what he meant by that.

She soon learned though.

Grayson leaned in and put his mouth on hers. It was just a touch, barely qualifying as a kiss, but this was Grayson. He could make her melt with a simple brush of his mouth and she'd forget all the arguments she had going through her head about why she couldn't do this. Kissing would only lead to more complications.

Still, Eve moved closer.

She hooked her arm around the back of his neck and eased him down to her. His mouth pressed harder, and that barely-a-kiss became a real one.

He snapped her to him, body to body, and took her mouth the way he always had. He was clever and thorough, and any thought of resisting him flew right out of her mind.

In fact, she did the opposite of resisting.

Eve got even closer, sliding her hands down his back

and adjusting their positions so that the kiss turned to full body contact. Yes, there were clothes between them, but she knew his body so well that she had no trouble filling in the blanks of how it would feel to have him naked against her.

"You still can't?" he mumbled against his mouth.

She couldn't answer because the kiss turned French and scalding hot. If she'd had breath left to speak, she wouldn't have used it to state the obvious because clearly she *could*.

Couldn't she?

This wouldn't be lab sex for the purpose of getting her pregnant. This would be like old times. And then what?

Eve forced herself to consider *then what*.

Grayson cursed, and for a moment she thought he had reached the same *then what?* roadblock that she had. It took her a moment to realize he was cursing because his phone was ringing. She hadn't heard it over the roar in her head.

"It's Nate," Grayson let her know after he glanced down at the screen. He flipped the cell open and jabbed the speaker button. He also leaned against the kitchen counter and tried to level his breathing.

Eve did the same, though it would take more than some deep breaths to get back to normal.

"Please tell me you have good news," he greeted Nate.

"Well, it's news," Nate explained. "I'll let you decide if it's good or not. Just got the preliminary DNA results, and Nina Manning was indeed Sophia Collier."

So there it was—the proof that at least some of the

Colliers weren't going to like because that proof was also motive.

"I did a statewide search of labs that had tested Sophia's DNA," Nate continued, "and I couldn't find any record that Cicely had requested a test."

Another lie, and Eve was betting that Cicely would just lie again when Grayson questioned her about it.

Eve huffed. Would they ever learn the truth so that Sophia's killer could be brought to justice and so that she could finally get on with her life?

She looked at Grayson and felt his kiss still burning her mouth. Maybe getting on with her life wasn't even possible. That kiss had proven that she would never get Grayson out of her blood and out of her system.

Never.

"But someone else did request a test on Sophia's DNA," Nate added. That caught Eve's attention. "That happened just three days before Sophia was murdered."

"Who?" Grayson and Eve asked in unison.

"Sebastian," Nate answered.

Eve saw the surprise in Grayson's eyes. Sebastian had denied that Nina was his sister, but yet he obviously knew the truth because he'd had her DNA tested.

"You're positive about this?" Grayson pressed.

"Positive, and I have proof. Sebastian tried to cover up the payment for the test by using cash, but the lab has 24/7 surveillance. We have footage of him going into the lab and then picking up the results."

"What kind of a timeline are we looking at for this? Did Sebastian have the DNA results before Nina was murdered?" Grayson wanted to know.

"Oh, yeah," Nate assured him. "He had them all right. Less than twenty-four hours after he got the results that confirmed Nina was his sister, someone killed her."

Grayson shook his head, mumbled something. "Then as far as I'm concerned, that makes Sebastian Collier our number-one suspect."

Eve agreed, and judging from the sound he made, apparently so did Nate.

"So what do you want me to do?" Nate asked Grayson.

Grayson didn't even hesitate. "Pick up Sebastian and put him in a holding cell. I'll be at SAPD first thing in the morning to read him his rights and arrest him."

Chapter 15

Grayson downed the shot of whiskey. It was strong stuff, Mason's private stash, and it burned his eyes and throat. What it didn't do was clear his head.

But then, that was asking a lot from a shot of whiskey.

The details of the case kept running through his head. Thoughts of Eve kept running through his body. Neither would give him much peace tonight, even though the house was whisper-quiet and would likely stay that way because it was going on midnight.

"Midnight," he mumbled.

Since he had an early-morning trip to SAPD to question and arrest Sebastian, he should be sleeping. Heck, Eve probably was. She'd called it a night well over an hour ago.

Good thing, too, because before her good-night

Grayson had been on the verge of resuming the make-out session that Nate's call had interrupted.

He shouldn't have touched her.

And he damn sure shouldn't have kissed her.

He should have just walked away and let fate sort out the details of what was to come in the next week or so. But the sight of those tears in her eyes had shaken him. Grayson considered himself a strong man, but he wasn't strong enough to keep her at arm's length when she'd been crying.

He poured himself another shot and took it in one gulp. Still no relief. So he gave up on the whiskey and headed out of the den and to his bathroom for a shower. He stripped along the way, dropping his clothes on the bedroom floor, and he kept the water ice-cold.

That didn't work, either.

There was a furnace of heat in his body, and there was only one cure for what he felt.

Eve.

Damn her. Damn *him*.

Grayson knew that pretty much any woman could satisfy his body, but there was only one woman who could satisfy *him*. And that was Eve.

For most of his life, she'd been what had fired him up and cooled him down—sometimes in the same minute. She'd been the one woman he couldn't get out of his head. And no amount of whiskey or cold water was going to cure that. No. There was only one cure, and she was right across the hall.

Grayson cursed and put on his jeans. No sense trying to talk himself out of jumping off this Texas-size cliff. He was going to jump all right, and this could be a fall that would hurt for the rest of his life.

He didn't knock on the guestroom door. Didn't want anything to slow him down and stop him. Well, that was the plan anyway, but his mouth went dry when he spotted her. Not asleep as he'd thought she would be. No. Eve was wide-awake, lying in bed, the ice-white covers draped loosely over her breasts and the rest of her.

Grayson shut the door. And went to her.

"The right thing would be for me to go back to my room," he told her.

Her mouth trembled slightly and turned into the hint of a smile. "Grayson, for once in your life, don't do the right thing, okay?"

She caught on to his hand, pulled him closer. Grayson obliged and leaned down for a kiss. He'd kissed her a thousand times, maybe more, but each time always felt like the first. That punch hit him hard in the chest and then below the belt.

How could he want anyone this much?

And worse, why would he want her this much even after he'd had her?

Grayson kept the kiss simple, though his body was revved up way past the kissing stage. Still, he needed this. The feel of her mouth against his. The sweet silk of her lips. Her taste. He needed it all, and apparently Eve did, too, because she kept inching him closer.

The covers shifted, and the sheet slipped off her breasts. No bra. Just Eve's bare breasts. He met her gaze and saw the little spark there.

Grayson used just the tip of his index finger to draw the covers down. He got an interesting show as he revealed every inch of her. Bare stomach. Bare hips. He heard himself choke back a groan.

No panties.

"I like to sleep naked," she whispered.

"I like that you like to sleep naked." He tried to chuckle. Failed at that, too.

"No." Eve tightened the grip on his hand. "Don't you dare have any doubts about this."

Oh. He had doubts, but he wasn't going to do anything about them. Grayson did what he did best. He took control of the situation. He raked back the rest of the covers, exposing every bit of Eve's naked body.

Yeah, she was beautiful.

He hadn't had to see her naked to remember that, but this trip down memory lane was a good one.

Grayson put his knee on the bed, the feather mattress giving way to his weight. He let himself ease into a fall and kissed her on the way down until his body was pressed hard against hers. The fit was right. Perfect. And it created pressure in all the right places.

"Jeans," she mumbled and fumbled for his zipper.

Grayson let her deal with that so he could make some headway with what he'd started. And what he'd started was a full-body kiss.

He trailed the kisses down her throat to her breasts. Yeah. That taste hadn't changed. He took her nipple into his mouth, and the zipper fumbling stopped, just as he figured it would. Eve moaned, arched her back and shoved her fingers into his hair to pull him closer.

"Yes." She repeated it and wrapped her legs around him.

His jeans were still between them, but Eve got the position and the pressure just right for this to go to the next level.

"Make me crazy, Grayson," she whispered and then laughed, low and husky.

He was too involved in the kissing to laugh, but he smiled when he slid his body through her leg lock and kissed her where she really wanted to be kissed. Right in the center of all that wet heat.

But Eve didn't stay on just the receiving end. She ran her hands over his shoulder and into his hair. Her legs caressed his back…and lower.

She knew exactly how to drive him crazy, too. And how to pleasure him. After all, they'd spent their teen years making out in his truck. Kisses only, at first. Lots of kisses.

Then, the touches.

He'd given Eve her first climax with his hand in her panties. They'd lost their virginity on her seventeenth birthday. They'd both been clumsy and awkward. But they'd both learned a lot over the years.

"Too crazy," she let him know when she was close to climaxing.

She caught on to him, pulling him back up so she could go after his zipper again. She wasn't playing this time. She was hot and ready so Grayson helped her, and she used her feet and hands to work the jeans off his hips.

"Commando," she said when she noticed he wasn't wearing his usual boxers. She smiled when she looked down between their bodies and no doubt saw that he was hard as stone. "That's my Grayson."

She froze and got that deer-in-the-headlights look. As if she'd crossed some line and tried to take them back to a place they could never go again. And maybe she had with that *my Grayson*. But he didn't care a flying fig about lines. He'd crossed the biggest line of all just by coming into her room.

He pinned her hands to the bed. Pinned her body, too. She would want his full weight on her so Grayson obliged, and he pushed himself inside her.

Mercy.

The pleasure was blinding.

It was like coming home for Christmas.

Eve arched her back and pressed her head against the pillow. She rocked her hips into his, causing him to go deep and hard into her. He was probably too rough. That thought was just a flash, and soon he couldn't think at all.

He moved inside her. Faster. Harder. Deeper. Until she was so close to climax. Until everything was a blur.

Everything except Eve.

Everything inside him pinpointed on her. Just her. The primal ache clawed away at him. This need as old as man. The need to take and claim.

But there were other needs, too.

And it was that need that sent Grayson in search of a kiss. He wanted the taste of her in his mouth when he lost all reason. When she slipped over the edge.

Eve came in a flash, when Grayson was deep inside her, when his mouth took hers.

Grayson said her name. It came from a place deeper than the primal need that had brought them to this point.

Somewhere in his brain, it registered that this was going to complicate the hell out of things. But that was only a split-second thought. Eve's legs tightened around him. She pulled him closer, and her climax brought on his.

Grayson felt his body surrender. Felt that slam of

pleasure that was beyond anything he ever deserved to feel. Something so perfect. So amazing.

So Eve.

Chapter 16

"**Y**ou did what?" Grayson snapped to the person on the other end of the phone.

Eve thought the caller might be Nate, but she wasn't sure, and she couldn't tell from the conversation what Grayson was snapping about now. But there was no doubt, he was snapping.

Eve stared out the car window, sipped her coffee and debated—again—what she should say to Grayson once he had finished this call. Or if she should say anything. After all, he certainly hadn't volunteered much about coming to her bed for one of the most amazing nights of her life.

In fact, he had avoided the subject.

Of course, he'd been on the phone most of the morning and during the entire drive from the ranch to San Antonio. So that was his excuse, but she had to wonder, if it hadn't been for the calls, would he have come up with another reason for them not to talk?

"You're positive this isn't some kind of ruse so Sebastian can escape?" Grayson demanded.

Mercy, that didn't sound good, and she didn't think it was a good sign when Grayson turned off the interstate two exits before the one for SAPD headquarters. Grayson had been on his way to arrest Sebastian, but there had obviously been a change of plans.

"No," Grayson continued. Except that wasn't a bark or a snarl. He mumbled it. "Eve's with me. There wasn't anyone at the ranch to stay with her. The ranch hands have already left for their Christmas break."

Even though he practically mumbled that part, too, she heard the frustration. Grayson hadn't wanted her to come along when he questioned Sebastian. He'd wanted her tucked safely away at the ranch, but both Dade and Mason were still in town working the details of Nina's murder. Or rather Sophia Collier's murder. And with Bessie and the ranch hands off the grounds, Grayson had reluctantly brought her along to arrest and interrogate Sebastian.

Not the ideal way to spend Christmas Eve.

Of course, the danger was almost certainly over for her now that the photos she'd taken were in the hands of the authorities. Sebastian had no reason to kill her. Well, unless he was hell-bent on getting some kind of revenge because she'd inadvertently incriminated him, and now that he was in police custody, even that wasn't possible.

She hoped.

This could all be over soon, especially if Grayson managed to get a confession from Sebastian. Or if something hadn't gone wrong with his arrest. Judging from

Grayson's sour expression and change of direction, that wasn't just possible but likely.

Grayson slapped his phone shut and took the turn for San Antonio Memorial Hospital.

Her heart dropped.

"Is someone hurt?" she asked and then held her breath.

He shook his head. "Claude's doctor doesn't think he'll last much longer so he requested the family's presence at Claude's bedside. That includes Sebastian."

Since Claude was critical, the doctor's request was reasonable, or at least it would have been if Sebastian weren't a murder suspect.

"An SAPD officer is escorting Sebastian," Grayson let her know. "They should arrive at the hospital any minute now."

And that explained why Grayson took the final turn toward San Antonio Memorial. It wasn't a large hospital but was in one of the more affluent neighborhoods of the city. No surprise about that, considering Claude was a millionaire many times over.

"Did Nate say if Claude was talking?" Eve asked.

"He's lucid." Grayson paused. "And he wants to see me."

Strange. Claude certainly hadn't wanted to see Grayson when he'd been ordered to SAPD headquarters. "Do you think he'll make a deathbed confession?"

Grayson's scowl deepened. "Maybe. But if he does, it'll probably be for one reason—not to tell the truth, but to save his son."

Of course. With Claude dying, it wouldn't matter if he confessed to a murder he didn't commit. But then, it was possible that he had indeed killed Sophia since there was no tangible proof that Claude knew she was his biological daughter. And even if he had known, he could have killed her when he realized she wasn't the darling little girl he wanted in his family.

There was no street parking, just a multilevel parking garage so Grayson drove in and looked for a spot. He took the first one available, at the back of the second level.

Grayson glanced around. So did Eve. And somewhere amid the glancing, their gazes collided.

There.

Eve saw it in his eyes then—the conversation he'd been avoiding all morning.

"Do I need to apologize?" Grayson tossed out there like a gauntlet.

She thought about her answer. "No. Do I?" She tossed that proverbial gauntlet right back at him.

He cursed, looked away and scrubbed his hand over his face. "I'm the one who went to your bed."

"And I could have said no," Eve reminded him.

But that was a lie. She'd never been able to say no to Grayson, and she wouldn't have started last night. Still, this had caused more tension between them, and that's the last thing they needed when they were within minutes of facing the Colliers.

And facing a possible pregnancy.

Eve certainly hadn't been thinking about getting pregnant when Grayson had climbed into bed with her. She'd been thinking about making love with him, but now that it was the morning after, she knew that last night had increased her chances of getting the baby she'd always wanted.

However, it hadn't helped her *relationship* with Grayson.

She could feel his uneasiness, and she had to do something to diffuse it.

"What happened between us doesn't have to mean anything," she settled for saying, but those words hurt. Because it sure as heck had meant something to her. It meant that Grayson had still wanted her enough to risk plenty by coming to her like that.

He looked at her, as if he might dispute her not-mean-anything offer, but he only shook his head. "We'll talk about this later."

Eve caught on to his arm when he started to bolt. "No need." That hurt, too, but she had to give Grayson an out. He'd done her a huge favor by having sex with her, and she didn't want him to feel guilty or tormented.

She leaned over and brushed a chaste kiss on his cheek. "I already know how you feel about fatherhood, about a lot of things." Eve had to take a deep breath before continuing. "And I know when this investigation is over, your life can get back to normal."

Something flashed through his metal-gray eyes, and his face tightened. For a moment she thought they might have that blowup they'd been skirting around all morning. But he didn't toss out any more gauntlets or launch into an argument. He eased her hand off his arm and stepped from the car.

Eve could only sigh and do the same.

The garage wasn't just dank, it was cold, and Eve pulled her coat tighter against her. She had no scarf or gloves. She'd forgotten to pick those up when they'd been at her condo the day before, and women's clothing was in short supply at the Ryland ranch. Eve had made do with the gray pants and sweater that she'd packed, but she had been forced to wear the same red coat that had survived their trek through the woods.

Ahead of her, Grayson pulled the sides of his buck-skin jacket together, as well. No festive red for him. He was wearing his usual jeans and dark shirt. Practically a uniform for him. He'd also worn his badge and shoulder holster, of course, which meant because he was armed, they would have to go through security inside.

She fell in step alongside Grayson as they walked to the elevator that would take them into the hospital, but they didn't get far before Grayson stopped. He lifted his head and looked around, just as he'd done when he had first parked. She looked, too, but only saw the sea of cars in the dimly lit space.

"Is something wrong?" Eve asked.

Grayson didn't answer. He glanced around again and caught on to her to get her moving to the elevator. It was clear he was hurrying now, but Eve didn't know why.

"I got a bad feeling," Grayson mumbled.

That put her on full alert because she knew from experience that Grayson's instincts were usually right.

And they were.

The sound zinged through the garage. It wasn't a blast. Eve wasn't sure what it was until the window shattered on the car next to them. Then she knew.

Oh, God.

Someone had fired at them.

Grayson cursed and shoved Eve to the side between two parked cars. He followed, moving directly in front of her, and in the same motion, he drew his gun.

What the hell was happening now?

The danger to Eve should be over. Finished. She was

no longer a threat to Sophia's killer since her photos had gone public. Obviously, the shooter wasn't aware of that.

Because another shot came right at them.

Not a loud blast but more like a swish. That meant the gunman was using a weapon rigged with a silencer.

This had to be connected to Sophia's murder. They couldn't be that unlucky to now be the victims of a random attack. Maybe someone didn't want them hearing whatever deathbed confession Claude was likely to make. If so, then it was even more vital that Grayson speak to the dying man.

Grayson pushed Eve flat on the concrete floor and tried to pinpoint the origin of those two shots. He also tried to spot the gunman. There was no sign of anyone, but he thought maybe the shots had come from a black van on the other side of the parking lot. It wasn't a huge space, only about fifty feet across, but with the vehicles jammed together, there were plenty of places for a would-be killer to hide.

"Call Nate and tell him we need backup," Grayson told Eve. Without taking his attention off that black van, he grabbed his phone from his jacket pocket and handed it to her.

Another shot.

This one smacked into the headlight of the car right next to them. The glass shattered, flying through the air, and Grayson had to duck down and shield his eyes.

Almost immediately, he heard footsteps.

Behind him, he also heard Eve call Nate and request assistance, but Grayson shut out what she was saying and concentrated on those footsteps. Someone was running, and he caught just a glimpse of that someone before they ducked out of sight.

The person was dressed head-to-toe in black and was wearing a black baseball cap that obstructed the shooter's face.

It could be anyone.

And that *anyone* ducked between two other vehicles—a white pickup truck and a red sports car.

"Nate's on the way," Eve relayed. "He said he'll seal off the exits to the garage and do a silent approach."

Good. He needed his brother because this situation could get more dangerous than it already was. If anyone came out of that elevator, the gunman would probably shoot to kill so there'd be no witnesses to this attack. Plus, someone driving into the garage could also become a target. Right now though Grayson's biggest concern was Eve, and getting her safely out of there.

He lifted his head a fraction and listened for any sound of movement or more footsteps. None on both counts. Just Eve's too-fast breathing, and she was mumbling something that sounded like a prayer. She was obviously terrified, and it didn't help that this was the third attempt to kill her. In fact, it was probably worse now because she might be pregnant.

But Grayson pushed that thought out of his mind.

He needed to focus, and he couldn't do that if he thought about the baby he'd possibly made with Eve.

The next shot got his full attention. It didn't slam into the car as the others had. This one was aimed at the ground, and it ripped through the concrete just a few feet in front of them. The shooter had obviously gotten himself in a better position to deliver a fatal shot.

Grayson needed to throw him off-kilter as much as he could. That wouldn't be easy since he only had his sidearm. There was extra ammunition in his car, but that was yards away and would be too dangerous to try to reach. That meant he had to make every shot count while maneuvering the gunman as far away from Eve as possible.

Grayson waited for the next shot, and he didn't have to wait long. It, too, tore into the floor and sent a cloud of debris and dangerous concrete bits right at them. He ducked out of cover for just a second and then fired in the direction of the shooter.

He hit the red sports car.

The shot bashed into the front end, and almost immediately the alarm went off. It was a piercing roar that was almost deafening. And worse. It blocked out any sound of the gunman's footsteps.

"Stay down!" Grayson warned Eve when he felt her move behind him.

He knew for a fact that she didn't have her gun with her because he'd talked her out of bringing it. Now, he wished he hadn't. He didn't want Eve up and returning fire, but it would have been nice to have the extra ammunition.

Even with the distraction of the car alarm, Grayson saw where the next shot landed. This one hadn't been aimed at them but rather the overhead lights. The gunman took out the ones near the elevator and stairwell, plunging that area into total darkness.

That could be good or bad.

Good because Nate would likely make his approach using the stairs, and the darkness would help conceal him. But that same darkness could also conceal the shooter if he tried to escape. Grayson didn't want this SOB to get away. He wanted to end this now.

Two more shots came at Eve and him, one right behind the other.

The gunman had moved again. This time to the right. Hell. The gunman was moving toward those stairs. Not only would that give him an escape route, it would also give him a better angle to fire more of those lethal bullets.

"What's going on up there?" someone called out. "I'm the security guard for the hospital."

"Sheriff Grayson Ryland. We're under fire. Stay back!"

But the words had no sooner left Grayson's mouth when he saw something out of the corner of his eye. To his left. There was a man in a dark gray uniform. The security guard, no doubt. He had his weapon drawn and had ducked down a little, but he was still making his way toward them.

The gunman obviously saw him, too.

Because a shot went in that direction.

The guard dove to the ground, but he was literally out in the open and therefore an easy target. Grayson had to do something, so he came out of cover, estimated the position of the shooter, and sent a bullet his way.

Because of the blasted car alarm, he couldn't tell if the gunman even reacted. Maybe he'd managed to hit the bastard, or at the very least maybe he had gotten the guy to back off so the guard could scramble to safety.

"You need to get down!" Eve snarled, and she put her hand on his back to push Grayson to the ground again.

It wasn't a second too soon.

The next bullet that was fired would have slammed right into him if Eve hadn't pulled him down with her.

However, Grayson didn't have time to thank her because everything seemed to happen at once. Another shot went toward the security guard who was trying to scramble away.

And then there was the movement in the stairwell.

For one horrifying moment, Grayson thought it was the gunman getting away. But this person wasn't dressed all in black.

It was Nate.

His brother was sneaking up the stairs, trying to get a drop on the gunman. But it was dark, and Nate was out of position. Unlike the gunman, who was probably only a few feet away.

"Watch out!" Grayson yelled to his brother.

But it was already too late.

Grayson couldn't hear the shot that the gunman fired, but he saw the end result.

A bullet slammed right into Nate's chest.

Chapter 17

Eve screamed, but the sound of her voice was drowned out by the blaring car alarm.

Her scream didn't warn Nate in time. Neither did Grayson's shouted warning to his brother. And because they'd failed, she watched in horror as the bullet hit Nate.

He flew backward from the impact.

"Oh, God." And Eve kept repeating it like a hysterical mantra.

Had he been killed?

She thought of his baby daughter, Kimmie, who would be an orphan if Nate died. And it would be partly her fault. If she just hadn't taken that damn picture then there would have been no attempts to kill her. All of this had started because of that.

Eve automatically bolted toward Nate so she could

help him, but Grayson latched onto her and pulled her back to the ground. Good thing, too. Because the shots came at them again. This time, however, they were non-stop. Frenzied. They pelted into the cars on either side of them and the concrete floor in front of them.

Eve covered her head with her hands, but she couldn't stay behind the shelter of the vehicles for long. "We have to help Nate," she shouted, though she was certain that Grayson already knew that.

Because Grayson was practically lying on top of her, she could feel the rock-hard muscles of his body, and his chest was pumping from the adrenaline. His gaze volleyed between the stairwell and the area where the gunman was likely hiding. He was primed and ready to fight, but he would also do whatever it took to save his brother.

Eve couldn't see Nate, nor could she hear him, but she prayed he'd somehow managed to survive the gunshot and the fall. Either could have been fatal.

She saw some movement at the other end of the parking lot and spotted another uniformed security guard on the stairwell. He had his gun ready, thank God, but he didn't seem to be in any better position than Grayson was to stop this. Still, he might be able to do some good if the shooter moved.

Finally, the shots stopped. Maybe because the gunman had to reload. Or, God forbid, maybe because he was escaping. The thought of that sickened Eve. She didn't want a killer to get away.

But right now, Nate was their first priority.

Grayson eased off her and inched toward the car to their right. He was probably thinking of making a run to the stairs, but she prayed he wouldn't do that. He could end up like Nate, or worse.

Since she still had Grayson's phone, she called nine-one-one to report an officer down, though someone was likely already aware of that. She doubted that Nate had come alone. But she immediately rethought that. Maybe that's exactly what Nate had done. Maybe he'd rushed to help his brother and her and hadn't considered the consequences.

She would have reacted the same way if it meant saving Grayson.

The moment she ended the call, Eve saw Grayson's gaze swing to the left. And she soon saw why. The first security guard was crawling toward them. She saw the blood on his shoulder and knew that he, too, had been shot. They had to get an ambulance up here right away, but that couldn't happen until the gunman had been stopped.

Grayson latched on to the guard and pulled him next to Eve. The man was clearly in pain, and even though he was clutching his gun, he had both it and his hand pressed to the wound. It didn't take medical training to know he'd already lost too much blood. Eve pushed aside his hand so she could apply some pressure.

"Wait here," Grayson ordered. "Use the gun if you have to." His eyes met hers, and she could see that it was indeed an order.

But, God, what was he going to do?

Please.

She didn't want him out there in the open, making himself an easy target. She wanted him to stay behind cover, even though cover didn't mean safety. Not with those bullets flying everywhere.

Her heart was pounding against her chest now, and her breath was so thin that she felt light-headed. Despite the cold, there was a fine mist of clammy sweat on her face. She felt sick, but she tried to fight off the feeling of dread. They would survive this, somehow, because there was no other alternative. It couldn't end here for Grayson and Nate.

Grayson took the gun from the security guard and handed it to her. Eve latched on to it, but she was shaking her head. "You can't go out there."

He shook his head, too. "I don't have a choice. This has to stop."

That was it. No other explanation. Grayson maneuvered around her and the guard and went behind them. He disappeared when he ducked around the front of the car to her right.

Well, at least he wasn't going to charge out into the center of the garage. He was obviously trying to get to the stairwell, and maybe the security guard could provide some backup. However, that still meant Grayson was moving closer and closer to the gunman, and she was betting the gunman would be looking for them to do just that. Shooting Nate could have all been designed to draw Grayson and her out into the open.

If so, it had worked.

Eve couldn't hear what the security guard was mumbling, but he squirmed, his face tightening in pain. She pressed harder on the wound to try to stop the flow of blood, but she also kept watch of the area near the black van where the last shots had originated.

"This is Sergeant O'Malley, SAPD." The man's voice boomed from a bullhorn. It sounded as if he was at street level. "Put down your weapon and surrender."

Backup. Thank God. But since there was no response from the shooter, Eve doubted he would just do as the sergeant had demanded.

By her calculations it'd been a minute, maybe more, and the gunman hadn't fired. Eve had no idea if that was good or bad, but it was certainly easier to think without those bullets bashing into the cement and other cars.

And because it was easier to think, tears sprang to her eyes.

Eve blinked them back. She couldn't give in to the worry and fear, but she was terrified for Grayson. For Nate. For this wounded security guard whom she didn't even know.

But who was out there doing this?

Sebastian? Maybe. But only if he'd managed to get away from his police escort. Of course, either Claude or Sebastian could have hired a gunman. It was possible Claude wasn't even in critical condition but instead had orchestrated this to get Grayson and her into a position so they could be killed.

That brought her back to why again.

If they could just figure out who'd fired shots at them, then knowing the *who* would tell them the *why*.

Eve finally spotted Grayson again. He was seven cars over to her right and was inching his way to the stairwell. She held her breath, waiting for another shot.

Nothing.

The seconds crawled by so slowly that she could feel them ticking off in her head. Finally, she saw some movement in the stairwell.

Nate.

Thank God he was moving. However, he wasn't just moving. He had his gun aimed and ready and was mak-

ing his way back up the stairs. Not easily. He, too, was
wincing, and Eve soon realized why. His shirt was open,
but there was no blood. Only a Kevlar vest.

Relieved, she let out her breath in a rush. Nate
hadn't been shot. The impact of the bullet had probably knocked him down the stairs. He looked shaken
up but very much alive.

So that was one prayer that'd been answered.

The security guard moved again, the muscles in his
body going stiff, and Eve looked down at him to see
what had caused that reaction. His eyes were wide and
not focused on her.

But rather behind her.

Oh, God.

That was the only thought that had time to form in
her head because Eve felt a hand grip on to her shoulder. She didn't have time to move. There was no time
to react.

Before someone pressed the barrel of a gun to her
head.

Grayson's heart went to his knees.

This couldn't be happening.

He'd had just a split second of relief because his
brother was alive, but that relief went south in a hurry
when he saw Eve. She was no longer where Grayson
had left her—crouched with the injured security guard
between the two cars. She was standing now.

And she wasn't alone.

Someone was behind her, their arm curved around
Eve's neck, and that someone had a gun pointed directly at Eve's head. The person had a second gun next

to Eve's neck. Both weapons were positioned to deliver a fatal shot.

Grayson couldn't see the person's face, only the black baseball cap. But he could see Eve's. The color had drained from her cheeks, and she was looking around as if trying to figure out how to escape.

But Grayson didn't want her to move.

Not with that gun pressed to her head.

"Drop your weapon and surrender," Sergeant O'Malley called out again.

Grayson was thankful for the backup, but he didn't want the sergeant's demand to make this bad situation worse.

He took aim, and with his attention nailed to the gunman's hand, Grayson inched closer.

"There's no need to do this," Grayson shouted. "Let her go."

If the gunman responded, Grayson didn't hear it. He wished like the devil that the car alarm would stop. He had to try to negotiate Eve's release, and it was hard to do that when he couldn't hear what was going on.

"Eve is no threat to you," Grayson tried again, all the while moving closer.

He didn't have a clean shot, not with the gunman using Eve as a human shield, but he needed to get as close as possible because it was likely this SOB was planning an escape. After all, Eve was still alive, and there had to be a reason for that. The gunman had taken her hostage.

But why?

Grayson was certain he would soon learn the answer, but he hoped he wouldn't learn it too late. Eve couldn't die. She just couldn't. Someway, somehow, he had to put himself in a position where he could save her.

He glanced over his shoulder at his brother. Nate wasn't following him but instead had crouched down and was making his way to the other side of the garage toward the black van and the red car with the blaring alarm.

Good move.

His brother might get a better angle on a shot that way, and Nate could also possibly block an attempted escape. The second security guard could help with that, too, since he was covering the other end of the garage. Grayson couldn't let the gunman get Eve out of there because once he no longer had any use for a hostage, the shooter would almost certainly kill her.

"The security guard needs medical attention," Grayson shouted to the gunman. Since the guy wasn't moving, he wanted to try a different approach. "Why don't you end this now so we can get an ambulance up here?"

Still nothing. But the guy was moving a little and looking around. Grayson didn't like the edgy movement because it proved the gunman was nervous and way out of his comfort zone.

Grayson stopped but kept his gun lifted and aimed. "Step out so I can see you." And he tried to make it sound like an order. Hard to do with that gun right at Eve's head.

"What should I do?" she mouthed.

But Grayson shook his head. He didn't want her to do anything. Not yet anyway. But if it came down to it, he hoped she could drop out of the way so that Nate or he would have a clean shot.

Grayson glanced around to see the best way to approach this, and while he was still studying the situation, just like that the car alarm stopped. Maybe the battery had given out or perhaps Nate had managed to disarm it. Either way, it was now deadly silent.

The gunman lifted his head, just a little, and even though Grayson still couldn't see his face, he didn't think it was his imagination that the guy wasn't pleased with the silenced alarm. But Grayson was certainly thankful for it. Maybe now he could hear this bozo's voice and figure out who he was dealing with. If it wasn't Sebastian, then maybe one of the Colliers had hired a triggerman.

"SAPD has the building surrounded," Grayson tossed out there. "You can't escape. But what you can do is let Eve go, and we can talk about a peaceful surrender."

No answer, but he hadn't expected one.

The guy finally moved. Well, he moved the gun away from Eve's head anyway, and for a moment Grayson thought he might surrender. He didn't.

He lowered the gun, pointing it down to the floor, and he fired.

Hell.

Grayson couldn't see exactly what had happened, but judging from the look of sheer horror on Eve's face and from her scream, the gunman had shot the security guard at point-blank range.

Things had just gone from bad to worse.

The gunman moved again, quickly this time. He put the gun back against Eve's head and he pushed her forward. He followed with the front of his body pressed to Eve's back.

The gunman was heading for that black van.

Nate was there, somewhere. Hopefully, in a position to stop a getaway attempt.

"You won't be able to drive out of here," Grayson warned.

But he'd barely had time to issue that warning when the gunman shifted his weapon.

He fired at Grayson.

Grayson jumped to the side, just in time, and he landed hard against the concrete floor. His shoulder jammed, the pain shooting through him, but he ignored it and came up ready to fire.

The gunman fired first, and the shot pinned Grayson down behind the back of a small truck.

"I have to kill you, you know," the gunman said.

Or rather the gunwoman. Because that was a female voice. A familiar one.

"Cicely?" Grayson spat out. She was the last of the Colliers that he had suspected. "Why the hell are you doing this?"

"Because you all have to die." Cicely's voice was eerily calm, but there was nothing calm about her expression when she met his gaze over Eve's shoulder. "Step out and die like a man, Sheriff Ryland. The other one, too." She tossed a look in Nate's direction. "And that other security guard."

She was just going to kill them all?

Why?

"Your son is in custody for Sophia's murder," Grayson tossed out there. He was testing the waters, trying to get Cicely to talk. And he was also hoping to distract her.

What he didn't intend to do was surrender.

"That's a mistake. He didn't kill his sister." Cicely's voice broke on the last word. "I know because I did it."

Eve gasped, and that was pretty much Grayson's reaction. "You killed your own daughter?"

A hoarse sob tore from Cicely's mouth. "It was an accident, but I don't expect you to believe that."

"I do." And Grayson wasn't lying. He did believe her. "Why did you do it?"

With Eve still in a body lock against her, Cicely continued to inch toward the black van. "I'll tell you, but it won't save you. Nothing will."

Grayson would prove her wrong, somehow.

"I begged Sophia to come home to me, but she just laughed. She wanted money, you see. Claude's money and mine. She didn't want us. Didn't want to be family again."

"So you killed her?" Eve asked in disbelief.

Cicely jammed the gun harder against Eve's head. "I told you that was an accident," Cicely practically yelled. "Sophia said her foster mother confessed to her who she really was—a Collier. The foster mother wanted to try and get money out of us. But Sophia gave her an overdose of insulin to get her out of the way."

Grayson didn't think Sophia's motives were pure, that she did that in order to protect her biological parents. "Sophia did that so she wouldn't have to share the cash with her foster mother?" he asked.

Cicely nodded. "Then, when Sophia and I were arguing, I pushed her, and she fell and hit her head." Another sob. "I had Leon dispose of the body. But Leon remembered that someone at the rodeo had been taking pictures. Pictures that would link him to Sophia. And eventually link her back to me. Leon tried to get them back from Eve, and then you killed him."

"Because he tried to kill us," Grayson reminded her. "Eve did nothing wrong. She was only doing her job when she took the pictures."

"Yes, but I couldn't have the police thinking Sebastian had anything to do with this. He's innocent, you know." She pulled in a shaky breath. "Now step out, Sheriff, and drop your gun so I can do what I have to do to protect my son."

"You mean so you can kill me," he answered flatly.

Eve frantically shook her head. "Stay put," she told Grayson.

Cicely fired at shot at him. "If you stay put or hold on to your gun, I'll make it painful for Eve. You're not the sort of man to cower behind a car while the woman you love is screaming in pain."

Grayson ignored that *woman you love* part and got ready to move. He would leave cover. There was no question about that. He wouldn't let this insane woman hurt Eve. But he couldn't just let Cicely kill him either, because he had to live so that he could rescue Eve. He wouldn't do her any good if he was dead.

"I'm coming out," Grayson let Cicely know. He glanced over at Nate who was ready to fire, as well.

Grayson slid out his gun first, not too far away. He needed to be able to reach for it. And then he stood.

At the exact moment that Eve shouted, "No!"

Eve rammed her elbow against Cicely and darted to the side. But Grayson didn't have time to get off a clean shot. Because Cicely darted to the side, too, and the woman didn't release the grip she had on Eve.

Grayson yelled for Eve to get out of the way, but the sound he heard turned his blood to ice.

The sound of the shot that Cicely fired.

Not at Grayson. Nor at Nate.

Grayson's world tipped on its axis when the bullet slammed into Eve.

Chapter 18

Eve heard the shot.

She also heard Grayson call out to her.

But she couldn't answer. She couldn't do anything except slide to the floor.

The pain was instant, searing, and it sliced through her right side like a red-hot stiletto. She grabbed at the fire and felt the warm blood against her fingers.

She'd been shot.

That fact registered somewhere in her mind. It also registered that she needed to tell Grayson to get down so that he, too, wouldn't be shot. But Eve couldn't make herself speak.

Was she in shock?

Or worse, was she dying?

Ironically, she could deal with the thought of her death, but not of Grayson's. She didn't want his life to end here in this cold, dank garage.

Because she was in love with him.

Always had been. Always would be.

And that's why she had to save him. At least one of them had to make it out of here alive.

"Eve?" Grayson called out. "Are you all right?"

She tried to answer, but Cicely was still beside her, crouched down, with a gun in each hand. She jammed the gun to Eve's head again.

"Tell him to come to you," Cicely demanded.

Eve shook her head. She had to do something to buy a little time. "They'll put you in jail," she managed to say to the woman who'd just shot her. "They'll give you the death penalty. All of this will be for nothing."

"No," Cicely quickly disagreed. Her eyes were wild, her gaze firing between Grayson and Nate. "Annabel is tied up in that black van. When the Rylands and you are dead, I'll shoot her and make it look like a suicide. I've already forced her to write the note, and trust me, it'll be no hardship killing that bimbo witch. She stole my husband. And my life. She deserves to die a thousand deaths."

Oh, God. Cicely wasn't just crazy, she was smart. If Eve couldn't fight back and stop her, Cicely might just get away with this. Worse, Cicely was trying to maneuver herself into a better position to kill again.

Cicely tucked the gun she'd been holding in her left hand into the waist of her pants. That meant she could use that hand to put a tight grip around Eve's neck. Cicely wasn't choking her, exactly, but it was close. Eve was already light-headed enough, but it was obvious Cicely was going to do anything to force Eve to cooperate.

"Tell the sheriff to come to you," Cicely repeated. "And make sure he's unarmed."

She would die before she did that because Cicely intended to kill them all anyway. Eve wouldn't be the reason Grayson took a bullet.

"You're not just killing me," Eve whispered. "I'm pregnant. You're killing my child, too. Maybe a daughter. It would be like killing Sophia all over again."

Cicely blinked, and with that blink Eve saw the hesitation in the woman's eyes. Her gaze dropped to Eve's stomach and then to the blood on the side of Eve's gray sweater. It wasn't much more than a split second of time, but that brief lapse was all that Eve needed.

She latched on to Cicely's wrist.

It was risky, but at this point anything she did or didn't do was risky. All she knew was that every drop of blood she lost put Grayson, Nate, her possible pregnancy and herself in danger. Besides, Cicely had killed both Sophia and the security guard, and Eve knew she wouldn't hesitate to kill again.

Cicely made a feral sound, part scream and part groan, and she struggled to throw off Eve's grip. Eve held on and tried to wrench the gun from Cicely's right hand. Of course, the woman had a second gun that she could use, but Eve would deal with that later. For now, she needed a weapon so she could fight back.

"Eve?" Grayson called out.

The sound of the struggle must have alerted him because Eve heard his frantic footsteps. He was running to try and save her.

Or maybe running to his death.

Eve clamped onto Cicely's gun because she knew that Grayson's life depended on it.

Grayson cursed, and even though Eve couldn't see him from her position, he was close by. Cicely was aware of that, too, because she bashed the gun against Eve's head and then pointed the weapon at Grayson.

Cicely fired.

The fear and adrenaline slammed through Eve, and despite the blow Cicely had delivered to her head, she kept fighting.

"Grayson!" Nate called out.

Nate sounded terrified, and that spiked the fear inside Eve. Did that mean he'd just witnessed his brother being shot?

Oh, God.

Eve couldn't risk thinking about that now. She had to stay in the fight. Despite the pain and the fear, she had to keep fighting.

"Come closer and he dies," she heard Cicely say, and she let go of Eve.

Eve swiveled around and realized Cicely was talking to Nate as he approached them. He had obviously retrieved his weapon and now had it trained on Cicely.

But Cicely had her gun aimed at Grayson.

Another smart move because Nate wouldn't do anything to risk his brother being killed.

Nate froze, but he didn't lower his gun, and he glanced behind him at the stairwell. Hopefully, there were backup officers there and ready to respond.

And then there was Grayson.

He, too, was ready to respond, but he was no longer the calm, collected lawman. Grayson said her name.

Eve.

It was a hoarse whisper filled with concern. No doubt from the blood.

"I'm okay," Eve said to him, even though she had no idea if that was true. She might have lost the chance to be a mother, but worse, she might lose Grayson. "I'm so sorry," she managed to say.

He shook his head. "For what?"

Too many things for her to say here. Besides, there was nothing she could say that would allow them to go back and undo everything. This was their fate, and unfortunately it was in the hands of a crazy woman hell-bent on covering up the murder of her own daughter.

"Eve needs a doctor," Grayson told Cicely. "End this now."

"It ends when you're all dead." But Cicely didn't sound as convinced of that as she had just moments earlier. She glanced at Eve. "I didn't know about your baby. If I had, I would have found a way to leave you out of this."

"Baby?" Nate mumbled. That obviously shocked him, but he didn't take his attention off Cicely.

Later, Eve would have to explain.

If there was a later.

The pain shot through her side again, and Eve felt the fresh trickle of warm blood. Grayson noticed it, too, because she saw his body tense. He was getting ready to have a shoot-out with Cicely. And he could no doubt kill her. But could he do that before she fired a lethal shot at him?

Eve couldn't take that risk. She had to do something, and she used her own body. She kicked at Cicely, and she put every ounce of her strength behind it. The heel of her shoe connected with the woman's shin, and Cicely howled in pain.

It wasn't much of an attack, but Grayson made the most of it.

He dove at Cicely, his muscled body ramming right

into the woman, and he slammed her back into the adjacent car.

Cicely made a gasping sound, fighting for the air that Grayson had knocked from her, but that didn't stop her from trying to aim her gun at his head.

"Watch out!" Eve shouted.

Grayson latched on to both of Cicely's hands and bashed them against the car's body. Her gun clattered to the floor, and Grayson snatched the other weapon from the waist of her pants. He tossed it on the floor, as well.

Nate moved in and kicked both of Cicely's weapons away, but even unarmed, Cicely didn't give up. She continued to fight until Grayson turned her around and pushed her hard against the car's fender.

A sob racked through Cicely, and she went limp.

"Take Cicely," Grayson immediately told Nate. "I'm getting Eve to the E.R."

He kept his forearm on Cicely to hold her until Nate switched places with him. Grayson didn't waste a second. He scooped Eve up in his arms.

"How bad?" he asked.

She wanted to lie. Eve wanted to tell him that everything would be all right, but the fight had taken the last of her breath. She opened her mouth, but no sound came out.

Grayson raced to the stairwell where the other officers were pouring up the steps. One of those officers latched onto Cicely, yanked her hands behind her back and cuffed her.

Grayson looked down at Eve as he ran toward the E.R. doors. He was so worried. And scared. She realized that was the first time she'd seen fear in Grayson's eyes.

Everything started to move in slow motion, and the edges of her vision turned gray. At first. Then, darker.

She fastened her gaze on Grayson and fought to keep her eyes open. But she failed at that, too.

Her eyelids fluttered down, and the last thing Eve saw was Grayson's face.

Grayson was afraid if he stopped moving, he would explode.

So he turned and once again paced across the surgical waiting room of the San Antonio hospital. It didn't help his raw nerves, nor did it ease the massive knot in his stomach, but he couldn't sit and wait as his brothers were doing.

Nate and Dade were on the far side of the room. Nate was on the phone, but both Dade and he were staring at a TV where *It's a Wonderful Life* was playing. Grayson doubted they were actually watching the movie, but they were trying to maintain a calm, business-as-usual facade. For his sake no doubt.

They knew he was ready to explode.

Mason, being Mason, didn't even attempt a facade. He was in a chair on the opposite side of the room, and he was glaring at anything and everything—including Jimmy Stewart on the screen. He was especially glaring at the hall where a nurse had appeared earlier to tell them that Eve was finally being taken to surgery.

Two hours.

That's how long it'd been since Eve had been in the hospital. Grayson hadn't known that one hundred and twenty minutes could feel like a lifetime, but he damn sure knew it now. Every one of those minutes had crawled by.

"She'll be okay," Nate assured him.

Dade mumbled his agreement, but it didn't sound remotely convincing. Mason's glare deepened.

The glare wasn't for Eve. Mason wasn't fond of too many people, but he cared as much for Eve as Grayson's other brothers did. No, this glare was for Cicely, for what the woman had nearly done to Eve. But the good thing in all of this was that Cicely was locked away at the SAPD facility and couldn't come after any of them again.

"Claude Collier's condition has stabilized," Nate reported when he ended the call. "Annabel's still being checked out over in the E.R., but she's going to be okay. Just some bruises and scratches from where Cicely attacked her and stuffed her in the van."

It was the wrong attitude for a lawman to have, but Grayson didn't give a flying fig about the Colliers. He only wanted good news about Eve.

At the sound of footsteps in the hall, his brothers stood, and Grayson turned to see Dr. Andrew Masters making his way toward him. Grayson had met the lanky no-nonsense doctor briefly when Eve had first been rushed into the E.R.

Grayson narrowed the distance between the doctor and him. "Is she okay?" he asked. But he wasn't sure he could take hearing any bad news.

The doctor nodded. "Eve should be fine."

"Should be?" Mason growled, taking the tone and the words right out of Grayson's mouth. "What the hell does that mean?"

The doctor gave a weary huff and looked at Grayson. "Physically, she'll be all right. The surgery didn't take long at all."

"Then what did?" That growl came from Dade. "It's been two hours."

"She had to be examined and prepped. The bullet entered her right side and made a clean exit. It didn't hit any vital organs, which makes her a very lucky woman."

Lucky. Yes, she was, but Grayson didn't feel so lucky. Eve had come damn close to dying.

"You said *physically* Eve will be all right?" Nate questioned.

Dr. Masters glanced at Grayson. A funny kind of glance. Had Eve told him about the possible pregnancy?

No doubt.

She might not have actually mentioned that Grayson could be her baby's father, but the doctor wasn't an idiot. He had almost certainly put one and one together when he's seen Grayson's reaction to her being shot.

"Eve wants to see you," the doctor said to Grayson. "But don't stay long. I want her to get plenty of rest." Then, he turned that authoritative gaze on the rest of the Rylands. "You can all come back in the morning."

The trio looked as if they might argue, but Nate finally caught on to his brothers' arms. "Grayson will see to Eve," he reminded them.

Yeah. He'd done a stellar job of that in the past forty-eight hours, hadn't he? He'd had sex with her, twice, and had nearly gotten her killed.

Grayson took a deep breath and followed the doctor to the post-op room at the end of the hall. Everything in the room was watery white, including Eve. There wasn't a drop of color in her cheeks. Still, she managed a smile of sorts when she saw him.

"You've got five minutes," the doctor instructed, "and then I don't want her to have any more visitors until tomorrow. Don't worry. After what Eve's been through, she'll sleep during that time anyway."

Grayson prayed that was true, that she would sleep with no nightmares. He stood zero chance of that happening for him. Every time he closed his eyes, he would see the attack. It would torment him, and he would try to figure out what he could have done to prevent it. In his nightmares, he would stop Cicely's bullet from hitting Eve.

But saving her from that bullet was a day late and a dollar short.

"You look worried," she mumbled. Her words were slurred, and her eyes bleary.

"I am worried." Grayson walked closer. She looked too fragile to touch, but he skimmed his fingers down her arm, barely making contact with her skin. "The doctor said you were going to be okay."

"Yes." The half smile faded. "It's too early to know if that's true."

"The baby," he whispered.

She gave a shaky nod. "The trauma probably put an end to any pregnancy."

Of course. Her body had been through a lot. Too much. He didn't know much about the biology of conception, but the blood loss and the shock from the attack could have caused her body to shut down.

Being shot was hardly conducive to making a baby.

"Dr. Masters said I should brace myself for the worst," she added. "So that's what I've done."

It made him ache to hear her say that, to see the resignation in her exhausted eyes.

"I'm sorry," Grayson said, because he didn't know what else to say.

She lifted her chin, though it was shaky, too. "I just wanted to thank you, for everything. That's why I asked to see you."

That hurt, as well. And it also riled him to the core. Grayson didn't want to be thanked for doing a half-assed job at protecting her. "Don't—"

"I know. You don't want to talk about it." She pulled in a slow breath and fought to keep her eyes open. "That's okay."

No. It wasn't *okay*. Far from it. He should tell her...

But tell her what, exactly?

Tell her that he wasn't sorry about sleeping with her? That was a moot point now that the gunshot wound had compromised her already slim chances of getting pregnant.

Maybe he should explain to her that he was sorry he hadn't stopped Cicely from shooting her? Or that the only thing he wanted was for her to be happy? She deserved happiness. She deserved a lot more than he could have ever given her.

But Grayson didn't say any of those things. He just stood there, looking at Eve, and knowing he couldn't do or say anything to make it better.

"Go home to your family." Her voice had no sound now. Even though her eyes drifted down, she smiled that sad half smile again. "Have a good life, Grayson."

The words went through him like ice. Like the dark cold he felt deep within his soul when he thought he'd lost Eve in that parking garage.

Because the words sounded like a goodbye.

And Grayson knew that's exactly what it was.

Well, he had his answer. Eve might have been groggy

from the surgical drugs, but he hadn't seen any doubt in her eyes, and she damn sure hadn't asked him to stay.

Have a good life, Grayson.

With those words slamming through his head, Grayson did as Eve wanted. He walked away.

Chapter 19

The pain seared through her when she eased off the hospital bed and into the wheelchair, but Eve tried not to react visibly. She didn't want Dr. Masters to see the pain on her face because he would only give her more hassle about leaving. And there was no way she wanted to spend the rest of Christmas day in a hospital.

Besides, if she stayed, she would go stark-raving mad. Every moment she was in that bed, she thought of Grayson and of the life that she'd nearly gotten to have as a mother.

"You know how I feel about this," the doctor grumbled. It was a paraphrase of the grumble he'd been doling out since she'd insisted on going home.

So yes, she did know how the doctor felt. He wanted her to stay put one more day, even at the risk of her sanity. However, the moment he signed the release papers, Eve snatched them from his hand.

Dr. Masters gave her a flat look. "At least tell me you'll be with family or friends, that you aren't going home alone."

"I won't be alone," she lied.

His flat look intensified. "You told the nurse to tell the Rylands that you couldn't have any visitors, that you were in too much pain."

"I lied about that." And that was the truth.

She had told that lie not because of the pain. Well, not the physical pain anyway, but she couldn't bear the thought of saying goodbye to Grayson again. Once she was home and had recovered, she would email his brothers and thank them for, well, for being there when it counted most.

Dr. Masters scribbled something on another piece of paper and handed it to her. "A script for pain meds and antibiotics," he explained.

The antibiotics were a necessity but not the drug for pain. The pain was right there, stabbing through her, but she didn't want to put any more drugs in her body in case there was the minuscule chance that she might be pregnant.

Yes, it was a pipe dream, but Eve was going to hold on to it until a pregnancy test proved otherwise.

"I can't talk you out of this?" the doctor asked. He grabbed the back of her wheelchair when Eve tried to wheel herself toward the door.

"No. I've made up my mind."

He gave a heavy sigh, followed by a nod, and he stepped behind her so he could wheel her toward the door. With any luck, the taxi she'd called would be waiting and could take her to her condo. She'd also phoned the super because she didn't have her keys. He had promised to meet her there and let her in. Then she could get some cash to pay the taxi driver.

"What should I tell the Rylands when they show up?" Dr. Masters asked.

And they would show up. "Tell them I made a miraculous recovery and that I'm spending the holiday with friends."

The doctor made a sound of disapproval but wheeled her out anyway.

"The taxi is meeting me at the back of the building," she let him know.

Another sound of disapproval, but he went in that direction anyway. Eve looked over her shoulder. No sign of Grayson. And she tried to convince herself that was a good thing.

The tears came anyway.

She blinked them back and realized that the pain in her side was nothing compared to the piercing ache in her heart. Damn her. She had known not to get too close to Grayson, and she'd done it anyway.

Again.

The doors slid open as they approached, and the cold wind nearly robbed her of her breath. So did the man who stepped out onto the walkway. Not Grayson.

Dade.

He was there, right next to the taxi that was waiting for her. Dade smiled, flashing those killer dimples that had probably coaxed many women into his bed. The dimples had never worked on Eve because to her Dade would always be the brother she'd never had.

"I asked at the front desk," Dade explained, "and the nurse said you were checking out early. Since I didn't see you out front, I figured I'd check back here."

He tipped his head to the taxi. "Going somewhere?" It was a friendly enough question, but there was concern in his voice.

"I need to get home." Eve kept it at that. She gave the doctor a nod of reassurance that all was well, and he went back inside.

"Right. You need to get home," Dade repeated. He blew out his breath as if resigned to the fact that they weren't going to have a real discussion here. "Want me to drive you?"

She shook her head. "It's Christmas and you should be with your family. The taxi will get me home just fine."

Another nod. He reached in his jeans' pocket, pulled out something and walked closer. "Your Christmas present," he announced. "Sorry, but I didn't have time to wrap it." Dade caught on to her hand and dropped something into her palm.

A silver concho.

Eve knew exactly what this was. One of the silver conchos that Boone Ryland had given to all six of his sons before he'd walked out on them and their mother.

She looked at Dade and shook her head. "I thought you threw yours in the creek."

Dade shrugged. "I had this one made for you a while back but never got around to giving it to you. I figured this was a good time."

Her mind slipped back to all those years ago, and she could see the hurt teenager whose father had run out on him. The concho was a reminder of both the pain from that loss and the family that Boone Ryland had made.

"Thank you," she managed to say despite the massive lump in her throat.

"I always thought you should have one," Dade added. "And if you decide to throw it in the creek, put a bullet in it or drape it around a picture frame, it's your right." He stooped down so he was eye level with her, and he caught on to her shoulders. "Eve, you're a Ryland, and you belong with Grayson."

The tears threatened again, and she hoped that Dade thought the cold wind was responsible. "I can't have Grayson," she said. She put the concho on her lap so her hands would be free to wheel the chair to the taxi door.

But Dade took over. "Because Grayson's too stubborn and proud."

"No. Because he's Grayson." She managed a smile when Dade helped her into the back of the taxi. She made sure she had hold of the concho, and then closed her hand around it.

Dade brushed a kiss on her forehead. "I can't do anything to change your mind?"

She didn't even have to think about this. "No."

Eve had seen Grayson's reaction the night before. He felt guilty for her injury and guilty that the bullet had almost certainly cost her a baby. That guilt would eat away at him, and he would come to her and try to make things right.

Eventually, they'd land in bed again.

And eventually the old feelings and wounds would resurface, and Grayson would resent her for forcing a relationship on him that he didn't want.

"I can tolerate a lot of things in life," she whispered to Dade. "But I refuse to be the person who brings Grayson Ryland to his knees. I love him too much for that."

Thankfully, Dade didn't argue. He didn't question

her or her logic. He simply smiled, shut the taxi door and waved goodbye.

Eve pressed her hand and the concho to her heart, hoping it would ease the pain. But that was asking a lot from a little piece of silver, even if this piece of silver was one of the most precious gifts she'd ever received. She definitely wouldn't throw it in the creek or put a bullet in it. She would keep it close to her heart.

Eve waited until the driver was out of the parking lot before she broke down and cried.

Chapter 20

Grayson cursed. He'd actually punched a singing Christmas tree and rammed it into the trash can.

He'd thought it was a reasonable reaction at the time. The tree was stupid, sitting on the dispatcher's desk at the sheriff's office and bursting into that same tinny "Jingle Bell" tune every time anyone walked past it. Well, Grayson was tired of it. Plus, it was nearly two weeks past Christmas, and if he'd had any holiday spirit, it was long gone.

Still, he'd punched a Christmas tree.

And that's when he knew this had to end.

His mood was well past the surly stage, and even the usually even-tempered Nate had demanded that Grayson *do something*. Grayson hadn't needed to figure out what his brother meant. He knew.

He had to see Eve.

So he'd forced himself into his new truck and started driving.

However, now that he was parked in front of her condo in San Antonio, Grayson was rethinking his impulsiveness. He probably should have called or emailed first. Heck, he darn sure should have sorted out his feelings and what he wanted to say to her.

What if she told him to take a hike?

That wasn't the only worry on his mind. Still, he had to see for himself that she was okay, that she had recovered both physically and mentally from the shooting.

He was about to get out of his truck, when the front door to her condo opened, and Eve backed out. She had on jeans, a dark red sweater top, and she was dragging something.

A Christmas tree.

Not a fake singing one but a real one with dry, browning branches. No ornaments, but there were a few strands of silver tinsel that caught the cold January wind and the afternoon sun. Since she was struggling with it and since he was pretty sure she shouldn't be twisting and turning her body like that, Grayson hurried over to help her.

She must have heard his footsteps because she let go of the tree and whirled around as if she'd expected to be attacked.

Hell.

She'd been having those nightmares about the shooting.

But her expression quickly went from alarm to a smile. Not the weak half-assed smile that she'd given him in the hospital. This was a real one. An Eve smile that lit up her whole face. That smile caused him to freeze.

Oh, man. She was beautiful. Always had been, always would be. And he would always feel as if it he'd been sucker-punched when he saw her.

"Grayson," she said on a rise of breath.

"Eve." His voice didn't sound any steadier than hers.

They stood there, staring, waiting. And because Grayson had to have something to do with his hands, he grabbed the trunk of the dead tree.

"Where do you want this to go?" he asked.

She motioned toward the Dumpster at the end of the parking lot where there were several other discarded Christmas trees. "The recycling truck is supposed to pick them up today," she let him know.

Grayson headed in that direction, and Eve followed along beside him. He looked for any signs of pain or limited movement, but there weren't any.

"I'm okay," she assured him as if reading his mind. "I had my post-op check up last week, and the doctor said I was healing nicely."

"Good." He cursed himself when he repeated it.

Grayson didn't hurry because he didn't want Eve to hurry to keep up with him, but he didn't dawdle, either. It was cold and blustery, and despite her *healing nicely* remark, he didn't want her outside any longer than necessary—especially since she wasn't wearing a coat. He tossed the tree next to the others and headed back.

"Would you like to come in?" she asked. The invitation was tentative, like her body language. She wasn't fidgeting exactly, but it was close.

"Yeah. I'd like to talk." And say what exactly, Grayson didn't know.

Well, except for asking her the results of the pregnancy test she'd taken. Of course, if by some miracle that result had been positive, she would have already told him.

Maybe.

And Grayson had to accept that maybe she had already written him out of her life. It seemed that way in the hospital.

Eve walked into the condo ahead of him and shut the door once he was inside, but didn't sit. She stuffed her hands into the back pockets of her jeans, causing her sweater to tighten across her breasts.

Something he shouldn't have noticed.

However, he also noticed her necklace. Not an ordinary one. It was a familiar concho with the double *R* brand of his family's ranch.

"Dade gave it to me for Christmas," she said, following his gaze. "He had it made years ago."

Funny, his brother hadn't mentioned a thing about seeing Eve or giving her a Christmas present. After Eve had left the goodbye note at the hospital, Grayson had thought all the Rylands had respected her wishes to be left alone.

Apparently not.

And he would take that up with Dade when he got home.

"The concho doesn't have bad memories for me like it does for you and your brothers," Eve explained. She shifted her weight, glanced away. "When I see it, I don't think of your father leaving. I think of all the memories of when he was there. When things were good."

Leave it to Eve to find the silver lining.

Grayson reached out and slid his fingers beneath

the concho pendant. But it wasn't just the pendant he touched. His knuckles brushed against her breasts. She made a slight shivering sound and stepped back. Grayson let go of the concho and stepped back, too.

"Sorry," she mumbled. But then her chin came up. "I guess it's stupid to apologize for an involuntary response. I'm always going to feel an attraction for you, Grayson, and saying I'm sorry won't make it go away."

No. But admitting the attraction only reminded him that he felt the same about her. Not that he needed a reminder. Just seeing her had the heat sliding through him.

"Always?" he questioned. Oh, yeah. This was playing with fire all right.

She met his gaze head-on. "Always."

Their gazes held, and so many things passed between them. Questions. But very few answers, only the obvious one about this simmering heat. Yes, it would always be there.

"How are you, really?" he asked.

The corner of her mouth lifted. "Well, I'm not in any shape to haul you off to my bed, but I'm healing."

That didn't cool him down. Oh, man. He was stupid to keep at this, but Grayson had no choice. He needed to get to the bottom of this once and for all.

"Do you want to haul me off to your bed?" he asked.

He didn't quite get the reaction he'd hoped for. Eve huffed, and her hands came out of her pockets and went on her hips. "Yes. Happy now?" She didn't wait for his answer. Not that he had one. "What's this visit really about?"

He didn't have an answer for that, either. But he knew he sure as hell needed one. Grayson couldn't go back to kicking Christmas trees or to his nonstop surly mood. He had to resolve this situation once and for all.

"Well?" she prompted. She wasn't tapping her foot, but it was close.

Grayson tried to wrap his mind around his feelings, but Eve huffed again.

"I'm in love with you," she tossed out there like profanity. "I've tried not to be, but I can't make my feelings go away. So, there! Learn to deal with it." Another huff. "Would you like to know what I've been dreaming about for the past two weeks?"

Not the shooting. Grayson prayed it wasn't that.

"About *you*," she tossed out, as well.

Grayson was relieved. Sort of. "I've dreamed about you, too."

He had to gather his breath because he knew these next few minutes would be the most important of his life. Everything was about to change.

And it all hinged on Eve.

"I'm in love with you, too." He said the words fast, like pulling off a bandage, and he was surprised that it hadn't hurt one bit. Just the opposite.

Grayson felt relieved.

That relief didn't extend to Eve, however. Her eyes widened. Her mouth dropped open. "When did you realize that?" she asked.

"A long time ago. It just took me a while to get around to saying it." And because it'd taken him too long, he decided to repeat it. "I love you, Eve."

She didn't say a word. She just stood there, mouth open, and then the tears sprang to her eyes. Grayson moved first, but she was faster. Eve launched herself into his arms.

He took things from there.

Grayson kissed her, and for the first time in his life, he didn't hold anything back. He loved her, and he wanted her to know that. He must have succeeded because the kiss quickly turned fiery hot.

Eve coiled her arms around him, pulling him closer, but Grayson kept things gentle. Or at least he tried. Hard to stay gentle with the kiss going French and with Eve pressed against him. It wasn't easy, but Grayson pulled back to remind her of her injury.

"You're not in any condition for sex," he reminded her.

"Maybe not our normal version of sex." She put her mouth right against his ear because she was obviously a twisted woman who knew that would torture him in the best kind of way.

Grayson groaned and gladly gave in to the torture. He lifted his hands in surrender while she went after his neck.

Oh, yeah.

Eve knew every inch of his body, and within seconds had him rethinking that no-sex-right-now rule.

She pulled back slightly, met his gaze and gave him a nudge with her body that had his eyes crossing. "But remember, I'm in love with you," Eve confessed, "and we can find a way to make this happen."

He froze. And Eve noticed. She went stiff, too, and some panic raced through those jeweled blue eyes. "I was talking about sex when I said we can find a way."

"Were you?" he challenged.

More panic. She stepped back, as she'd always done in the past because she didn't want to put him in a corner. Well, Grayson was sure of two things—he was crazy in love with Eve, and he wanted to be in that *corner*.

He caught on to the silver concho pendant again, and because he wanted to hear that little shiver of arousal, he let his fingers trail over her right nipple.

He smiled when he heard the sound.

And then Grayson let go of the pendant and dropped to his knees.

Eve's sexy shiver turned to a gasp. "What are you doing?"

Grayson didn't even have to think about this. "I'm asking you to marry me."

The room was suddenly way too quiet. No more shivery sounds. No gasps. Eve just stared at him, and for one horrifying moment, he thought she would turn him down.

She certainly didn't say yes.

"Why are you asking me now?" she wanted to know.

Grayson had to release the breath he was holding so he could speak. "Uh, is that a trick question?"

"No." Eve was quick with that assurance but not with the answer to his proposal.

He shrugged. "I thought it was obvious. I'm asking because I love you. Because you're already part of the family, but I wanted to make it official. And because I want you in my bed every night."

She stared at him, as if waiting for more.

What?

That wasn't enough?

Grayson eased her down to her knees so they were face-to-face and so he could kiss her. She apparently needed a reminder of that love she'd professed for him just minutes earlier.

The kiss was long, satisfying and left them both breathless. "Say yes," he insisted.

But she didn't. She pulled back again. "Is this about the attempt to get me pregnant?"

"No." And he hoped she could see that was the honest to goodness truth. "This is about being in love with you. We can discuss the details of our future later, but for now I need an answer, and I need that answer to be yes. Because I can't imagine living the rest of my life without you."

Now, she made a sound. No shiver, but a melting sigh, and her smile returned. Eve slid her arms around him.

"Yes," she finally said. "Because I can't imagine living without you, either."

Grayson wasn't sure which he felt first—relief or happiness, but it was the happiness that filled every part of him.

Eve had said yes!

He wanted to whoop for joy and celebrate, but first he needed another kiss. Their mouths met, barely a touch at first, but in their case familiarity bred lust because this kiss quickly turned scalding hot.

Grayson wanted to tell his brothers about the engagement, but after a few more of those kisses, he knew his brothers would have to wait. Right now, he wanted to make love—gently—to his fiancée.

He got up, scooped Eve into his arms and headed for her bedroom. The kisses didn't stop. In fact, they got more heated as Eve pressed her mouth to his chin and then his throat.

"Wait!" she said the moment he eased her onto the bed.

Hell. That wasn't a word he wanted to hear. "You

can't take back your yes," he let her know. "You're marrying me." And he hoped she didn't argue.

"I didn't mean wait about that. Of course I want to marry you. I've wanted that since I was sixteen."

And that made Grayson smile.

He eased them onto the bed and then rolled her on top of him. "Then why did you say wait?" But his gaze dropped to her side. "Oh. Second thoughts about sex?"

"No." She made it sound as if he'd lost his mind. "I want sex. Trust me, I really want to have sex with you. But I have to tell you something first."

Her smile faded until she looked anything but happy.

Grayson froze again. In fact, he was reasonably sure that every muscle in his body locked up so he couldn't move. "What's wrong?"

"Uh…" And a moment later, she repeated it. She also licked her lips and bunched up her forehead. "The test was, well, it was positive."

It took a few seconds for that to sink in through the worry and the haze in his mind. "You're pregnant?" And that was something he thought he'd *never* hear himself ask Eve.

She nodded. Swallowed hard.

Eve eyed him as if he were a stick of dynamite about to go off. "I should have told you the minute you got on your knees, but I was so surprised. And happy. The only thing I could think of was saying yes. I didn't think that this baby could change everything."

He caught on to her arm. "Wait a minute." The thoughts and words were flying at him so fast that it took Grayson a moment to speak. "You think a baby could change the way I feel about you?"

She blinked back tears. "Does it?"

Oh, man. He had some explaining to do. Grayson decided to start that explanation with a kiss. He gently pulled her down to him and did just that.

"Yes, it changes how I feel about you," he admitted. He slid his hand over her stomach. "It makes me love you even more."

Her breath swooshed out and she snapped him to her. Probably too hard. But Grayson couldn't make himself let go of her.

"But this messes up the plans you had for your life," she reminded him.

"Screw the plans." In fact, he was looking forward to a little chaos, especially the kind of chaotic love that a wife and a child would give him. He hadn't realized until now that having Eve and this child gave him something he'd never had—completion.

His life would be complete with them.

He wouldn't just have brothers. Wouldn't just be part of the Rylands. He would have his *own* family.

"So you're happy?" she asked.

Grayson wanted no room for doubt. "I'm the happiest man on earth." And he pulled her into his arms so he could hold her and kiss her.

He could have sworn he felt everything in the universe go into some kind of perfect cosmic alignment.

Or maybe that was just his heart.

Either way, this was right. No, it was better than that. It was perfect.

And Grayson wanted to hold on to Eve and his baby like this forever.

* * * * *

We hope you enjoyed reading

THE MAVERICK

by *New York Times* bestselling author

DIANA PALMER

and

GRAYSON

by *USA TODAY* bestselling author

DELORES FOSSEN

Both were originally **Harlequin® Desire** and **Harlequin® Intrigue** series stories!

Harlequin Desire stories feature sexy, romantic heroes who have it all: wealth, status, incredible good looks... everything but the right woman. Add some secrets, maybe a scandal, and start turning pages!

Powerful heroes...scandalous secrets...burning desires.

Look for six *new* romances every month from **Harlequin Desire!**

Available wherever books are sold.

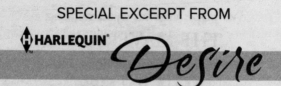
Claire looked completely panicked by the thought of
Luca having access to her child.

Their child.

It seemed so wrong for him to have a child with a
woman he'd never met. But now that he had a living,
breathing daughter, he wasn't about to sit back and
pretend it didn't happen. Eva was probably the only child
he would ever have, and he'd already missed months of
her life. That would not continue.

"We can and we will." Luca spoke up at last. "Eva
is my daughter, and I've got the paternity test results to
prove it. There's not a judge in the county of New York
who won't grant me emergency visitation while we await
our court date. They will say when and where and how
often you have to give her to me."

Claire sat, her mouth agape at his words. "She's just
a baby. She's only six months old. Why fight me for her
just so you can hand her over to a nanny?"

Luca laughed at her presumptuous tone. "What makes
you so certain I'll have a nanny for her?"

HDEXP0216

"You're a rich, powerful, unmarried businessman. You're better suited to run a corporation than to change a diaper. I'm willing to bet you don't have the first clue of how to care for an infant, much less the time."

Luca just shook his head and sat forward in his seat. "You know very little about me, *tesorino*, you've said so yourself, so don't presume anything about me."

Claire narrowed her gaze at him. She definitely didn't like him pushing her. And he was pushing her. Partially because he liked to see the fire in her eyes and the flush of her skin, and partially because it was necessary to get through to her.

Neither of them had asked for this to happen to them, but she needed to learn she wasn't in charge. They had to cooperate if this awkward situation was going to improve. He'd started off nice, politely requesting to see Eva, and he'd been flatly ignored. As each request was met with silence, he'd escalated the pressure. That's how they'd ended up here today. If she pushed him any further, he would start playing hardball. He didn't want to, but he would crush her like his restaurants' competitors.

"We can work together and play nice, or my lawyer here can make things very difficult for you. As he said, it's your choice."

"What are you suggesting, Mr. Moretti?" her lawyer asked.

"I'm suggesting we both take a little time away from our jobs and spend it together."

Don't miss
THE CEO'S UNEXPECTED CHILD
by Andrea Laurence, available March 2016 wherever
Harlequin® Desire books and ebooks are sold.

www.Harlequin.com

HDEXP0216

HARLEQUIN™ *Desire*

Powerful heroes…scandalous secrets…burning desires.

THE CEO'S UNEXPECTED CHILD

BILLIONAIRES AND BABIES

ANDREA LAURENCE

Use this coupon to save

$1.00

on the purchase of any Harlequin® Desire book.

Available wherever books are sold, including most bookstores, supermarkets, drugstores and discount stores.

- ✂

Save $1.00

on the purchase of any Harlequin® Desire book.

Coupon valid until April 30, 2016.
Redeemable at participating outlets in the U.S. and Canada only.
Not redeemable at Barnes & Noble stores. Limit one coupon per customer.

52613470

5 65373 00076 2 (8100)0 12140

NYTCOUP0216

Turn your love of reading into
rewards you'll love with

Harlequin My Rewards

**Join for FREE today at
www.HarlequinMyRewards.com**

Earn **FREE BOOKS** of your choice.

Experience **EXCLUSIVE OFFERS** and contests.

Enjoy **BOOK RECOMMENDATIONS**
selected just for you.

PLUS! Sign up now
and get **500** points
right away!

Earn
FREE
REWARDS
HarlequinMyRewards.com
Join
Today!

MYR16R